DEBBIE MACOMBER

Forever Under The Mistletoe

When Christmas Comes and *Christmas Letters*

mira

mira™

ISBN-13: 978-0-7783-3402-6

Forever Under the Mistletoe

Mira
22 Adelaide St. West, 41st Floor
Toronto, Ontario M5H 4E3, Canada
www.Harlequin.com

Printed in U.S.A.

CONTENTS

Praise for the novels of #1 *New York Times* bestselling author Debbie Macomber

"It's impossible not to cheer for Macomber's characters.... When it comes to creating a special place and memorable, honorable characters, nobody does it better than Macomber."
—*BookPage*

"Macomber's writing and storytelling deliver what she's famous for—a smooth, satisfying tale with characters her fans will cheer for and an arc that is cozy, heartwarming and ends with the expected happily-ever-after."
—*Kirkus Reviews* on *Starting Now*

"Debbie Macomber is...a bona fide superstar."
—*Publishers Weekly*

"Readers won't be able to get enough of Macomber's gentle storytelling."
—*RT Book Reviews*

"No one tugs at readers' heartstrings quite as effectively as Macomber."
—*Chicago Tribune*

"Romantic, warm, and a breeze to read."
—*Kirkus Reviews* on *Cottage by the Sea*

"The reigning queen of women's fiction."
—*Sacramento Bee*

WHEN CHRISTMAS COMES

One

"What do you mean you won't be home for Christmas?" Emily Springer was sure she couldn't have heard correctly. She pressed the telephone receiver harder against her ear, as though that would clarify her daughter's words.

"Mom, I know you're disappointed..."

That didn't even begin to cover it. Emily had scraped and sacrificed in order to save airfare home for her only daughter, a student at Harvard. They always spent the holidays together, and now Heather was telling her she wouldn't be back for Christmas.

"What could possibly be more important than Christmas with your family?" Emily asked, struggling to hide her distress.

Her daughter hesitated. "It's just that I've got so much going on during those two weeks. I'd love to be home with you, I really would, but... I can't."

Emily swallowed past the lump in her throat. Heather was twenty-one; Emily realized her daughter was becoming an independent adult, but for the last eleven years it had been just the two of them. The thought of being separated from her only child over Christmas brought tears to her eyes.

"You've got all the neighbor kids to spoil," Heather continued.

Yes, the six Kennedy children would be more than happy to gobble up Emily's homemade cookies, candies and other traditional holiday treats. But it wouldn't be the same.

"I was home a few months ago," Heather reminded her next.

Emily opened her mouth to argue. True, her daughter had spent the summer in Leavenworth, but she'd been busy working and saving money for school. If she wasn't at her library job, she was with her friends. Emily knew that Heather had her own life now, her own friends, her own priorities and plans. That was to be expected and natural, and Emily told herself she should be proud. But spending Christmas on opposite sides of the country was simply too hard—especially for the two of them, who'd once been so close.

"What about the money I saved for your airfare?" Emily asked lamely, as if that would change anything.

"I'll fly out for Easter, Mom. I'll use it then."

Easter was months away, and Emily didn't know if she could last that long. This was dreadful. Three weeks before Christmas, and she'd lost every shred of holiday spirit.

"I have to hang up now, Mom."

"I know, but…can't we talk about this? I mean, there's got to be a way for us to be together."

Heather hesitated once more. "You'll be fine without me."

"Of course I will," Emily said, dredging up the remnants of her pride. The last thing she wanted was to look pathetic to her daughter—or to heap on the guilt—so she spoke with an enthusiasm she didn't feel. Disappointment pounded through her with every beat of her heart. She had to remember she wasn't the only one who'd be alone, though. Heather would be missing out, too. "What about you?" Emily asked. Caught up in her own distress, she hadn't been thinking about her daughter's feelings. "Will you be all alone?"

"For Christmas, you mean?" Heather said. Her voice fell slightly, and it sounded as if she too was putting on a brave front. "I have friends here, and I'll probably get together with them—but it won't be the same."

That had been Emily's reaction: *It won't be the same.* This Christmas marked the beginning of a new stage in their relationship. It was inevitable—but Christmas was still Christmas, and she vowed that wherever Heather was in future years, they'd spend the holiday together. Emily squared her shoulders. "We'll make it through this," she said stoutly.

"Of course we will."

"I'll be in touch soon," Emily promised.

"I knew you'd be a trouper about this, Mom."

Heather actually seemed proud of her, but Emily was no heroine. After a brief farewell, she placed the portable phone back in the charger and slumped into the closest chair.

Moping around, Emily tried to fight off a sense of depression that had begun to descend. She couldn't concentrate on anything, too restless to read or watch TV. The house felt…bleak. Uncharacteristically so. Maybe because she hadn't put up the Christmas decorations, knowing how much Heather loved helping her.

They had their own traditions. Heather always decorated the fireplace mantel, starting with her favorite piece, a small almost-antique angel that had belonged to Emily's mother. While she did that, Emily worked on the windowsills around the dining room, arranging garlands, candles and poinsettias. Then together, using the ornaments Emily had collected over the years, they'd decorate the Christmas tree. Not an artificial one, either, despite warnings that they were safer than fresh trees.

It sometimes took them half a day to choose their Christmas tree. Leavenworth was a small Washington town tucked in the foothills of the Cascade Mountains, and it offered a stunning array of firs and pines.

This year, without Heather, there would be no tree. Emily wouldn't bother. Really, why go to that much effort when she'd be the only one there to enjoy it. Why decorate the house at all?

This Christmas was destined to be her worst since Peter had died. Her husband had been killed in a logging accident eleven years earlier. Before his death, her life had been idyllic—exactly what she'd wanted it to be. They'd been high-school sweethearts and married the summer after graduation. From the start, their marriage was close and companionable. A year later Heather had arrived. Peter had supported Emily's efforts to obtain her teaching degree and they'd postponed adding to their family. The three of them had been contented, happy with their little household—and then, overnight, her entire world had collapsed.

Peter's life insurance had paid for the funeral and allowed her to deal with the financial chaos. Emily had invested the funds wisely; she'd also continued with her job as a kindergarten teacher. She and Heather were as close as a mother and daughter could be. In her heart, Emily knew Peter would have been so proud of Heather.

The scholarship to Harvard was well deserved but it wasn't enough to meet all of Heather's expenses. Emily periodically cashed in some of her investments to pay her daughter's living costs—her dorm room, her transportation, her textbooks and entertainment. Emily lived frugally, and her one and only extravagance was Christmas. For the last two years, they'd somehow managed to be together even though Heather had moved to Boston. Now this…

Still overwhelmed by her disappointment, Emily wandered into the study and stared at the blank computer screen. Her friend Faith would understand how she felt. Faith would give her the sympathy she needed. They communicated frequently via email. Although Faith was ten years younger, they'd become good friends. They were both teachers; Faith had done her student teaching in Leavenworth and they'd stayed in touch.

Faith—braver than Emily—taught junior-high literature. Emily cringed at the thought of not only facing a hundred thirteen-year-olds every school day but trying to interest them in things like poetry. Divorced for the past five years, Faith lived in the Oakland Bay area of San Francisco.

This news about Heather's change in plans couldn't be delivered by email, Emily decided. She needed immediate comfort. She needed Faith to assure her that she could get through the holidays by herself.

She reached for the phone and hit speed dial for Faith's number. Her one hope was that Faith would be home on a Sunday afternoon—and to Emily's relief, Faith snatched up the receiver after the second ring.

"Hi! It's Emily," she said, doing her best to sound cheerful.

"What's wrong?"

How well Faith knew her. In a flood of emotion, Emily spilled out everything Heather had told her.

"She's got a boyfriend," Faith announced as if it were a foregone conclusion.

"Well, she has mentioned a boy named Ben a few times, but the relationship doesn't sound serious."

"Don't you believe it!"

Faith tended to be something of a cynic, especially when it came to relationships. Emily didn't blame her; Faith had married her college boyfriend and stayed in the marriage for five miserable years. She'd moved to Leavenworth shortly after her divorce. Her connection with Emily had been forged during a time of loneliness, and they'd each found solace in their friendship.

"I'm sure Heather would tell me if this had to do with a man in her life," Emily said fretfully, "but she didn't say one word. It's school and work and all the pressures. I understand, or at least I'm trying to, but I feel so…so cheated."

"Those are just excuses. Trust me, there's a man involved."

Not wanting to accept it but unwilling to argue the point, Emily sighed deeply. "Boyfriend or not," she muttered, "I'll be alone over the holidays. How can I possibly celebrate Christmas by myself?"

Faith laughed—which Emily didn't consider very sympathetic. "All you have to do is look out your front window."

That was true enough. Leavenworth was about as close to Santa's village as any place could get. The entire town entered the Christmas spirit. Tourists from all over the country visited the small community, originally founded by immigrants from Germany, and marveled at its festive atmosphere. Every year there were train rides and Christmas-tree-lighting ceremonies, three in all, plus winter sports and sleigh rides and Christmas parades and more.

Emily's home was sixty years old and one block from the heart of downtown. The city park was across the street. Starting in early December, groups of carolers strolled through the neighborhood dressed in old-fashioned regalia. With the horse-drawn sleigh, and groups of men and women in greatcoats and long dresses gathered under streetlamps, the town looked like a Currier & Ives print.

"Everyone else can be in the holiday spirit, but I won't—not without Heather," Emily said. "I'm not even going to put up a tree."

"You don't mean that," Faith told her bracingly.

"I do so," Emily insisted. She couldn't imagine anything that would salvage Christmas for her.

"What you need is a shot of holiday cheer. Watch *Miracle on 34th Street* or—"

"It won't help," Emily cried. "Nothing will."

"Emily, this doesn't sound like you. Besides," Faith said, "Heather's twenty-one. She's creating her own life, and that's completely appropriate. So she can't make it this year—you'll have *next* Christmas with her."

Emily didn't respond. She couldn't think of anything to say.

"You need your own life, too," Faith added. "I've

been after you for years to join the church singles group."

"I'll join when you do," Emily returned.

"Might I remind you that I no longer live in Leavenworth?"

"Fine, join one in Oakland."

"That's not the point, Em," her friend said. "You've been so wrapped up in Heather that you don't have enough going on in *your* life."

"You know that's not true!" Emily could see that talking to Faith wasn't having the desired effect. "I called because I need sympathy," Emily said, her tone a bit petulant even to her own ears.

Faith laughed softly. "I've failed you, then."

"Yes." Emily figured she might as well tell the truth. "Of all people, I thought you'd understand."

"I'm sorry to disappoint you, Em."

Her friend didn't *sound* sorry.

"I actually think being apart over the holidays might be good for you—and for Heather."

Emily was aghast that Faith would suggest such a thing. "How can you say that?"

"Heather might appreciate you more and you might just discover that there are other possibilities at Christmas than spending it with your daughter."

Emily knew she'd adjust much more easily if she wasn't a widow. Being alone at this time of year was hard, had been hard ever since Peter's death. Perhaps Faith was right. Perhaps she'd clung to her daughter emotionally, but Emily felt that in her circumstances, it was forgivable.

"I'll be fine," she managed, but she didn't believe it for a moment.

"I know you will," Faith said.

Even more distressed than before, Emily finished the conversation and hung up the phone. Never having had children, Faith didn't understand how devastating Heather's news had been. And if Emily *was* guilty of relying on her daughter too much, Christmas was hardly the time of year to deal with it. But wait a minute. She'd encouraged Heather's independence, hadn't she? After all, the girl was attending school clear across the country. Surely a few days at Christmas wasn't too much to ask.

Emily decided a walk would help her sort through these complicated emotions. She put on her heavy wool coat, laced up her boots and wrapped her hand-knitted red scarf around her neck. She'd knitted an identical scarf for her daughter, although Heather's was purple instead of red, and mailed it off before Thanksgiving. Finally she thrust her hands into warm mittens. It'd snowed overnight and the wind was cold enough to cut to the bone.

The Kennedy kids—ranging from six years old to thirteen—had their sleds out and were racing down the hill in the park. In order of age and size, they scrambled up the steep incline, dragging their sleds behind them. When they reached the top, they all waved excitedly at Emily. Sarah, the youngest, ran over to join her.

"Hello, Mrs. Springer." The youngster smiled up at her with two bottom teeth missing.

"Sarah," Emily said, feigning shock. "Did you lose those two teeth?"

The girl nodded proudly. "My mom pulled them out and I didn't even cry."

"Did the tooth fairy visit?"

"Yes," Sarah told her. "James said there wasn't any such thing, but I put my teeth under my pillow and in the morning there was fifty cents. Mom said if I wanted to believe in the tooth fairy, I could. So I believed and I got two quarters."

"Good for you."

With all the wisdom of her six years, Sarah nodded. "You've got to believe."

"Right," Emily agreed.

"In Santa, too!"

As the youngest, Sarah had four older brothers and a sister all too eager to inform her that Santa Claus and his helpers bore a strong resemblance to Mom and Dad.

"Do *you* believe, Mrs. Springer?"

Right now that was a difficult question. Emily was no longer sure. She wanted to believe in the power of love and family, but her daughter's phone call had forced her to question that. At least a little…

"Do you?" Sarah repeated, staring intently up at Emily.

"Ah…" Then it hit her. She suddenly saw what should've been obvious from the moment she answered the phone that afternoon. "Yes, Sarah," she said, bending down to hug her former kindergarten student.

It was as simple as talking to a child. Sarah understood; sometimes Emily hadn't. *You've got to believe.* There was always a way, and in this instance it was for Emily to book a flight to Boston. If Heather couldn't join her for Christmas, then she'd go to Heather.

The fact that this answer now seemed so effortless unnerved her. The solution had been there from the first, but she'd been so caught up in her sense of loss she'd been blind to it.

Emily had the money for airfare. All she needed was to find a place to stay. Heather would be so surprised, she thought happily. In that instant Emily decided not to tell her, but to make it a genuine surprise—a Christmas gift.

Emily reversed her earlier conviction. What could've been the worst Christmas of her life was destined to be the best!

Two

Charles Brewster, professor of history at Harvard, pinched the bridge of his nose as he stared at the computer screen. Stretching his neck to see the clock hidden behind two neatly stacked piles of paper, he discovered that it was three o'clock. Charles had to stop and calculate whether that was three in the afternoon or three at night. He often lost track of time, especially since he had an inner office without windows.

And especially since it was December. He hated the whole miserable month—the short days with darkness falling early, the snow, the distractedness of his students and colleagues. *Christmas.* He dreaded it each and every year. Cringed at the very mention of the holidays. Rationally he knew it was because of Monica, who'd chosen Christmas Eve to break off their relationship. She claimed he was distant and inattentive, calling him the perfect example of the absentminded professor. Charles admitted she was probably right, but he'd loved her and been shocked when she'd walked out on him.

Frowning now, Charles realized it was happening already. Christmas was coming, and once again he'd be forced to confront the memories and the bitterness. The truth was, he rarely thought of Monica anymore except at Christmas. He couldn't help it. Boston during December depressed him. In fact, he associated Christmas, especially Christmas in the city, with unhappiness and rejection. It was as if those emotions had detached themselves from Monica and just become part of the season itself.

Standing up, he strolled out of his office and noticed that all the other History Department offices were dark and empty. It must be three at night, then, which meant he hadn't eaten dinner yet. Funny, he distinctly remembered Mrs. Lewis bringing him a tuna sandwich and a cup of hot coffee. His assistant was thoughtful that way. On the other hand, that might've been the day before. Frankly, Charles no longer remembered. His stomach growled, and he rummaged through his desk drawers for a snack. He located a candy bar, eating it hungrily, with only the briefest consideration of how old it might be.

It was too late to head home now, Charles decided. If he left the building, Security would be on him so fast he wouldn't make it to the front door. He'd have to haul out all his identification and explain why he was still here and… No, it was easier just to stay.

He returned his attention to the computer screen and his work. He'd recently been contracted to write a textbook. He'd agreed to a tight deadline because he knew it would help him get through the holidays. Now he wondered if he'd taken on too much.

The next time he glanced up from the computer, Mrs. Lewis had stepped into the office. "Professor Brewster, were you here all night?"

Charles leaned back in his chair and rubbed his hand along his face. "It seems I was."

Shaking her head, she placed a cup of hot, black coffee on his desk.

He sipped it gratefully. "What day is this?" It was a question he asked often—so often that it didn't even cause the department secretary's brow to wrinkle.

"Tuesday, December fourteenth."

"It's the fourteenth already?" He could feel the panic rising.

"Yes, Professor. And you have three student appointments today."

"I see." But all Charles saw was trouble. If his mother wasn't pestering him, then it was his students. He sighed, suddenly exhausted. He'd spent the better part of fifteen hours writing his American history text, focusing on the Colonial era, the Revolutionary War and the country's founding fathers. Much of his work that night had been about the relationship between Thomas Jefferson and Aaron Burr. It wouldn't be light reading, but he knew his history and loved it. If he met his deadline, which Charles was determined to do, and turned in the completed manuscript shortly after the first of the year, it would be published and ready for use by the start of the 2006 autumn classes. High aspirations, but Charles knew he could meet the challenge.

"Your mother just phoned again," Mrs. Lewis informed him. She'd left his office and returned to set the mail on his desk.

Charles sighed. His mother's intentions were good, but she worried about him far too much. For years now, she'd been after him to join her in Arizona for the holidays. Personally, Charles would rather have his fingernails pulled out than spend Christmas with his mother. She suffocated him with her concern and irritated him with her matchmaking efforts. Try as he might, he couldn't make her understand that he wasn't interested in another relationship. His one and only attempt at romance had practically demolished him. After Monica's Christmas Eve defection, he'd shielded himself from further involvement. He was content with his life, although his mother refused to believe it. He didn't *want* a relationship. Women made demands on his time; they were a luxury he couldn't afford if he planned to get ahead in his profession. He wanted to write and teach and there simply weren't enough hours in the day as it was. Frankly that suited him just fine.

If Ray would do him the favor of marrying, Charles would be off the hook. Unfortunately his older brother seemed to be a confirmed bachelor. That left Charles—and his mother wasn't giving up without a fight. At every opportunity she shoved women in his path. Twice in the last six months she'd sent the daughters of friends to Boston to lure him out of his stuffy classroom, as she called it. Both attempts had ended in disaster.

"She wants to know your plans for the holidays."

Charles stiffened. This was how their last conversation had begun. His mother had casually inquired about his plans for Labor Day, and the next thing he knew she'd arranged a dinner engagement for him with one of those young women. That particular one had been a twenty-four-year-old TV production assistant in New York; to say they had nothing in common was putting it mildly. "What did you tell my mother?" he asked.

"That you were occupied and unable to take the call."

From the way Mrs. Lewis's lips thinned, Charles

guessed she wasn't pleased at having to engage in this small deception. "Thank you," he muttered.

"She insisted I must know about your plans for Christmas," Mrs. Lewis said in a severe voice.

Apprehension shot up his back. "What did you say?"

Mrs. Lewis crossed her arms and stared down at him. "I said I am not privy to your private arrangements, and that for all I knew you were going out of town."

Actually, that didn't sound like a bad plan. He needed an escape, and the sooner the better. If his mother's behavior was true to pattern, she was about to sic some woman on him. As soon as Mrs. Lewis had made that comment about traveling, the idea took root in his mind. It would do him good to get out of the city. He didn't care where he went as long as it was away from Boston, away from his seasonal misery. Someplace quiet would suit him nicely. Someplace where he could work and not worry about what time or day it happened to be.

"Hmm. That has possibilities," he murmured thoughtfully.

The older woman didn't seem to know what he was talking about. His students often wore the same confused look, as if he were speaking in a foreign language.

"Traveling." The decision made now, he stood and reached for his overcoat. "Yes."

Her gaze narrowed. "Excuse me?"

"That was an excellent idea. I'm leaving town for the holidays." All he wanted was peace and quiet; that should be simple enough to arrange.

"Where?" Mrs. Lewis stammered, following him out of his office.

He shrugged. "I really don't care."

"Well, I could call a travel agent for recommendations."

"Don't bother."

A travel agent might book him into some area where he'd be surrounded by people and festivities centered on the Christmas holidays. Any contact with others was out of the question. He wanted to find a place where he'd be completely alone, with no chance of being disturbed. And if possible, he wanted to find a place where Christmas wasn't a big deal.

He told Mrs. Lewis all this, then asked her for suggestions. He turned down Vermont, Aspen, Santa Fe and Disney World.

Disney World!

At her despairing look, he sighed again. "Never mind," he said. "I'll do it myself."

She nodded and seemed relieved.

Later that day, Charles had to admit that finding an obscure location for travel on such short notice was difficult. Taking his briefcase with him, he walked to his condo, not far from the university area. But after he'd showered, heated up a microwave lasagna for his dinner and slept, he tackled the project with renewed enthusiasm. It was now shortly after 8:00 p.m.

After calling half a dozen airlines, he realized he was seeking the impossible. Not a man to accept defeat, Charles went online to do his own investigative work. It was while he was surfing the Internet that he found a site on which people traded homes for short periods.

One such notice was from a woman who'd posted a message: Desperately Seeking Home in Boston for Christmas Holidays.

Charles read the message twice, awed by his good

fortune. This woman, a schoolteacher in a small town in Washington State, sought a residence in Boston for two weeks over the Christmas holidays. She could travel after December 17th and return as late as December 31st.

The dates were perfect for Charles. He started to get excited. This might actually work without costing him an arm and a leg. Since he didn't have to register in a hotel, his mother would have no obvious means of tracking him. Oh, this was very good news indeed.

Charles answered the woman right away.

From: "Charles Brewster" <hadisbad@charternet.net>
To: "Emily Springer" <springere@aal.com>
Sent: December 14, 2004
Subject: Trading Places

Dear Ms. Springer,
I'm responding to the DESPERATELY SEEKING IN BOSTON advertisement shown on the Trading Homes Web site. I live in Boston and teach at Harvard. My condo is a two-bedroom, complete with all modern conveniences. You can email me with your questions at the address listed above. I eagerly await your reply.
Sincerely,
Charles Brewster

Before long Charles received a response. Naturally, she had a number of questions. He had a few of his own, but once he was assured that he'd be completely alone in a small Eastern Washington town, Charles agreed to the swap. He supplied references, and she offered her own.

A flurry of emails quickly passed between them as

they figured out the necessary details. Emily seemed to think she owed him an explanation as to why she was interested in Boston. He didn't tell her that he didn't care about her reasons.

He certainly didn't mention his own. He rather enjoyed the notion of spending time in a town called Leavenworth. If he remembered correctly, a big federal prison was situated in the area. As far as Charles was concerned, that was even better. The less celebrating going on, the happier he'd be. He could spend the holidays in a nice, quiet prison town without any Christmas fuss.

His remaining concern was buying a plane ticket, but once again the online travel sites came to his rescue. Charles had no objection to flying a red-eye, since half the time he didn't know whether it was day or night.

"Everything's been arranged," he announced to Mrs. Lewis the following morning.

She responded with a brief nod. "So you have decided to travel."

"I have."

She held up her hand. "Don't tell me any of the details."

He stared at her. "Why not?"

"In case your mother asks, I can honestly tell her I don't know."

"Excellent idea." He beamed at the brilliance of her suggestion. For once, he was going to outsmart his dear, sweet matchmaker of a mother and at the same time blot Christmas from the calendar. School was closing for winter recess and if she couldn't reach him, she'd assume he wasn't answering his phone, which he rarely did, anyway—even before caller ID. And suppose his mother found some way to get hold of Mrs. Lewis during the Christmas holidays? It wouldn't matter, because Mrs. Lewis didn't know a thing! This was more satisfactory by the minute.

For two blessed weeks in December, he was going to escape Christmas and his mother in one fell swoop.

No question about it, life didn't get any better than this.

Three

The bell rang, dismissing Faith Kerrigan's last junior-high literature class of the afternoon. Her students were out of the room so fast, anyone might think the building was in danger of exploding. She could understand their eagerness to leave. When classes were dismissed for winter break at the end of the week, she'd be ready—more than ready.

"Faith?" Sharon Carson stuck her head in the doorway. "You want to hit the mall this afternoon?"

Faith cringed. The crowds were going to be horrendous, and it would take a braver woman than she to venture into a mall this close to the holidays. One advantage of being single was that Faith didn't have a lot of Christmas shopping to do. That thought, however, depressed her.

She was an aunt three times over, thanks to her younger sister. Faith loved her nephews, but she'd always dreamed of being a mother herself one day. She'd said goodbye to that dream when she divorced. At the time she hadn't realized it; she'd blithely assumed she'd remarry, but to this point she hadn't met anyone who even remotely interested her. She hadn't guessed it would be that difficult to meet a decent man, but apparently she'd been wrong. Now thirty, she'd begun to feel her chances were growing bleaker by the day.

"Not tonight, Sharon, but thanks."

Her fellow teacher and friend leaned against the door of her classroom. "You're usually up for a trip to the mall. Is something bothering you?"

"Not really." Other than the sorry state of her love life, the only thing on Faith's mind was getting through the next few days of classes.

"Are you sure?" Sharon pressed.

"I'm sure." Faith glanced over at her and smiled. She was tall, the same height as Faith at five foot eight, and ten years older. Odd that her two best friends were forty. Both Emily and Sharon were slightly overweight, while Faith kept her figure trim and athletic. Emily was an undiscovered beauty. She was also the perfect kindergarten teacher, patient and gentle. She looked far younger than her years, with short curly brown hair and dark eyes. Unlike Faith, she wasn't interested in sports. Emily felt she got enough physical exercise racing after five-year-olds all day and had no interest in joining the gym or owning a treadmill. Come to think of it, Faith wasn't sure Leavenworth even had a gym.

Faith ran five miles three times a week and did a seven-mile-run each weekend. She left the races to those who enjoyed collecting T-shirts. She wasn't one of them. The running habit had started shortly after her separation, and she'd never stopped.

"You haven't mentioned Emily lately. What's up with her?" Sharon asked and came all the way into the room. The summer before, when Sharon and her family had taken a trip north to Washington State, Faith had suggested they visit Leavenworth. As soon as Emily learned Faith's friend would be in the area, she'd insisted on showing them the town. Emily was the consummate host and a fabulous cook. Sharon had come back full of tales about Leavenworth and Emily.

"I talked to her on Sunday." Faith began erasing the blackboard, but paused in the middle of a sweeping motion. "Funny you should mention her, because she's been on my mind ever since."

"I thought you two emailed back and forth every day."

"We do—well, almost every day." Faith had sent Emily an email the day before and hadn't heard back, which told her Emily was especially busy. No doubt there'd be a message waiting for her once she got home.

She turned to face Sharon. "I think I might've offended her." Now that she thought about it, Faith realized she probably had. "Emily phoned, which she rarely does, to tell me Heather won't be coming home for Christmas. I told Emily it was time Heather had her own life and to make the best of it." Given the opportunity, she'd gladly take back those words. "I can't believe I wasn't more sympathetic," Faith said, pulling out the desk chair to sit down. She felt dreadful. Her friend had phoned looking for understanding, and Faith had let her down.

"Don't be so hard on yourself," Sharon said. She slipped into one of the student desks.

"Emily doesn't want to be alone over Christmas, and who can blame her?"

"No one wants to be alone at Christmas."

Faith didn't; in fact she'd made plans to visit Penny

and join in the festivities with her nephews. "I was completely and utterly insensitive. Poor Emily." No wonder she hadn't answered Faith's email.

"What are you going to do?" Sharon asked.

"What makes you think I'm going to do anything?"

A smile crept over Sharon's face. "Because I know you. I can tell from the look in your eyes."

"Well, you're right. I have an idea."

"What?"

Faith was almost beside herself with glee. "I'm going to surprise Emily and visit her for Christmas."

"I thought you were spending the holidays with your sister."

"I was, but Penny will understand." The truth, Faith realized, was that Penny might even be grateful.

"It's pretty hard to book a flight at this late date," Sharon said, frowning.

"I know.... I haven't figured that out yet." Booking a flight could be a problem, but Faith was convinced she'd find a way, even if it meant flying in the dead of night. There had to be a flight into the Seattle-Tacoma airport at some point between Friday night and Christmas Day.

"My sister-in-law works for a travel agent. Would you like her number?"

"Thanks, Sharon."

They walked to the faculty lounge together and got their purses out of their lockers. Sharon pulled out her cell phone, then scrolled down until she found the number. Faith quickly made a note of it.

"If there's a flight to be had, Carrie will find it," Sharon assured her.

"Thanks again."

"Are you going to call Emily and let her know your

plans?" Sharon asked as they left the school building, walking toward the parking lot.

"Not yet. I don't want to get her hopes up if this turns out to be impossible."

"If worse comes to worst, I suppose you could always drive."

"I don't think so." Faith had done it often enough to realize she didn't want to take the Interstate in the middle of winter. The pass over the Siskiyous could be hellish this time of year. It wasn't a trip she wanted to make on her own, either.

"Don't worry—Carrie will get you a flight," Sharon said confidently.

As soon as she was in her car, Faith pulled out her own cell phone and dialed the travel agency. Carrie was extremely helpful and promised to get back to her as soon as she could.

Now that she had a plan, Faith was starting to feel excited. She called her sister soon after she arrived home, and the instant Penny picked up the phone, Faith could hear her three nephews fighting in the background. It sounded as if they were close to killing one another by the time the conversation ended.

Penny had made a token display of disappointment, but Faith didn't think her sister was too distressed. And Faith had to admit she was looking forward to a different kind of holiday herself. One without bickering kids—much as she loved them—and the same old routines. Still, her family was important to her, and she'd promised to visit right after New Year's.

Because she had someplace to go and family to be with, Faith hadn't really listened to what Emily had tried to tell her, hadn't really understood. Emily adored her daughter, of course, but Heather's absence was only part of the problem. What bothered her just as much was the prospect of spending perhaps the most significant holiday of the year by herself. In retrospect, Faith was astonished she hadn't recognized that earlier. She was a better friend than this and she was about to prove it.

After Faith had finished talking to her sister, she immediately sat down at her computer and logged on to the Internet. To her surprise Emily hadn't left her a message. Undeterred, she sent one off.

From: "Faith"<fkerriganinca@network.com>
To: "Emily"<springere@aal.com>
Sent: Thursday, December 16, 2004
Subject: Gift to arrive

Dear Emily,
I haven't heard from you all week. Forgive me for not being more of a friend.
Look for a present to arrive shortly.
Get back to me soon.
Love,
Faith

Half an hour later, the travel agent phoned. "I've got good news and bad news."

"Did you get me a flight?"

"Yes, that worked out fine. I got you into Seattle, but all the flights into Wenatchee are full. That's the bad news." Leavenworth was a few hours outside Seattle, but Faith could manage that easily enough with a rental car.

"I'll book a car," she said.

"I thought of that, too," Carrie went on to explain, "but this is a busy time of year for car rental agencies. The only vehicle available in all of Seattle is a seven-person van."

"Oh." Faith bit her lower lip.

"I reserved it because it was the last car left, but I can cancel the reservation if you don't want it."

Faith didn't take more than a few seconds to decide. "No, I'll take it."

On December twenty-fifth, she intended to be with Emily in Leavenworth. Not only that, she intended to bring Christmas with her—lock, stock and decorations.

Have Yule, will travel.

Four

In Emily's opinion, everything had worked out perfectly—other than the fact that she hadn't been able to reach Heather to let her know she was arriving. Not that it mattered. Heather would be as thrilled as she was. When Christmas came, the two of them would be together.

Early Sunday morning, Emily caught the short commuter flight out of Wenatchee and landed thirty minutes later at Sea-Tac Airport. Within an hour, Emily was on a nonstop flight from Seattle to Boston.

A mere seven days following her conversation with Heather, Emily was on her way across the entire United States to spend Christmas with her daughter. At the same time Charles Brewster, who sounded like a stereotypical absentminded history professor, was on his way to Leavenworth. Apparently their paths would cross somewhere over the middle of the country, her plane headed east and his headed west.

Emily would spend two glorious weeks with Heather, and Charles would have two weeks to explore Washington State—or do whatever he wanted. They were due to trade back on January first.

Two glorious weeks in Boston. Emily realized Heather had to work on papers and study, but she didn't mind. At least they'd be able to enjoy Christmas Day together and that was what mattered most.

The one negative was that Emily didn't know her daughter's schedule. Emily had repeatedly attempted to contact her, but Heather hadn't returned her messages. Tracy, Heather's roommate, hadn't said anything outright, but Emily had the feeling Heather didn't spend much time in her dorm room. She was obviously working longer hours than she'd let on. Actually, surprising her would be a good thing, Emily thought as she called Heather from Charles Brewster's condo. It would force her to take some time off and—

Surprise her she did.

"Mother," Heather cried into the receiver loudly enough to hurt Emily's eardrum. "You *can't* be in Boston."

Emily realized her arrival was a shock, but Heather seemed more dismayed than pleased.

"I didn't know you had a cell phone," Emily said. It would've saved them both a great deal of frustration had she been able to reach Heather earlier. She'd called the dorm room as soon as she'd landed and Tracy had given Emily a cell number.

"The phone isn't mine," Heather protested. "It belongs to a…friend."

"Ben?"

"No," she said. "Ben is old news."

Information she hadn't bothered to share with her mother, Emily mused. "Where are you?"

"That's not important." Heather sounded almost angry. "Where are you?"

Emily rattled off the address, but it didn't sound as if Heather had written anything down. Charles Brewster's condo had proved to be something of a disappointment—not that she was complaining. She'd found it easily enough and settled into the guest room, but it was modern and sterile, devoid of personality or any sign of Christmas.

"I'm so eager to see you," Emily told her daughter. She'd been in town for several hours and they still hadn't connected. "Why don't you come here, where I'm staying and—"

"I'd rather we met at the Starbucks across the street from my dormitory."

"But…" Emily couldn't understand why her daughter wouldn't want to come to her. Her attitude was puzzling, to say the least.

"Mother." Heather paused. "It would be better if we met at Starbucks."

"All right."

"Are you far from there?"

Emily didn't know her way around Boston, but the Harvard campus was within walking distance of the condo. Emily figured she'd find the coffee place without too much trouble, and she told Heather that.

"Meet me there in an hour," Heather snapped.

"Of course, but—"

The line went dead and Emily stared at the receiver, shocked that her own daughter had hung up on her. Or maybe the phone had gone dead. Maybe the battery had run out….

With a little while before she had to leave, Emily

walked around the condominium with all its modern conveniences. The kitchen was equipped with stainless steel appliances and from the look of it, Emily doubted anyone had so much as turned on a burner. The refrigerator still had the owner's manual in the bottom drawer and almost nothing else. As soon as she could manage it, Emily would find a grocery store.

Everything about the condo was spotless—and barren. Barren was a good word, she decided. Charles Brewster apparently didn't spend much time in his luxurious home. In her opinion his taste in furniture left something to be desired, too. All the pieces were modern, oddly shaped and in her opinion, uncomfortable. She suspected he'd given a designer free rein and then found the look so discordant that he left home whenever possible.

There wasn't a single Christmas decoration. Thank goodness Emily had brought a bit of Christmas cheer with her. The first thing she unpacked was their hand-knit Christmas stockings.

Emily's mother, who'd died a couple of years before Peter, had knit her stocking when Emily was five years old, and she'd knit Heather's, too. It just wouldn't be Christmas without their stockings. She hung them from the mantel, using a couple of paperweights she found in the study to secure them. The angel was carefully packaged in a carry-on. She unwrapped that and set it on the mantel, too. Then she arranged a few other favorite pieces—a tiny sled with a little girl atop, a Santa Heather had bought with her own money when she was ten, a miniature gift, gaily wrapped.

Her suitcases were empty now, but several Christmas decorations remained to be placed about the condo.

Emily thought she'd save those until later, when Heather could take part. That way it'd be just like home.

Assuming it would take her no more than thirty minutes to walk to Starbucks, Emily put on her coat, then stepped out of the condo, took the elevator to the marble foyer and hurried onto the sidewalk. Although it was only midafternoon, it resembled dusk. Dark ominous clouds hung overhead and the threat of snow was unmistakable.

Perhaps Heather would suggest a walk across the campus in the falling snow. They could pretend they were back home.

Emily arrived at Starbucks in fifteen minutes and bought a cup of coffee. While she waited for her daughter, she sat at the table next to the window and watched the young people stroll past. Although classes had officially been dismissed for winter break, plenty of students were still in evidence.

A large motorcycle roared past, and Emily winced at the loud, discordant sound. She sipped her coffee, watching the Harley—she assumed it was a Harley because that was the only brand she'd ever heard of. The motorcycle made a U-turn in the middle of the street and pulled into an empty parking space outside the coffee shop. Actually, it wasn't a real space, more of a gap between two parked cars.

The rider turned off the engine, climbed off the bike and removed his black bubblelike helmet. He was an unpleasant-looking fellow, Emily thought. His hair was long and tied at the base of his neck in a ponytail, which he'd flipped over his shoulder. He was dressed completely in black leather, much of his face covered with a thick beard.

A second rider, also dressed in black leather, slipped off the bike and removed a helmet. Emily blinked, certain she must be seeing things. If she didn't know better, she'd think the second person was her own daughter. But that wasn't possible. Was it?

Heather's twin placed her hand on the man's forearm, said something Emily couldn't hear and then headed into Starbucks alone. The Harley man stayed outside, guarding his bike.

Once the door opened and the girl walked inside, it was all too obvious that she was indeed Heather.

Aghast, Emily stood, nearly tipping over her coffee. "Heather?"

"Why didn't you let me know you were coming?" her daughter demanded.

"It's good to see you, too," Emily mumbled sarcastically.

Heather's eyes narrowed. "Frankly, Mother, it's *not* good to see you."

Emily swallowed a gasp. In her wildest imaginings, she'd never dreamed her daughter would say such a thing to her. Without being aware of it, Emily sank back into her chair.

Heather pulled out the chair across from her and sat down.

"Who's your…friend?" Emily asked, nodding toward the window.

"That's Elijah," Heather responded, defiance in every word.

"He doesn't have a last name?"

"No, just Elijah."

Emily sighed. "I see."

"I don't think you do," Heather said pointedly. "You should've told me you were coming to Boston."

"I tried," Emily burst out. "I talked to Tracy five times and left that many messages. Tracy said she'd let you know I'd phoned."

"She did…."

"Then why didn't you return my calls?"

Heather dropped her gaze. "Because I was afraid you were going to send me on a guilt trip and I didn't want to deal with it."

"Send you on a *guilt* trip?"

"You do that, you know? Make me feel guilty."

Despite her irritation, Emily did her best to remain calm. Now she understood why her daughter had insisted they meet at the coffee shop. She didn't want Emily to make a scene, which she admitted she was close to doing.

"I left five messages," Emily reminded her.

"I know—but I've been staying with friends and didn't realize you'd phoned until Tracy got in touch with me."

Staying with friends? Yeah, right. Emily's gaze flew out the window. Her daughter and that…that Neanderthal?

"I love him," Heather said boldly.

Emily managed to stay seated. "If that's the case, why don't you bring him inside so we can meet?"

"Because…" Heather hesitated and then squared her shoulders as if gathering her courage. "I didn't want him to hear what you're planning to say."

"About what?" This made no sense whatsoever.

"None of that matters. I'm leaving town with Elijah. In other words, I won't be in Boston over the holidays."

Emily shook her head slightly, wondering if she'd heard correctly. "I beg your pardon?"

"Elijah and I and a couple of other friends are riding down to Florida."

"For Christmas?" Emily *knew* something was wrong with her hearing now. There simply had to be. "On motorcycles?"

"Yes, for Christmas. And yes, on motorcycles. We're sick of this weather and want to spend our holiday on the beach."

Emily was completely speechless.

"You don't have anything to say?" Heather asked angrily. "I figured you'd have lots of opinions to share."

Emily's mouth opened and closed twice while she gathered her thoughts. "I traded homes with a stranger, traveled across the country and now you're telling me you won't be here for Christmas?" Her voice rose on the last word.

Heather's eyes flashed. "That's exactly what I'm saying. I'm of age and I make my own decisions."

Emily's jaw sagged in dismay. "You mean you're actually going to abandon me here—"

"You didn't bother to check your plans with me before you boarded that plane, did you, Mother? That's unfortunate because I've made other arrangements for Christmas. As far as I'm concerned, this problem is all yours."

"You said you had to work." That clearly had been a blatant lie.

"There you go," Heather cried. "You're trying to make me feel guilty."

"If you'd been honest—"

"You don't want me to be honest!" Heather challenged.

The truth of it was, she was right. Emily would rather not know that her daughter was associating with a member of some motorcycle gang.

"Go then," Emily said, waving her hand toward the door. "Have a wonderful time."

Heather leaped out of the chair as if she couldn't get away fast enough. "You can't blame me for this!"

"I'm not blaming you for anything," she said tiredly. Heaven forbid her daughter should accuse her of throwing guilt.

"This is all your own doing."

Emily stared silently into the distance.

"Nothing you say is going to make me change my mind," Heather insisted, as if wanting her to argue.

Emily didn't imagine it would. She felt physically ill, but she held on to her dignity. Pride demanded that she not let her daughter know how badly she'd hurt her.

Rushing out the door, Heather grabbed the black helmet, placed it on her head and climbed onto the back of the motorcycle. Elijah with no last name was already on the bike and within seconds they disappeared down the street.

Emily's opinion of this coming Christmas did an about-face.

This was destined to be the worst one of her life. Not only was she alone, but she was in a strange town, without a single friend. And her daughter had just broken her heart.

Five

"For heaven's sake, what is this?" Charles stood outside the gingerbread house in the middle of Santa's village feeling total dismay. There had to be some mistake—some vast, terrible mistake. Nothing else would explain the fact that after flying three thousand miles, he'd landed smack-dab in the middle of Christmas Town, complete with ice-skating rink, glittering lights and Christmas music.

He closed his eyes, hoping, praying, this nightmare would vanish and he could settle down in a nice quiet prison community. When he opened them, it was even worse than Charles had imagined. A little kid was staring up at him.

"I'm Sarah," she announced.

He said nothing.

"I lost two teeth." She proceeded to pull down her lower lip in order to reveal the empty spaces in her mouth.

"Is this where Emily Springer lives?" Charles asked, nodding toward the house. He was uncomfortable around children, mainly because he didn't know any.

"She went to Boston to spend Christmas with her daughter," Sarah informed him.

"I know." So he was in the right town. Damn.

"She keeps the key under the flower pot if you need to get inside."

Charles cocked his eyebrows. "She told you that?"

"Everyone in town knows where the key is." As if to prove it, Sarah walked over to the porch, lifted up the pot and produced the key, which she proudly displayed.

A one-horse open sleigh drove past, bells ringing, resembling something straight off a Christmas card. It didn't get any more grotesque than this. Ice skaters circled the rink in the park directly across the street from him. They were dressed in period costumes and singing in three-part harmony.

Rolling his suitcase behind him and clutching his laptop, Charles approached the house. It reminded him of an illustration, too cozy and perfect to be true, with its scalloped edging and colorful shutters. The porch had a swing and a rocking chair. Had he been Norman Rockwell, he would have found a canvas and painted it. Charles sighed heavily. This must be his punishment for trying to avoid Christmas.

"My mom's bringing you cookies," Sarah told him as she followed him up the steps.

"Tell her not to bother."

"She does it to be neighborly."

"I don't want neighbors."

"You don't?"

The little girl looked crushed.

He didn't mean to hurt the kid's feelings, but he wasn't interested in joining a Christmas commune. He simply wasn't socially inclined. All he wanted was to be left alone so he could write—and ignore anything to do with Christmas. Clearly, he'd been mistaken about this town—where was the prison? Keeping to his all-work-and-no-Yule agenda was going to be more of a challenge than he'd planned.

"Thank your mother for me, but explain that I came here to work," he told the little girl, making an effort to mollify her with politeness.

"But it's *Christmas*."

"I'm well aware of the season," he said, stabbing the key into the lock. "Let your mother know I prefer not to be disturbed." He hoped the kid would take the hint, too.

Sarah jutted out her lower lip. "Okay."

Good, she got the message. Charles opened the front door and stepped inside. He should've been prepared.... If Leavenworth was Santa's village, then stepping into this house was like walking into a fairy tale. The furniture was large and old-fashioned and bulky, with lots of lace and doilies. He'd traded homes with Goldilocks. Well, with the Three Bears, anyway. A grandfather clock chimed in the living room and logs were arranged in the fireplace, ready for a match. A knitted afghan was draped across the back of the overstuffed sofa. A green and blue braided rug covered the hardwood floor.

"Oh, brother," Charles sighed, truly discouraged. He abandoned his suitcase and laptop in the entry and walked into the kitchen. Emily had left him a note propped against the holly wreath that served as a centerpiece on the round oak table. Charles was almost afraid to read it.

After a moment he reached for it, read it, then tossed

it in the garbage. She'd left him dinner in the refrigerator. All he had to do was heat it in the microwave.

Dinner. Cookies from the neighbor. "Jingle Bells" in a one-horse open sleigh gliding back and forth in front of the house. If *that* wasn't bad enough, the entire street, indeed the whole town, glittered with Christmas lights that blinked from every conceivable corner. This was madness. Sheer madness. He hadn't escaped Christmas; he'd dived headfirst into the middle of it.

The first thing Charles did before he unpacked was pull down every shade on every window he could find. That, at least, blocked out the lights. He found an empty bedroom, set his suitcase on a chair and took out the work materials he needed.

The doorbell chimed and he groaned inwardly, bracing himself for another confrontation with the Christmas kid. Or her mother, bearing gifts of cookies.

It wasn't a woman with a plate of cookies or the child who'd accosted him earlier. Instead there were *six* of them, six children who stared up at him in wide-eyed wonder. They were dressed in winter gear from head to toe, with only their eyes and noses visible behind thick wool scarves and hand-knit hats. Their noses were bright red and their eyes watery. Melting snow dripped puddles onto the porch.

"Do you want to come outside? Go sledding with us?" the oldest of the group asked, his scarf moving where his mouth must be.

"No." Charles couldn't think of anything more to add.

"We have an extra sled you can use."

"I—no, thanks."

"Okay," the second-tallest boy answered.

No one budged.

"You sure?" the first boy asked.

Someone shouted from nearby. An adult voice from what he could tell.

"That's our mom," one of the children said. The little girl from before.

"We were supposed to leave you alone," another girl told him. At least he thought it was a girl.

"You should listen to your mother."

"Do you?"

The kid had him there. "Not always."

"Us neither." The boy's eyes smiled at him and Charles realized he'd made a friend, which was unfortunate.

"Emily said you were a teacher, too."

"I'm writing a book and I won't have time to play in the snow." He started to close the door.

"Not at all?" The oldest boy asked the question with a complete sense of horror.

"It's Christmas," another reminded him.

The woman's voice sounded again, shriller this time.

"We got to go."

"Bye," Charles said and, despite himself, found that he was grinning when he closed the door. His amusement died a quick death once he was back inside the house. Despite his attempt to block out all evidence of Christmas, he was well aware that it waited right outside, ready to pounce on him the minute he peeked out.

Grumbling under his breath, he returned to the kitchen and grudgingly set his dinner in the microwave. Some kind of casserole, duly labeled "Charles." He resisted the urge to call Emily Springer and tell her exactly what he thought of her little Christmas deception.

He would, too, if she'd misled him—only she hadn't. He blamed himself for this. Because he'd just realized something—he'd confused Leavenworth, Washington, with Leavenworth, Kansas.

The doorbell chimed once more, and Charles looked at the ceiling, rolling his eyes and groaning audibly. Apparently he was going to have to be more forthright with the family next door. He stomped across the room and hauled open the front door. He wanted to make it clear that he didn't appreciate the disturbances.

No one was there.

He stuck his head out the door and glanced in both directions.

No one.

Then he noticed a plate of decorated cookies sitting on the porch. They were wrapped in red cellophane, which was tied with a silver bow. His first instinct was to pretend he hadn't seen them. At the last second, he reached down, grabbed the plate and slammed the door shut. He turned the lock, and leaned against the wall, breathing fast.

He was in the wrong Leavenworth, but he might as well be in prison, since he wouldn't be able to leave the house, or even open the door, for fear of being ambushed by Christmas carolers, cookies and children.

Not exactly what he'd had in mind…

Six

Bernice Brewster was beside herself with frustration. For two days she'd tried to reach her son Charles, to no avail. He refused to use a cell phone and the one she'd purchased for him sat in a drawer somewhere. She was sure he'd never even charged the battery.

Growing up in Boston, Charles had been fascinated by history, particularly the original Thirteen Colonies. Now look at him! Granted, that interest had taken him far; unfortunately it seemed to be his *only* interest. If he wasn't standing in front of a classroom full of students—hanging on his every word as she fondly imagined—then he was buried in a book. Now, it appeared, he was writing his very own.

Why, oh why, couldn't her sons be like her friends' children, who were constantly causing them heartache and worry? Instead, she'd borne two sons who had to be the most loving, kindest sons on God's green earth, but… The problem was that they didn't understand one of the primary duties of a son—to provide his parents with grandchildren.

Bernice couldn't understand where she'd gone

wrong. If there was anything to be grateful for, it was that Bernard hadn't lived long enough to discover what a disappointment their two sons had turned out to be in the family department.

Charles was the younger of the two. Rayburn, eight years his senior, lived in New York City and worked for one of the big publishers there. He insisted on being called Ray, although she never thought of him as anything but Rayburn. He was a gifted man who'd risen quickly in publishing, although he changed houses or companies so often she couldn't hope to keep track of where he was or exactly what he did. At last mention, he'd said something about the name of the publisher changing because his company had merged with another. The merger had apparently netted him a promotion.

Like his younger brother, however, Rayburn was a disappointment in the area of marriage. Her oldest son was married to his job. He was in his midforties now and she'd given up hope that he'd ever settle down with a wife and family. Rayburn lived and breathed publishing.

Charles, it seemed, was her only chance for grandchildren, slight though that chance might be. He was such a nice young man and for a while, years ago now, there'd been such promise when he'd fallen head over heels in love. Monica. Oh, yes, she remembered Monica, a conniving shallow little bitch who'd broken her son's heart. On Christmas Eve, yet.

What was wrong with all those women in Boston and New York? Both her sons were attractive; Rayburn and Charles possessed their father's striking good looks, not that either had ever taken advantage of that. Bernice suspected Rayburn had been involved with various women, but obviously there'd never been anyone special.

Sitting in her favorite chair with the phone beside her, Bernice wondered what to do next. This was a sorry, sorry state of affairs. While her friends in the Arizona retirement community brought out book after book filled with darling pictures of their grandchildren, she had nothing to show except photos of her Pomeranian, FiFi. There were only so many pictures of the dog she could pass around. Even she was tired of looking at photographs of FiFi.

Bernice petted the small dog and with a brooding sense that something was terribly wrong, reached for the phone. She pushed speed dial for Charles's number and closed her eyes with impatience, waiting for the call to connect.

After one short ring, someone answered. "Hello."

Bernice gasped. The voice was soft and distinctly female. She couldn't believe her ears.

"Hello?"

"Is this the residence of Charles Brewster?" Bernice asked primly. "Professor Charles Brewster?"

"Yes, it is."

Of course it was Charles's condominium. The number was programmed into her phone and Bernice trusted technology. Shocked, she slammed down the receiver and stared, horrified, at the golf course outside.

Charles had a woman at his place. A woman he hadn't mentioned to his own mother, which could mean only one thing. Her son didn't want her to know anything about this…this female. All kinds of frightening scenarios flew into her mind. Charles consorting with a gold digger—or worse. Charles held hostage. Charles… She shook her head. No, she had to take control here.

Still in shock, Bernice picked up the phone again and pushed the top speed-dial button, which would connect her with Rayburn's New York apartment. He was often more difficult to reach than Charles. Luck was with her, however, and Rayburn answered after the third ring.

"Rayburn," Bernice cried in near panic, not giving him a chance to greet her.

"Mother, what's wrong?"

"When was the last time you spoke with your brother?" she demanded breathlessly.

Rayburn seemed to need time to think about this, but Bernice was in no condition to wait. "Something is wrong with Charles! I'm so worried."

"Why don't you start at the beginning?"

"I *am,*" she cried.

"Now, Mother…"

"Hear me out before you *Now, Mother* me." The more she thought about a strange woman answering Charles's phone, the more alarmed she became. Ever since that dreadful Monica had broken off the relationship… Ever since her, he'd gone out of his way to avoid women. In fact, he seemed oblivious to them and rejected every attempt she'd made to match him up.

"Your brother has a woman living with him," she said, her voice trembling.

Silence followed her announcement. "Mother, have you been drinking hot buttered rum again?"

"No," she snapped, insulted he'd ask such a thing. "Hear me out. I haven't been able to get hold of Charles for two days. I left messages on his answering machine, and he never returned a single call."

Her son was listening, and for that Bernice was grateful.

"Go on," he said without inflection.

"Just now, not more than five minutes ago, I called Charles again. A woman answered the phone." She squeezed her eyes closed. "She had a…sexy voice."

"Perhaps it was a cleaning woman."

"On a Monday?"

"Maybe it was a colleague. A friend from the History Department."

Bernice maintained a stubborn silence.

"You're sure about this?" Rayburn finally said.

"As sure as I live and breathe. Your brother has a woman in his home—living there."

"Just because she answered the phone doesn't mean she's living with Charles."

"You and I both know your brother would never allow just anyone to answer the phone."

Rayburn seemed to agree; a casual visitor wouldn't be answering his brother's phone.

"Good for him," Rayburn said with what sounded like a chuckle.

"How can you say that?" Bernice cried. "It's obvious that this woman must be completely unacceptable."

"Now, Mother…"

"Why wouldn't Charles tell us about her?"

"I don't know, but I think you're jumping to conclusions."

"I'm not! I just know something's wrong. Perhaps she tricked her way into his home, killed him and—"

"You've been watching too many crime shows," Rayburn chastised.

"Perhaps I have, but I won't rest until I get to the bottom of this."

"Fine." Her oldest son apparently grasped how serious she was, because he asked, "What do you want me to do?"

"Oh, Rayburn," she said with a sob, dabbing her nose with a delicate hankie. "I don't know how I'd manage without my sons to look out for me."

"Mother…"

"Take the train to Boston and investigate this situation. Report back to me ASAP."

"I can phone him and handle this in five minutes."

"No." She was insistent. "I want you to check it out with your own eyes. God only knows what your brother's gotten himself into with this woman. I just know whoever it is must be taking advantage of Charles."

"*Mother.* This is Christmas week and—"

"I know what time of year it is, Rayburn, and I realize you have a life of your own. A life that's much too busy to include your mother. But I'll tell you right now that I won't sleep a wink until I hear what's happened to Charles."

There was a pause.

"All right," Rayburn muttered. "I'll take the train to Boston and check up on Charles."

"Thank God." She could breathe easier now.

Seven

The Boeing 767 bounced against the tarmac and jarred Faith Kerrigan awake. She bolted upright and realized that she'd just landed in Seattle. She glanced at her watch; it was just after seven. She'd had less than four hours' sleep the entire night.

She'd survive. Any discomfort would be well worth the look of joy and surprise on Emily's face when Faith arrived and announced she'd be joining her friend for Christmas.

Remembering that was a better wake-up than a triple-shot espresso. Although the flight—which was completely full—had left the Bay area at 5:00 a.m., Faith had been up since two. Her lone suitcase was packed to the bursting point and she'd stuffed her carry-on until the zipper threatened to pop. After filing off the plane and collecting her suitcase, she dragged everything to the car rental agency. Thankfully, an attendant was available despite the early hour.

Faith stepped up to the counter and managed a smile. "Hi."

"Happy holidays," the young woman greeted her.

The name tag pinned to her blouse identified her as Theresa.

With her confirmation number in hand, Faith leaned against the counter and asked, “Will you need my credit card?” She couldn’t remember if she’d given the number to her travel agent earlier.

Theresa nodded and slid over a sheaf of papers to fill out. Faith dug in the bottom of her purse for her favorite pen.

The girl on the other side of the counter reminded her of Heather, and she wondered briefly if Theresa was a college student deprived of spending Christmas with her family because of her job.

The phone pealed; Theresa answered immediately. After announcing the name of the agency, followed by “Theresa speaking,” she went silent. Her eyes widened as she listened to whoever was on the other end. Then, for some inexplicable reason, the young woman’s gaze landed on her.

“That’s terrible,” Theresa murmured, steadily eyeing Faith.

Faith shifted her feet uncomfortably and waited.

“No…she’s here now. I don’t know what to tell you. Sure, I can ask, but…yes. Okay. Let me put you on hold.”

Faith shifted her weight to the other foot. This sounded ominous.

Theresa held the telephone receiver against her shoulder. “There’s been a problem,” she said. Her dark eyes held a pleading look.

“What kind of problem?”

The young woman sighed. “Earlier we rented a van exactly like yours to a group of actors and, unfortunately, theirs broke down. Even more unfortunate, we don't have a replacement we can give them. On top of that, it doesn't look like the van they were driving can be easily fixed."

Faith could tell what was coming next. "You want me to give up the van I reserved."

"The thing is, we don't have a single car on the lot to give you in exchange."

Faith would've liked to help, but she had no other means of getting to Leavenworth. "The only reason I reserved the van is because it was the last car available."

"My manager is well aware of that."

"Where is this group headed?" All she needed the van for was to get to Leavenworth. Once Faith reached her destination, she'd be with Emily, who had her own vehicle. She explained that.

"I'm not sure, but my manager said this group gives charity performances across the region. They have appearances scheduled at nursing homes and hospitals."

Great, just great. If she didn't let them have her van, the entire state of Washington would be filled with disappointed children and old people, and it would be all her fault.

"In other words, if we could find a way to get you to Leavenworth, you'd be willing to relinquish the van?" Theresa sounded optimistic. "Let me find out if that's doable."

Faith waited some more while the clerk explained the situation. The young woman had an expressive face. Her eyes brightened as she glanced at Faith and smiled. Cupping her hand over the receiver, she said, "My manager's talking to the actors now, but it seems their next performance is in the general vicinity of Leavenworth."

"So they could drive me there?"

Theresa nodded. "They can drop you off." She smiled again. "My manager said if you agree to this, she'll personally make sure there's a car available for you later, so you can get back to Seattle."

"Okay." This was becoming a bit complicated, but she was willing to cooperate.

"She also wanted me to tell you that because you're being so great about all of this, there won't be any charge for whatever length of time you have one of our cars."

"Perfect." Faith was pretty sure the rental agency must be desperate to ask such a favor of her. Still, it was Christmas, a time for goodwill.

Theresa's attention returned to the phone. "That'll work. Great. Great."

Fifteen minutes later, Faith was driven to the off-site rental facility. Clasping her paperwork and pulling her suitcase, she half-carried, half dragged her carry-on bag.

"Can I help you?" a little person in an elf costume asked.

"I'm fine, but thank you," she responded, a little startled.

"I think you must be the woman the agency told us about."

"Us?"

"The others are inside."

"The actors?"

"Santa and six elves. I'm one of the elves."

Faith grinned and, bending slightly forward, offered the man her hand. "Faith."

"Tony."

Soon Faith was surrounded by the five other elves and Santa himself. The actors were delightful. Tony introduced each one to Faith. There was Sam, who played the role of Santa. He was, not surprisingly, a full two feet taller than the other cast members, and he had a full white beard and a white head of hair. He must pad his costume because he was trim and didn't look to be more than fifty. His helpers, all little people, were Allen, Norman, Betty, Erica and David. And Tony, of course. Before Faith had an opportunity to repeat their names in her mind, the luggage was transferred from the company van to the rental.

"We sure appreciate this," Sam told her as he slid into the driver's seat.

"I'm happy to help," Faith said, and she meant it.

At Sam's invitation, seconded by Tony, Allen and the others, Faith joined him up front; the six elves took the two rear seats.

"Is Leavenworth out of your way?" she asked.

Sam shook his head. "A little, but you won't hear me complaining." He glanced over at Faith. "We have a performance this afternoon in north Seattle at a children's hospital. If you need to be in Leavenworth before tonight, I could let you take the van with Tony. He has a license, but—"

Theresa hadn't mentioned a performance that day, but then she probably hadn't known about it either. Faith hesitated. No doubt Tony should be there for the show. Yes, she was tired and yes, she wanted to see her friend, but nothing was so pressing that she had to be in Leavenworth before five that evening.

"I'm surprising a friend," she admitted. "Emily isn't

expecting me. So I don't have to get there at any particular time."

"You mean she doesn't even know you're coming?"

"Nope." Faith nearly giggled in her excitement. "She's going to be so happy to see me."

"Then you don't mind attending the performance with us?"

"Not at all." Although she was eager to get to Leavenworth, Faith didn't feel she could deprive children of meeting Tony.

As it turned out, Faith was completely charmed by the performance. Santa and his helpers were wonderful with the sick children, and Tony even enlisted her to assist in the distribution of gifts. The performance was clearly the highlight of their Christmas celebration.

It wasn't until after four that they all piled back into the van. The elves chatted away, pleased everything had gone so well. Faith learned that Sam and his friends had been doing these charity performances for years. They all worked regularly as actors—with roles in movies, TV productions and commercials—but they took a break at Christmas to bring a bit of joy and laughter into the lives of sick children and lonely old people. Faith felt honored to have been part of it.

"I'm starving," Allen announced not long after they got on the freeway.

Erica and David chimed in. "Me, too."

Not wanting to show up at Emily's hungry, she agreed that they should stop for hamburgers and coffee. Sam insisted on paying for Faith's meal.

"You guys were just great," she said again, biting into her cheeseburger with extra pickles. Emily was going to love them, especially when she learned that they were performing at children's hospitals and retirement homes.

"Thanks."

"What's on the agenda for tomorrow?"

"We aren't due in Spokane until three," Sam told her.

Spokane was a long drive from Leavenworth, and they'd be driving at night. "Do you have hotel reservations?" Faith asked.

"Not until tomorrow," Sam confessed. "Our original plan was to spend the night in Ellensburg."

Faith mulled over this information and knew Emily would encourage her to ask her newfound friends to stay at the house overnight. The place had two extra bedrooms that were rarely used.

"Listen, I'll need to talk it over with my friend, but I'm sure she'd want me to invite you to spend the night." She grinned. "What if you all arrived in costume? I'll be her Christmas surprise—delivered by Santa and his elves. Are you game?"

"You bet," Sam said, and his six friends nodded their agreement.

They all scrambled back into the van, and Tony chuckled from the back seat. "One Christmas delivery, coming right up."

Eight

Emily was bored and sad and struggling not to break down. There was only one thing left to do—what she always did when she got depressed.

Bake cookies.

But even this traditional cure required a monumental effort. First, she had to locate a grocery store and because she didn't have a car, she'd have to haul everything to the condominium on her own. This was no easy task when she had to buy both flour and sugar. By the time she let herself back into the condo with three heavy bags, she was exhausted.

On the off chance that she might be able to reach Faith, she tried phoning again. After leaving six messages, Emily knew that if her friend was available, she would've returned the call by now. Faith must be at her sister's because she certainly wasn't at home.

Heather's roommate had apparently left town, too, because there was no answer at the dorm. Emily had to accept that she was alone and friendless in a strange city.

Once she began her baking project, though, her

mood improved. She doubted Charles had so much as turned on the oven. In order to bake cookies, she'd had to purchase every single item, including measuring cups and cookie sheets. Once the cookies were ready, Emily knew she couldn't possibly eat them all. It was the baking, not the eating, that she found therapeutic. She intended to pack his freezer with dozens of chocolate chip cookies.

Soon the condo smelled delectable—of chocolate and vanilla and warm cookies. She felt better just inhaling the aroma. As she started sorting through her Christmas CDs, she was startled to hear someone knocking at the door. So far she hadn't met a single other person in the entire building. Her heart hammered with excitement. Really, it was ridiculous to be this thrilled over what was probably someone arriving at her door—Charles's door—by mistake.

Emily squinted through the peephole and saw a man in a wool overcoat and scarf standing in the hallway. He must be a friend of Professor Brewster's, she decided. A rather attractive one with appealing brown eyes and a thick head of hair, or what she could see of his hair. She opened the door.

All he did was stare at her.

Emily supposed she must look a sight. With no apron to be found, she'd tucked a dish towel in the waistband of her jeans. Her Rudolph sweatshirt, complete with blinking red nose, had been a gift from her daughter the year before. She wore fuzzy pink slippers and no makeup.

"Can I help you?"

"Where's Charles?" he asked abruptly.

"And you are?"

"His brother, Ray."

"Oh…" Emily moved aside. "You'd better come in because this is a rather long story."

"It would seem so." He removed his scarf and stepped into the apartment. As soon as he did, he paused and looked around. "This *is* my brother's place?"

"Technically yes, but for the next two weeks it's mine. I'm Emily Springer, by the way."

"Hmm. I hardly recognized it." Ray glanced at the mantel where Emily had hung the two Christmas stockings and put the angel. "Would you mind if I sat down?"

"No. Please do." She gestured toward the low-slung leather chair that resembled something one would find on a beach.

Ray claimed the chair and seemed as uncomfortable as she'd been when she'd tried watching television in it.

"You might prefer the sofa," she said, although that meant they'd be sitting next to each other.

"I think I'll try it." He had to brace his hand on the floor before he could lever himself out of the chair. He stood, sniffed the air and asked, "Are you baking cookies?"

She nodded. "Chocolate chip."

"From scratch?"

Again she nodded. "Would you like some? I've got coffee on, too."

"Not yet." He shook his head. "I think you'd better tell me what's going on with my brother first."

"Yes, of course." Emily sat on the other end of the sofa, and turned sideways, knees together, hands clasped. She just hoped she could get through this without breaking into tears. "It all started when my daughter phoned to say she wouldn't be home for Christmas."

"Your daughter lives here in Boston?"

"Yes." Emily moistened her lips. "Heather attends Harvard." She resisted the urge to brag about Heather's scholarship.

"One of my brother's students?"

The thought had never occurred to Emily. "I don't think so, but I don't know." Apparently there was a lot she didn't know about her daughter's life.

"When I learned that Heather wouldn't be coming home for the holidays, I made the foolish decision to come to Boston, only I couldn't afford more than the airfare."

"In other words, you needed a place to stay?"

"Exactly, so I posted a message on a home-exchange site. Charles contacted me and we exchanged emails and decided to trade places for two weeks."

"My brother hates Christmas—that's why he wanted out of the city."

Emily's gaze shot to his. "He didn't mention that."

"Well, it's another long story."

"Then I'm afraid Leavenworth's going to be a bit of a shock."

"Explain that later."

"There's not much more to tell you. Charles is living in my home in Leavenworth, Washington, for the next two weeks and I'm here." She stopped to take a deep breath. "And Heather, my daughter, is in Florida with a man who looks like he might belong to the Hells Angels."

"I see."

Emily doubted that, but didn't say so. "Did Charles know you were coming?"

"No. Actually, my mother asked me to visit. She

called and you obviously answered the phone. Mother was convinced something had happened to Charles—that he'd gotten involved with some woman and… Never mind. But she insisted I get over here to, uh, investigate the situation."

"She'll be relieved."

"True," Ray said, "but truth be known, I'm a bit disappointed. It would do my brother a world of good to fall in love."

He didn't elaborate and she didn't question him further. Everything she knew about Charles had come from their email chats, which had been brief and businesslike.

Emily stood and walked into the kitchen. Ray followed her. "So you're alone in the city over Christmas?"

She nodded, forcing a smile. "It isn't exactly what I intended, but there's no going back now." Her home was occupied, and getting a flight out of Boston at this late date was financially unfeasible. She was stuck.

"Listen," Ray said, reaching for a cookie. "Why don't I take you to dinner tonight?"

Emily realized she shouldn't analyze this invitation too closely. Still, she had to know. "Why?"

"Well, because we both need to eat and I'd rather have a meal with you than alone." He paused to take a bite of the cookie, moaning happily at the taste. "Delicious. Uh—I didn't mean to sound ungracious. Let me try that again. Would you be so kind as to join me for dinner?"

"I'd love to," Emily said, her spirits lifting.

"I'll catch the last train back to New York, explain everything to my mother in the morning and we'll leave it at that. Now, may I have another one of these incomparable cookies?"

"Of course." Emily met his eyes and smiled. He was a likable man, and at the moment she was in need of a friend. "When would you like to leave?"

Ray checked his watch. "It's six-thirty, so any time is fine with me."

"I'd better change clothes." She pulled the towel free of her waistband, folded it and set it on the kitchen counter.

"Before you do," Ray said stopping her. "Explain what you meant about my brother being in trouble if he isn't fond of Christmas."

"Oh, that." A giggle bubbled up inside her as she told him about Leavenworth in December—the horse-drawn sleigh, the carolers and the three separate tree-lighting ceremonies, one for every weekend before Christmas.

Ray was soon laughing so hard he was wiping tears from his eyes. Just seeing his amusement made her laugh, too, although she didn't really understand what he found so hilarious.

"If only…if only you knew my b-brother," Ray sputtered. "I can just imagine what he thought when he arrived."

"I guess Charles and I both had the wrong idea about trading homes."

"Sure seems that way," Ray agreed, still grinning. "Why don't I have another cookie while you get ready," he said cheerfully. "I haven't looked forward to a dinner this much in ages."

Come to think of it, neither had Emily.

Nine

Charles worked at his laptop computer until late in the afternoon. He stopped only when his stomach started to growl. He was making progress and felt good about what he'd managed to accomplish, but he needed a break.

After closing down his computer, he wandered into the kitchen. An inspection of the cupboards and the freezer revealed a wide selection of choices, but he remembered his agreement with Emily. They were to purchase their own food. Emily had been kind enough to prepare yesterday's dinner for him, but he needed to fend for himself from here on out.

There was no help for it; he'd have to venture outside the comfort and security of Emily's house. He'd have to leave this rather agreeable prison and take his chances among the townspeople. The thought sent a chill down his spine.

Peeking through the drapes, Charles rolled his eyes. He was convinced that if he looked hard enough, he'd see Ebenezer Scrooge and the ghost of Marley, not to mention Tiny Tim hobbling down the sidewalk, complete with his crutch, and crying out, "God bless us everyone."

Once he'd donned his long wool coat and draped a scarf around his neck, he dashed out the door. He locked it behind him, although he wondered why he bothered. According to the kid next door, the entire town knew where Emily kept the key. Still, Charles wanted it understood that he wasn't receiving company.

Walking to his rental car, he hurriedly unlocked it and climbed inside before anyone could stop him. With a sense of accomplishment, he drove until he discovered a large chain grocery store. The lot was full, and there appeared to be some sort of activity taking place in front of the store.

Ducking his head against the wind, he walked rapidly across the parking lot toward the entrance.

A crowd had gathered, and Charles glanced over, wondering at all the commotion. He blinked several times as the scene unfolded before him. Apparently the local church was putting on a Nativity pageant, complete with livestock—a donkey, a goat and several sheep.

Just as he scurried by, the goat raised its head and grabbed the hem of his overcoat. Charles took two steps and was jerked back.

The goat was eating his coat. Apparently no one noticed because the three wise men had decided to make an appearance at the same time. Charles tried to jerk his hem free, but the goat had taken a liking to it and refused to let go. Not wanting to call attention to himself, he decided to ignore the goat and proceed into the store, tugging at his coat as he walked. Unfortunately the goat walked right along behind him, chewing contentedly.

Charles had hoped to dash in, collect his groceries and get out, all in fifteen minutes or less. Instead, everyone in the entire store turned to stare at him as he stumbled in, towing the goat.

"Mister, you've got a goat following you." Some kid, about five or six, was kind enough to point this out, as if Charles hadn't been aware of it.

"Go away." Charles attempted to shoo the goat, but the creature was clearly more interested in its evening meal than in listening to him.

"Oh, sorry." A teenage boy raced after him and took hold of the goat by the collar. After several embarrassing seconds, the boy managed to get the goat to release Charles's coat.

Before he drew even more attention, Charles grabbed a cart and galloped down the aisles, throwing in what he needed. He paused to gather up the back of his expensive wool coat, which was damp at the hem and looking decidedly nibbled, then with a sigh dropped it again. As he went on his way, he noticed several shoppers who stopped and stared at him, but he ignored them.

He approached the dairy case. As he reached for a quart of milk a barbershop quartet strolled up to serenade him with Christmas carols. Charles listened politely for all of five seconds, then zoomed into a check-out line.

Was there no escape?

By the time he'd loaded his groceries in the car and returned to Emily's home, he felt as if he'd completed the Boston marathon. Now he had to make it from the car to the house undetected.

He looked around to see if any of the neighborhood kids were in sight. He was out of luck, because he immediately caught sight of six or seven of the little darlings, building a snowman in the yard directly next to his.

They all gaped at him.

Charles figured he had only a fifty-fifty chance of making it to the house minus an entourage.

"Hello, mister."

They were already greeting him and he didn't even have the car door completely open. He pretended not to hear them.

"Want to build a snowman with us?"

"No." He scooped up as many of the grocery bags as he could carry and headed toward the house.

"Need help with that?" All the kids raced to his vehicle, eager to offer assistance.

"No."

"You sure?"

"What I want is to be left alone." Charles didn't mean to be rude, but all this Christmas stuff had put him on edge.

The children stared up at him, openmouthed, as if no one had ever said that to them in their entire lives. The little girl blinked back tears.

"Oh, all right," he muttered, surrendering to guilt. He hadn't intended to be unfriendly—it was just that he'd had about as much of this peace and goodwill business as a man could swallow.

The children gleefully tracked through the house, bringing in his groceries and placing them in the kitchen. They looked pleased when they'd finished. Everyone, that is, except the youngest—Sarah, wasn't it?

"I think someone tried to eat your coat," the little girl said.

"A goat did."

"Must've been Clara Belle," her oldest brother put in. "She's Ronny's 4-H project. He said that goat would latch on to anything. I guess he was right."

Charles grunted agreement and got out his wallet to pay the youngsters.

"You don't have to pay us," the boy said. "We were just being neighborly."

That "neighborly" nonsense again. Charles wanted to argue, but they were out the door before he had a chance to object.

Once Charles had a chance to unpack his groceries and eat, he felt almost human again. He opened the curtains and looked out the window, chuckling at the Kennedy kids' anatomically correct snowman. He wondered what his mother would've said had he used the carrot for anything other than the nose.

It was dark now, and the lights were fast appearing, so Charles shut the curtains again. He considered returning to work. Instead he yawned and decided to take a shower in the downstairs bathroom. He thought he heard something when he got under the spray, but when he listened intently, everything was silent.

Then the sound came again. Troubled now, he turned off the water and yanked a towel from the rack. Wrapping it around his waist, he opened the bathroom door and peered out. He was just about to ask if anyone was there when he heard a female voice.

"Emily? Where are you?" the voice shouted.

Charles gasped and quickly closed the door. He dressed as fast as possible, which was difficult because he was still wet. Zipping up his pants, he stepped out of the bathroom, hair dripping, and came face to face with—Santa Claus.

Both men shouted in alarm.

"Who the hell are you?" Santa cried.

"What are you doing in my house?" Charles demanded.

"Faith!" Santa shouted.

A woman rounded the corner and dashed into the hallway—then stopped dead in her tracks. Her mouth fell open.

"Who are *you?*" Charles shrieked.

"Faith Kerrigan. What have you done with my friend?"

"If you mean Emily Springer, she's in Boston."

"What?" For a moment it looked as if she was about to collapse.

Immediately six elves appeared, all in pointed hats and shoes, crowding the hallway.

Santa and six elves? Charles had taken as much as a Christmas-hating individual could stand. "What the hell is going on here?" he yelled, his patience gone.

"I… I flew in from the Bay area to surprise my friend for Christmas. She didn't say anything about going to Boston."

"We traded houses for two weeks."

"Oh…no." Faith slouched against the wall.

All six of the elves rushed forward to comfort her. Santa looked like he wanted to punch Charles out.

Charles ran his hand down his face. "Apparently there's been…a misunderstanding."

"Apparently," Faith cried as if that was the understatement of the century.

The doorbell chimed, and when Charles went to answer it, the Kennedy kids rushed past him and over to Faith. Their arms went around her waist and they all started to chatter at once, telling her about Heather not coming home and Emily going to Boston.

Adding to the mass confusion were the six elves, who seemed to be arguing among themselves about which one of them would have the privilege of bashing in Charles's nose.

Charles's head started to swim. He raised his arms and shouted in his loudest voice, "Everyone out!"

The room instantly went silent. "Out?" Faith cried. "We don't have anywhere to go. There isn't a hotel room between here and Spokane with a vacancy now."

Charles slumped onto the arm of the sofa and pressed his hand against his forehead.

"Where do you expect us to go?" Faith asked. Her voice was just short of hysterical. "I've only had a few hours' sleep and my friends changed their plans to drive me to Leavenworth and the van broke down and now—this."

"All right, all right." Charles decided he could bear it for one night as long as everyone left by morning.

The small group looked expectantly at him. "You can spend the night—but just tonight. Tomorrow morning, all of you are out of here. Is that understood?"

"Perfectly," Faith answered on their behalf.

Not a one of them looked grateful enough. "Count your blessings," Charles snapped.

Really, he had no other choice—besides kicking them out into the cold.

"Thank you," Faith whispered, looking pale and shaken.

Charles glared at the mixed ensemble of characters.

Santa, elves, kids and a surprisingly attractive woman stared back at him. "Remember, tomorrow morning you're gone. All of you."

Faith nodded and led Santa and his elves up the stairs.

"Good." First thing in the morning, all these people would be out of this house and out of his life.

Or so Charles hoped. He didn't have the energy to wonder why the tall guy and the six short ones were all in Christmas costume.

Ten

Early in the evening, Emily and Ray left the condominium. Although it was dark, Ray insisted on showing her the waterfront area. They walked for what seemed like miles, talking and laughing. Ray was a wonderful tour guide, showing her Paul Revere's house and the site of the Boston Tea Party. Both were favorites of his brother's, he pointed out, telling her proudly of Charles's accomplishments as a historian. From the harbor they strolled through St. Stephen's Church and Copp's Hill Burying Ground, which began in 1659 and was the city's second-oldest graveyard. They strolled from one site to the next. Time flew, and when Emily glanced at her watch, she was astonished to discover it was almost eight-thirty.

On Hanover Street, they stopped for dinner at one of Ray's favorite Italian restaurants. The waiter seated them at a corner table and even before handing them menus, he delivered a large piece of cheese and a crusty loaf of warm bread with olive oil for dipping.

"Have I completely worn you out?" Ray asked, smiling over at Emily. He started to peruse the wine list, which had been set in front of him.

Yes, she was tired, but it was a nice kind of tired. "No, quite the contrary. Oh, Ray, thank you so much."

He looked up, obviously surprised.

"A few hours ago, I was feeling utterly sorry for myself. I was staying in one of the most historic cities in our country and all I could think about was how miserable I felt. And right outside my door was all this." She made a wide sweeping gesture with her arm. "I can't thank you enough for opening my eyes to Boston."

He smiled again—and again she was struck by what a fine-looking man he was.

"The pleasure was all mine," he told her softly.

The waiter came with their water glasses and menus. By now, Emily was hungry, and after slicing off pieces of cheese for herself and for Ray, she studied the menu. Ray closed the wine list. After consulting with her, he ordered a bottle of Chianti and an antipasto dish.

As soon as the waiter took their dinner order, Ray leaned back in his seat and reached inside his suit jacket for his cell phone.

"I'd better give my mother a call. I was planning to do it tomorrow, but knowing her, she's waiting anxiously to hear about the strange woman who's corrupted her son."

"You or Charles?" Emily teased.

Ray grinned and punched out a single digit. He raised the small phone to his ear. "Hello, Mother."

His smile widened as he listened for a long moment. "I have someone with me I'd like you to meet."

He had to pause again, listening to his mother's lengthy response.

"Yes, this is the evil woman you feared had ruined your son. She might still do it, too."

"Stop it," Emily mouthed and gently kicked his shoe beneath the table.

"Not to worry—Charles is in Washington State. Here, I'll let Emily explain everything." He handed her the cell phone.

Emily had barely gotten the receiver to her ear when she heard the woman on the other end of the line demand, "To whom am I speaking?"

"Mrs. Brewster, my name is Emily Springer, and Charles and I traded homes for two weeks."

"You're living in Charles's condo?" She didn't seem to believe Emily.

"Yes, but just until after Christmas."

"Oh."

"Charles and I met over the Internet at a site set up for this type of exchange."

"I see." The woman went suspiciously silent.

"It's only for two weeks."

"You're telling me my son let you move into his home sight unseen? And that, furthermore, Charles has ventured all the way to the West Coast?" The question sounded as if it came from a prosecuting attorney who'd found undeniable evidence of perjury.

"Yes… I came to Boston to see my daughter." For the last few days, Emily had tried not to think about Heather, which was nearly impossible.

"Let me speak to Rayburn," his mother said next.

Emily handed the cell phone back to Ray.

Ray and his mother chatted for another few minutes before he closed the phone and stuck it inside his pocket.

By then the wine had been delivered and poured.

Emily reached for her glass and sipped. She enjoyed wine on occasion, but this was a much finer quality than she normally drank.

"Rayburn?" she said, teasing him by using the same tone his mother had used.

He groaned. "If you think that's bad, my little brother's given name is actually Hadley."

"Hadley?"

"Hadley Charles. The minute he was old enough to speak, he refused to let anyone call him Hadley."

Emily smiled. "I can't say I blame him."

"Rayburn isn't much of an improvement."

"No, but it's better than Hadley."

"That depends." Ray sipped his wine and sat up straighter when the waiter brought the antipasto plate. It was a meal unto itself, with several varieties of sliced meats, cheese, olives and roasted peppers.

That course was followed by soup and then pasta. Emily was convinced she couldn't swallow another bite when the main course, a cheese-stuffed chicken dish, was brought out.

When they'd finished, they lingered over another bottle of wine. Ray leaned forward, elbows resting on the table, and they talked, moving from one subject to the next. Emily had hardly ever met a man who was so easy to talk to. He seemed knowledgeable about any number of subjects.

"You're divorced?" he asked, as they turned to more personal matters.

"Widowed. Eleven years ago. Peter was killed when Heather was just a little girl."

"I'm sorry."

"Thank you." She could speak of Peter now without pain, but that had taken years. She was a different woman than she'd been back then, as a young wife and mother. "Peter was a good husband and a wonderful father. I still miss him."

"Is there a reason you've never remarried?"

"Not really. I got caught up in Heather's life and my job. Over the years I've dated now and then, but there was never any spark. What about you?"

He shrugged. "I've been consumed by my job for so long, I don't know what it is to have an ordinary life."

This interested Emily. "I've always wondered what an ordinary life would be like. Does anyone really have one?"

"Good point."

"Did you have any important relationships?"

"I dated quite a bit when I was in my twenties and early thirties. I became seriously involved twice, but both times I realized, almost from the first, that it wouldn't last."

"Sounds like a self-fulfilling prophecy to me."

He grinned as he picked up his wineglass. "My mother said almost those identical words to me. The thing is, I admired both women and, to some extent loved them, but deep down I suspect they knew it wouldn't last, either."

"And it didn't."

"Right. I put long hours into my job and I have a lot of responsibilities. I love publishing. No one's more excited than I am when one of our authors does well."

Emily had plenty of questions about the publishing world, but she knew Ray must have been asked these same questions dozens of times. They had this one evening together, and Emily didn't want to bore him with idle curiosity.

When they'd finished the second bottle of wine, Emily felt mellow and sleepy. Most of the other tables were vacant, and the crew of waiters had started changing tablecloths and refilling the salt and pepper shakers.

Ray noticed the activity going on around them, too. "What time is it?" he asked, sitting up and glancing at his watch with an unbelieving expression.

"It's ten to eleven."

"You're kidding!" He looked shocked.

"Well, you know what they say about time flying, etc."

He chuckled softly. "Tonight certainly was an enjoyable evening—but there's a problem."

"Oh?"

He downed the last of his wine and announced, "I'm afraid the next train doesn't leave for New York until tomorrow morning."

"Oh…right." Emily had entirely forgotten that Ray would have to catch the train.

He relaxed visibly, apparently finding a solution to his problem. "Not to worry, I'll get a hotel room. That shouldn't be too difficult."

Without a reservation, she wondered if that was true. Furthermore, she hated the thought of him spending that extra money on her account. "You don't need to do that."

"What do you mean?"

"Your brother's condo has two bedrooms."

He raised his eyebrows.

"I'm sleeping in the guest room, and I'm sure your brother wouldn't object to your taking his room."

Ray hesitated and looked uncertain. "Are you sure you're comfortable with that arrangement?"

"Of course."

That was easy to say after two bottles of wine. Had Emily been completely sober, she might not have—but really, what could it hurt?

She decided that question was best left unanswered.

Eleven

Heather Springer wrapped her arms tightly around Elijah's waist, the sound of the wind roaring in her ears. She laid her head against his muscular back and relished the feel of his firm body so close to her own. Three other Harleys, all with passengers, zoomed down the interstate on their way to the white sandy beaches of Florida.

Try as she might, Heather couldn't stop thinking about the bewildered look on her mother's face when she learned Heather had made her own plans for the Christmas holidays.

The least her mother could've done was let her know she was flying to Boston. It was supposed to be a big surprise—well, it definitely was that. Actually, it was more of a shock, and not a pleasant one. Heather had hoped for the proper time to tell her mother about Elijah. That opportunity, unfortunately, had been taken away from her.

Heather sighed. She was grateful when Elijah pulled into a rest area near Daytona Beach. He climbed off the

Harley and removed his helmet, shaking his head to release his long hair.

Heather watched as the other motorcycles pulled into nearby spaces. Heather was proud that Elijah led the way in this adventure. Being with him during the holidays was thrilling, and she wasn't about to let her stick-in-the-mud, old-fashioned mother ruin it.

Elijah was different from any boy Heather had ever dated. The others paled by comparison, especially Ben who was traditional and frankly boring. All he thought about was school and work and getting his law degree. For once, just once, she wanted to think about something besides grades and scholarship money. She wanted to *live.*

She'd met Elijah at Starbucks, and they'd struck up a conversation. That was in early October, and after meeting him everything had changed. Never before had she been in love like this. It was exciting and crazy and new. Elijah's world was completely unlike her own, and she knew their differences were what made him so attractive. He was dark, wild, dangerous—all she'd ever craved. She wanted to share his life, share everything with him. Heather felt pleased that he was introducing her to his friends, but she'd noticed he wasn't interested in meeting hers. That hadn't bothered her until recently. Heather didn't know the other bikers and their girlfriends very well, but she liked them and hoped for the chance to connect.

"Feel that sunshine," Elijah said. He closed his eyes and tilted his face toward the sun.

Heather removed her own helmet and slid off the Harley. "It's not as warm as I thought it would be." She didn't want to complain, but she'd assumed the temperature would be in the seventies; it was closer to the fifties. This wasn't exactly swimming-in-the-ocean kind of weather.

"Once we're in the Miami Beach area you'll be hot enough," Elijah promised. "Until then I'll keep you warm." He circled her waist with his massive arms.

She turned in his embrace, kissing him lightly.

"I thought we'd hang out here for a while," he murmured.

"That sounds good to me." Heather didn't want to admit how much her backside ached, especially when the others didn't seem to have any such complaint. She'd heard one of the girls comment that Heather was walking oddly and then giggle. Heather pretended not to hear. She wasn't one of them, but she badly wanted to be. Given a chance, she'd prove herself, she vowed.

Soon the eight of them were sprawled out on the grass. Elijah lay on his back, his head resting on Heather's lap. She sat leaning against a palm tree.

"You okay?" Elijah asked.

"Of course." She tried to make light of her feelings, rather than confess what she was really thinking.

"You've been pretty quiet."

Heather slipped her fingers through his hair. "I suppose."

"I bet it's your mother."

Heather sighed and realized she couldn't hide her thoughts any longer. "She might've said something, you know."

Elijah nodded. "You couldn't have known she was planning to fly in for Christmas."

Heather twirled a lock of his dark hair around her finger. "She didn't even hint at her plans. It's like she expected me to abandon everything just because she showed up in Boston."

"Parents are unreasonable."

"Yeah." Still, the sick feeling in the pit of her stomach refused to go away.

"It's better with just you and me," he whispered.

Heather didn't bother to mention that there were three other couples tagging along. In the beginning, it was supposed to be just the two of them. But as soon as word got out, several of Elijah's friends had asked to join them. He'd agreed without discussing it with Heather. She hadn't said anything, but she was disappointed.

She'd had their first Christmas together all planned out. Once they reached Miami or the Keys, she'd make this Christmas as special for him as her mother had always made the holiday for her. They'd decorate a tree, sing carols on the beach and open small gifts to each other.

Thinking about her mother depressed her.

"You've got that look again," Elijah muttered, frowning up at her.

"Sorry."

"Forget about her, okay?"

"I'm trying, but it's hard. I wonder what she's doing and who she's with." The thought of her mother all alone tugged at Heather's heart, and despite her best efforts, she couldn't stop feeling guilty. She steeled herself against those emotions. If anyone was to blame for this fiasco, it was her mother, not her!

"You've got to let go of this, or it'll ruin everything," Elijah warned.

"I know."

"You said you and your mother were tight."

"We used to be." Heather knew that nothing would be the same again, and she was glad, she told herself fiercely. Well, maybe not glad exactly, but relieved that her mother knew about Elijah.

"It's time she understood that you're your own woman and you make your own decisions."

Elijah was repeating the same things she'd told her mother, the same things she'd been saying to herself from the moment they left Boston. "You're right."

"Of course I'm right. She can't dictate to you anymore, you know."

Heather agreed in principle, but that didn't do a thing to ease the knot in her stomach. "I'd feel better if I talked to her."

"You already did."

That was true, but Heather had lingering doubts about their conversation. She'd been shocked and angry when she'd learned her mother was in town. Everything she'd worked toward all these weeks was in danger, and she refused to let her mother ruin her plans.

Elijah studied her, his gaze narrowed. "You've changed your mind, haven't you?"

"About what? Us?" Heather pressed her hands gently against the sides of Elijah's bearded face and stared down at him, letting her love for him fill her eyes. "Oh, Elijah, about us? Never." As if to prove her undying love and devotion, she lowered her mouth to his.

Elijah was a seductive kisser, and he brought his muscular arms around her neck and half lifted his head to meet her lips. His mouth was moist and sensual and before long, any thoughts of her mother vanished completely.

When Elijah released her, Heather kept her eyes closed and sighed softly.

"Are you still worried about your mother?" he teased.

"Mother? What mother?"

Elijah chuckled. "That's what I figured."

Oh, how she loved her motorcycle man.

"You ready to go?" he asked.

The prospect of climbing back on the Harley didn't thrill her, but she tried to sound enthusiastic. "Anytime you say."

Elijah rewarded her with a smile. "And the guys said you'd be trouble."

"Me?"

"College girls generally are."

"So I'm not your first college girl?"

He laughed, but the sound lacked amusement. "I've been around."

She ignored that. She didn't want to hear about any of his other women, because she was determined it would be different with her.

They were good for each other. With Elijah she could throw away her good-girl image and discover her real self. At the same time, she'd teach him about love and responsibility. She didn't know exactly how he made his money, although he always seemed to have enough for gas and beer. But Heather wasn't concerned about that right now; she was determined to enjoy herself.

In one graceful movement Elijah leaped to his feet and stood. As soon as he was upright, the others started to move, too. He was their unspoken leader, their guide to adventure. And Heather was his woman, and she loved it.

Elijah offered Heather his hand, which she took. She

brushed the grass and grit from her rear and started back across the grass and the parking lot to where he'd parked the Harley.

Elijah gave Heather her helmet. "You don't need to feel guilty about your mother," he said.

"I don't." But she did. "Still, I think I should call her."

"I thought you said she doesn't have a cell phone."

"She doesn't."

"Do you know where she's staying?"

"No…but—"

"It's out of the question, then, isn't it?"

Heather was forced to agree. Even if she wanted to, she realized in an instant of panic, she had no way of reaching her mother.

Twelve

"*How* much?" Faith Kerrigan couldn't believe what the airline representative on the phone was telling her. According to what he said, her flight back to California would cost nearly twice as much as her original ticket.

"That's if I can find you a seat," he added.

"Oh." Faith could feel a headache coming on. She pressed her fingertips to her temple, which didn't help.

"Do you want me to check for an available flight?" the man asked.

"I—no." Her other option was to wait until there was a rental car available, with a different agency if necessary, and then drive back to California. The fees couldn't possibly be as steep as what the airlines wanted to charge. One thing was certain—she couldn't stay in Leavenworth. She hauled out Emily's phone book and began to call the local car rental places.

This entire Christmas was a disaster. If only she'd talked to Emily before she booked her flight. Oh, no, she groaned to herself, that would have been far too sensible. She'd wanted to surprise her friend. Some surprise! Instead, *she* was the one who'd gotten the shock of her life.

Sam, Tony and the others tiptoed around the house as quietly as possible, not wanting to intrude on the curmudgeon. What an unlikable fellow he was! But at least he'd been kind enough not to cast them into the cold dark night. She reminded herself that he'd only delayed it until morning—which made it difficult to maintain much gratitude.

Faith hadn't seen Charles yet. The den door was closed and she could only assume he was on his computer, doing whatever it was he found so important.

"It's time we left," Sam announced once she was off the phone.

Faith still didn't know what she'd do, but the problem was hers and hers alone. Santa and the small troupe of elves gathered around and watched her with anxious expressions.

"Are you sure you'll be safe with *him?*" Tony motioned toward the closed door. Judging by the intense look he wore, he seemed to welcome the opportunity to share his opinion of Charles—with Charles himself.

Faith resisted the urge to kiss his forehead for being so sweet. "I'll be perfectly fine, don't you worry." She hoped she sounded more confident than she felt, but she wanted to send her friends off without burdening them with her troubles.

Sam hesitated, as if he wasn't convinced he should believe her. He scratched his white beard, frowning. "You have a way back to California?"

"Not quite, but I'm working on it. I've called the car rental agency, plus several others. I'm waiting to hear back."

Sam's frown deepened. He seemed about to suggest she join them, but Faith knew that would be impossible.

"You go on," she insisted, "and if I run into any trouble, I'll give you a call." She had his cell phone number. Faith still felt his reluctance, but eventually, after conferring with the others, Sam agreed.

Smiling bravely, she stood on the porch and watched as they climbed into the rental van and backed out of the driveway. She waved until they were out of sight. Her heart sank when she could no longer see them. Soon, far sooner than she was ready, she'd be facing Charles with the unwelcome news from the airlines. Perhaps he'd offer a suggestion, but it was all too clear that he wanted her gone.

Already the two oldest Kennedy children were outside, frolicking in the snow. "Wanna go sledding with us?" Thomas called out to her. He walked toward the park, dragging his sled behind him. His younger brother Jimmy followed, tugging his own sled.

"Maybe later," Faith shouted back. She didn't have the heart to tell him she probably wouldn't be in town much longer.

The cold cut through Faith and she rubbed her hands up and down her arms. She hurried back into the warm comfort of the house, leaning against the closed door as she considered her limited options. She was so deep in thought that it took her a moment to notice Charles standing on the far side of the room.

"Santa and his elves have left?" he asked. "Why were they wearing those outfits, anyway?" He sounded both curious and a touch sardonic.

"Oh—we went to a rest stop and they got changed.

We decided it would be part of Emily's Christmas surprise."

"Uh-huh."

Faith avoided eye contact.

"What about you? You're leaving today, too—aren't you?"

Faith raised her index finger and swallowed. "There's… a small problem."

"How small?"

"Well, actually, it's a rather large one." She told him how much it would cost to change her flight.

"*How* much?" He sounded as appalled as she was.

"The way it was explained to me is that this would be a new ticket. But the representative said that even if I was willing to pay the change fee, it was unlikely he could find me a seat. I could fly standby, but he told me there are hardly ever any standby seats at this time of year." Faith knew she was giving him more information than necessary, but it was critical that he understand her position.

Charles sighed as if this was too much to take in all at once. "Summarize, please," he snapped—as if she was some freshman in one of his classes, she thought resentfully. "Where does that leave you?"

"Well… I have a rental car…or rather I did until Sam and the elves needed it, so I ended up giving it to them." Again she explained far more than necessary, ending with the tale of the troupe's appearances at hospitals and nursing homes.

"So, you're saying they've left with the one and only van?"

She nodded. "I have calls into several rental agencies

now, and they're all looking for a car for me. But rest assured that once I do have a vehicle, I'll be out of here."

"Where will you go?"

She didn't have many options there, either. "Back to California."

Charles had the good grace to look concerned. "You'd be driving at this time of year and in this weather?"

"Do I have a choice?"

He sighed, turned abruptly and walked into the kitchen. "Let me think about this. There's got to be a solution that'd suit both of us."

She was glad he seemed to think there were other options, because she couldn't think of any. The one obvious solution—that she simply stay—was as unpalatable to her as it no doubt was to him.

After a few minutes, Charles returned to the den and closed the door. Apparently he hadn't come up with any creative ideas.

Faith's stomach growled, reminding her that she hadn't eaten since yesterday afternoon. Checking out the refrigerator, she found eggs, cheese and a few vegetables. She whipped up two omelets, then timidly knocked at the den door.

At Charles's gruff reply, she creaked open the door just enough to peer inside. "I made breakfast if you're interested."

"Breakfast? Oh. Yeah, sure."

She didn't need to ask him twice. Maybe half a minute later, Charles joined her at the table. He stared down at his plate, eyes widening as if this was the most delicious meal he'd seen in years.

He sat down and sampled the omelet. "You cook like this all the time?"

Faith wasn't sure what he was asking. "I know my way around a kitchen, if that's what you mean," she said cautiously.

"Every meal?"

"Not always, but I do enjoy cooking."

He ate several more bites, pausing between each one, a blissful expression on his face. "You'd be willing to leave me alone to do my work?"

"If that's a question, I suppose I could manage to keep out of your way." She'd begun to feel hopeful—maybe they *could* compromise.

He studied her narrowly, as if to gauge the truth of her words. "In that case you can stay. You prepare the meals, make yourself scarce, and we'll both cope with this as well as we can. Agreed?"

Faith doubted he knew how gruff and unfriendly he sounded. However… "I could do that."

"Good. I'm here to work. The last thing I'm interested in is Christmas or any of the festivities that seem to have taken over this town. Tell me, are these people crazy? No, don't answer that. Just leave me alone—except for meals, of course."

"Fine."

"I want nothing to do with Christmas. Got that?"

"Yes."

She had no idea what kind of work he was doing, but she'd gladly keep her distance. As for the Christmas part, he'd certainly made his point and she didn't need to hear it again.

"I'll probably have my meals in the den."

"Fine," she said again. As far as she was concerned, the less she had to do with him, the better.

Charles set his fork next to his plate and seemed to be waiting for something more from her.

"I'm willing to make the best of this situation if you are," she finally said. Neither was to blame. They were the victims of a set of unfortunate circumstances.

He nodded solemnly as if to seal their agreement. Then he pushed away from the table and stood. "I will tell you that this is one of the best omelets I've had in years."

She smiled, pleased to hear it. "Thank you." Then she hopped up from the table, taking her plate and cup. "What time would you like lunch?"

"I hadn't thought about it."

"Okay, I'll let you know when it's ready. Fair enough?"

"Certainly." He sounded distracted and eager to get back to his work.

"I'll pick up the groceries," she offered. "It's the least I can do."

His eyes brightened. "That would be appreciated. Just be careful of the goat."

"The goat?"

"Never mind," he muttered and returned to the den.

Thirteen

Bernice Brewster slept well for the first time in three days. At her age, she shouldn't be worrying about her adult children, but Charles was a concern. For that matter, so was Rayburn. Thankfully her older son had taken her apprehensions to heart and traveled to Boston to check on his younger brother.

Naturally there was a perfectly logical explanation as to why a woman had answered Charles's phone. She should've realized her sensible son wouldn't have some stray woman in the house. Charles was far too intelligent to be taken in by a gold digger. Granted, she'd like nothing better than to see him with the right woman—but there'd be nothing worse than seeing him with the wrong one. Like that Monica. Well, she was a fool and didn't deserve Charles.

Fortunately, Bernice now had the phone number in Washington State where Charles could be reached. She leaned toward the telephone and dialed.

One ring. Two.

"Hello," a female voice answered.

"Hello," Bernice responded, a little uncertainly. She

must have written the number down incorrectly. There was only one way to find out and that was to ask. "This phone number was given to me by Emily Springer. Is Charles Brewster there?"

The woman hesitated. "Yes, but he's unavailable at the moment."

Bernice swallowed a gasp and before she could think better of it, slammed down the telephone. Dear heaven, what was happening? Feeling light-headed, she waited until her pounding heart had settled down before she tried to call Rayburn at his apartment. She wanted to know what was going on and she wanted to know right this minute.

When Rayburn didn't answer, she tried his office and learned he was still in Boston.

"Why?" she demanded of his assistant. "Why is he still in Boston?"

"I'm sorry, Mrs. Brewster," the young woman said politely. "Mr. Brewster phoned the office this morning and that's what he said."

"He has his cell phone?" Of course he did, because he'd called her on it the night before.

"I believe he does."

Bernice carefully punched out the cell number and waited. The phone rang four times before her son answered.

"Ray Brewster."

"Rayburn," she gasped, overwhelmed by her children's odd behavior. His greeting had sounded far too friendly, as if he'd been laughing. Well, this was no laughing matter!

"Mother." The sound of her voice sobered him up

fast enough, she noticed. Something very suspicious was going on.

"Where *are* you?" she demanded.

"I'm forty-three years old. I no longer need to check in with you."

How dared he speak to her in that tone! She was about to say so when Rayburn chuckled.

"If you must know, I'm in Boston at Charles's condo."

"There's a *woman* there."

"I already know that, Mother."

Bernice gasped. "You spent the night with her?"

"I was in the same condo, not that it's any of your business."

Bernice pulled out her lace-edged hankie and clenched it tightly. "I… I have no idea where your father and I went wrong that both my sons—"

"Mother, take a deep breath and start over."

Bernice tried, she honestly tried, but her heart was pounding and her head spinning. "I phoned the number you gave me and…another woman answered."

"A woman? Are you sure you had the right number?"

"Of course I'm sure. I asked and she said Charles was unavailable."

"Hold on, let me ask Emily who it might be."

Emily, was it? "I see you're on a first-name basis with this—this house-stealer."

To her chagrin, Rayburn laughed. "Honestly, Mother, I think you missed your calling. You should've been on the stage."

Her husband used to make the same claim, and while she did have a good stage presence, she suspected Rayburn didn't mean it as a compliment.

Bernice could hear him in the background, but hard

as she pressed her ear against the receiver, she couldn't make out what was being said.

"Emily says she doesn't have a clue who would be answering the phone at her place. She'll call later and find out if you wish."

"If I *wish?*" Bernice repeated.

"All right, I'll get back to you."

Her son was about to hang up, but she still had more to say. "Rayburn," she shouted. "You behave yourself with this woman, understand?"

"Yes, Mother."

The phone line went dead.

"A woman answered?" Emily repeated after Ray ended the conversation with his mother. "Now, that's interesting."

"Who do you think it might be?"

Emily shrugged. "Don't know, but it'll be easy enough to find out." She went to the telephone and punched out her own number in Washington State.

The line was picked up almost right away. "Hello."

"Faith?" Emily shrieked. "Faith? Is it really you?"

"Emily?"

They both started talking at once, blurting out questions and answers, then each explained in turn. Even then, it took Emily a few moments to discern what had actually happened.

"Oh, no! You came to spend Christmas with me and I'm not there."

"You went to Boston to be with Heather and now she's in Florida?"

"Yes, but I can't think about it, otherwise I'll get too upset."

Faith was sympathetic. "I felt so badly for the way I brushed off your disappointment."

"And now you're trapped in Leavenworth."

"There are worse places to be this time of year," Faith said. She seemed to be in a good frame of mind. "Charles and I have reached an agreement," she went on to say. "I'm staying until after Christmas, and in exchange, I'll keep out of his way and cook his meals."

While her friend put a positive slant on the situation, Emily realized Faith had to be miserable. Alone—or virtually alone—at Christmas.

"What about you?" Faith asked.

"I'm stuck in Boston, but it's really a lovely town." Still, none of that mattered now. "Oh, Faith, what a good friend you are to go to all this trouble for me."

"Well, I tried."

Emily wanted to weep. Despite everything, it seemed she was destined to spend the holidays by herself. Still, she'd had a wonderful evening with Ray and felt attractive and carefree in a way she hadn't in years.

They talked for several minutes longer, making plans to call each other again. When she finished, Emily replaced the receiver and looked over at Ray, smiling.

"I take it she's someone you know?"

Emily told him what had happened. "I was lucky I caught her. Faith was on her way outside to go sledding with the neighbor kids. She's so good with children."

"Faith sounds like a fun-loving person."

"She is."

"She's staying, then?"

Emily nodded. "She and Charles have worked out a compromise." Emily felt guilty about the whole mess. Poor Charles. All he wanted was to escape Christmas and have time to work without interruption. But, between Faith and the Kennedy children, Emily figured the poor man wouldn't have a moment's peace.

Ray drank the rest of his coffee and set his mug aside. "I guess I'd better head back to New York."

Emily knew it was too much to hope that he'd stay on. "I can't let you go without breakfast," she said brightly.

Ray seemed almost relieved at being given an excuse to linger. "Are you sure I'm not disrupting your plans?"

"Plans? What plans? I'm here for another week and I don't know a soul in town." She opened the cupboard, looking for ideas, and found an old-fashioned waffle iron. She brought it down, oiled it and plugged it in.

"I wondered what happened to Mom's old waffle iron," Ray said as he leaned against the counter. He watched Emily assemble ingredients.

"Are you hungry?" he asked.

She shrugged as she cracked an egg against the side of the bowl. "Not really… The truth is, I'm just delaying the inevitable." It probably wasn't polite to be this truthful, but she was beyond pretense. The minute Ray walked out that door, she'd be alone again and she'd enjoyed his company.

"Actually, I'm not hungry, either."

"You aren't?" The question came out in a rushed whisper.

Ray shook his head. "I was looking for an excuse to stay."

He and Emily exchanged a grin.

"Do we actually need an excuse?" he asked.

Emily didn't know how to answer or even if she should. "Do you have to go back to New York?"

"At the moment I can't think of a single compelling reason."

"Would you be interested in staying in Boston for Christmas? With me?" Normally she wasn't this direct, but she had little to lose and so much to gain.

"I can't imagine anyone I'd rather spend Christmas with."

Fourteen

On a mission now, Faith walked down Main Street in Leavenworth and headed for her favorite grocery. Even after a number of years away, she was astonished by the number of people who remembered her. Five years earlier, she'd done her student teaching in Leavenworth and worked in Emily's classroom.

Newly divorced, emotionally fragile and struggling to pick up the pieces of her life, she'd come to this out-of-the-way community. The town had welcomed her, and with Emily as her friend, she'd learned that life does continue.

The three months she'd spent with Emily had been like a reprieve for Faith, providing a much-needed escape from her badly bungled life. Once her student teaching was completed, she'd moved back to Seattle and soon afterward graduated with her master's degree in education. Diploma in hand, she'd gone to California to be closer to family.

Although she'd moved away from Leavenworth, Faith had stayed in contact with Emily. Their friendship had continued to grow, despite the physical distance between them and the difference in their ages. In fact, Faith felt she could talk to Emily in ways she couldn't talk to her mother. They were colleagues, but not only that, they'd both experienced the loss of a marriage, albeit for very different reasons and in very different ways.

They made a point of getting together every summer. Usually they met in Seattle or California. The long-distance aspect of the relationship hadn't been a hindrance.

Faith's family and friends were important to her; romance, though, was another matter. She was rather frightened of it. Her marriage had burned her and while she'd like to be settled and married with children, that didn't seem likely now.

As she walked through town, Faith waved at people she recognized. Some immediately waved back; one woman stopped and stared as if she had yet to place her. The living Nativity wasn't scheduled until the afternoon, so she was safe from the goat Charles had mentioned. She'd figured out that the infamous Clara Belle—she remembered Emily's hilarious story about a farm visit with her kindergarten class—had to be the goat in question.

Thinking of Charles made her smile. He was an interesting character. If he hadn't already told her, she would've guessed he was an academic. He fit the stereotype of the absentminded professor perfectly—a researcher who became so absorbed in his work, he needed someone to tell him when and where he needed to be.

He did have a heart, though. Otherwise she'd probably be hitchhiking back to California by now. As long as she made herself invisible, they would manage.

Once inside the store, she got a grocery cart and wandered aimlessly down the aisle, seeking inspiration for dinner. She decided on baked green peppers stuffed with a rice, tomato soup and ground beef mixture. The recipe was her mother's but Faith rarely made it. Cooking for one was a chore and it was often easier to pick up something on the way home from school. Fresh cranberries were on sale, so she grabbed a package of those, although she hadn't decided what to do with them. It seemed a Christmassy thing to buy. She'd find a use for them later.

She'd come up with menus for the rest of the week this afternoon, and write a more complete grocery list then.

On the walk home, Faith discovered the Kennedy kids and about half the town's children sledding down the big hill in the park. If her arms hadn't been full, she would've stopped and taken a trip down the hill herself.

The kids were so involved in their fun that they didn't notice her. Breathless, Faith brought everything into the kitchen. She removed her hat and gloves and draped her coat over the back of a chair. Unpacking the groceries, she sang a Christmas song that was running through her mind.

The door to the den flew open and Charles stood in the doorway glaring at her.

Faith stopped midway to the refrigerator, a package of ground beef in her hand. "Was I making too much noise?" she asked guiltily. In her own opinion, she'd been quiet and subdued, but apparently not.

"I'm trying to work here," he told her severely.

"Sorry," she mouthed and tiptoed back to the kitchen counter.

"You aren't planning to do anything like bake cookies, are you?" He wrinkled his nose as if to say he wasn't interested.

"Uh, I hadn't given it any thought."

"In case you do, you should know I don't want to be distracted by smells, either."

"Smells?" With an effort, Faith managed not to groan out loud.

"The aroma of baking cookies makes my stomach growl."

He wasn't kidding, and Faith found that humorous, although she dared not show it. She was able to stay here only with his approval and couldn't afford to jeopardize her position. "Then rest assured. I won't do anything to make your stomach growl."

"Good." With that, Charles retreated into the den, closing the door decisively.

Faith rolled her eyes. What was she supposed to do all day? Sit in a corner and knit? Play solitaire? If that little bit of commotion had bothered His Highness, then she couldn't see this arrangement working. And yet, what was the alternative?

The awful part was that she felt an almost overwhelming urge to bang lids together. Standing in the middle of the kitchen, she had to bite her lower lip to restrain herself from singing at the top of her lungs and stomping her feet.

This was crazy. Ludicrous. Still, it was all she could do not to behave in the most infantile manner. If she was going to behave like a child, then she might as well join the children. This close to Christmas, they had a lot of pent-up energy.

Dressed in hat, gloves and her coat once again, Faith went outside. The snow on the front lawn was untouched. A fresh layer had fallen overnight, and with time on her hands, she made an impulsive decision to build a snowman. She grinned as she looked at the specimen in the neighbor's yard.

Starting with a small hand-size ball of snow, she rolled it across the lawn, letting it grow larger and fuller with each sweep.

"Do you want me to help?" Sarah asked, appearing at her side.

Sarah was a favorite of Emily's, Faith knew. As the youngest in a big family, she'd learned to hold her own.

"I sure do."

The little girl beamed as Faith resumed the snow-rolling task. "The bottom part of the snowman has to be the biggest," Sarah pointed out, obviously taking on supervisory responsibilities.

"Right."

"Dylan says it's the most important part, too."

Dylan, if Faith remembered correctly, lived down the street and was a good friend to one of the Kennedy boys.

"Are you building a fort?" Thomas shouted, hurrying across the street from the park. He abandoned his sled near the front porch.

"This is a nice friendly snowman," Faith assured him.

Thomas narrowed his eyes. "Looks more like a snow fort to me."

"It's a ball," Sarah primly informed her brother, hands on her hips. "Anyone can see that."

"I don't think so." Thomas raced over to his own yard and started rolling snow. He was quickly joined by his brothers. The boys worked feverishly at constructing their fort.

Sarah and Faith hurried to catch up, changing their tactics. There were four boys against the two of them, but what they lacked in numbers they made up for in cunning. While Faith built their defensive wall, Sarah rolled snowballs, stacking them in neat piles out of sight of her brothers.

"Now, boys," Faith said, standing up and strolling to the middle of the battleground between their two yards. "I'm telling you right now that it's not a good thing to pick a fight with girls."

"Yeah, because they tattle."

"Do not," Sarah screeched.

"Do, too."

Faith stretched out her arms to silence both sides. "Sarah and I were innocently building a friendly snowman for Mrs. Springer's front yard when we were accused of constructing a snow fort."

"It *is* a snow fort," Thomas insisted, pointing accusingly at the wall of snow.

"It became one when you started building yours," Faith said. "But before we go to war, I feel honor bound to look for some means of making peace."

"No way!" Mark cried.

"Hear me out," Faith urged. "First of all, it's unfair. There are more of you than of us."

"I ain't going over to the girls' side," Mark protested.

"We don't want any boys, anyway," Sarah shouted back.

Again Faith silenced them. "You don't want peace?"

"No!" Thomas tossed a snowball straight up and batted it down with his hand as if to prove his expertise.

"Forget it," Mark seconded.

"Then we have to make it a fair fight."

The boys were silent, apparently waiting for one of them to volunteer. No one did.

"I suggest that in order to even things up, the boys' side is restricted to the use of one hand. Agreed?"

The boys grinned and nodded.

"Your left hand," she added.

Their laughter and snickers quickly died out. "Ah, come on…"

Not giving the group a chance to argue, Faith tossed the first snowball, which landed just short of the snow fortification. Before the boys had time to react, she raced back to Sarah. The little girl was crouched behind the shelter and had accumulated a huge pile of snowballs.

Soon they were all laughing and pelting each other with snow. Faith managed to land several wildly thrown snowballs, but she was on the receiving end just as often. At one point she glanced toward the house and saw Charles looking out the living-room window.

Oh, no. Even a snowball fight was too much racket for him. Unfortunately, the distraction cost her. Thomas, who was fast becoming accustomed to pitching snowballs left-handed, scored a direct hit. The snowball struck her square in the chest. Snow sprayed up into her face, and Faith made a show of sputtering.

"Gotcha," Thomas cried and did a jig of triumph, leaping up and down with his arms above his head.

Faith glanced at the house again and saw Charles laughing. She did a double take. The man could actually laugh? This was news. Perhaps he wasn't so stuffy, after all. Perhaps she'd misread him entirely.

Was that possible?

Fifteen

"This is the Old North Church?" Emily stood outside Christ Church, made famous in the Longfellow poem. "The 'one if by land, two if by sea' church?"

"The very one," Ray assured her. "Boston's oldest surviving religious structure."

Emily tilted back her head and looked to the very top of the belfry. "If I remember my history correctly, a sexton…"

"Robert Newman."

She nodded. "He warned Paul Revere and the patriots that the British were coming."

"Correct. You may go to the head of the class."

Emily had always been fascinated by history. "I loved school. I was a good student," she said. A trait her daughter had inherited.

"I can believe it," Ray said, guiding her inside the church.

They toured it briefly, and Emily marveled as Ray dramatically described that fateful night in America's history.

"How do you know so much about this?"

Ray grinned. "You mean other than through Charles, who's lived and breathed this stuff from the time he was a kid?"

"Yes."

"The truth is that, years ago, I edited a book—a mystery novel, actually—in which the Old North Church played a major role in the plot."

Emily was so enraptured by Boston's history that she'd forgotten Ray was an important figure in New York publishing.

"As a matter of fact, I have plenty of trivia in the back of my mind from my years as a hands-on editor."

As they walked, Ray described a number of books he'd edited and influential authors he'd worked with. Apparently he no longer did much of that. Instead he had a more administrative role.

Emily found it very easy to talk to Ray, and the hours melted away. It seemed they'd hardly left the condominium, but it was already growing dark. She admired the Christmas lights and festive displays, which weren't like those in Leavenworth, but equally appealing.

They stopped for a seafood dinner and then walked around some more, taking in the sights and sounds of the season. As Emily told him about Leavenworth, Ray grew more amused with each anecdote. "I wish I could be there to see Charles's reaction."

Emily continued to feel guilty about Ray's brother—and about Faith—but she couldn't have known. Her one wish was that Faith and Charles would be as compatible as she and Ray.

Being with him these last few days before Christmas made all the difference in the world. If not for Ray, she'd probably be holed up in the condo baking dozens of cookies and feeling sorry for herself.

"Despite all the mix-ups, I'm glad I'm here," she told him.

"I'm glad you're here, too," Ray said. "I'm enjoying your company so much. Do you want to know what else I'm enjoying?"

Emily could only guess. "Being in Boston again?"

"Well, that too. But what I mean is that I'm completely free of phone calls."

The first thing Ray had done, once he'd contacted his office and informed his assistant that he wouldn't be returning until after the holidays, was turn off his cell phone.

"You might have missed an important call," she reminded him.

"Tough. Whoever's in the office can handle it this time. I'm unavailable." He laughed as he said it.

Emily laughed because he did, but from the little she'd learned about his work, it was a hectic series of meetings and continual phone calls. Ray must be under constant pressure, dealing with agents' and authors' demands, in addition to various vice presidents, sales and marketing personnel, advertising firms and more. Although he held a prominent position with the company and obviously interacted with many people, he seemed as lonely as she was. He'd told her that aside from his work and a few social commitments, he had no reason to rush back to New York. Indeed, he seemed eager to stay here in Boston.

"Coffee?" he asked when they reached the Starbucks where she'd had her last encounter with Heather.

Emily hesitated, but then agreed. After all these

hours of walking, she was exhausted and her feet hurt. Yet, at the same time, she was invigorated by everything she'd seen and done—and utterly charmed by Ray.

While he stepped up to the counter to order their drinks, she secured a table. As luck would have it, the only vacant one was the same table she'd occupied while waiting to meet her daughter. Her thoughts inevitably flashed to Heather, and Emily wondered where she was now and what she was doing. No, it was probably best not to know.

A few minutes later, Ray joined her with two tall cups of coffee. He slipped into the seat across from her. "Time like this is a luxury for me," he said.

"I want you to know how much I appreciate—"

He took her hand, stopping her. "What I'm trying to say, I guess, is that I've avoided it."

Emily frowned, uncertain she understood his meaning.

"I loved being with you today, talking and laughing with you. The truth is, I can't remember any day I've enjoyed more in a very long while."

"But I'm the one who's indebted to you."

"No," he said emphatically. "*I'm* the one who owes *you.* I'd forgotten," he said quietly, "what it's like to give myself a free day. To do something that's not related to work." He paused. "There seems to be a great deal in my life that I've let slide. I needed this wake-up call."

"In other words, I'm an alarm clock?"

He grinned. "You're more than that."

They were flirting with each other, she realized. Normally, conversations such as this terrified her. She'd married her high-school sweetheart and had rarely dated since Peter's death. Her daughter, sad as it was to admit, had more experience with men than she did.

Despite her determination not to, she was worrying about Heather again. Tears filled her eyes.

"Are you okay?"

Embarrassed, she nodded. Wiping the tears from her cheeks, she offered him a watery smile. "I was just thinking about my daughter."

"She's with friends, isn't she?"

"So she says." Emily rolled her eyes.

"Everyone has to grow up sooner or later, and among other things, that means learning how to judge other people's intentions." He shrugged. "Some lessons are more painful than others."

Sniffling a little, Emily agreed. "I can't think about Heather, otherwise I'll get upset. It's just that I had all these plans for the two of us over Christmas."

"What kind of plans?"

It seemed a little silly to tell Ray about them now. "I packed our favorite Christmas ornaments, so we could decorate a tree the same way we do every year."

"You and I could get a tree."

"You'd be willing to do that?"

"It's Christmas, isn't it? I haven't put up a tree in years."

"No tree?"

He chuckled. "Too much bother to do it on my own, but I'd love to help you. First thing in the morning, we'll buy a tree."

Her spirits brightened instantly.

"Anything else?"

"I always roast the traditional turkey, but I felt that since we were in Boston we should cook lobster. I love lobster tail with lots of melted butter. I've never prepared a whole lobster, though. I thought it'd be fun to go to a fish market and pick one out."

"That sounds like an excellent idea. Lobster for two."

"This is great!" Emily crowed happily.

After finishing their coffee, they walked back to the condominium hand in hand. By the time they rode up in the elevator, Ray had his arm around her. Being this close to him felt…natural. She rested her head against his shoulder.

Ray unlocked the door and swung it open, but he didn't immediately reach for the light switch. When Emily stepped into the living room, Ray turned her into his arms. He closed the front door with his foot, and they stood in near darkness, the only light seeping in through the blinds. She leaned against him, eyes drifting shut.

Ray's palm cradled her cheek, his touch gentle. He rubbed his thumb across her lips and Emily sighed, wanting him to kiss her, afraid he wouldn't—yet afraid he would.

Standing on her toes, she slipped her arms around his neck and whispered, "Thank you for the most wonderful day."

"Thank *you.*" His lips found hers then, and it was sweet and sensual all at once.

He brought her full against him as their mouths met again and again, one unhurried kiss following another. Emily's senses spun out of control but she pulled back, fearful of what might happen if they allowed this to continue.

Ray exhaled shakily. "I'm not sure that was a good idea, but I'm not sorry. Not at all…"

Emily kissed the side of his jaw. “Me, neither,” she whispered.

She felt his smile. “Don’t worry, Ray, I promise not to ravish you,” she teased.

“Damn.”

“Well…” Emily laughed softly. “I could reconsider.”

It was Ray’s turn to be amused. “You ready for the lights?”

“I suppose.”

When Ray touched the switch, the room instantly went from dark to bright. But he didn’t immediately release her.

When they separated and moved farther into the room, Emily noticed the flashing message light on the phone. Ray noticed it, too. Emily’s hopes soared—could it be Heather?—but then she remembered that her daughter didn’t know where she was staying.

Ray pushed the caller ID button and groaned. “Four calls,” he muttered, “and they’re all from my mother.”

Sixteen

Southern Florida in December was paradise. There was no other word for it. The beach was flawless, the water blue and clear and warm, the sunshine constant. It was as close to heaven as anyone who'd spent a winter in Boston could imagine.

What Heather didn't know was why she felt so miserable in such a perfect setting. She had every reason in the world to be happy, but she wasn't. To make matters worse, Elijah was growing irritated with her moods.

"Get me a beer," her hero called from where he was stretched out beneath a palm tree on the beach, one of his stalwart companions beside him.

Heather got up from the beach towel where she was sunbathing and walked back into their motel room. She opened the small refrigerator and brought out a cold beer. Without a word she delivered it to Elijah. He looked at his friend, nodded, and the other man stood up and left.

"Let's talk," Elijah said, patting the sand next to him.

"About what?" Heather crossed her arms stubbornly.

"Sit down," he ordered. He pointed at the empty space his friend had just vacated.

Reluctantly Heather joined him.

"All right," he muttered after opening the beer. He took a long swig and wiped the back of his hand across his mouth. "What's wrong?"

"Nothing."

"Don't give me that. You haven't been yourself since we left Boston."

Heather didn't say anything. He knew she felt terrible about leaving her mother behind. If he couldn't figure it out, then she wasn't going to tell him.

"I thought you'd like Florida." Elijah made it sound like an accusation, as if he'd done everything humanly possible to provide for her happiness.

"What's not to like?"

Elijah nodded. "Exactly—so what's the problem?"

"You're right. I'm not happy."

He wrapped his arm around her neck, the cold beer bottle dangling between two fingers. "What is it, babe?"

Heather cringed at his use of the word *babe,* but she'd given up trying to convince Elijah to call her anything else. What particularly irritated her was that she suspected it was the term he used with all his girlfriends.

"If you must know, I'm worried about my mother."

Elijah tightened his grip around her neck by taking another healthy swig of beer. "I thought we already talked that out."

"We talked." He seemed to think it was a closed subject. Heather wished it was, but none of this was turning out the way she'd hoped. The motel was a dump, she was sick of fast food, the other women didn't like her, and…

"What is it now?"

She shook her head, letting her long hair swing. "Nothing."

"Don't give me that," he said again. "You've been in a piss-poor mood from the get-go." He spread his arms and looked out at the rolling waves of the ocean. "Here we are in paradise and you're whining about your mother." He made it sound ludicrous.

Maybe it was, but Heather couldn't help herself. "I'm just worried about her."

"You're *worried* about Mommy?" Now he made it seem like one big joke and that infuriated her even more.

"You don't have a clue," Heather cried. Vaulting to her feet, she tore down the beach, kicking up sand. A few minutes later, she was out of breath and started walking, her eyes filled with tears.

"Wait up," Elijah shouted.

She was surprised he'd come after her. Heather waited for him and then fell into his arms, weeping softly. Elijah held her in his muscular embrace.

"All right, babe, tell me all about it."

"You don't understand."

He kissed the side of her neck. "I can't be happy when you're miserable, you know."

And that made Heather remember why she loved him. Taking a deep breath, she tried to explain.

"Mom was born and raised in this dinky town in Washington State. This is her first trip to the East Coast."

"Get out of here! Her first trip?"

Heather nodded. "I left her all by herself."

"She loves you, right?"

"Of course. She's my mother."

"And you love her?"

"Of course—why else would I feel so awful?"

"Don't you think she'd want you to be happy?" Elijah asked as if following his logic was a simple thing.

"Yes, I suppose, but..." Heather felt confused and unsure. "I wish it was that easy."

"It is," he argued. "Just don't think about her."

"She's probably miserable and alone, and I did this to her."

"Babe," he said, more gruffly this time. "You didn't ask her to fly to Boston, did you?" When she shook her head, he muttered, "Then get a grip. The others are starting to complain."

"Who?"

"Peaches, for one."

Heather had tried to make friends with the women but they were impossible. She was a college girl, so they disliked and mistrusted her on sight.

"Peaches would complain about me no matter what I said or did."

"That's not true," Elijah asserted.

"Yes, it is. It's the same with the others." She didn't mention the way the other girls had made fun of her. Heather wasn't accustomed to riding on a motorcycle for long periods of time and suffered a bad case of TB, better known as tired butt.

"Walk with me," Heather suggested, tugging at his arm.

Elijah hesitated. His only concession to the beach was a sleeveless T-shirt. Even in the Miami sunshine, he wore his leather pants and boots.

"Just for a little way," Heather coaxed.

Elijah glanced over his shoulder and then nodded. "Not far, all right?"

"Sure." At the moment Heather would have promised him anything. They hadn't been alone since they'd left Boston. Even the motel room was shared with another couple. Naturally she was stuck with Peaches, who made no effort to hide her disdain for Heather.

They walked for a while, until Elijah decided they'd gone far enough, and sat down in the sand. "Tell me about *your* mother," Heather said, pressing her head against his shoulder.

Elijah was silent for a moment. "Not much to tell. She's a regular mother, or I think she would've been if she'd stayed around."

"I'm sorry." Heather felt bad for bringing up unhappy memories.

"It was a bummer after she left, but I survived."

"What was Christmas like for you?"

Elijah pulled out his pack of cigarettes, lit one up and took a drag before responding. "It wasn't any Santa down the chimney, if that's what you mean."

"How so?"

"Did I mention my dad took off a year before my mother?"

"No." Heather felt worse than ever.

"No big deal. We had good foster parents, and the state always made sure we had at least one gift under the tree."

Heather slid her arm around his waist.

"What about you?" he asked.

"You don't want to know."

"Sure I do," he countered.

Heather wasn't sure where to start. "I told you about Leavenworth, right?"

"Yeah, it's a Bavarian kind of town, you said."

"Right. Christmas is a big deal there and with my mother, too. I think she always wanted to make up for the fact that my dad died when I was young, so she really did the Christmas thing up big. We had dozens of traditions." Heather grew sad again, just thinking about all she was missing.

"You're a big girl now," Elijah told her. "Traditions are for kids."

Heather nodded but she wanted to tell him that people didn't outgrow their need for a Christmas stocking or decorating a tree or hot apple cider on Christmas Eve.

Elijah sighed. "Are you okay now?"

She shrugged. "I guess."

"Good." He stabbed his cigarette into the sand and then stood. Extending his hand to her, Elijah helped Heather to her feet.

"Thank you," she whispered, kissing him.

"That's much better," he said. He placed one arm around her waist and drew her close. "Forget about your mother."

Heather doubted she could. Despite everything, she knew her mother was all alone in Boston, completely miserable without her.

Seventeen

Faith basted the roasting chicken and closed the oven door as quietly as possible. Rather than mash the potatoes with the mixer, she decided to use the hand utensil in an effort to cut down on noise. As far as she could discern, the cranky professor had enjoyed her cooking the night before. The stuffed green peppers had disappeared in short order.

By six, the house was dark and dreary. Faith went from room to room, drawing the curtains and turning on lights. She played solitaire for an hour. Then she finished the dinner preparations and set the table for one. Before serving herself, she sautéed the green beans with bacon bits and onion, sliced the gelatin salad and carved the roast chicken. Then she lit two candles on the dining-room table and filled her own plate from the dishes in the kitchen. The closed den door discouraged her from letting Charles know dinner was ready. Once she'd eaten, she'd make up a plate for him and leave it on the kitchen counter; he could warm it up in the microwave when he was hungry. That was what she'd done yesterday.

Faith sat down at the far end of the dining-room table and spread the linen napkin across her lap. Emily always used real cloth napkins. Faith admired that about her friend. Living on her own, Faith tended to treat meals as a necessary evil, but when she dined with Emily, meals were an event to be savored and shared. So, in Emily's house and in Emily's honor, Faith would keep up this tradition.

Reaching for the merlot she'd bought that day, she started to pour herself a glass, then stopped, the bottle suspended, when she realized Charles had emerged from the den. He stood in the dining room, looking a bit disoriented. He stared at her as if he'd forgotten she was in the house.

Faith stood. "Would you like me to get you a plate?"

Charles frowned at the grandfather clock. "I had no idea it was six-thirty." The clock marked the half hour with a resounding clang, punctuating his words. "Uh, do you mind if I join you?" he asked.

Faith was too shocked to reply. "P-please do," she stuttered after an embarrassingly long pause.

Charles went into the kitchen for a plate and served himself from the various dishes she'd prepared, then returned to the dining room. He sat at the opposite end of the table.

They remained awkward with each other. He made a polite comment about the food; she responded with equal politeness.

Silence! Faith desperately wished she had the nerve to put on a Christmas CD—maybe a Celtic Christmas recording Emily had. Or an instrumental of classic carols.

She cleared her throat. "Would you like some merlot?" she offered. She preferred red wine to white, which was why she chose to drink a red with chicken.

"Thank you."

Before she could stand, he got up and retrieved a second wineglass from the kitchen, poured his wine and sat down.

An uneasy silence settled between them once again. Faith picked up her fork and resumed eating.

"How did your snow war end yesterday afternoon?" Charles asked in a casual voice.

"Successfully—for the girls," Faith told him in cordial tones. "The boys surrendered when they saw they were outwitted and overpowered by us."

Charles nodded. "I had a feeling the boy team needed my assistance."

This time, Faith managed to hide her shock.

He glanced at her and grinned—actually grinned. "My aim is excellent, if I do say so myself."

"Oh." She couldn't think of a thing to say. What suddenly filled her mind was a vision of Charles Brewster throwing snowballs, surrounded by a swarm of young boys.

"So you survived the adventure unscathed."

"I sure did." She wasn't telling him how much her shoulders ached and she'd ended up taking aspirin before retiring last night, nor did she mention that she'd soaked in a hot tub for twenty minutes. Today she'd gone shopping, list in hand, and when she returned, she'd lounged in front of the fireplace with a good book and a cup of warm cocoa, keeping as still as possible.

"You enjoyed seeing me get plowed, didn't you?" she asked, again in the most conversational of tones.

"Dare I admit that I did?" He smiled once more,

and it transformed his face, reminding Faith of her reaction to his laughter the day before. *Had* she been wrong about him?

"I wish you had joined us," she told him impulsively.

"I was tempted."

"Why didn't you?"

He shrugged and lifted his wineglass. "Mainly because I've got work to do—but that isn't the only reason I'm here." He gestured at the window. "Hard as it is to believe, I came here to avoid Christmas."

Had her mouth been full, Faith would have choked. "You came to *Leavenworth* to avoid Christmas?"

He shrugged again. "I thought it would be a nice quiet prison community."

"That's Leavenworth, Kansas."

"I eventually remembered that."

Faith couldn't keep from laughing.

"I'm delighted you find this so amusing."

"Sorry, I don't mean to make fun of your situation, but it really is kind of funny."

"It's your situation, too," he said. "You're stuck here, just like I am."

Faith didn't need any reminders. "What are you working on?" she asked in an effort to change the subject.

"I'm a history professor at Harvard, specializing in the early-American era."

It made sense that he taught at Harvard, Faith supposed; he lived in Boston, after all.

"I'm contracted to write a textbook, which is due at my publisher's early in the new year."

"How far are you with it?"

"Actually, it's finished. I was almost done when I

arrived, and my goal is to polish the rough draft in the remaining time I'm here."

"Will you be able to do that?"

"I'm astonished at all the writing I've accomplished since I got here. I finished the rough draft about fifteen minutes ago." He couldn't quite suppress a proud smile.

"Then congratulations are in order," she said, raising her wineglass to salute him.

Charles raised his glass, too, and they simultaneously sipped the merlot.

"Actually, early American history is a favorite subject of mine," Faith told him. "I teach English literature at the junior-high level but I include some background in American history whenever I can. Like when I teach Washington Irving. The kids love 'The Legend of Sleepy Hollow.'"

"Don't we all?"

After that, they launched into a lively discussion, touching on the Boston Tea Party, Longfellow's poetry, writings of the Revolutionary War period and the War of 1812.

"You know your history," he said. "And your American literature."

"Thank you." She heard the admiration in his voice and it warmed her from the inside out. "I like to think I can hold my own in snowball fights and battles of wits and words."

"No doubt you can." Charles stood and carried both plates into the kitchen. "Shall we finish our wine in the living room?" he surprised her by asking.

"That would be lovely."

The fire had died down to embers, so Charles added another log. He sat in the big overstuffed chair and stretched out his long legs, crossing them at the ankle. Faith sat on the rug by the fireplace, bringing her knees up to her chin as she reveled in the warmth.

"I've always loved this town," she said.

"Thus far, I haven't been very impressed," Charles said, a little sardonically. "But my predicament hasn't turned out to be nearly as disastrous as I feared."

Faith couldn't have held back a smile if she tried. "I don't think I'll ever forget the look on your face when I showed up with Santa and the elves."

"I don't think I'll ever forget the look on yours when I walked out of that bathroom."

"I was expecting Emily."

"I wasn't expecting anyone."

They both laughed.

"You're not nearly so intimidating when you laugh."

"Me, intimidating?" Charles asked as if she were joking.

"You can be, you know."

He seemed puzzled by that, shaking his head.

"I suspect you don't get angry often," she went on, "but when you do…"

"When I do," he said, completing her thought, "people know it."

He'd certainly made his feelings known shortly after her arrival. "I really appreciate your letting me stay," she told him.

"Actually, after a meal like that and last night's too, I think I'm the fortunate one."

"I've enjoyed cooking the last couple of days. I don't do much of it anymore. Usually I grab something on my way home from school."

"Me, too," he said. "You live alone?"

Faith nodded. "I've been divorced for more than five years." She was too embarrassed to admit how short-lived her marriage had been. "What about you?"

"I've never been married."

"Are you involved with anyone?" Faith asked the question before she had time to think about what it might reveal.

Charles shook his head. "No, my work's always been my life."

Suddenly the room seemed to grow very warm. Faith looked up and found Charles studying her as if seeing her for the first time.

Uncomfortable under his scrutiny, Faith came gracefully to her feet. "I'd better do the dishes," she said.

"Wait." Charles stood, too. "I'll help."

"No, really, that isn't necessary." Faith didn't understand *why* it was so important to put distance between them, but it was. She knew that instinctively. They'd shared a wonderful meal, found common ground, discussed history and even exchanged a few personal facts. They were attracted to each other. She felt it; he felt it, too, Faith was sure, and it unnerved her.

"Okay," Charles said. He stood no more than a foot away from her.

The tension between them seemed to throb like a living thing. It took Faith a moment to realize that Charles was responding to her statement about not needing help with the dishes.

She started to walk away, abandoning her wine, when he caught her hand. She stood frozen, half-facing the kitchen, her fingers lightly held in his. She sensed that if she turned back, he'd probably kiss her. He'd given her the choice.

Slowly, almost against her will, Faith turned. Charles drew her into the circle of his arms and brought his mouth down on hers.

The kiss was wonderful. They strained against each other, wanting, needing to give more, receive more, *feel* more.

When it was over, they stared at each other as if equally perplexed.

"Wow," Faith mumbled.

"You're telling me!"

Charles pulled her back into his embrace and held her tightly. "I'm ready to be wowed again. How about you?"

Faith's heart fluttered with excitement. This was the best surprise yet, she mused, as she closed her eyes and tilted her mouth toward his.

Eighteen

Emily had the bacon sizzling and muffins baking by the time Ray came out of his brother's bedroom. His hair was still wet from the shower, and he wore a fresh set of clothes. Emily assumed they'd come out of Charles's closet, because Ray hadn't brought a suitcase. Apparently the two brothers were close enough in size for Ray to wear his brother's clothes.

"Good morning," she greeted him cheerfully.

Ray muttered something indistinguishable and stumbled over to the coffeepot. He poured himself a mug. "Are you always this happy in the morning?" he asked, after his first restorative sip.

"Always," Emily said, just as cheerfully as before.

Ray stared at her. "I've heard there are two kinds of people in the world. Those who wake up and say 'Good Morning, God' and those who say 'Good God, Morning.'"

Emily laughed. "You don't need to tell me which one you are."

"Or you." He settled on the stool by the counter, propped up his elbows and slowly sipped his coffee.

When he'd finished his first cup, he was smiling again and eager for breakfast.

Emily set their plates on the counter and joined him, bringing the coffeepot for refills.

"Are you still interested in getting a Christmas tree?" she asked, as Ray dug into his bacon and eggs.

"Definitely, but first I think I'd better call my mother."

They'd listened to the messages the night before. Bernice Brewster made it sound imperative that she speak to her oldest son *immediately*.

After breakfast, Ray went to retrieve the portable phone.

"It's barely six in Arizona," she warned.

"Mom's an early riser and trust me—she's waiting with bated breath to hear from me."

He knew his mother well, because almost as soon as he'd dialed, Bernice was on the line. While they exchanged greetings, Emily scraped off the plates and set them in the dishwasher. She could only hear one end of the conversation, but Ray seemed to have trouble getting a word in edgewise. After a while, he placed the receiver carefully on the counter and walked away. He leaned against one of the stools, arms crossed, and waited patiently for his mother to finish her tirade. Even from the other side of the kitchen, Emily could hear the woman ranting.

"Ray," she whispered, half amused and half shocked at what he'd done.

He poured himself a third mug of coffee and shrugged elaborately.

After a few minutes, he lifted the receiver and pretended to be outraged. "Yes, Mother. Yes, of course, it's *dreadful.*" He rolled his eyes. "What do I plan to do about it? Frankly, nothing. Charles is over twenty-one and for that matter, so am I. Have a wonderful Christmas—your gift should arrive by the 24th. I'll be in touch. Bye now." He listened a few seconds more and then turned off the phone.

"Did you, uh, reassure your mother?" Emily asked.

"I doubt it." Ray chuckled. "She wanted to know what's going on with Charles. I didn't tell her, because basically I don't know. Besides, hard though it is for my mother to grasp, it's none of her business who Charles is with."

Still, Emily understood the other woman's concerns. "She's worried that both her sons are with strange women." She gave a short laugh. "Not *strange,* but strangers."

He smiled, too. "You know, frankly I think she'd be overjoyed if she met you. You're exactly the kind of woman she's wanted to introduce me to all these years."

Emily wasn't sure what to make of his comment. "Is that good or bad?"

"Good," he assured her and briefly touched her cheek. "Very good."

As soon as they'd cleaned up the kitchen, they put on their winter coats and ventured outside. The sky was dull gray, threatening snow. Arms linked, they walked several blocks until they found a Christmas-tree lot.

"Merry Christmas." The lot attendant, a college student from the look of him, wandered over when they entered. He didn't seem especially busy, Emily noticed, but with only three days until Christmas most people had their trees up and decorated.

"Hello," Emily said, distracted by Ray who was

straightening a scraggly fir that leaned against the makeshift wire fence. She shook her head at the pathetic little tree with its broken limbs and one bald side.

"Do you want your tree tall or small?" the young man asked. His breath made foggy wisps in the air.

"Medium-sized," Emily said.

He stared at her with narrowed eyes. "Would you mind telling me where you got that scarf?"

Emily turned away from the Christmas trees to look at the young man. "I knit it. Why?"

He shrugged. "I had a friend who had a similar one. That's all."

A chill raced down Emily's spine. "Your friend wouldn't happen to be Heather Springer, would she?"

"Yeah," he said excitedly. "How'd you know?"

"She's my daughter."

"You're Heather's mother?" He whipped off his glove and thrust out his hand. "I'm Ben Miller," he told her. "Heather and I were in art history together."

Ben Miller… Ben Miller… She had it! "Didn't you and Heather date for a while?"

"Yeah." He replaced his glove and rubbed his hands together. "I apparently wasn't…dangerous enough for her."

"Dangerous?"

"Never mind." Ben shook his head. "She's seeing Elijah now. Elijah with no last name." He spit out the words. "From what I hear, she's headed down to Florida with him and a bunch of his no-account friends."

The urge to defend Heather rose quickly, but died within the space of a single heartbeat. Emily could tell that he'd been hurt by Heather's actions—just as she herself had been. "Heather'll be back soon, I'm sure," she murmured. It was the best she could do.

"You came out to spend Christmas with her and she left anyway?" Ben sounded thoroughly disgusted.

"Yes…"

"You know, when Heather told me her plans for Christmas, I assumed it wouldn't take her long to see that she's making a mistake."

Emily'd hoped so, too.

"But if she could turn her back on her own mother at Christmas, then she isn't the person I thought she was." Ben's eyes hardened. "To tell you the truth, I don't care if I ever see her again." He walked over to another section of the lot. "There are a couple of nice trees over here," he said, all business now.

Emily and Ray followed him.

"Give her time," Emily said, squeezing his forearm with one mittened hand.

Ben glanced at her. "She isn't interested in me anymore."

Emily hung her head, fearing her daughter hadn't given her a single thought, either.

Sensing her mood, Ray placed his hand on Emily's shoulder. "You okay?" he asked.

She nodded. Nothing she said or did now would make a difference to what Heather had done or how Emily felt about it. But Ben seemed like a decent, hardworking young man and she felt bad that her daughter had so obviously hurt him.

"With Christmas this close, we don't have much to choose from," Ben apologized. He picked through several trees, then chose a tall, full one. "This is probably a little bigger than you wanted, but it's the best I've got."

Ray looked skeptical and circled the tree. "What do you think?" he asked Emily.

"It's perfect." She winked at Ben.

"We'll take it," Ray said and reached for his wallet.

Without a car they were forced to carry the tree back to the condominium. They walked in single file, Ray holding the trunk in one hand and a stand in the other, and Emily behind him, supporting the treetop. They must've been something of a spectacle, because they got lots of stares along the way.

Once inside the condo, they saw the message light blinking again. Ray checked the caller ID and groaned. "It's my mother. Again."

"Are you going to call her back?"

"Of course, but not anytime soon."

Emily smiled. While Ray fit the tree in the stand, she took out the decorations she'd brought from Seattle.

"You got all that in a single suitcase?" Ray marveled when she spread everything out.

"Two very large suitcases if you must know. Don't forget the stuff already on the mantel."

He shook his head, but Emily could tell he was enjoying this.

The living room was compact, and after a long debate, they decided the best place for the tree was by the window, although that entailed moving the furniture around.

"It's beautiful," Emily told him. She handed him the first decoration—a felt snowman complete with knitted scarf. "I made that for Heather the year she was in kindergarten," Emily explained.

Ray placed it on a tree limb and picked up a second

ornament. "Does every one of these have some significance?"

Emily nodded. "Each and every one."

"That's wonderful."

She was surprised he'd appreciate her sentimentality. "You don't think I'm silly to treasure these ornaments?"

"Not at all. You've given your daughter a lovely tradition."

At the mention of Heather, Emily bit her lip, overwhelmed by sadness.

Ray wrapped his arms around her. "My guess is she's got just enough freedom to be miserable," he said softly.

Emily doubted it, but she was grateful for his encouragement.

"Everything's going to work out for the best," he assured her. "Just wait and see."

Emily hoped he was right.

Nineteen

Faith woke up to the sound of Charles rummaging around in the kitchen. Grabbing her housecoat, she hurried down the stairs.

"Morning," he said, grinning sheepishly. "I hope I didn't wake you."

Faith rubbed the sleep from her eyes. He had to be joking. But then she glanced at the kitchen clock and couldn't believe she'd slept this late. It was the deepest, most relaxed sleep she'd had in months. She hadn't realized how tired she'd been.

"Coffee?" Charles lifted the glass pot.

"Please." She tightened the belt of her velour robe and sat down at the table, shaking the hair away from her face. Charles brought her a mug, which he'd filled with coffee. She added cream and held it in both hands, basking in the warmth that spread through her palms. They'd spent the most enjoyable evening talking and drinking wine and…

"What are your plans for today?" he asked.

Faith hadn't given it much consideration. "Maybe I'll walk into town a bit later."

Charles mulled that over. "Would you object to company?"

"You?" she gasped.

He shrugged in a self-conscious manner. "Unless you'd rather I didn't come with you."

"But I—what about your work?" Naturally she'd enjoy his company but Charles had insisted he was in Leavenworth to work and didn't want to be distracted from his purpose.

"I was up early this morning and got quite a bit done."

"Oh."

"I felt I should leave the project for a while, now that the rough draft is done. I'd like to give my mind a rest."

"Oh." All at once Faith seemed incapable of words consisting of more than one syllable.

"So—it seems I have the luxury of some free time."

"Oh." She sipped her coffee. "But I thought you hated Christmas?"

"I do. For…various reasons. It's far too commercial. The true meaning's been lost in all the frenzy of the season."

"Christmas is what each one of us makes it," Faith felt obliged to tell him.

"Exactly."

Faith swallowed. "I was going into town to do some shopping. Uh, Christmas shopping," she added. She met his eyes as she looked for some indication that he'd be interested in accompanying her. Men were notoriously impatient when it came to browsing through stores. And an avowed Christmas-hater…

He didn't say anything for a moment, then set his

mug aside. "I see. Well, in that case, I've got other projects I can work on."

"Oh." She couldn't disguise her disappointment.

Charles frowned. "*Would* you like my company?"

"Very much," she said quickly.

"Then I read you wrong."

"I'm just afraid it wouldn't interest you," she explained.

"I'd enjoy being out in the fresh air. I'll get my coat." He was like a kid eager to start a promised adventure.

"Whoa." Faith raised one hand. "Give me time. I've got to shower and dress, and I wouldn't mind a little something to eat first."

"Okay." He seemed amenable enough to that.

Faith wasn't quite sure what had prompted the change in him, but she wasn't complaining. She poured cereal and milk into a bowl, and ate every bite. Drinking the last of her coffee, she hurried back up the stairs and grabbed her jeans, a sweater and fresh underwear. She showered, dressed and dried her hair. When she came out of the bathroom, she found her boots, put them on and laced them up.

"Charles?" He didn't seem to be anywhere around. "Charles," she called, more loudly this time.

By chance she happened to glance out the window—to discover him surrounded by half a dozen neighborhood boys and Sarah. The children were apparently trying to talk him into something, but Charles clearly wasn't interested. Several times he shook his head and gestured dismissively with his gloved hands.

Faith threw on her coat and dashed out of the house, fastening her buttons as she went. She could see that Charles had begun to sweep the snow off the porch steps and had apparently been interrupted in his task by the children.

"Hi, Faith," Thomas called out. "You want to go sledding with us?"

"Ah…" She looked to Charles for some indication of his feelings. "What about you?"

Charles shook his head. "The last time I was on a sled, I was thirteen years old and too young to know better."

"It's fun," Thomas Kennedy promised.

"Go down the hill just once and you'll see what we mean." Mark's young voice was filled with excitement.

"You just gotta," Sarah insisted, tugging at Charles's hand.

Several of the older kids had lost interest in persuading Charles; they were already across the street, pulling their sleds.

"Come on," Faith said. "You need to do this or you'll lose face with the kids."

"Faith, I'm not sure it's a good idea."

"It'll be fun. You'll see."

"Faith, listen, I'm not entirely comfortable with this."

"They'll pester you until you give in, you realize?"

Charles seemed to need more convincing. "I'll go first," she told him. "Just do what I do, and you won't have a problem."

"People can get killed sledding," he mumbled to no one in particular.

She looked both ways before crossing the street. "People get killed on their way to work, too."

"This isn't encouraging."

"I'll go first," she said again.

"No," he countered as they trudged up the hill. "If this has to be done, I'll do it."

Thomas proudly showed Charles how to lie flat on the sled and how to steer with his arms. Charles still seemed unsure, but he was enough of a sport to lie prone, his feet hanging over the sled. He looked up at Faith with an expression that said if he died, it would be her fault.

"Are your life insurance premiums paid up?" she teased.

"Very funny," he grumbled.

Faith laughed, but her amusement soon turned to squeals of concern as the sled started down the snowy hill. Because of his weight, Charles flew downward at breakneck speed. His momentum carried him much farther than the children and straight toward the playground equipment.

"Turn!" she screamed. "Charles, turn the sled!" He couldn't hear her, so she did the only thing she could—and that was run after him. She stumbled and fell any number of times as she vaulted down the hill. Before long, she was on her backside, sliding down the snow and slush with only the thin protection of her jeans. The icy cold seeped through her clothes, but she didn't care. If anything happened to him, she'd never forgive herself.

Charles disappeared under the swing set and continued on for several feet before coming to a stop just short of the frozen pond.

"Charles, Charles!" Faith raced after him, oblivious now to her wet bottom and the melting snow running down her calves.

Charles leaped off the sled. His smile stretched from ear to ear as he turned toward her. "That was *incredible!*"

"You were supposed to stop," she cried, furious with him and not afraid to let him know it.

"Then you should have said so." He was by far the calmer one.

"You could've been hurt!"

"Yes, I know, but weren't you the one who said I could just as easily die on my way to work?"

"You're an idiot!" She hurled herself into his arms, nearly choking him. She felt like bursting into tears of relief that he was safe and unhurt.

Charles clasped her around the waist and lifted her off the ground. "Hey, hey, I'm fine."

"I know... I know—but I expected you to stop where the kids do."

"I will next time."

"Next time?"

"Come on," he said, and set her down. "It's your turn."

"No, thanks." Faith raised both her hands and took a step backward. "I already had a turn. I went down the hill on my butt, chasing after you."

He laughed, and the sound was pure magic. He kissed her cold face. "Go change clothes. As soon as you're ready we'll go into town."

"Are you staying in the park?"

Charles nodded. "Of course. A man's got to do what a man's got to do."

Shaking her head, she sighed. What on earth had she created here? One ride down the hill, and Charles Brewster was a thirteen-year-old boy all over again.

Twenty

Heather could hardly hear a thing over all the noise in the Hog's Breath Tavern in Key West, Florida. Peaches was eyeing Elijah with the voluptuous look of a woman on the prowl. Heather gazed across the room rather than allow herself to be subjected to such blatant attempts to lure Elijah away.

Slipping off the bar stool, she squeezed past crowded tables in a search for the ladies' room. This entire vacation wasn't anything like she'd imagined. She'd pictured sitting with Elijah on a balmy beach, singing Christmas carols and holding each other close. His idea of fun was riding twelve hours a day on his Harley with infrequent breaks, grabbing stale sandwiches in a minimart, and drinking beer with people who disliked and distrusted her.

Inside the restroom, Heather waited in line for a stall. Once she was hidden by the privacy of the cubicle, she buried her face in her hands. It was time to admit she'd made a mistake—hard as that was on her pride—but she'd had about as much as she could take of Elijah and his so-called friends.

When she left the ladies' room, Elijah was back at the bar with a fresh beer, which he raised high in the air when he saw her, evidently to tell her where he was. As if she hadn't figured it out by now. If Elijah didn't have a beer in his hand, then he was generally with a woman and most of the time it wasn't her.

"Babe," he said, draping his arm around her neck. "Where'd you go?"

"To the powder room."

He slobbered a kiss on the corner of her mouth. "Want another beer?"

"No, thanks."

"Hey, this is a party."

Maybe—but she wasn't having any fun. "So it seems."

His smile died and a flash of anger showed in his eyes. "What's your problem?"

Frankly, at this point there were too many to list. "Can we talk?" she asked.

"Now?" He glanced irritably around.

"Please."

"Sure, whatever." Frowning, he slid off the stool. With his arm still around her neck, he led the way outside. "You don't like Key West?" he asked as soon as they were outside. His tone suggested that anyone who couldn't have a good time in this town was in sad shape.

"What's not to like?" This had become her standard response. And she did like Key West. But the things she wanted to do—take history walks, visit Hemingway House, check out bookstores—were of no interest to the others.

"Well, then?" Elijah took another swallow of beer

and pitched the bottle into a nearby trash can. "You've been in a sour mood ever since we got here."

"Maybe I don't like you clinging to Peaches."

His laugh was short and abrupt. "You're jealous. Damn, I should've figured as much."

"Not really." She hadn't fully analyzed her feelings. The only emotion she'd experienced watching the two of them had been disgust. That, and sadness at her own misguided choices.

"So what's the big deal?" he demanded.

"There isn't one."

They stopped walking and faced each other. Elijah crossed his arms, leaning against his motorcycle as the din of raised voices and loud music spilled out from the Hog's Breath. Elijah looked longingly over his shoulder, as if he resented being dragged away from all the fun. The partyers continued their revelry, apparently not missing either of them.

"Dammit, tell me what you want."

His impatience rang in her ears. "What are your—our plans for Christmas Day?"

"Christmas Day?" Elijah said. He seemed confused by the question. "What do you mean?"

"You know, December twenty-fifth? Two days from now? What are we going to do to celebrate Christmas?"

He looked at her, his eyes blank. "I haven't thought that far ahead. Why?"

"Why?" she repeated. "Because it's important to me."

He considered this. "What would you like to do?"

Her throat clogged with emotion as she remembered the way she'd celebrated Christmas with her mother, all the special traditions that had marked her childhood.

She hadn't realized how much she'd miss those or how empty the holidays would feel without her family.

"I was hoping," Heather said, being as forthright and honest as she could, "that we'd find a small palm tree on the beach and decorate it like a real Christmas tree."

This seemed to utterly baffle Elijah. "Decorate it with what? Toilet paper?"

"I…don't know. Something. Maybe we could find sea shells and string those and cut out paper stars."

Elijah shrugged. "Would that make you happy?"

"I… I don't know. I dreamed of sitting in the sand with you and looking up at the night sky, singing Christmas carols."

Elijah rubbed his hand over his face. "I don't sing, and even if I did, I don't know the words to any of those carols. Well, maybe the one about the snowman. What the hell was his name again? Frisky?"

"Frosty."

"Yeah, Frosty."

"But you can hum, can't you?" Heather had a fairly decent voice. It didn't matter if he sang or not; all that mattered was being together and in love and sharing something important. Maybe creating a new tradition of their own…

"Heather, listen," Elijah said as he unfolded his arms and slowly straightened. "I'm not the kind of guy who decorates palm trees with paper stars or sings about melting snowmen."

"But I thought—"

"What?" He slapped his hand against the side of his head in frustration. "*What* were you thinking?"

"I like to party, too, but a steady diet of it grows old after a while."

"Says who?"

"Me," she cried. She'd never asked Elijah where he got his money, but she was beginning to think she should. "You didn't even consult me about having all these other people along."

"Hey," Elijah snapped, thrusting up both palms in a gesture of surrender. "You didn't *consult* me about all this Christmas junk you're so keen on, either."

He was right, but his sarcasm didn't make her feel any better. "I thought it would be just the two of us."

"Well, it isn't. I've got friends, and I'm not letting any woman get between me and my people."

"Your…people?"

"You know what I mean."

Unfortunately, Heather was beginning to understand all too well.

"Peaches warned me about college girls," he muttered.

"Ben warned me about you," she returned.

"Who the hell is Ben?"

"A friend." Heather wanted to kick herself for not listening, but it was too late for that.

"College girls are nothing but trouble."

"You didn't used to think that," Heather reminded him. "Not about me." From the moment they met, he'd said he didn't want to get involved with a college girl, and she'd taken that as a challenge to change his mind. She'd wanted to prove…what? She didn't know. Possibly how incredibly foolish she could be.

"I didn't used to think about a lot of things," Elijah said emphatically. "I've got a weakness for good girls, but the first thing they want to do is change me. Thing is, I'm content just the way I am. I'm not ever going to sit under any Christmas tree and sing silly songs. The sooner you accept that, the better."

Heather looked down the road and nodded. "I'm never going to be happy living like this." Her wide gesture took in the bar, the motorcycles, a group of hysterically laughing people clambering out of a cab.

"Like what?"

"Like this," she said. "Life is more than one big party, you know?"

"No, I don't," he countered.

"Fine." It wouldn't do any good to argue. "I'm leaving."

"You won't get any argument from me, but I'm not taking you to Boston, if that's what you want."

"No." She'd never ask that of him. "I'll catch a bus to Miami in the morning and fly back."

"What about money?" he asked, and the way he said it made it clear she was on her own.

"I'll be fine."

Elijah snorted. "Mommy's credit card to the rescue, right?"

Heather did have an emergency credit card her mother had given her, and she'd be forced to use it. In three years, she'd never had reason to do so, but she did now. Still, she was determined to pay back every last penny.

"Yes, Mommy's credit card. I'm fortunate to have a mother."

Elijah considered that for a moment, then nodded in agreement. "That's probably the reason you're in college. You had parents who gave a damn about you."

"I'm sorry it didn't work out for us," she told Elijah, sad now.

He shrugged casually. “Don’t worry about it. We had a few good times.”

“No hard feelings?”

Elijah shook his head. “You’ll be all right, and so will I.”

Heather knew that what he said was true. She should also have known, when she left Boston, that this arrangement would never work. Now she had two days to get back there and find her mother. Her poor, desperate mother in a strange town, without any friends…

Twenty-One

The phone rang as Ray and Emily sat by the Christmas tree, both cross-legged, sipping wine and listening to a Christmas concert on the radio.

"Don't answer that," he warned. "It might be my mother."

Emily smiled and hopped up to check caller ID. "It's my phone number back in Washington," she said, picking up the receiver. "Hello?"

"Emily? It's Faith."

"Oh, Faith," Emily said, instantly cheered. "It's so good to hear from you."

"Is everything all right?" her friend asked.

"Everything is positively wonderful." Emily looked over to where Ray sat with his wineglass.

"It is here, too," Faith confessed.

"What about Charles?" Emily was sure she hadn't heard her friend correctly. Faith actually sounded happy, but that couldn't be possible, since she was stuck with a Christmas-hating curmudgeon.

"Oh, Emily, Charles has been just *great.* He wasn't

in the beginning, but then I realized he's just like everyone else, only a little more intense."

"Really?"

"Yes. In fact, this morning he went sledding with the Kennedy kids. Thomas talked him into it. He was reluctant at first, but once he got started there was no stopping him."

"Charles?" Although they'd never met, Emily had heard enough about Ray's brother to find this bit of news truly astonishing.

"Then Charles and I walked downtown and browsed the stores and he bought the cutest little birdhouse for your yard. It's got a snowy roof and a bright-red cardinal on top."

"*Charles* did that?"

"Yes, and then we had a fabulous lunch. He's working now, or at least that's what he said he was doing, but I think he's taking a nap."

Emily smiled. This definitely wasn't the man Ray had described. From everything he'd told her, Charles was the classic absentminded professor, as stuffy and staid as they come. And he hated Christmas. Something—or someone—had turned his world upside down, and Emily had a very good idea who that might be.

"Faith," Emily murmured, "are you interested in Charles? As a man?"

Her friend didn't answer right away. "Define interested."

"Romantically inclined."

That caught Ray's notice; he stood and walked over to the phone, sitting down on a nearby stool.

"I don't know." Faith's answer revealed her indecision. "Well, maybe." She sounded uncertain, as if she was surprised by her feelings and a little troubled. This relationship must be developing very quickly; Emily could identify with that.

"I think it's wonderful that the two of you are getting along so well."

"He's not at all the way he first seemed," Faith told her. "First impressions can be deceptive, don't you think?"

"Of course."

"But I didn't phone to talk about myself." Faith seemed even more flustered now. "I just wanted to see how you're doing."

Emily's gaze drifted to Ray. "Like I said, this is turning out to be a wonderful Christmas."

Her announcement was followed by a short pause. "Charles's brother is still there?"

"Yes." Emily didn't elaborate.

"So the two of you are hitting it off?"

"We are. We're getting along really well."

As if to prove how well, Ray came to stand behind Emily. He slipped his arms around her waist and kissed the back of her neck. Tiny shivers of delight danced down her spine and she closed her eyes, savoring his warmth and attention.

"Have you heard from Heather?" Faith asked.

Emily's eyes flew open. "Not a peep, but I don't expect to since she doesn't have this phone number."

"I guess she'll call after Christmas," Faith said.

Emily managed a few words of assent, then changed the subject. "It was so sweet of you to come to Leavenworth for Christmas. I just wish you'd let me know."

"And ruin the surprise?" Faith teased.

"Just like I surprised Heather."

Faith laughed softly. "I'll check in with you later. Bye for now."

"Okay. Talk to you soon." Emily hung up the phone and sighed as she turned to Ray to explain the call. "As you could tell, that was Faith."

"What's all this about my brother?"

He released her and Emily leaned against the kitchen counter. "Charles apparently spent the morning sledding with the neighborhood kids."

Ray shook his head, frowning. "That's impossible. Not Charles. He'd never knowingly choose to be around kids."

"That's not all. After sledding, the two of them went Christmas shopping—and he bought me a gift. A birdhouse."

Ray's frown grew puzzled. "This is a joke, right?"

"Not according to Faith."

"Charles? My *brother,* Charles?"

"The very same. Apparently she tired him out, because he's napping."

"I've got to meet this friend of yours. She must be a miracle worker." He paused. "You're sure about all this?"

"That's what Faith told me, and I've never known her to exaggerate."

"Something must've happened to my brother. Maybe I should call him myself."

"Don't you think this is a good thing?" Emily asked. "Judging by everything you've said, your brother seems to have a single focus. His work. He wanted to escape Christmas and finish his book."

Ray nodded, but his expression had started to relax.

"It's interesting when you put it that way," he said thoughtfully.

"How so?"

"It sounds as if you're describing me."

This surprised Emily. From the beginning, she'd viewed Charles as an introvert, in contrast to Ray, who was personable and outgoing.

"For years now, Christmas has meant nothing but a few extra days off. Every year, I send the obligatory gift to my mother—usually the latest big mystery and maybe a new coffee-table book with lots of scenic pictures. I attend a few parties, have my assistant mail out greeting cards, make a restaurant reservation for the twenty-fifth. But I haven't felt any real spirit until today. With you."

Emily's heart warmed at his words.

"I never go for even an hour without thinking about work or publishing. We've spent the entire day together, and I haven't once missed hearing my cell ring."

Emily had no idea their Christmas-tree adventure had meant so much to him. He'd seemed eager to hear about her homemade decorations and the traditions she had with her daughter. Later she'd felt a bit silly to be talking so much and certain she'd bored him with her endless stories. She was glad she hadn't.

Ray looked away as if he'd said more than he intended. "Are you ready for dinner? What about that Mexican place we passed?"

"I'm starving." Mexican food sounded divine and the perfect ending to a perfect day.

"Me, too. That's what you get for walking my feet off this afternoon," he said. "Now you have to feed me."

After they'd finished putting the final touches on

the tree, they'd gone out for a light lunch of pizza and salad, then walked and walked. They'd had no real destination, but enjoyed being out of doors. They'd talked incessantly and Emily was surprised they had so much to discuss. She was a voracious reader and Ray questioned her about her favorite books and authors. Emily had questions of her own about the publishing industry, which fascinated her. She noticed, though, that neither of them talked much about their private lives. Their conversations skirted around their thoughts and feelings, but the more time they spent together, the more they revealed.

Twenty-Two

Faith replaced the telephone receiver, and a happy feeling spread through her. What had felt like a disaster a few days earlier now seemed to be working wonderfully well—for her *and* her dearest friend.

As if her thoughts had awakened him, Charles opened the door to the den and stepped out, still yawning.

"Just as I suspected," Faith teased. "You *were* napping."

"I intended to revise the first chapter," he muttered, rubbing his eyes, "but the minute I sat down in that warm, quiet room, I was lost. Thank goodness there's a comfortable sofa in there or I would've fallen asleep with my head on the keyboard."

Faith had taken more than one nap in Emily's comfortable den, perhaps her favorite room in the house. In the early years, it had been Heather's bedroom, but as she grew up, Heather had wanted more privacy and claimed the room at the top of the stairs. Emily had transformed her daughter's former bedroom into a library, with books in every conceivable place. A desk and computer took up one wall, and the worn leather couch another. A hand-knit afghan was draped over its back for those times when reading led to napping.… She'd spent many a lazy winter afternoon on that couch, Faith recalled.

"What have you been up to?" Charles asked.

"I called Emily in Boston to see how she's doing," she told him.

Charles poured a mug of coffee. "Is she having any problems?"

"No. In fact, it seems your brother's decided to stay on."

"Stay on what?"

"In Boston with Emily."

Charles's eyes widened as he stared at her. "Let me see if I'm hearing you right. My brother didn't return to New York?"

"Nope." Faith loved the look of absolute shock. She wondered if Ray had shown the same degree of astonishment when he learned how well his brother had adjusted to Leavenworth and being with her.

"Has something happened in New York that I don't know about?" Charles asked.

"What do you mean?"

"Has the city been snowed in or has there been a train strike? That sort of thing?"

"Not that I've heard. I had the radio on earlier and they didn't mention anything. Why?"

"Why? Because my brother is a dyed-in-the-wool workaholic. Nothing keeps him away from his desk."

"Well, he's taking a few days off to spend with Emily."

Charles took a sip of coffee, as though he needed

time to mull over what she'd told him. "Your friend must be one hell of a woman."

"She is." That was the simple truth.

Still distracted, Charles pulled out a kitchen chair and sat down. He glanced around and seemed to notice for the first time that she'd been busy. "You put up those decorations?"

"I didn't think you'd mind." She felt a bit uneasy about that now. Emily had a number of Christmas things she hadn't bothered to display this year; she'd obviously taken the rest of them to Boston. Faith had brought a few of her own decorations, as well. While everything was quiet, she'd unpacked the special ones and displayed them throughout the house. The tiny Christmas tree with red velvet bows stood on the mantel, and so did a small manger scene that Heather had loved since childhood. Emily's Christmas teapot, white china with holly decorations, now held pride of place on the kitchen counter.

Charles wandered into the dining room, Faith on his heels. "What's this?" he asked, motioning toward the centerpiece on the dining-room table.

"A cottonball snowman. Heather made it for Emily when she was eight. She was so proud of it, which is why Emily's kept it all these years."

Charles seemed puzzled, as if he couldn't quite grasp the beauty of the piece. Bells chimed softly from outside and Faith looked out the large picture window to see the horse-drawn sleigh gliding past.

"Charles, let's go for a sleigh ride," she said impulsively. For Faith, it was a highlight of the first and only Christmas she'd spent in Leavenworth—until now. It was the Christmas following her divorce. The sleigh ride, which she'd taken alone, had comforted her. That, and Emily's friendship, had made a painful Christmas tolerable, even pleasant. Her sleigh ride had shown her that being alone could bring its own contentment, its own pleasures. And spending Christmas Day with Emily and Heather had taught her that friendship could lend value to life.

Charles seemed startled by her invitation, then shook his head. "No, thanks."

"It's even more fun than sledding," she coaxed.

Still he declined.

"Well, come and stand in line with me while I wait my turn."

For a moment she thought he'd refuse, but then he nodded. "As long as the line isn't too long."

"Okay."

Dressed in their coats, boots, scarves and gloves, they strolled downtown, walking arm in arm. Night had settled over the small town, and festive activities abounded. The carolers in period costumes were out, standing on street corners singing. The Salvation Army band played Christmas music in the park, as ice skaters circled the frozen pond. Glittering multicolored lights brightened the streets and the town was bustling with shoppers.

Fortunately, the line for the sleigh ride wasn't too long and while she waited, Charles bought them cups of creamy hot chocolate. "I'm so glad I remembered the sleigh ride," she said, holding her hot chocolate with gloved hands.

"Why's that?" Charles asked.

She shrugged, sipping at her chocolate. "I think I mentioned that I did my student teaching in Leavenworth—that's when I met Emily. Those months were hard on me emotionally. I'd only recently been divorced and I was feeling pretty bad. Before me, no one in my family had ever gotten a divorce."

"No one?"

"Not in my immediate family. My parents, grandparents and sister were all happily married, and it really hurt my pride to admit that I'd made a mistake. I blamed myself because I hadn't listened when my parents warned me about Douglas."

"What happened?"

"My husband had a problem—he needed the approval and love of other women. Even now, I believe he loved me to the best of his ability, but Douglas could never be tied to a single woman."

"I see."

"I forgave him the first time he was unfaithful, although it nearly killed me, but the second time I knew this would always be a pattern with him. I thought—I hoped that if I got out of the marriage early enough, I'd be all right, but… I wasn't. I'm not."

Charles moved closer to her, and Faith looked down, tears blurring her eyes. She blinked them away and tried to compose herself, sipping the hot cocoa.

"Why aren't you all right? What do you mean?" he asked.

"I can't trust men anymore. I'm afraid of relationships. Look at me," she whispered. "Five years later, and I rarely date. All my dreams of marriage and family are gone and—" Resolutely she closed her mouth. What had possessed her to tell him this? "Listen," she told him, forcing a cheerful note into her voice, "forget I said anything."

Charles didn't answer right away. "I don't know if I can."

"Then pretend you have. Otherwise I'm going to feel embarrassed."

"Why should you?"

She shook her head. She hardly ever mentioned her divorce, not to anyone. Yet here she was, standing in the middle of this vibrant town in the most joyous season of the year, fighting back tears—spilling her heart to a man she hardly knew.

The sleigh glided up to the stop and the bells chimed as the chestnut mare bowed her head. The driver climbed down from his perch and offered Faith his hand. "Just one ticket," she said, about to give him the money.

"Make that two," Charles said, paying the driver. Without explaining why he'd changed his mind, he stepped up into the sleigh and settled on the narrow bench next to Faith.

The driver leaped back into the seat and took the reins.

Faith spread the woolen blanket over their laps. "What made you decide to come?" she asked.

He stared at her for a long moment. "I don't know… I just didn't want to leave you." He slid his arm around her shoulders and held her close. Warmth seeped into her blood. She hadn't realized how cold she was, but now Charles Brewster sat beside her in a one-horse open sleigh, two days before Christmas, and she felt warm, happy…and complete.

Twenty-Three

Emily woke the morning of Christmas Eve and stared up at the bedroom ceiling, musing that this was by far the most unusual Christmas of her life.

Not since the first Christmas following Peter's death had she dealt with such complex emotions during the holidays. For one thing, she'd been forced to acknowledge that Heather was an adult now, making her own decisions without the counsel of her mother.

As if *that* wasn't strange enough, Emily was in emotionally unfamiliar territory, living with a man she'd only known a few days. She sat up in bed and reviewed their time together. Ray was a hotshot New York publisher badly in need of a vacation, a career bachelor by all accounts. She was a widow and a small-town kindergarten teacher. Their meeting was accidental, as amusing as it was unexpected. They got along well, laughed together, and enjoyed each other's company. Much as she wanted to continue the relationship, Emily was realistic enough to accept that in a few days they'd both go back to their individual lives, three thousand miles apart. She decided then and there to make the most of their remaining time together.

After a quick shower, she dressed and emerged from the bedroom to discover that Ray was already up and reading the morning paper. The coffee was made. When she entered the kitchen, he lowered the newspaper and smiled.

"What's on the agenda for today?" he asked.

Emily wasn't sure. Back in Leavenworth, she'd be delivering charity baskets in the afternoon. Then, after a dinner of homemade clam chowder with Heather, followed by hot apple cider, she'd get ready for the Christmas Eve service at church. Home again, they'd go to bed, looking forward to a lazy Christmas morning, when they'd open their gifts and enjoy a late breakfast.

"I don't know what to do today," she said, feeling at a loss. "This year is completely unlike any I've ever experienced."

"What would you *like* to do?"

They'd spent their days sightseeing, and while Emily had thoroughly enjoyed this tour of American history, she wanted to concentrate on the season now.

"I'd like to bake cinnamon rolls," she said, coming to the decision quickly. "I do every year, specially for breakfast on Christmas morning. I think that would put me in the holiday spirit more than anything."

"Sounds fantastic. While you're doing that, I'll shop for our Christmas dinner. What shall we have?"

Emily shrugged. "A turkey might be a bit much for just the two of us."

"Didn't you say something about lobster earlier?" Ray asked.

She nodded, smiling. "Lobster would be perfect."

Emily must've realized she'd want to bake bread, because she'd tossed in a packet of yeast when she'd bought the supplies for her cookie-baking venture. She began to systematically search the kitchen cupboards for bowls and pans.

When Ray finished reading the paper, he put on his overcoat. On his way out the door, he came into the kitchen, where Emily was busy assembling ingredients. The recipe was a longtime family favorite, one she knew by heart. Ray took her by the shoulders and turned her so she couldn't avoid looking at him.

"I know this Christmas isn't anything like you anticipated, and I'm sorry about that. But it's the best Christmas I've had since I was a kid—the year my dad got me the red racing bike I so desperately wanted."

"Oh, Ray," she whispered, "that's the nicest thing anyone's said to me in a long, long time." Unable to resist, she slipped her arms around his waist and hugged him. She hadn't been this intimate with a man in years, nor had she felt such longing. He didn't kiss her and, although she was disappointed, she applauded his restraint. There'd be time later to enjoy the sweetness of each other's company.

Whistling, Ray left the condo, and as soon as she'd mixed the dough, Emily set it in a slightly warmed oven to rise. Pulling on her coat, gloves and scarf, she hurried out the door. She wanted to buy Ray a Christmas gift and while she was at it, she needed to stop at the grocery store.

The weather was exactly as it should be: cold and clear, with snow falling lightly. Everyone seemed to be bustling about, intent on last-minute Christmas shopping. There was an infectious spirit of joy and goodwill wherever she went.

Ninety minutes later, when Emily returned to the condo, her arms were laden with packages and groceries. She hummed a Christmas carol as she waited for the elevator. She hoped Ray had returned, too, but when she walked inside, the condo was silent and empty.

As quickly as she could, she unloaded her packages, hung up her coat and hid Ray's present in the bedroom to be wrapped that afternoon. She turned on the gas fireplace, and gentle flames flickered over the artificial log. She went to the radio next, and an instant later, the condo was filled with the glorious sounds of holiday music.

Ray didn't come back for another hour; among his purchases was a couple of deli sandwiches. Emily had been so busy, she'd forgotten to eat breakfast and it was now well past lunchtime.

"I think I should probably put these lobsters in water," he said, setting a large box on the counter. He filled the sink. "Should I add salt?"

"Salt?"

"They live in salt water. They might need it."

"I don't think so." Emily was preoccupied with unwrapping the sandwiches. Not until she turned around did she notice two huge lobsters looking directly at her. "They're alive!" She felt sorry for them and while Ray carried their sandwiches to the table, she released the rubber bands holding their claws together. Poor things, it seemed a shame to keep them prisoner.

Ray got two cold sodas from the refrigerator. "I wasn't sure about getting live lobsters, but I figured I could always exchange them if you'd rather."

"Ah..." Emily was afraid to admit she'd never cooked a live lobster in her life. Nor had she ever eaten anything more than a lobster tail. "This should be...well, a challenge."

"We'll figure it out," Ray said.

Emily agreed. They were both hungry and didn't attempt conversation until they'd finished lunch. To all outward appearances, they were like a long-married couple anticipating each other's needs. Ray handed her a napkin, she gave him the pepper mill, all without exchanging a word.

"Since neither of us knows that much about cooking lobsters, perhaps I should exchange these for cooked ones," Ray suggested once they'd eaten.

"That might be best." She took their empty plates into the kitchen and let out a small cry.

"What?" Ray demanded.

"One of the lobsters is missing."

"What do you mean, missing?"

"There's only one in the sink."

"That's impossible."

"I'm telling you there's only one lobster in the sink."

Ray entered the kitchen and stared into the sink. "One of the lobsters is missing."

Emily placed her hand on her hip. "The editor's eye misses nothing," she teased.

"Where could it have gone?"

"That's for you to find out. I've got dough to knead." She moved to the oven and was about to remove the bowl when she felt something attach itself to her pant leg. Glancing down she saw the lobster.

"Ah... Ray." She held out her leg. "I found the lobster."

"I can see that." He squatted down and petted the creature's head as if it were his favorite pet.

"You might want to detach him from my pant leg."

Ray frowned. "How did the rubber band get off his claws?"

"Er… I took them off. It seemed cruel."

"I see."

"Ray, this is all very interesting, but I'd prefer not to be worrying about this lobster crawling up my leg." She was trying hard not to giggle.

"If you have any ideas on how to remove him, let me know."

Emily tried to shake her leg, but the lobster was firmly affixed. Ray started to laugh then, and she found it impossible not to join him.

"What are we going to do?" she asked between giggles.

"I don't know." Ray bent down and tugged at her jeans, but the lobster wasn't letting go. "Maybe you should take off your pants."

"Oh, sure."

"I'm not kidding."

By then, they were nearly hysterical with laughter. Emily leaned against the kitchen counter, her hand over her mouth, tears running down her cheeks. Ray sat on the floor.

"You've got yourself quite a mess here."

"Just return me with the lobster." Emily could picture it now: Ray walking into the fish market, with her slung over his shoulder, the lobster dangling from her pant leg.

They burst into laughter again.

There was a knock at the door, and Ray, still laughing, left the room. It must be one of the neighbors, Emily supposed, someone else who lived on this floor. She went with Ray, not about to let him escape without helping her first. They had their arms around each other and were nearly doubled over with laughter when he opened the door.

An older woman stood on the other side, wearing a fur coat and an elaborate hat with a protruding feather. Cradled in the folds of her fur was a white Pomeranian. The dog took one look at Emily and growled.

"Ray!"

"Mother!"

After a few seconds' silence, he asked, "How did you get in?"

"Some nice young man opened the door for me." She glared at Emily. "And who's this?" Bernice Brewster demanded.

Ray looked at Emily and started laughing all over again. "Do you mean Emily or were you referring to the lobster?"

Twenty-Four

Faith hoped it would snow on Christmas Eve; to her disappointment the day was cold and bright, but there was no sign of snow. Charles had gone out on some errand, and she'd stayed home, her favorite Christmas CD playing as she flipped through Emily's cookbooks, looking for Christmas dinner ideas. Really, she should've thought about this earlier. Charles had suggested a roast, and she was beginning to think that was a good plan. Since she'd never made a turkey, she was a little intimidated by the prospect.

Sipping a cup of coffee, she read through one recipe after another, searching for inspiration. The more she read, the hungrier she got.

The phone rang, and she sighed, half wondering if she should answer. It wouldn't be for her. Still, habit and curiosity demanded she pick up the receiver.

"Merry Christmas," she greeted the unknown caller.

"Mom?" a small quizzical voice returned.

"Heather?"

"You're not my mother," Heather cried.

"This is Faith."

"Faith!" Heather sounded beside herself. "What are you doing in Washington? Where's my mom?"

"I came to surprise your mother, only she isn't here."

"Mom's still in Boston?"

"Yes," Faith said. "Where are you?"

"Boston."

Faith frowned. "I thought you went to Florida with some guy on a Harley."

"I did, but we…we had a parting of the ways. Where's my mother?"

"She's staying in Charles Brewster's condominium. I don't have the address but I understand it isn't that far from the Harvard campus."

"Not Professor Brewster?"

"One and the same. Why?"

"You mean to say he's in Leavenworth, and you are, too?" Heather asked incredulously.

Faith smiled at the comedy of errors. "Yes. I arrived shortly after Charles did. I came with Santa and the elves and then—"

"Who?"

"Never mind, it's complicated. But listen, everything's fine. Charles has been absolutely marvelous about all of this. He agreed to let me stay here until my original departure date." Faith hated to think what might've happened if he'd insisted she leave. She might still have been at the airport, waiting for a standby seat.

"You're talking about *Professor* Brewster?"

"Yes. Professor Charles Brewster."

"You say he's been…marvelous?" Heather seemed genuinely surprised.

"Yes." In fact, he'd been more than that, but Faith wasn't about to share any of the details with Heather.

"He *isn't* marvelous," Heather insisted. "He gave my roommate a C when she worked hard on every assignment and studied for every test. Well, okay, she fell asleep in his class, but who can blame her? The guy's boring."

"I happen to think he's a fascinating man," Faith said sharply, "so please keep your complaints to yourself."

"Faith?" Heather said, her voice dropping. "Are you…interested in Dr. Brewster?"

"That's none of your business."

Heather gave a short, abrupt laugh. "You are! I don't believe it. Just wait until Tracy hears this. Does the professor feel the same way about you? No, don't answer that 'cause I'll bet he does." She laughed again, as if this was the funniest thing she'd heard in weeks.

"It isn't that amusing," Faith said, surprised by her need to defend Charles.

But Heather had already moved on to her own concerns. "So Mom's still in Boston," she said.

"Yes, she couldn't fly home without paying a high-priced penalty."

"That's wonderful." Heather sighed with relief. "Don't say anything to her, okay?"

"Yes, but there's something you—"

"I want to surprise her, so promise you won't say a word."

Faith leaned against the kitchen counter and raised her eyes to the ceiling, resisting the urge to laugh. "You have my word of honor. I won't let her know."

"Great. Thanks, Faith. Say hello to the professor for me."

"Sure."

"I'm going to be my mom's Christmas surprise." With that, Heather terminated the call.

Faith's smile grew. Heather was about to discover a surprise of her own.

Just then, the front door opened and Charles staggered into the house, his arms stacked high with packages. Blindly he made his way into the dining room, piling the festively wrapped gifts on the table. Bags hung from his arms, and he set those next to the boxes.

"Good grief!" Faith rushed forward to help him. "What have you done?"

"I went shopping." His smile was as bright as sun on snow. He looked downright boyish, with a swath of brown hair falling over his brow, his eyes sparkling.

"Who are all these gifts for?"

"The Kennedy kids get a bunch of them and there are a couple in here for you and…" He seemed decidedly pleased with himself.

"Charles." He resembled Scrooge the day after his nightmare, rushing about buying gifts. Faith half listened for Tiny Tim.

"I got something else for Emily, too, in appreciation for trading places with me."

This was quite a switch from his initial attitude. "The way I remember it, you said you'd walked into the middle of a Christmas nightmare." Faith couldn't restrain a smile. "And then I showed up."

"That was no nightmare," he said softly. "That was a gift."

Faith didn't know what to say. His intensity flustered her and she felt the heat rush into her cheeks. After the sleigh ride, something had happened between them, something that was difficult to put into words.

She sensed that sharing her pain and the bitter disappointment of her divorce had, in some strange way, released *him.* Charles hadn't said anything, but Faith realized words were often inadequate when it came to conveying emotions. She'd noticed the changes in him last night and even more so this morning.

"You got presents for the Kennedy kids?" she asked, pointing to the packages.

He nodded. "Did you know their dad got laid off last month?"

The kids hadn't said anything to her, but apparently they had to Charles.

"They didn't tell me, either," he told her before she could comment, "but I overheard Mark and Thomas talking about it. And then, early this morning, I saw someone deliver a food basket to the house. With six children, it's got to be tough this time of year."

"What a sweet thing to do. If you want, I'll help you write up gift cards and deliver them."

He nodded and the boyish, pleased look was back. "I enjoyed myself today. I didn't know Christmas could be this much fun. It's always been a time I dreaded."

"But why?"

Charles glanced away. "It's a long story, and a boring one at that."

"Involving a woman, no doubt."

He shrugged.

Faith waited expectantly. She'd shared her pain with him; the least he could do was trust her enough to divulge his.

"I see," she said after an awkward moment. She turned back to the kitchen.

Charles followed her. "If you want to know—"

"No, it isn't necessary," she broke in. "Really."

"It was a devastating experience, and I'd prefer not to discuss it."

"I understand," she said and she did. Faith reassured him with a smile, gathering up the cookbooks and replacing them on the shelf.

"Her name was Monica."

Faith pretended not to hear.

"I loved her and I was sure she loved me."

"Charles, really, you don't need to explain if you'd rather not."

He threw off his coat and sat at the table. "But I would. Please." He gestured to the chair across from him.

Faith pulled it out and sat down. He took her hands, holding them in his own. "I adored her and assumed she felt the same way about me. I bought an engagement ring and planned to give it to her on Christmas Day. Thankfully I never had the opportunity to ask her to marry me."

"Thankfully?"

Charles's fingers tightened around hers. "She told me on Christmas Eve that she found me dull and tedious. I learned later that she'd met someone else."

Faith knew he didn't want her sympathy and she didn't offer it. "I think she was an extremely foolish woman."

Charles raised his eyes until they met hers. "I *am* dull and tedious."

"No," she countered swiftly. "You're brilliant and absentminded and quite possibly the kindest man I know."

A slow smile touched his mouth. "And you," he said. "You're the most marvelous woman I've ever met."

Twenty-Five

"Alone at last," Ray muttered as he shut the condo door. He'd walked his mother outside and waited with her until the taxi arrived to take her to the Four Seasons Hotel.

"Ray!" Emily said. "Your mother is hilarious."

"Believe me, I know. She's also meddling and demanding."

"But she loves you and worries about you."

"I should be worrying about *her,*" Ray said. "I can't believe she'd fly here without telling me."

"She tried," Emily reminded him. "If I remember correctly, she left four messages, none of which you returned."

Ray looked up at the ceiling and rolled his eyes. "Guilty as charged."

"She does have impeccable timing, though, doesn't she?" Emily doubted she'd ever forget the expression on Bernice's face when Emily appeared at the front door with a lobster attached to her pant leg. The Pomeranian had started barking like crazy, and pandemonium had immediately broken out. Bernice wanted answers and Emily wanted the lobster off her leg and the dog had taken an immediate dislike to both the lobster and Emily. FiFi had leaped out of Bernice's arms, grabbing hold of Emily's other pant leg, and she was caught in a tug-of-war between the lobster and the lapdog.

Everything eventually got sorted out, but until Ray was able to rescue Emily and assure his mother that all was well, it had been a complete and total circus.

"This isn't the way I intended to spend Christmas Eve," Ray said.

"It was wonderful," Emily told him. His mother had known exactly what to do with the lobsters and she'd taken over in the kitchen, issuing orders and expecting them to be obeyed. Ray and Emily had happily complied. That evening, the three of them had feasted on the lobsters and a huge Caesar salad.

After dinner, they'd gathered in front of the fireplace, sipping wine and listening to Christmas music, and Bernice had delighted Emily with tales of her two sons growing up. Emily had enjoyed the evening immensely. And while he might complain, Ray seemed to take pleasure in their visit with his mother, too.

"She insists on taking us out for Christmas dinner," Ray said.

"That would be lovely."

"I'll bet you've never eaten at a hotel on Christmas Day in your life."

"True, but nothing about this Christmas is normal."

Ray walked over to where she stood by the tree. "Do you mind sharing the day with my mother and me?"

Emily smiled. "I consider myself fortunate to be with you both." She was sorry she couldn't be with her daughter, but she'd come a long way since Heather had announced she wouldn't be flying home for the holidays. She was far more prepared to accept Heather's independence, for one thing; it was a natural, healthy process and it was going to happen anyway, so she saw no point in fighting it.

"You're right, this isn't the Christmas Eve I expected," she added, "but I've had such a fabulous time in Boston and I owe it all to you."

"I should be the one thanking you," he whispered, drawing her into his arms. His kisses were gentle but thorough, coaxing and sensual. Emily's knees were weak by the time he released her.

"I have something for you," he said, stroking her arms. He seemed unable to stop touching her, and Emily was equally loath to break away from him.

"I have something for you, too," she told him.

"Me first."

"Okay." They separated and went to their respective bedrooms to retrieve their gifts. A few minutes later, as they sat beneath the Christmas tree, he handed her a small beribboned box. Emily stared at the beautifully wrapped present and then at Ray.

"Open it," he urged.

Her pulse going wild, she tore away the red satin bow and the wrapping paper. The jeweler's box surprised her. This looked expensive.

"Ray?" Her eyes flew up to meet his.

"Open it," he said again.

Slowly, Emily lifted the lid and swallowed a gasp. Inside was a cameo, about the size of a silver dollar.

"It's on a chain," Ray said.

"I love cameos," she whispered, and wondered how he could possibly have known. "Did I mention that?"

She had two precious cameos that were among her most treasured possessions. The first had belonged to her grandmother and the second, a small one about the size of a dime, held an even deeper significance. Peter had given it to her on their fifth wedding anniversary. Now she had a third.

"I didn't know, but I saw this one and somehow I was sure you'd like it."

"Oh, Ray, I do. Thank you so much."

He helped her remove it from its plush bed. Emily turned her back to him and lifted her hair so he could connect the chain. This cameo was the most perfect gift he could possibly have given her. The fact that he'd sensed, after such a short acquaintance, how much it would appeal to her, was truly touching.

"This is for you," she said shyly, handing him her present. The day before, they'd strolled past an antique store that specialized in rare books. That morning, she'd gone inside to investigate and discovered a first edition of the science-fiction classic *Dune* by Frank Herbert. It was autographed, and because this was Christmas Eve, she'd been able to talk the dealer down to a reasonable price.

In one of their many conversations, Ray had said that he'd enjoyed science fiction as a teenager. She watched as he eagerly ripped off the paper. When he saw the novel, his eyes grew wide.

"It's autographed," she told him, smiling.

Ray's mouth sagged open. "I loved *Dune* as a kid. I read it so many times the pages fell out."

Reverently he opened the book. "How did you know?" The whispered question revealed his own astonishment that she could find him such a fitting gift.

"I listened."

"You listened with your heart." His fingertips grazed her cheek as his eyes held hers. Slowly he glided his hand around the nape of her neck and brought her closer to thank her with a kiss.

Emily opened her lips to his. Their kisses were warm, moist, each more intense than the one before. Ray leaned back, gazing at her for several breath-stopping moments. Then he wrapped his arms around her and held her hard against him.

"Ray?"

He answered her with another kiss, and any sensible thoughts she might have had vanished the moment his lips met hers. He lowered her to the carpet, leaning over her.

Emily slid her arms around his neck. Excitement tingled through her, and passion—so long dormant, so deeply buried—came to life.

Ray's hand cupped her breast and she gasped with pleasure. She was afraid and excited at the same time. He began to unfasten her blouse and when she saw that his fingers trembled, she gently brushed them aside and unbuttoned it herself. Just as she reached the last button, there was a knock at the door.

Ray looked at her. Startled, Emily looked at him.

"Your mother?" she asked.

He shrugged and got to his feet. "I doubt it." He walked across the room. "Whoever it is, I'll get rid of them." From her vantage point, she couldn't see the door, but she could hear him open it.

Emily waited. At first nothing happened, and then she heard Heather's shocked voice.

"Who are you?"

"Ray Brewster. And you are?"

Heather sidestepped Ray and walked into the condo. Emily quickly bunched her blouse together and stared up at her daughter's horrified expression.

"Mother?" Heather screeched.

Emily was sure her face was as red as the lobster she'd had for dinner that very night.

Twenty-Six

When Faith woke on Christmas morning, it was snowing, just as she'd hoped. Tossing aside the covers, she leaped out of bed, thrust both arms into her housecoat and bounded down the stairs. Happiness bubbled up inside her—it was Christmas Day!

From their short time together, Faith knew Charles wasn't a morning person, but she couldn't bear to let him sleep in on a morning as special as this.

After putting on the coffee and waiting impatiently for enough of it to filter through to fill a cup, she swiftly removed the pot and stuck the mug directly under the drip. Then, coffee in hand, she walked down the hallway to the room in which Charles slept.

Knocking at the door, she called, "Wake up, it's Christmas! You can't escape me this morning."

She could hear him grumbling.

"Charles, it's snowing! Come on, get up now."

"What time is it, anyway?"

"Seven-thirty. I have coffee for you. If you want, I can bring it in."

"Do I have a choice?"

She laughed and admitted that he really didn't. If he chose to sleep longer, she'd simply rattle around the kitchen making lots of noise until he got up.

"All right, all right, come in."

He didn't sound too pleased, but Faith didn't care. When she creaked open the door, she discovered Charles sitting up in bed. His hair was disheveled and a book had fallen onto the floor.

"Merry Christmas," she said, handing him the coffee.

His stare was blank until he took his first sip. "Ahh," he breathed appreciatively. Then he gave her an absent grin. "Merry Christmas, Faith. Did Santa arrive?"

"Oh… I didn't think to look."

"Let me finish my coffee and shower, and then I'll take a peek under the tree with you."

"You're on," she said and backed out of the room before she could do something silly and completely out of character—like throw her arms around his neck and kiss him. With the two of them alone in Emily's cozy house, the atmosphere had become more and more intimate….

A half hour later, Faith had dressed and was frying bacon for their breakfast when Charles appeared. He wore a dress shirt and sweater vest.

"Merry Christmas!" he said again.

"You, too." She made an effort not to look at him for fear she'd be too easily distracted.

"So, did you check under the tree?" Charles asked.

"Not yet." She slid the bacon onto the platter and wiped her hands.

"You look very nice," Charles said. "I generally don't notice much of anything before ten. I don't know if it's the day or if it's you." His comment was as casual as if he were discussing the weather.

"Me?" she whispered.

"You're an attractive woman." He cleared his throat. "Very attractive."

"Oh."

"It's true."

Flustered now, she offered him a tentative smile. "Breakfast is ready." She carried the crisp bacon over to the kitchen table, which she'd already set using a poinsettia-covered tablecloth. The juice was poured and the toast made; scrambled eggs were heaped in a dish. A quiche lorraine sat in the center of the table. And she'd brewed fresh coffee, the aroma pervading the room. She'd prepared far more than the two of them could possibly eat, but she supposed the quiche would make a nice lunch tomorrow.

"I'm so glad it's snowing," she said excitedly.

"Why wouldn't it snow today? It's snowed every day since I got here."

"Not true," she countered, but then admitted he was right. It *had* snowed every day at some point. Watching the thick white flakes drifting down was a holiday ideal. She felt like a child again.

"Oh, my," she said, unaware that she'd spoken aloud.

"What?"

Faith shook her head, not wanting to answer. She realized that she'd forgotten what it felt like to be happy. It was as though a fog had lifted and the world had become newly vivid, the colors clear and pure. Her gaze flew across the table and she looked at Charles. She knew immediately that he was responsible for her change of attitude. Spending these days with him had opened her to the joy of the season and the promise of love. The divorce had robbed her of so much, shredded her self-confidence, undercut trust and faith and made her doubt herself. It had taken her a long time to deal with the loss, but she was stronger now. She could expect good things in her life. She could anticipate happiness.

"Faith?" he asked with a quizzical expression. "What is it?"

She glanced quickly away and dismissed his question with another shake of her head. "Nothing important."

"Then tell me."

She smiled. "I was just thinking how happy I am to be here, having breakfast with you on Christmas morning."

Charles let the comment rest between them for a long moment. "With me?"

She giggled because he sounded so shocked. "Yes, Charles, with you. Is that so strange?"

"As a matter of fact, yes. I'm not accustomed to anyone enjoying my company."

"Well, I do." She reached for an extra strip of bacon to create a distraction for herself.

Charles set his fork aside and sat back in his chair, staring across the table as if she'd taken his breath away.

Faith grew uncomfortable under his scrutiny. "What is it?" she demanded.

He grinned. "I was just thinking that I could love you."

"Charles!"

"This isn't a joke—I'm completely sincere. I'm halfway in love with you already. But I know what you're going to say."

"I'm sure you don't."

"Yes, I do," he insisted. "You're thinking it's much too

soon and I couldn't possibly know my feelings yet. Two weeks from now, our encounter will be just a memory."

That *was* what she was thinking, although Faith badly wanted to stay in touch with Charles once they parted. But there was more to her reaction than that.

"I'm just so happy," she said, "and I realized I haven't been in a long time."

"Happy with me?"

She nodded.

"Could we...you know, call each other after the holidays?" He seemed almost afraid of her response.

"I'd like that."

His eyes sparkled with undisguised pleasure. "I was recently approached by Berkeley about a teaching position," he confided. "Is that anywhere close to you?"

"It's very close."

He took in that information with a slight nod. "Good. That's good."

The doorbell chimed, and Faith dropped her napkin on the table, rising to her feet. "I'll get it." She suspected it was one or more of the Kennedy kids, coming to thank Charles for the gifts. She wondered what he'd bought her; from all the hints he'd been dropping, she suspected it was something special. She'd found a small antique paperweight for him, and that, too, was under the tree.

When she opened the door, it wasn't the Kennedy kids she saw. Instead, there stood Sam with the six helpers crowding around him. They looked as if all they needed was a word of encouragement before rushing inside and attacking Charles en masse.

"Sam!" she cried and was instantly crushed in a big hug.

"We came to check up on you," Tony said, peering inside the house.

"Yes," Allen added. "We wanted to make sure Scrooge was good to you."

"Everything's fine," she assured her friends, bringing them into the house—and bringing them up to date. By that time, Charles had joined them in the living room.

Santa's elves peered up at him suspiciously.

Tony took a step closer. "She said you've had an attitude adjustment. Is that true?"

Charles nodded, a solemn expression on his face. "Faith won me over."

Sam chuckled. "We thought we'd give you a ride back to Seattle, Faith, so you can catch your flight tomorrow afternoon."

"I'll drive her." Charles moved to her side, placing his arm around her shoulders.

"We're just finishing breakfast but there's plenty if you haven't eaten."

"We haven't," Sam said promptly, and the seven of them rushed into the kitchen.

"Can you stay for dinner?" Charles asked, surprising Faith with the invitation.

"No, no, we don't want to intrude. Besides, we have to head out soon for flights of our own. The only reason we came was to make sure everything was all right with Faith."

"I'm having a wonderful Christmas," Faith told her friends.

And I'm going to have a wonderful life.

Twenty-Seven

"I've never eaten at the Four Seasons in my life," Emily said anxiously, "Christmas or not." She was sure there'd be more spoons at a single place setting than she had in her entire kitchen.

"It's where Mother always stays when she's in town," Ray told her. His hand rested on the small of her back as he directed her into the huge and elegantly decorated hotel lobby, dominated by a massive Christmas tree.

Emily glanced around, hoping to see Heather. Her daughter had been shocked to find her and Ray together. Although mortified that Heather had caught her half-undressed—well, with her blouse unfastened, anyway—Emily had hurriedly introduced them. Then, summoning all the panache she could muster, she'd announced that she hadn't slept with him.

Her cheeks flamed at the memory of how she'd managed to embarrass all three of them in one short sentence.

"Do you see Heather?" Emily asked, scanning the lobby.

"No," Ray murmured, "but I'm not looking for her."

The two people she held so dear hadn't exactly gotten off on the right foot, and Emily blamed herself.

Ray had tried to explain that the condo actually belonged to his brother, Professor Brewster, but Heather had been too flustered and confused to respond. The scene had been awkward, to say the least. Complicating everything, Heather had immediately stumbled out.

She'd rushed after Heather to invite her to the hotel for Christmas dinner. Her daughter had pretended not to hear, then stepped into the elevator and cast Emily a disgusted look. She'd shaken her head disapprovingly, as if the last place on earth she wanted to be was with her mother and that…*man*.

Emily had gone back into the apartment with her stomach in knots. She still felt ill; her stomachache hadn't abated since last night and she'd hardly been able to force down any breakfast.

"She'll be here any minute," Ray told her.

"Do you think so?" Emily's voice swelled with anticipation and renewed hope.

Ray exhaled loudly. "Actually, I was referring to my mother."

"Oh." Her shoulders deflated.

"Heather will make her own decision," Ray said, giving her shoulder a reassuring squeeze.

"I know." Emily had already realized that, but it was hard not to call her and smooth things out, despite Heather's rude behavior. To be estranged from her only child on Christmas Day was almost more than Emily could bear. If she hadn't heard from her by early evening, she knew she'd break down and call.

"Rayburn!" His mother stepped out of the elevator, minus FiFi the Pomeranian. She held out her arms to her son as she slowly glided across the lobby. Several heads turned in their direction.

"Mother likes to make an entrance," Ray said under his breath.

"So I noticed."

Bernice Brewster hugged Ray as if it'd been years since their last meeting, and then shifted her attention to Emily. Clasping both of Emily's hands, the older woman smiled benevolently.

"I am so pleased that my son has finally found someone so special."

"Mother, stop it," Ray hissed under his breath.

Emily quite enjoyed his discomfort. "Ray's the special one, Mrs. Brewster."

"I do agree, but it takes the right woman to recognize what a prize he is."

"What time is the dinner reservation?" Ray asked in an obvious attempt to change the subject.

"Three-thirty," his mother informed him. "I do hope you're hungry."

"I'm famished," Emily said, although it wasn't true. Worried as she was about Heather, she didn't know if she could eat a single bite. "I, uh, hope you don't mind, but I invited my daughter to join us.... She didn't know if she could make it or not."

Ray gripped her hand at the telltale wobble in her voice.

"Is anything wrong, my dear?" Mrs. Brewster asked.

"I—Heather and I had a bit of a disagreement."

"Children inflict those on their parents every now and then." Ray's mother looked pointedly in his direction. "Isn't that right, Rayburn?"

Ray cleared his throat and agreed. "It's been known to happen. Every now and then, as you say."

"Don't you worry," the older woman said, gently patting Emily's forearm. "We'll ask the maître d' to seat us at a table for four and trust your daughter has the good sense to make an appearance."

"I hope she does, too."

Ray spoke to the maître d' and they were led to a table with four place settings. Emily was surprised by the number of people who ate dinner in a restaurant on Christmas Day. Aujourd'hui was full, with a long waiting list, if the people assembled near the front were any indication.

The maître d' seated Mrs. Brewster, and Ray pulled out Emily's chair. She was half seated when she saw Heather. Her daughter rushed into the restaurant foyer, glancing around the tables until she caught sight of Emily. A smile brightened her pretty face, and she came into the room, dragging a young man. It took Emily only a moment to recognize Ben.

Emily stood to meet her daughter.

"Mom!" Heather threw her arms around Emily's neck. "I'm so glad I found you."

Emily struggled with emotion. "I am, too." She could hardly speak since her throat was clogged with tears.

"Hi," Heather said, turning to Ray. She extended her hand. "We sort of met last night. I'm Heather."

Ray stood, and they exchanged handshakes. "Ray." He motioned to his mother. "This is my mother, Bernice Brewster."

"And this is Ben Miller," Heather said, slipping her arm around the young man's waist. She pressed her head against his shoulder, as if they were a longtime couple.

Emily was curious about what had happened to Elijah No-Last-Name, but figured she'd learn the details later.

"Please," Mrs. Brewster said, gesturing to the table. "I would like both of you to join us."

Immediately an extra chair and place setting were delivered to the table, and not a minute later everyone was seated.

"This place is really something," Heather said with awe. "You wouldn't believe some of the roadside dumps I ate at while I was in Florida. Thanks so much for including us."

"It's good to see you again," Emily said, smiling at Ben.

The college student grinned, and answered Heather's unspoken question. "Your mother and Ray bought a Christmas tree from me a few days ago."

"Oh."

"When did you two…" Emily began, but wasn't sure how to phrase what she wanted to ask.

"When I left last night, I was pretty upset," Heather confessed, reaching for her water glass. She didn't drink from it but held on to it tightly. "I don't really know why I took off the way I did." She turned to Ray's mother. "I guess I didn't expect to find my mother with a man, you know?"

"Rayburn isn't just a regular run-of-the-mill man," Bernice said with more than a trace of indignation.

"I know—well, at first I didn't, but I'm over that now." Heather drew in a deep breath. "When I left the condo, I wasn't sure where to go or what to do, so I started walking and—"

"I saw her," Ben interrupted, "kind of wandering aimlessly down the street."

"You were still at the Christmas-tree lot?" Ray asked.

Ben nodded. "For those last-minute shoppers. Technically I should've closed about an hour earlier, but I didn't have anywhere to be, so I stuck around."

"It was a good thing, too," Heather said, her eyes brimming with gratitude. "I don't know what I would've done without Ben."

"I closed down the lot, and then Heather and I found somewhere to have coffee and we talked."

"Ben told me just what I needed to hear. He said I was being ridiculous and that my mother was entitled to her own life."

The waiter appeared then, and handed everyone elegant menus. Heather paused until he'd finished.

"It's just that I never thought my mother would ever be interested in a man other than my father," she continued in a low voice as Bernice perused the wine list. "I was…shocked, you know?"

Beneath the table, Ray took Emily's hand and they entwined their fingers.

"You *are* interested in Ray, aren't you?" Heather asked her mother.

The entire room seemed to go silent, as though everyone was waiting for Emily's reply. "Well…"

Mrs. Brewster leaned closer. So did Ray.

"I—I guess you could s-say I'm interested," she stammered. Now that the words were out, she suddenly felt more confident. "As a matter of fact, yes, I am. Definitely. Yes."

Mrs. Brewster released a long sigh. "Is it too early to discuss the wedding?"

"Yes." Ray and Emily spoke simultaneously and then both smothered their laughter.

"We've just met," Ray reminded everyone. "Let's not get ahead of ourselves, okay?"

"But you are smitten, aren't you?" Ray's mother asked with such eagerness that Emily couldn't disappoint her.

"Very much," she said, smiling at the old-fashioned word.

"And Rayburn?"

"I'm smitten, too."

"Good." Mrs. Brewster turned to Heather next. "I think a pale green and the lightest of pinks for the wedding colors, don't you agree?"

Heather nodded. "Perfect."

"May or June?"

Heather sneaked a look at her mother and winked. "June."

Ray brought his head closer to Emily's and spoke behind the menu. "They're deciding our future. Do you object?"

Emily grinned, and a warm, happy feeling flowed through her. "Not especially. What about you?"

Ray grinned back. "I've always been fond of June."

"Me, too."

"My mother will drive us both crazy," he warned.

"I like her," Emily whispered. "I even like FiFi."

Ray studied Bernice and then sighed. "Mother *is* a sweetheart—despite everything."

The waiter approached the table. "Merry Christmas," he said formally, standing straight and tall, as if it was his distinct pleasure to serve them on this very special day of the year.

"May I offer you a drink to start off with?"

"Champagne!" Bernice called out. "Champagne all round."

"Champagne," the others echoed.

"We have a lot to celebrate," Bernice pronounced. "Christmas, a homecoming—and a wedding."

Epilogue

"This is so festive, isn't it?" Faith had seen pictures of Rockefeller Center, but that didn't compare to actually standing here, watching the skaters in their bright winter clothes. Some were performing elaborate twirls and leaps; others clung timidly to the sides. They all seemed to be having a good time.

"I knew you'd love it," Emily said.

"What I'd love to do is skate." Not that she would in what Charles referred to as her "delicate" condition. She rubbed her stomach with one hand, gently reassuring her unborn child that she wouldn't do anything so foolish when she was six months pregnant. In the other hand she held several shopping bags from Saks.

The two friends continued down the avenue, weaving in and out of the crowd. Emily, too, carried packages and bags.

"I still can't imagine you living in New York City and actually loving it, especially after all those years in Leavenworth," Faith said. She was happy for Emily and Ray, but she'd been astonished when Emily had announced last spring that she was moving across the country.

"What I discovered is that New York is just a collection of small communities. There's Brooklyn and SoHo and the Village and Little Italy and Harlem and more."

"What about teaching? Is that any different?"

Emily shook her head. "Children are children, and the kindergartners here are just like the ones in Leavenworth. Okay, so they might be a bit more sophisticated, but in many ways five-year-olds are the same everywhere."

"What's new with Ray?"

Emily's lips turned up in a soft smile. "He works too hard. He brings his work home with him and spends far too many hours at the office, but according to everyone I've met, he's better now than ever."

"Better?"

Her friend blushed. "Happier."

"That," said Faith, "is what regular sex will do for you."

"Faith." Emily nudged her and laughed.

"It certainly worked with Charles."

"If you're going to talk about your love life, I don't want to hear it."

Faith enjoyed watching Emily blush. She'd never seen her this radiant. Life had certainly taken an interesting turn for them both, she reflected. Just a year earlier, they'd been lonely and depressed, facing the holidays alone. A mere twelve months later, each was married—and, to pile happiness on top of happiness, they were practically sisters now. Faith's baby was due in March, and Charles was about as excited as a man could get at the prospect of becoming a father.

His mother was pretty pleased with herself, too. Faith and Emily had both come to love Bernice Brewster. She'd waited nearly seventy years for daughters, and she lavished her daughters-in-law with gifts and occasional bits of motherly wisdom and advice. Well, perhaps more than occasional, but Faith had no objection and she doubted Emily did, either.

"When will Heather get here?" Faith asked, looking forward to seeing her.

"Tomorrow afternoon. She's taking the train down."

"How is she?"

Emily rearranged her shopping bags. "Heather's doing really well."

"Did you ever find out what happened with Elijah and the ill-fated Florida trip? I know she didn't want to talk about it for a while...."

Emily frowned. "Apparently he drank too much and he didn't like to eat in real restaurants. His idea of fine dining was a hot dog at a roadside stand. In addition to all that, he apparently had a roving eye, which Heather didn't approve of."

"That girl always was high maintenance," Faith teased. "What about her and Ben?"

"Who knows?" Emily said with a shrug. "She claims they're just friends but they seem to spend a lot of time together. Ben's going on to law school after graduation."

"Good for him."

"He might come down and spend Christmas with us, too."

"You'll have a houseful, with Heather and maybe Ben." Despite the invitation to spend Christmas in New York at their apartment, Charles and Faith had booked a room at the Warwick Hotel. Bernice was due to arrive, as well. She, of course, would be staying at the Plaza.

Faith doubted there was anyplace more romantic than New York at Christmastime.

She and Emily walked into the Warwick and down the steps to the small lobby. Ray and Charles stood when they came into the room. Even now, after all these months, Faith's heart fluttered at the sight of her husband. His eyes brightened when he saw her. The unexpected happiness she'd discovered last Christmas had never left. Instead, it had blossomed and grown. She was loved beyond measure by a man who was worthy of her devotion.

"Looks like you bought out Saks Fifth Avenue," Charles said as he took the packages from her hands.

"Just the baby department, but Charles, I couldn't help myself. Everything was so cute."

"Buying anything is a big mistake," Ray told them, helping Emily with her shopping bags. "Mother's waited all these years to spoil her first grandchild. My guess is she has stock in Toys 'R' Us by now."

"Don't forget a certain aunt and uncle, too," Emily murmured.

Faith wrapped her arm around Charles's and laid her head against his shoulder.

Emily read her perfectly. "Listen, why don't you two go to your room and rest for a little while? Faith needs to put her feet up and relax. Ray and I will have a drink and catch up. Then, when you're ready, we'll go out for dinner."

Faith nodded, grateful for her friend's sympathy and intuition.

Charles led the way to the elevator. He didn't speak until they were inside. "You overdid it, didn't you?"

"Only a bit. I'll be fine as soon as I sit down with a cup of herbal tea."

Her husband tucked his arm protectively around her and waited until they were back in the room to kiss her.

Then he ordered tea.

"Did you two have a chance to visit?" Ray asked as Emily removed her coat and slung it over the back of her chair. They'd entered the bar, securing a table near the window. "Or was shopping at the top of your priority list?"

"Actually, we did some of both. It's just so good to see Faith this happy."

The waitress came by, and Ray ordered a hot buttered rum for each of them.

"I can't believe the changes in her," Emily said. "She's so much more confident."

"I was going to say the same thing about Charles," her husband said with a bemused grin. "I hardly recognize my own brother. Until he met Faith, all he cared about was history—in fact, I think he would've preferred to live in the eighteenth century. I feel like I finally have a brother again."

The waitress brought their drinks and set them on the table, along with a bowl of salted nuts.

"Do you suppose they're talking about us in the same way?" Emily asked. "Are we different people now than we were a year ago?"

"I know I am," Ray said.

"I think I am, too."

Emily reached for a pecan, her favorite nut, and then for no discernible reason started to laugh.

"What's so funny?"

"Us. Have you forgotten the day we met?"

Ray grinned. "Not likely."

"I was so miserable and upset, and then you happened along. I glommed on to you so fast, I can only imagine what you must've thought."

"*You* glommed on to me?" he repeated. "That's not the way I remember it." Ray grabbed a handful of nuts. "As I recall, I found out that my brother had traded homes with this incredibly lovely woman. The explanation was reasonable. All I had to do was reassure my mother everything was fine and catch the train back to New York."

Emily lowered her eyes and smiled. "I'm so glad you ended up staying."

"You think I missed the last train by accident?"

"You didn't?"

"Not by a long shot. As my mother would say, I was smitten. I still am."

"That's comforting to hear."

"Christmas with you last year was the best of my life."

"Except for the Christmas you got the red racer."

"Well, that was my second-best Christmas."

"And this year?"

"When Christmas comes, I'll let you know."

"You do that," Emily whispered, raising her glass in a toast to the most wonderful Christmas gift of her life.

* * * * *

CHRISTMAS LETTERS

Prologue

Zelda O'Connor Davidson
76 Orchard Avenue
Seattle, Washington
Christmas, 2006

Dear Family and Friends:

Merry Christmas, everyone!

Let me warn you—this Christmas letter won't be as clever as last year's. My sister, Katherine (whom you may know better as K.O.), wrote that one for me but, ironically, she hasn't got time to do this year's. Ironic because it's due to the popularity of that particular letter that she's managed to start a little business on the side—writing Christmas letters for other people! (She offered to write mine, of course, but I know that between her work doing medical transcriptions, her job search and her Christmas letters, it would be a real stretch to find the time.)

So, here goes. The twins, Zoe and Zara, have recently turned five. They're looking forward to starting kindergarten next September. It's hard to believe our little girls are almost old enough for school! Still, they keep themselves (and us!) busy. So do our assorted pets—especially the dogs, two Yorkies named Zero and Zorro.

I'm still a stay-at-home mom and Zach's still working as a software programmer. This year's big news, which I want to share with all of you, has to do with a wonderful book I read. It changed my family's life. It's called *The Free Child* and it's by Dr. Wynn Jeffries. My sister scoffs at this, but Dr. Jeffries believes that children can be trusted to set their own boundaries. He also believes that, as parents, we shouldn't impose fantasies on them—fantasies like Santa Claus. Kids are capable of accepting reality, he says, and I agree! (See page 146 of *The Free Child*.)

So, this Christmas will be a different kind of experience for us, one that focuses on family, not fantasy.

Zach and the girls join me in wishing all of you a wonderful Christmas. And remember, a free child is a happy child (see page 16).

Love and kisses,

Zelda, Zach, Zoe and Zara

(and a wag of the tail from Zero & Zorro)

One

It *was* him. Katherine O'Connor, better known as K.O., was almost positive. She squinted just to be sure. He looked identical to the man on the dust jacket of that ridiculous book, the one her sister treated like a child-rearing bible. Of course, people didn't really look like their publicity photos. And she hadn't realized the high and mighty Dr. Wynn Jeffries was from the Seattle area. Furthermore, she couldn't imagine what he was doing on Blossom Street.

She'd never even met him, but she distrusted him profoundly and disliked him just as much. It was because of Dr. Jeffries that she'd been banned from a local bookstore. She'd had a small difference of opinion with the manager on the subject of Wynn's book. Apparently the bookseller was a personal friend of his, because she'd leaped to Dr. Jeffries's defense and had ordered K.O. out of the store. She'd even suggested K.O. take her future book-purchasing business elsewhere, which seemed unnecessarily extreme.

"K.O.," Bill Mulcahy muttered, distracting her. They sat across from each other at the French Café, filled to capacity during the midmorning rush. People lined up for coffee, and another line formed at the bakery counter. "Did you get all that?" he asked.

"Sure," K.O. said, returning her attention to him. "Sorry—I thought I saw someone I knew." Oh, the things she was willing to do for some extra holiday cash. One witty Christmas letter written on her sister's behalf, and all of a sudden K.O. was the most sought-after woman at her brother-in-law's office. They all wanted her to write their Christmas letters. She'd been shocked to discover how much they'd willingly plunk down for it, too. Bill Mulcahy was the third person she'd met with this week, and his letter was the most difficult so far. Leno or Letterman would've had a hard time finding anything amusing about this man's life.

"I don't know what you're going to write," Bill continued. "It's been an exceptionally bad year. As I explained earlier, my son is in a detention home, my daughter's living with her no-good boyfriend and over Thanksgiving she announced she's pregnant. Naturally, marriage is out of the question."

"That *is* a bit of a challenge," K.O. agreed. She widened her eyes and stared again at the man who waited in the long line at the cash register. It *was* him; she was convinced of it now. The not-so-good doctor was—to put it in appropriately seasonal terms—no Santa Claus. He was a child psychologist who'd written a book called *The Free Child* that was the current child-rearing rage.

To be fair, K.O. was single and not a mother. The only child-rearing experience she'd had was with her identical twin nieces, Zoe and Zara, whom she adored. Until recently, anyway. Overnight the five-year-olds had become miniature monsters and all because her sister had followed the "Free Child" rules as set out by Dr. Jeffries.

"My wife," Bill said, "is on the verge of a breakdown."

K.O. pitied the poor woman—and her husband.

"We've written Christmas letters for years and while life wasn't always as perfect as we—well, as we implied…" He let the rest fade away.

"You painted the picture of a model family."

"Yes." Bill cleared his throat and offered her a weak smile. "Patti, that's my wife, chose to present a, shall we say, rosier depiction of reality." He exhaled in a rush. "We never included family pictures and if you met my son, you'd know why. Anyone looking at Mason would know in a minute that this kid isn't a member of the National Honor Society." He released his breath again and shook his head sadly. "Mason's into body piercing," Bill added. "He pierced his eyebrows, his nose, his lips, his tongue, his nipples—"

K.O. stopped him before he went any lower. "I get it."

"You probably don't, but that's lucky for you. Oh, and he dyed his hair green."

"Green?"

"He wears it spiked, too, and he…he does this thing with paint." Bill dropped his voice.

K.O. was sure she'd misunderstood. "I beg your pardon?"

"Mason doesn't call it paint. It's some form of cosmetic he smears across his face. I forget the actual significance of the black smudges under his eyes and across his cheeks," Bill said. "To me it looks like he's some teenage commando."

Yes, this letter would indeed be a challenge. "Have

you thought about skipping your Christmas letter this year?" K.O. asked hopefully.

"Yeah, I'd like to, but as I said, Patti's emotional health is rather fragile. She claims people are already asking about our annual letter. She's afraid that if we don't send it the same as we do every year, everyone will figure out that we're pitiful parents." His shoulders drooped. "In other words, we've failed our children."

"I don't think you've necessarily failed," K.O. assured him. "Most teenagers go through a rebellious stage."

"Did you?"

"Oh, sure."

"Did you pierce anything?"

"Well, I had my ears pierced…."

"That's not the same thing." He peered at her earrings, visible through her straight blond hair, which she wore loosely tied back. "And you only have one in each ear—not eight or ten like my son." He seemed satisfied that he'd proved his point. "Then you'll write our Christmas letter and smooth over the rough edges of our year?"

K.O. was less and less confident that she could pull this off. "I don't know if I'm your person," she said hesitantly. How could she possibly come up with a positive version of such a disastrous year? Besides, this side job was supposed to be fun, not real work. It'd begun as a favor to her sister and all of a sudden she was launching a career. At some stage she'd need to call a halt—maybe sooner than she'd expected.

Her client shifted in his seat. "I'll pay you double what you normally charge."

K.O. sat up straight. Double. He said he'd pay double?

"Would four days be enough time?" she asked. Okay, so she could be bought. She pulled out her Day-Timer, checked her schedule and they set a date for their next meeting.

"I'll give you half now and half when you're finished."

That seemed fair. Not one to be overly prideful, she held out her hand as he peeled off three fifty-dollar bills. Her fingers closed around the cash.

"I'll see you Friday then," Bill said, and reaching for his briefcase, he left the French Café carrying his latte in its takeout cup.

Looking out the windows with their Christmas garland, she saw that it had begun to snow again. This was the coldest December on record. Seattle's normally mild climate had dipped to below-freezing temperatures for ten days in a row. So much for global warming. There was precious little evidence of it in Seattle.

K.O. glanced at the coffee line. Wynn Jeffries had made his way to the front and picked up his hot drink. After adding cream and sugar—lots of both, she observed—he was getting ready to leave. K.O. didn't want to be obvious about watching him, so she took a couple of extra minutes to collect her things, then followed him out the door.

Even if she introduced herself, she had no idea what to say. Mostly she wanted to tell him his so-called Free Child movement—no boundaries for kids—was outright lunacy. How could he, in good conscience, mislead parents in this ridiculous fashion? Not that she had strong feelings on the subject or anything. Okay, so maybe she'd gone a little overboard at the bookstore that day, but she couldn't help it. The manager had been touting the benefits of Dr. Jeffries's book to yet another unsuspecting mom. K.O. felt it was her duty to let the poor woman know what might happen if she actually followed Dr. Jeffries's advice. The bookseller had strenuously disagreed and from then on, the situation had gotten out of hand.

Not wanting him to think she was stalking him, which she supposed she was, K.O. maintained a careful distance. If his office was in Seattle, it might even be in this neighborhood. After the renovations on Blossom Street a few years ago, a couple of buildings had been converted to office space. If she could discreetly discover where he practiced, she might go and talk to him sometime. She hadn't read his book but had leafed through it, and she knew he was a practicing child psychologist. She wanted to argue about his beliefs and his precepts, tell him about the appalling difference in her nieces' behavior since the day Zelda had adopted his advice.

She'd rather he didn't see her, so she dashed inconspicuously across the street to A Good Yarn, and darted into the doorway, where she pretended to be interested in a large Christmas stocking that hung in the display window. From the reflection in the window, she saw Dr. Jeffries walking briskly down the opposite sidewalk.

As soon as it was safe, she dashed from the yarn store to Susannah's Garden, the flower shop next door, and nearly fell over a huge potted poinsettia, all the while keeping her eyes on Dr. Jeffries. He proved one thing, she mused. Appearances were deceiving. He looked so…so normal. Who would've guessed that beneath that distinguished, sophisticated and—yes—handsome exterior lay such a fiend? Perhaps *fiend* was too strong a word. Yet she considered Wynn Jeffries's thinking to be nothing short of diabolical, if Zoe and Zara were anything to judge by.

No way!

K.O. stopped dead in her tracks. She watched as Wynn Jeffries paused outside her condo building, her very own building, entered the code and strolled inside.

Without checking for traffic, K.O. crossed the street again. A horn honked and brakes squealed, but she barely noticed. She was dumbfounded.

Speechless.

There had to be some mistake. Perhaps he was making a house call. No, that wasn't right. What doctor made house calls in this day and age? What psychologist made house calls *ever?* Besides, he didn't exactly look like the compassionate type. K.O. bit her lip and wondered when she'd become so cynical. It'd happened around the same time her sister read Dr. Jeffries's book, she decided.

The door had already closed before she got there. She entered her code and stepped inside just in time to see the elevator glide shut. Standing back, she watched the floor numbers flicker one after another.

"Katherine?"

K.O. whirled around to discover LaVonne Young, her neighbor and friend. LaVonne was the only person who called her Katherine. "What are you doing, dear?"

K.O. pointed an accusing finger past the elegantly decorated lobby tree to the elevator.

LaVonne stood in her doorway with her huge tomcat, named predictably enough, Tom, tucked under her arm. She wore a long shapeless dress that was typical of her wardrobe, and her long graying hair was drawn back in a bun. When K.O. had first met her, LaVonne had reminded her of the character Auntie Mame. She still did. "Something wrong with the elevator?" LaVonne asked.

"No, I just saw a man..." K.O. glanced back and noticed that the elevator had gone all the way up to the penthouse suite. That shouldn't really come as a shock. His book sales being what they were, he could easily afford the penthouse.

LaVonne's gaze followed hers. "That must be Dr. Jeffries."

"You know him?" K.O. didn't bother to hide her interest. The more she learned, the better her chances of engaging him in conversation.

"Of course I know Dr. Jeffries," the retired accountant said. "I know everyone in the building."

"How long has he lived here?" K.O. demanded. She'd been in this building since the first week it was approved for occupation. So she should've run into him before now.

"I believe he moved in soon after the place was renovated. In fact, the two of you moved in practically on the same day."

That was interesting. Of course, there was a world of difference between a penthouse suite and the first-floor, one-bedroom unit she owned. Or rather, that the bank owned and she made payments on. With the inheritance she'd received from her maternal grandparents, K.O. had put a down payment on the smallest, cheapest unit available. It was all she could afford at the time—and all she could afford now. She considered herself lucky to get in when she did.

"His name is on the mailbox," LaVonne said, gesturing across the lobby floor to the mailboxes.

"As my sister would tell you, I'm a detail person." It was just the obvious she missed.

"He's a celebrity, you know," LaVonne whispered conspiratorially. "Especially since his book was published."

"Have you read it?" K.O. asked.

"Well, no, dear, I haven't, but then never having had children myself, I'm not too concerned with child-raising. However, I did hear Dr. Jeffries interviewed on the radio and he convinced me. His book is breaking all kinds of records. Apparently it's on all the bestseller lists. So there must be *something* to what he says. In fact, the man on the radio called Dr. Jeffries the new Dr. Spock."

"You've got to be kidding!" Jeffries's misguided gospel was spreading far and wide.

LaVonne stared at her. "In case you're interested, he's not married."

"That doesn't surprise me," K.O. muttered. Only a man without a wife and children could possibly come up with such ludicrous ideas. He didn't have a family of his own to test his theories on; instead he foisted them on unsuspecting parents like her sister, Zelda, and brother-in-law, Zach. The deterioration in the girls' behavior was dramatic, but Zelda insisted this was normal as they adjusted to a new regimen. They'd "find their equilibrium," she'd said, quoting the book. Zach, who worked long hours, didn't really seem to notice. The twins' misbehavior would have to be even more extreme to register on him.

"Would you like me to introduce you?" LaVonne asked.

"No," K.O. responded immediately. Absolutely not. Well, maybe, but not now. And not for the reasons LaVonne thought.

"Do you have time for tea?" LaVonne asked. "I wanted to tell you about the most recent class I attended. Fascinating stuff, just fascinating." Since her retirement, LaVonne had been at loose ends and signed up for a variety of workshops and evening classes.

"I learned how to unleash my psychic abilities."

"You're psychic?" K.O. asked.

"Yes, only I didn't know it until I took this class. I've learned so much," she said in wonder. "So much. All these years, my innate talent has lain there, unused and unfulfilled. It took this class to break it free and show me what I should've known all along. *I can see into the future.*" She spoke in a portentous whisper.

"You learned this after one class?"

"Madame Ozma claims I have been blessed with the sight. She warned me not to waste my talents any longer."

This *did* sound fascinating. Well...bizarre, anyway. K.O. would have loved to hear all about the class, but she really needed to start work. In addition to writing Christmas letters—which she did only in November and December—she was a medical transcriptionist by training. It paid the bills and had allowed her to put herself through college to obtain a public relations degree. Now she was searching for a job in PR, which wasn't all that easy to find, even with her degree. She was picky, too. She wanted a job with a salary that would actually meet her expenses. Over the years she'd grown accustomed to a few luxuries, like regular meals and flush toilets.

Currently her résumé was floating around town. Anytime now, she was bound to be offered the perfect job. And in the meanwhile, these Christmas letters gave her some useful practice in creating a positive spin on some unpromising situations—like poor Bill Mulcahy's.

"I'd love a cup of tea, but unfortunately I've got to get to work."

"Perhaps tomorrow," LaVonne suggested.

"That would be great."

"I'll call upon my psychic powers and look into your future if you'd like." She sounded completely serious.

"Sure," K.O. returned casually. Perhaps LaVonne could let her know when she'd find a job.

LaVonne's eyes brightened. "I'll study my class notes and then I'll tell you what I *see* for you."

"Thanks." She reached over and scratched Tom's ears. The big cat purred with pleasure.

With a bounce in her step, LaVonne went into her condo, closing the door with a slam that shook her Christmas wreath, decorated with golden moons and silver stars. K.O. headed for her own undecorated door, which was across the hall. Much as she disapproved of her sister's hero, she could hardly wait to tell Zelda the news.

Two

K.O. waited until she'd worked two hours straight before she phoned her sister. Zelda was a stay-at-home mom with Zoe and Zara, who were identical twins. Earlier in the year Zelda and Zach had purchased the girls each a dog. Two Yorkshire terriers, which the two girls had promptly named Zero and Zorro. K.O. called her sister's home the Land of Z. Even now, she wasn't sure how Zelda kept the girls straight, let alone the dogs. Even their barks sounded identical. *Yap. Yap* and *yap* with an occasional *yip* thrown in for variety, as if they sometimes grew bored with the sound of their own yapping.

Zelda answered on the third ring, sounding frazzled and breathless. "Yes?" she snapped into the phone.

"Is this a bad time?" K.O. asked.

"Oh, hi." The lack of enthusiasm was apparent. In addition to everything else, Dr. Jeffries's theories had placed a strain on K.O.'s relations with her younger sister.

"Merry Christmas to you, too," K.O. said cheerfully. "Can you talk?"

"Sure."

"The girls are napping?"

"No," Zelda muttered. "They decided they no longer need naps. Dr. Jeffries says on page 125 of his book that children should be allowed to sleep when, and only when, they decide they're tired. Forcing them into regimented nap-and bedtimes, is in opposition to their biological natures."

"I see." K.O. restrained the urge to argue. "Speaking of Dr. Jeffries…"

"I know you don't agree with his philosophy, but this is the way Zach and I have chosen to raise our daughters. When you have a family of your own, you can choose how best to parent your children."

"True, but…"

"Sorry," Zelda cried. It sounded as if she'd dropped the phone.

In the background, K.O. could hear her sister shouting at the girls and the dogs. Her shouts were punctuated with the dogs' yapping. A good five minutes passed before Zelda was back.

"What happened?" K.O. asked, genuinely concerned.

"Oh, nothing."

"As I started to say, I saw Dr. Jeffries."

"On television?" Zelda asked, only half-interested.

"No, in person."

"Where?" All at once she had Zelda's attention.

"On Blossom Street. You aren't going to believe this, but he actually lives in my building."

"Dr. Jeffries? Get out of here!"

Zelda was definitely interested now. "Wait—I heard he moved to Seattle just before his book was published." She took a deep breath. "Wow! You really *saw* him?"

"Uh-huh."

"Oh, my goodness, did you talk to him? Is he as handsome in person as he is in his photo?"

Feeling about him the way she did, K.O. had to consider the question for a moment. "He's fairly easy on the eyes." That was an understatement but looks weren't everything. To her mind, he seemed stiff and unapproachable. Distant, even.

"Did you tell him that Zach and I both read his book and what a difference it's made in our lives?"

"No, but..."

"K.O., could you... Would it be too much to get his autograph? Could you bring it on the fifteenth?"

K.O. had agreed to spend the night with the twins while Zelda and Zach attended his company's Christmas party. Her sister and brother-in-law had made arrangements to stay at a hotel downtown, just the two of them.

"All the mothers at the preschool would *die* to have Dr. Jeffries's autograph."

"I haven't met him," K.O. protested. It wasn't like she had any desire to form a fan club for him, either.

"But you just said he lives in your building."

"Yes."

"Are you sure it's him?"

"It looks like him. Anyway, LaVonne said it was."

Zelda gave a small shout of excitement. "If LaVonne says it's him, then it must be. How could you live in the same building as Dr. Jeffries and not know it?" her sister cried as though K.O. had somehow avoided this critical knowledge on purpose. "This is truly amazing. I've *got* to have his autograph."

"I'll...see what I can do," K.O. promised. This was

not good. She'd hoped to find common ground with her sister, not become a…a go-between so Zelda could get her hero's autograph. Some hero! K.O.'s views on just about everything having to do with parenting were diametrically opposed to those purveyed by Dr. Wynn Jeffries. She'd feel like a fraud if she asked for his autograph.

"One more thing," Zelda said when her excitement had died down. "I know we don't agree on child-rearing techniques."

"That's true, but I understand these are your daughters." She took a deep breath. "How you raise them isn't really any of my business."

"Exactly," Zelda said emphatically. "Therefore, Zach and I want you to know we've decided to downplay Christmas this year."

"Downplay Christmas," K.O. repeated, not sure what that meant.

"We aren't putting up a tree."

"No Christmas tree!" K.O. sputtered, doing a poor job of hiding her disapproval. She couldn't imagine celebrating the holiday without decorating a tree. Her poor nieces would be deprived of a very important tradition.

"I might allow a small potted one for the kitchen table." Zelda seemed a bit doubtful herself. She *should* be doubtful, since a Christmas tree had always been part of their own family celebration. The fact that their parents had moved to Arizona was difficult enough. This year they'd decided to take a cruise in the South Pacific over Christmas and New Year's. While K.O. was happy to see her mother and father enjoying their retirement, she missed them enormously.

"Is this another of Dr. Jeffries's ideas?" K.O. had

read enough of his book—and heard *more* than enough about his theories—to suspect it was. Still, she could hardly fathom that even Wynn Jeffries would go this far. Outlaw Christmas? The man was a menace!

"Dr. Jeffries believes that misleading children about Santa does them lasting psychological damage."

"The girls can't have Santa, either?" This was cruel and unusual punishment. "Next you'll be telling me that you're doing away with the tooth fairy, too."

"Why, yes, of course. It's the same principle."

K.O. knew better than to argue with her sister. "Getting back to Christmas…" she began.

"Yes, Christmas. Like I said, Zach and I are planning to make it a low-key affair this year. Anything that involves Santa is out of the question."

Thankfully her sister was unable to see K.O. roll her eyes.

"In fact, Dr. Jeffries has a chapter on the subject. It's called 'Bury Santa Under the Sleigh.' Chapter eight."

"He wants to bury Santa Claus?" K.O. had heard enough. She'd personally bury Dr. Jeffries under a pile of plowed snow before she'd let him take Christmas away from Zoe and Zara. As far as she was concerned, his entire philosophy was unacceptable, but this no-Santa nonsense was too much. Here was where she drew her line in the snow—a line Wynn Jeffries had overstepped.

"Haven't you been listening to *anything* I've said?" Zelda asked.

"Unfortunately, I have."

Her doorbell chimed. "I need to go," K.O. told her sister. She sighed. "I'll see what I can do about that autograph."

"Yes, please," Zelda said with unmistakable gratitude. "It would mean the world to me if you could get Dr. Jeffries's autograph."

Sighing again, K.O. replaced the receiver and opened the door to find her neighbor LaVonne standing there. Although *standing* wasn't exactly the right word. LaVonne was practically leaping up and down. "I'm sorry to bother you but I just couldn't wait."

"Come in," K.O. said.

"I can't stay but a minute," the retired CPA insisted as she stepped over the threshold, clutching Tom. "I did it!" she exclaimed. "I saw the future." She squealed with delight and did a small jig. "I saw the future of your love life, K.O. It happened when I went to change the kitty litter."

"The...kitty litter." That was fitting, since it was where her love life happened to be at the moment. In some kind of toilet, anyway.

"Tom had just finished his business," LaVonne continued, gazing lovingly at her cat, "and there it was, plain as day."

"His business?" K.O. asked.

"No, no, the future. You know how some people with the *gift* can read tea leaves? Well, it came to me in the kitty-litter box. I know it sounds crazy but it's true. It was right there in front of me," she said. "You're going to meet the man of your dreams."

"Really?" K.O. hated to sound so disappointed. "I don't suppose you happened to see anything in the kitty litter about me finding a job?"

LaVonne shook her head. "Sorry, no. Do you think I should go back and look again? It's all in the way it's arranged in the kitty litter," she confided. "Just like tea leaves."

"Probably not." K.O. didn't want to be responsible for her neighbor sifting through Tom's "business" any more than necessary.

"I'll concentrate on your job prospects next."

"Great." K.O. was far more interested in locating full-time employment than falling in love. At twenty-eight she wasn't in a rush, although it *was* admittedly time to start thinking about a serious relationship. Besides, working at home wasn't conducive to meeting men. Zelda seemed to think that as a medical transcriptionist K.O. would meet any number of eligible physicians. That, however, hadn't turned out to be the case. The only person in a white coat she'd encountered in the last six months had been her dentist, and he'd been more interested in looking at her X-rays than at her.

"Before I forget," LaVonne said, getting ready to leave. "I'd like you to come over tomorrow for cocktails and appetizers."

"Sure." It wasn't as if her social calendar was crowded. "Thanks."

"I'll see you at six." LaVonne let herself out.

"Concentrate on seeing a job for me," K.O. reminded her, sticking her head in the hallway. "The next time you empty the litter box, I mean."

LaVonne nodded. "I will," she said. As she left, she was mumbling to herself, something K.O. couldn't hear.

The following morning, K.O. set up her laptop on a window table in the French Café, determined to wait for Dr. Jeffries. Now she felt obliged to get his autograph, despite her disapproval of his methods. More importantly, she had to talk to him about Christmas. This clueless man was destroying Christmas for her nieces—and for hundreds of thousands of other kids.

She had no intention of knocking on his door. No, this had to seem unplanned. An accidental meeting. Her one hope was that Wynn Jeffries was hooked on his morning latte. Since this was Seattle, she felt fairly certain he was. Nearly everyone in the entire state of Washington seemed to be a coffee addict.

In an effort to use her time productively, K.O. started work on the Mulcahy Christmas letter, all the while reminding herself that he was paying her double. She had two ideas about how to approach the situation. The first was comical, telling the truth in an outlandish manner and letting the reader assume it was some sort of macabre humor.

Merry Christmas from the Mulcahys, K.O. wrote. She bit her lip and pushed away a strand of long blond hair that had escaped from her ponytail. *Bill and I have had a challenging year. Mason sends greetings from the juvenile detention center where he's currently incarcerated. Julie is pregnant and we pray she doesn't marry the father. Bill, at least, is doing well, although he's worried about paying for the mental care facility where I'm receiving outpatient therapy.*

K.O. groaned. This *wasn't* humorous, macabre or otherwise. It was difficult to turn the Mulcahys' disastrous year into comedy, especially since the letter was purportedly coming from them.

She deleted the paragraph and tried her second approach.

Merry Christmas from the Mulcahys, and what an— interesting? unexpected? unusual?—*year it has been for our lovely family.* K.O. decided on eventful. *Bill and I are so proud of our children, especially now as they approach adulthood. Where have all the years gone?*

Mason had an opportunity he couldn't turn down and is currently away at school. Our son is maturing into a fine young man and is wisely accepting guidance from authority figures. Our sweet Julie is in her second year of college. She and her boyfriend have decided to deepen their relationship. Who knows, there might be wedding bells—and perhaps even a baby—in our daughter's future.

So intent was she on putting a positive spin on the sad details of Bill Mulcahy's year that she nearly missed Wynn Jeffries. When she looked up, it was just in time to see Dr. Jeffries walk to the counter. K.O. leaped to her feet and nearly upset her peppermint mocha, an extravagance she couldn't really afford. She remained standing until he'd collected his drink and then straightening, hurried toward him.

"Dr. Jeffries?" she asked, beaming a winsome smile. She'd practiced this very smile in front of the mirror before job interviews. After her recent cleaning at the dentist's, K.O. hoped she didn't blind him with her flashing white teeth.

"Yes?"

"You are Dr. Jeffries, Dr. Wynn Jeffries?"

"I am." He seemed incredibly tall as he stood in front of her. She purposely blocked his way to the door.

K.O. thrust out her hand. "I'm Katherine O'Connor. We live in the same building."

He smiled and shook her hand, then glanced around her. He seemed eager to escape.

"I can't tell you what a surprise it was when LaVonne pointed out that the author of *The Free Child* lived in our building."

"You know LaVonne Young?"

"Well, yes, she's my neighbor. Yours, too," K.O. added. "Would you care to join me?" She gestured toward her table and the empty chairs. This time of day, it was rare to find a free table. She didn't volunteer the fact that she'd set up shop two hours earlier in the hope of bumping into him.

He checked his watch as if to say he really didn't have time to spare.

"I understand *The Free Child* has hit every bestseller list in the country." Flattery just might work.

Wynn hesitated. "Yes, I've been most fortunate."

True, but the parents and children of America had been most *un*fortunate in her view. She wasn't going to mention that, though. At least not yet. She pulled out her chair on the assumption that he wouldn't refuse her.

He joined her, with obvious reluctance. "I think I've seen you around," he said, and sipped his latte.

It astonished her that he knew who she was, while she'd been oblivious to his presence. "My sister is a very big fan of yours. She was thrilled when she heard I might be able to get your autograph."

"She's very kind."

"Her life has certainly changed since she read your book," K.O. commented, reaching for her mocha.

He shrugged with an air of modesty. "I've heard that quite a few times."

"Changed for the *worse,*" K.O. muttered.

He blinked. "I beg your pardon?"

She couldn't contain herself any longer. "You want to

take Santa away from my nieces! *Santa Claus.* Where's your heart? Do you know there are children all over America being deprived of Christmas because of *you?*" Her voice grew loud with the strength of her convictions.

Wynn glanced nervously about the room.

K.O. hadn't realized how animated she'd become until she noticed that everyone in the entire café had stopped talking and was staring in their direction.

Wynn hurriedly stood and turned toward the door, probably attempting to flee before she could embarrass him further.

"You're no better than…than Jim Carrey," K.O. wailed. She meant to say the Grinch who stole Christmas but it was the actor's name that popped out. He'd played the character in a movie a few years ago.

"Jim Carrey?" He turned back to face her.

"Worse. You're a…a regular Charles Dickens." She meant Scrooge, darn it. But it didn't matter if, in the heat of her anger, she couldn't remember the names. She just wanted to embarrass him. "That man," she said, stabbing an accusatory finger at Wynn, "wants to bury Santa Claus under the sleigh."

Not bothering to look back, Wynn tore open the café door and rushed into the street. "Good riddance!" K.O. cried and sank down at the table, only to discover that everyone in the room was staring at her.

"He doesn't believe in Christmas," she explained and then calmly returned to the Mulcahys' letter.

Three

The confrontation with Wynn Jeffries didn't go well, K.O. admitted as she changed out of her jeans and sweater later that same afternoon. When LaVonne invited her over for appetizers and drinks, K.O. hadn't asked if this was a formal party or if it would be just the two of them. Unwilling to show up in casual attire if her neighbor intended a more formal event, K.O. chose tailored black slacks, a white silk blouse and a red velvet blazer with a Christmas tree pin she'd inherited from her grandmother. The blouse was her very best. Generally she wore her hair tied back, but this evening she kept it down, loosely sweeping up one side and securing it with a rhinestone barrette. A little lip gloss and mascara, and she was ready to go.

A few minutes after six, she crossed the hall and rang LaVonne's doorbell. As if she'd been standing there waiting, LaVonne opened her door instantly.

K.O. was relieved she'd taken the time to change. Her neighbor looked lovely in a long skirt and black jacket with any number of gold chains dangling around her neck and at least a dozen gold bangles on her wrists.

"Katherine!" she cried, sounding as though it'd been weeks since they'd last spoken. "Do come in and meet Dr. Wynn Jeffries." She stepped back and held open the door and, with a flourish, gestured her inside.

Wynn Jeffries stood in the center of the room. He held a cracker raised halfway to his mouth, his eyes darting to and fro. He seemed to be gauging how fast he could make his exit.

Oh, dear. K.O. felt guilty about the scene she'd caused that morning.

"I believe we've met," Wynn said stiffly. He set the cracker down on his napkin and eyed the door.

Darn the man. He looked positively gorgeous, just the way he did on the book's dust jacket. This was exceedingly unfair. She didn't *want* to like him and she certainly didn't want to be attracted to him, which, unfortunately she was. Not that it mattered. She wasn't interested and after their confrontation that morning, he wouldn't be, either.

"Dr. Jeffries," K.O. murmured uneasily as she walked into the room, hands clasped together.

He nodded in her direction, then slowly inched closer to the door.

Apparently oblivious to the tension between them, LaVonne glided to the sideboard, where she had wine and liquor bottles set on a silver platter. Sparkling wineglasses and crystal goblets awaited their decision. "What can I pour for you?" she asked.

"I wouldn't mind a glass of merlot, if you have it," K.O. said, all the while wondering how best to handle this awkward situation.

"I do." LaVonne turned to Wynn. "And you, Dr. Jeffries?"

He looked away from K.O. and moved to stand behind the sofa. "Whiskey on the rocks."

"Coming right up."

"Can I help?" K.O. asked, welcoming any distraction.

"No, no, you two are my guests." And then as if to clear up any misconception, she added, "My *only* guests."

"Oh," K.O. whispered. A sick feeling attacked the pit of her stomach. She didn't glance at Wynn but suspected he was no more pleased at the prospect than she was.

A moment later, LaVonne brought their drinks and indicated that they should both sit down.

K.O. accepted the wine and Wynn took his drink.

With her own goblet in hand, LaVonne claimed the overstuffed chair, which left the sofa vacant. Evidently Dr. Jeffries was not eager to sit; neither was K.O. Finally she chose one end of the davenport and Wynn sat as far from her as humanly possible. Each faced away from the other.

"Wynn, I see you tried the crab dip," LaVonne commented, referring to the appetizers on the coffee table in front of them.

"It's the best I've ever tasted," he said, reaching for another cracker.

"I'm glad you enjoyed it. The recipe came from Katherine."

He set the cracker down and brushed the crumbs from his fingers, apparently afraid he was about to be poisoned.

K.O. sipped her wine in an effort to relax. She had a feeling that even if she downed the entire bottle, it wasn't going to help.

"I imagine you're wondering why I invited you here

this evening," LaVonne said. Phillip, her white Persian, strolled regally into the room, his tail raised, and with one powerful thrust of his hind legs, leaped into her lap. LaVonne ran her hand down the length of his body, stroking his long, white fur. "It happened again," she announced, slowly enunciating the words.

"What happened?" Wynn asked, then gulped his drink.

Dramatically, LaVonne closed her eyes. "The sight."

Obviously not understanding, Wynn glanced at K.O., his forehead wrinkled.

"LaVonne took a class this week on unleashing your psychic abilities," K.O. explained under her breath.

Wynn thanked her for the explanation with a weak smile.

LaVonne's shoulders rose. "I have been gifted with the sight," she said in hushed tones.

"Congratulations," Wynn offered tentatively.

"She can read cat litter," K.O. told him.

"That's not all," LaVonne said, raising one hand. "As I said, it happened again. This morning."

"Not with the litter box?" K.O. asked.

"No." A distant look came over LaVonne as she fixed her gaze on some point across the room.

Peering over her shoulder, K.O. tried to figure out what her neighbor was staring at. She couldn't tell—unless it was the small decorated Christmas tree.

"I was eating my Raisin Bran and then, all of a sudden, I knew." She turned slightly to meet K.O.'s eyes. "The bran flakes separated, and that was when two raisins bobbed to the surface."

"You saw...the future?" K.O. asked.

"What she saw," Wynn muttered, "was two raisins in the milk."

LaVonne raised her hand once more, silencing them. "I saw the *future.* It was written in the Raisin Bran even more clearly than it'd been in the cat litter." She pointed a finger at K.O. "Katherine, it involved *you.*"

"Me." She swallowed, not sure whether to laugh or simply shake her head.

"And you." LaVonne's finger swerved toward Wynn. Her voice was low and intent.

"Did it tell you Katherine would do her utmost to make a fool of me at the French Café?" Wynn asked. He scooped up a handful of mixed nuts.

As far as K.O. was concerned, *nuts* was an appropriate response to her neighbor's fortune-telling.

LaVonne dropped her hand. "No." She turned to K.O. with a reproachful frown. "Katherine, what did you do?"

"I…" Flustered, she looked away. "Did…did you know Dr. Jeffries doesn't believe in Santa Claus?" There, it was in the open now.

"My dear girl," LaVonne said with a light laugh. "I hate to be the one to disillusion you, but there actually *isn't* a Santa."

"There is if you're five years old," she countered, glaring at the man on the other end of the sofa. "Dr. Jeffries is ruining Christmas for children everywhere." The man deserved to be publicly ridiculed. Reconsidering, she revised the thought. "He should be censured by his peers for even *suggesting* that Santa be buried under the sleigh."

"It appears you two have a minor difference of opinion," LaVonne said, understating the obvious.

"I sincerely doubt Katherine has read my entire book."

"I don't need to," she said. "My sister quotes you chapter and verse in nearly every conversation we have."

"This is the sister who asked for my autograph?"

"Yes," K.O. admitted. Like most men, she concluded, Dr. Jeffries wasn't immune to flattery.

"She's the one with the children?"

K.O. nodded.

"Do you have children?"

LaVonne answered for her. "Katherine is single, the same as you, Wynn."

"Why doesn't that surprise me?" he returned.

K.O. thought she might have detected a smirk in his reply. "It doesn't surprise me that you're single, either," she said, elevating her chin. "No woman in her right mind—"

"My dears," LaVonne murmured. "You're being silly."

K.O. didn't respond, and neither did Wynn. "Don't you want to hear what I saw in my cereal?"

Phillip purred contentedly as LaVonne continued to stroke his fluffy white fur.

"The future came to me and I saw—" she paused for effect "—I saw the two of you. Together."

"Arguing?" Wynn asked.

"No, no, you were in love. Deeply, deeply in love."

K.O. placed her hand over her heart and gasped, and then almost immediately that remark struck her as the most comical thing she'd ever heard. The fact that LaVonne was reading her future, first in cat litter and now Raisin Bran, was ridiculous enough, but to match K.O. up with Wynn— It was too much. She broke into peals of laughter. Pressing her hand over her mouth, she made an effort to restrain her giggles.

Wynn looked at her curiously.

LaVonne frowned. "I'm serious, Katherine."

"I'm sorry. I don't mean to be rude. LaVonne, you're my friend and my neighbor, but I'm sorry, it'll never happen. Never in a million years."

Wynn straightened. "While Katherine and I clearly don't see eye to eye on any number of issues, I tend to agree with her on this."

LaVonne sighed expressively. "Our instructor, Madam Ozma, warned us this would happen," she said with an air of sadness. "Unbelievers."

"It isn't that I don't believe you," K.O. rushed to add. She didn't want to offend LaVonne, whose friendship she treasured, but at the same time she found it difficult to play along with this latest idea of hers. Still, the possibility of a romance with just about anyone else would have suited her nicely.

"Wynn?" LaVonne said. "May I ask how you feel about Katherine?"

"Well, I didn't officially meet her until this morning."

"I might've given him the wrong impression," K.O. began. "But—"

"No," he said swiftly. "I think I got the right impression. You don't agree with me and I had the feeling that for some reason you don't like me."

"True…well, not exactly. I don't know you well enough to like *or* dislike you."

LaVonne clapped her hands. "Perfect! This is just perfect."

Both K.O. and Wynn turned to her. "You don't really know each other, isn't that correct?" she asked.

"Correct," Wynn replied. "I've seen Katherine around the building and on Blossom Street occasionally, but we've never spoken—until the unfortunate incident this morning."

K.O. felt a little flustered. "We didn't start off on the right foot." Then she said in a conciliatory voice, "I'm generally not as confrontational as I was earlier today. I might've gotten a bit…carried away. I apologize." She did feel guilty for having embarrassed him and, in the process, herself.

Wynn's dark eyebrows arched, as if to say he was pleasantly surprised by her admission of fault.

"We all, at one time or another, say things we later regret," LaVonne said, smiling down on Phillip. She raised her eyes to K.O. "Isn't that right, Katherine?"

"Yes, I suppose so."

"And some of us," she went on, looking at Wynn, "make hasty judgments."

He hesitated. "Yes. However in this case—"

"That's why," LaVonne said, interrupting him, "I took the liberty of making a dinner reservation for the two of you. Tonight—at seven-thirty. An hour from now."

"A dinner reservation," K.O. repeated. Much as she liked and respected her neighbor, there was a limit to what she was willing to do.

"It's out of the question," Wynn insisted.

"I appreciate what you're doing, but…" K.O. turned to Wynn for assistance.

"I do, as well," he chimed in. "It's a lovely gesture on your part. Unfortunately, I have other plans for this evening."

"So do I." All right, K.O.'s plans included eating

in front of the television and watching *Jeopardy,* and while those activities might not be anything out of the ordinary, they did happen to be her plans.

"Oh, dear." LaVonne exhaled loudly. "Chef Jerome Ray will be so disappointed not to meet my friends."

If Wynn didn't recognize the name, K.O. certainly did. "You know Chef Jerome Ray?"

"Of Chez Jerome?" Wynn inserted.

"Oh, yes. I did his taxes for years and years. What most people don't realize is that Jerome is no flash in the pan, if you'll excuse the pun. In fact, it took him twenty years to become an overnight success."

The Seattle chef had his own cooking show on the Food Network, which had become an immediate hit. His techniques with fresh seafood had taken the country by storm. The last K.O. had heard, it took months to get a reservation at Chez Jerome.

"I talked to Jerome this afternoon and he said that as a personal favor to me, he would personally see to your dinner."

"Ah..." K.O. looked at Wynn and weighed her options.

"Dinner's already paid for," LaVonne said in an encouraging voice, "and it would be a shame to let it go to waste."

A nuked frozen entrée and *Jeopardy,* versus one dinner with a slightly contentious man in a restaurant that would make her the envy of her friends. "I might be able to rearrange my plans," K.O. said after clearing her throat. Normally she was a woman of conviction. But in these circumstances, for a fabulous free dinner, she was willing to compromise.

"I think I can do the same," Wynn muttered.

LaVonne smiled brightly and clapped her hands. "Excellent. I was hoping you'd say that."

"With certain stipulations," Wynn added.

"Yes," K.O. said. "There would need to be stipulations."

Wynn scowled at her. "We will *not* discuss my book or my child-rearing philosophies."

"All right," she agreed. That sounded fair. "And we'll…we'll—" She couldn't think of any restriction of her own, so she said, "We refuse to overeat." At Wynn's frown, she explained, "I'm sort of watching my weight."

He nodded as though he understood, which she was sure he didn't. What man really did?

"All I care about is that the two of you have a marvelous dinner, but I know you will." LaVonne smiled at them both. "The raisins have already assured me of that." She studied her watch, gently dislodged Phillip and stood. "You'll need to leave right away. The reservation's under my name," she said and ushered them out the door.

Before she could protest or comment, K.O. found herself standing in the hallway with Wynn Jeffries, her dinner date.

Four

If nothing else, K.O. felt this dinner would afford her the opportunity to learn about Wynn. Well, that and an exceptional dining experience, of course. Something in his background must have prompted a child-rearing ideology that in her opinion was completely impractical and threatened to create a generation of spoiled, self-involved brats. Although she didn't have children of her own, K.O. had seen the effect on her nieces ever since Zelda had read that darn book. She was astonished by how far her sister had been willing to go in following the book's precepts, and wondered if Zach understood the full extent of Zelda's devotion to *The Free Child.* Her brother-in-law was quite the workaholic. He was absorbed in his job and often stayed late into the evenings and worked weekends.

Chez Jerome was only a few blocks from Blossom Street, so K.O. and Wynn decided to walk. She retrieved a full-length red wool coat from her condo while Wynn waited outside the building. The moment she joined him, she was hit by a blast of cold air. A shiver went through her, and she hunched her shoulders against the wind. To her surprise, Wynn changed places with her, walking by the curb, outside the shelter of the buildings, taking the brunt of the wind. It was an old-fashioned gentlemanly action and one she hadn't expected. To be fair, she didn't know *what* to expect from him. With that realization came another. He didn't know her, either.

They didn't utter a single word for the first block.

"Perhaps we should start over," she suggested.

Wynn stopped walking and regarded her suspiciously. "You want to go back? Did you forget something?"

"No, I meant you and me."

"How so?" He kept his hands buried in the pockets of his long overcoat.

"Hello," she began. "My name is Katherine O'Connor, but most people call me K.O. I don't believe we've met."

He frowned. "We did earlier," he said.

"This is pretend." Did the man have to be so literal? "I want you to erase this morning from your memory and pretend we're meeting for the first time."

"What about drinks at LaVonne's? Should I forget that, too?"

"Well." She needed to think this over. That hadn't been such a positive experience, either. "Perhaps it would be best," she told him.

"So you want me to act as if this is a blind date?" he asked.

"A blind date," she repeated and immediately shook her head. "I've had so many of those, I need a Seeing Eye dog."

He laughed, and the sound of it was rich and melodious. "Me, too."

"You?" A man this attractive and successful required assistance meeting women?

"You wouldn't believe how many friends have a compulsion to introduce me to *the woman of my dreams.*"

"My friends say the same thing. *This* is the man you've been waiting to meet your entire life. Ninety-nine percent of the time, it's a disaster."

"Really? Even you?" He seemed a little shocked that she'd had help from her matchmaking friends.

"What do you mean *even you?*"

"You're blond and beautiful—I thought you were joking about those blind dates."

She swallowed a gasp of surprise. However, if that was the way he saw her, she wasn't going to argue.

He thrust out his hand. "Hello, Katherine, my name is Jim Carrey."

She laughed and they shook hands. They continued walking at a leisurely pace, and soon they were having a lively conversation, exchanging dating horror stories. She laughed quite a few times, which was something she'd never dreamed she'd do with Wynn Jeffries.

"Would you mind if I called you Katherine?" he asked.

"Not at all. Do you prefer Wynn or Dr. Jeffries?"

"Wynn."

"I've heard absolutely marvelous things about Chez Jerome," she said. Not only that, some friends of K.O.'s had recently phoned to make dinner reservations and were told the first available opening was in May.

"LaVonne is certainly full of surprises," Wynn remarked. "Who would've guessed she had a connection with one of the most popular chefs in the country?"

They arrived at the restaurant, and Wynn held the

door for her, another gentlemanly courtesy that made her smile. This psychologist wasn't what she'd expected at all. After hearing his theories about Christmas, she'd been sure he must be a real curmudgeon. But in the short walk from Blossom Street to the restaurant, he'd disproved almost every notion she'd had about him. Or at least about his personality. His beliefs were still a point of contention.

When Wynn mentioned LaVonne's name to the maître d', they were ushered to a secluded booth. "Welcome to Chez Jerome," the man said with a dignified bow.

K.O. opened her menu and had just started to read it when Jerome himself appeared at their table. "Ah, so you are LaVonne's friends."

K.O. didn't mean to gush, but this was a real honor. "I am so excited to meet you," she said. She could hardly wait to tell Zelda about this—even though her sister would be far more impressed by her meeting Wynn Jeffries than Jerome.

The chef, in his white hat and apron, kissed her hand. The entire restaurant seemed to be staring at them and whispering, wondering who they were to warrant a visit from the renowned chef.

"You won't need those," Jerome said and ostentatiously removed the tasseled menus from their hands. "I am preparing a meal for you personally. If you do not fall in love after what I have cooked, then there is no hope for either of you."

Wynn caught her eye and smiled. Despite herself, K.O. smiled back. After a bit of small talk, Jerome returned to the kitchen.

Once the chef had gone, Wynn leaned toward her and teased, "He makes it sound as if dinner is marinated in

Love Potion Number Nine." To emphasize the point, he sang a few lines from the old song.

K.O. smothered a giggle. She hated to admit it, but rarely had she been in a more romantic setting, with the elegant linens, flattering candlelight and soft classical music. The mood was flawless; so was their dinner, all four courses, even though she couldn't identify the exact nature of everything they ate. The appetizer was some kind of soup, served in a martini glass, and it tasted a bit like melted sherbet. Later, when their waiter told them the soup featured sea urchin, K.O. considered herself fortunate not to have known. If she had, she might not have tasted it. But, in fact, it was delicious.

"Tell me about yourself," she said to Wynn when the soup dishes were taken away and the salads, which featured frilly greens and very tart berries, were delivered.

He shrugged, as though he didn't really have anything of interest to share. "What would you like to know?"

"How about your family?"

"All right." He leaned back against the luxurious velvet cushion. "I'm an only child. My mother died three years ago. My father is Max Jeffries." He paused, obviously waiting to see if she recognized the name and when she didn't, he continued. "He was a surfer who made a name for himself back in the late sixties and early seventies."

She shook her head. Surfing wasn't an activity she knew much about, but then she really wasn't into sports. Or exercise, either. "My dad's the captain of his bowling team," she told him.

He nodded. "My parents were hippies." He grinned. "True, bona fide, unreconstructed hippies."

"As in the Age of Aquarius, free love and that sort of thing?" This explained quite a bit, now that she thought about it. Wynn had apparently been raised without boundaries himself and had turned out to be a successful and even responsible adult. Maybe he figured that would be true of any child raised according to his methods.

Wynn nodded again. "Dad made it rich when he was awarded a patent for his surfboard wax. Ever heard of Max's Waxes?" He sipped his wine, a lovely mellow pinot gris. K.O. did, too, savoring every swallow.

"I chose my own name when I was ten," he murmured.

It was hardly necessary to say he'd lived an unconventional life. "Why did you decide on Wynn?" she asked, since it seemed an unusual first name.

"It was my mother's maiden name."

"I like it."

"Katherine is a beautiful name," he commented. "A beautiful name for a beautiful woman."

If he didn't stop looking at her like that, K.O. was convinced she'd melt. This romantic rush was more intense than anything she'd ever experienced. She wasn't even prepared to *like* Wynn, and already she could feel herself falling for this son of a hippie. In an effort to break his spell, she forced herself to look away.

"Where did you grow up?" she asked as their entrées were ceremoniously presented. Grilled scallops with wild rice and tiny Brussels sprouts with even tinier onions.

"California," he replied. "I attended Berkeley."

"I lived a rather conventional life," she said after swooning over her first bite. "Regular family, one sister, two parents. I studied to become a medical transcriptionist, worked for a while and returned to college. I have a degree in public relations, but I'm currently working from home as a transcriptionist while looking for full-time employment. I'd really like to work as a publicist, but those jobs are rare and the pay isn't all that great." She closed her eyes. "Mmm. I think this is the best meal I've ever had." And she wasn't referring *just* to the food.

He smiled. "Me, too."

A few minutes later, he asked, "Your sister is married with children?"

"Identical twin girls. Zoe and Zara. I'm their godmother." When she discussed the twins, she became animated, telling him story after story. "They're delightful," she finally said. Dessert and coffee arrived then. An unusual cranberry crème brûlée, in honor of the season, and cups of exquisite coffee.

"So you like children?" Wynn asked when they'd made serious progress with their desserts.

"Oh, yes," she said, then added a qualifier, "especially well-behaved children."

His eyebrows arched.

Seeing how easy it was to get sidetracked, she said, "I think children are a subject we should avoid."

"I agree." But Wynn's expression was good-natured, and she could tell he hadn't taken offense.

Even after a two-and-a-half-hour dinner, K.O. was reluctant to leave. She found Wynn truly fascinating. His stories about living in a commune, his surfing adventures—including an encounter with a shark off the coast of Australia—and his travels kept her enthralled. "This has been the most wonderful evening," she told him. Beneath the polished exterior was a remarkable human being. She found him engaging and unassuming and, shock of shocks, *likeable.*

After being assured by Jerome that their meal had already been taken care of, Wynn left a generous tip. After fervent thanks and a protracted farewell, they collected their coats. Wynn helped K.O. on with hers, then she wrapped her scarf around her neck.

When they ventured into the night, they saw that snow had begun to fall. The Seattle streets were decorated for the season with sparkling white lights on the bare trees. The scene was as festive as one could imagine. A horse-drawn carriage passed them, the horse's hooves clopping on the pavement, its harness jingling.

"Shall we?" Wynn asked.

K.O. noticed that the carriage was traveling in the opposite direction from theirs, but she couldn't have cared less. For as long as she could remember, she'd wanted a carriage ride. "That would be lovely." Not only was Wynn a gentleman, but a romantic, as well, which seemed quite incongruous with his free-and-easy upbringing.

Wynn hailed the driver. Then he handed K.O. into the carriage before joining her. He took the lap robe, spread it across her legs, and slipped his arm around her shoulders. It felt like the most natural thing in the world to be in his embrace.

"I love Christmas," K.O. confessed.

Wynn didn't respond, which was probably for the best, since he'd actually put in writing that he wanted to bury Santa Claus.

The driver flicked the reins and the carriage moved forward.

"It might surprise you to know that I happen to feel the same way you do about the holidays."

"But you said—"

He brought a finger to her lips. "We agreed not to discuss my book."

"Yes, but I *have* to know…."

"Then I suggest you read *The Free Child.* You'll understand my philosophies better once you do. Simply put, I feel it's wrong to mislead children. That's all I really said. Can you honestly object to that?"

"If it involves Santa, I can."

"Then we'll have to agree to disagree."

She was happy to leave that subject behind. The evening was perfect, absolutely perfect, and she didn't want anything to ruin it. With large flakes of snow drifting down and the horse clopping steadily along, the carriage swaying, it couldn't have been more romantic.

Wynn tightened his arm around her and K.O. pressed her head against his shoulder.

"I'm beginning to think LaVonne knows her Raisin Bran," Wynn whispered.

She heard the smile in his voice. "And her cat litter," she whispered back.

"I like her cats," he said. "Tom, Phillip and…"

"Martin," she supplied. The men in her neighbor's life all happened to be badly spoiled and much-loved cats.

The carriage dropped them off near West Lake Center. Wynn got down first and then helped K.O. "Are you cold?" he asked. "I can try to find a cab if you'd prefer not to walk."

"Stop," she said suddenly. All this perfection was

confusing, too shocking a contrast with her previous impressions of Dr. Wynn Jeffries.

He frowned.

"I don't know if I can deal with this." She started walking at a fast pace, her mind spinning. It was difficult to reconcile this thoughtful, interesting man with the hardhearted destroyer of Christmas Zelda had told her about.

"Deal with *what?*" he asked, catching up with her.

"You—you're wonderful."

He laughed. "That's bad?"

"It's not what I expected from you."

His steps matched hers. "After this morning, I wasn't sure what to expect from you, either. There's a big difference between the way you acted then and how you've been this evening. *I* didn't change. You did."

"I know." She looked up at him, wishing she understood what was happening. She recognized attraction when she felt it, but could this be real?

He reached for her hand and tucked it in the crook of his arm. "Does it matter?" he asked.

"Not for tonight," she said with a sigh.

"Good." They resumed walking, more slowly this time. She stuck out her tongue to catch the falling snow, the way she had as a child. Wynn did, too, and they both smiled, delighted with themselves and each other.

When they approached their building on Blossom Street, K.O. was almost sad. She didn't want the evening to end for fear she'd wake in the morning and discover it had all been a dream. Worse, she was afraid she'd find out it was just an illusion created by candlelight and gorgeous food and an enchanting carriage ride.

She felt Wynn's reluctance as he keyed in the door

code. The warmth that greeted them inside the small lobby was a welcome respite from the cold and the wind. The Christmas lights in the lobby twinkled merrily as he escorted her to her door.

"Thank you for one of the most romantic evenings of my life," she told him sincerely.

"I should be the one thanking you," he whispered. He held her gaze for a long moment. "May I see you again?"

She nodded. But she wasn't sure that was wise.

"When?"

K.O. leaned against her door and held her hand to her forehead. The spell was wearing off. *"I don't think this is a good idea."* That was what she'd *intended* to say. Instead, when she opened her mouth, the words that popped out were, "I'm pretty much free all week."

He reached inside his overcoat for a PDA. "Tomorrow?"

"Okay." How could she agree so quickly, so impulsively? Every rational thought told her this relationship wasn't going to work. At some point—probably sooner rather than later—she'd have to acknowledge that they had practically nothing in common.

"Six?" he suggested.

With her mind screaming at her to put an end to this *now,* K.O. pulled out her Day-Timer and checked her schedule. Ah, the perfect excuse. She already had a commitment. "Sorry, it looks like I'm booked. I have a friend who's part of the Figgy Pudding contest."

"I beg your pardon?"

"Figgy Pudding is a competition for singing groups. It's a fund-raising event," she explained, remembering that he was relatively new to the area. "I told Vickie I'd come and cheer her on." Then, before she could stop herself, she added, "Want to join me?"

Wynn nodded. "Sure. Why not."

"Great." But it wasn't great. During her most recent visit with Vickie, K.O. had ranted about Dr. Jeffries for at least ten minutes. And now she was going to be introducing her friend to the man she'd claimed was ruining America. Introducing him as her…*date?*

She had to get out of this.

Then Wynn leaned forward and pressed his mouth to hers. It was such a nice kiss, undemanding and sweet. Romantic, too, just as the entire evening had been. In that moment, she knew exactly what was happening and why, and it terrified her. She liked Wynn. Okay, *really* liked him. Despite his crackpot theories and their total lack of compatibility. And it wasn't simply that they'd spent a delightful evening together. A charmed evening. No, this had all the hallmarks of a dangerous infatuation. Or worse.

Wynn Jeffries! Who would've thought it?

Five

The phone woke K.O. out of a dead sleep. She rolled over, glanced at the clock on her nightstand and groaned. It was already past eight. Lying on her stomach, she reached for the phone and hoped it wasn't a potential employer, asking her to come in for an interview that morning. Actually, she prayed it *was* a job interview but one with more notice.

"Good morning," she said in her best businesslike voice.

"Katherine, it's LaVonne. I didn't phone too early, did I?"

In one easy motion, K.O. drew herself into a sitting position, swinging her legs off the bed. "Not at all." She rubbed her face with one hand and stifled a yawn.

"So," her neighbor breathed excitedly. "How'd it go?"

K.O. needed a moment to consider her response. LaVonne was obviously asking about her evening with Wynn; however, she hadn't had time to analyze it yet. "Dinner was incredible," she offered and hoped that would satisfy her friend's curiosity.

"Of course dinner was incredible. Jerome promised

me it would be. I'm talking about you and Wynn. He's very nice, don't you think? Did you notice the way he couldn't take his eyes off you? Didn't I tell you? It's just as I saw in the kitty litter and the Raisin Bran. You two are *meant* for each other."

"Well," K.O. mumbled, not knowing which question to answer first. She'd prefer to avoid them all. She quickly reviewed the events of the evening and was forced to admit one thing. "Wynn wasn't anything like I expected."

"He said the same about you."

"You've talked to him?" If K.O. wasn't awake before, she certainly was now. "What did he say?" she asked in a rush, not caring that LaVonne would realize how interested she was.

"Exactly that," LaVonne said. "Wynn told me you were nothing like he expected. He didn't know what to think when you walked into my condo. He was afraid the evening would end with someone calling the police—and then he had a stupendous night. That was the word he used—*stupendous*."

"Really." K.O. positively glowed with pleasure.

"He had the look when he said it, too."

"What look?"

"The *look,*" LaVonne repeated, emphasizing the word, "of a man who's falling in love. You had a good time, didn't you?"

"I did." K.O. doubted she could have lied. She *did* have a wonderful evening. Shockingly wonderful, in fact, and that made everything ten times worse. She wanted to view Wynn as a lunatic confounding young parents, a grinch out to steal Christmas from youngsters all across America. How could she berate him and detest him if she was in danger of falling in love with him? This was getting worse and worse.

"I knew it!" LaVonne sounded downright gleeful. "From the moment I saw those raisins floating in the milk, I knew. The vision told me everything."

"Everything?"

"Everything," LaVonne echoed. "It came to me, as profound as anything I've seen with my psychic gift. You and Dr. Jeffries are perfect together."

K.O. buried her face in her hand. She'd fallen asleep in a haze of wonder and awakened to the shrill ring of her phone. She couldn't explain last night's feelings in any rational way.

She wasn't attracted to Wynn, she told herself. How could she be? The man who believed children should set their own rules? The man who wanted to eliminate Santa Claus? But she was beginning to understand what was going on here. For weeks she'd been stuck inside her condo, venturing outside only to meet Christmas-letter clients. If she wasn't transcribing medical records, she was filling out job applications. With such a lack of human contact, it was only natural that she'd be swept along on the tide of romance LaVonne had so expertly arranged for her.

"Wynn told me you were seeing him again this evening," LaVonne said eagerly.

"I am?" K.O. vaguely remembered that. "Oh, right, I am." Her mind cleared and her memory fell into place like an elevator suddenly dropping thirteen floors. "Yes, as it happens," she said, trying to think of a way out of this. "I invited Wynn to accompany me to the Figgy Pudding event at West Lake Plaza." She'd *invited* him. What was she thinking? *What was she thinking?* Mentally she slapped her hand against her forehead. Before this afternoon, she had to find an excuse to cancel.

"He's very sweet, isn't he?" LaVonne said.

"He is." K.O. didn't want to acknowledge it but he was. He'd done it on purpose; she just didn't know *why.* What was his purpose in breaking down her defenses?

She needed to think. She pulled her feet up onto the bed and wrapped one arm around her knees. He *had* been sweet and alarmingly wonderful. Oh, he was clever. But what was behind all that charm? Nothing good, she'd bet.

"I have more to tell you," LaVonne said, lowering her voice to a mere whisper. "It happened again this morning." She paused. "I was feeding the boys."

K.O. had half a mind to stop her friend, but for some perverse reason she didn't.

"And then," LaVonne added, her voice gaining volume, "when I poured the dry cat food into their bowls, some of it spilled on the floor."

"You got a reading from the cat food?" K.O. supposed this shouldn't surprise her. Since LaVonne had taken that class, everything imaginable provided her with insight—mostly, it seemed, into K.O.'s life. Her love life, which to this point had been a blank slate.

"Would you like to know how many children you and Wynn are going to have?" LaVonne asked triumphantly.

"Any twins?" K.O. asked, playing along. She might as well. LaVonne was determined to tell her, whether she wanted to hear or not.

"Twins," LaVonne repeated in dismay. "Oh, my goodness, I didn't look that closely."

"That's fine."

LaVonne took her seriously. "Still, twins are definitely a possibility. Sure as anything, I saw three children. Multiple births run in your family, don't they? Because it might've been triplets."

"Triplets?" It was too hard to think about this without her morning cup of coffee. "Listen, I need to get off the phone. I'll check in with you later," K.O. promised.

"Good. You'll give me regular updates, won't you?"

"On the triplets?"

"No," LaVonne returned, laughing. "On you and Wynn. The babies come later."

"Okay," she said, resigned to continuing the charade. Everything might've been delightful and romantic the night before, but this was a whole new day. She was beginning to figure out his agenda. She'd criticized his beliefs, especially about Christmas, and now he was determined to change hers. It was all a matter of pride. *Male* pride.

She'd been vulnerable, she realized. The dinner, the wine, Chef Jerome, a carriage ride, walking in the snow. *Christmas.* He'd actually used Christmas to weaken her resolve. The very man who was threatening to destroy the holiday for children had practically seduced her in Seattle's winter wonderland. What she recognized now was that in those circumstances, she would've experienced the same emotions with just about any man.

As was her habit, K.O. weighed herself first thing and gasped when she saw she was up two pounds. That fabulous dinner had come at a price. Two pounds. K.O. had to keep a constant eye on her weight, unlike her sister. Zelda was naturally thin whereas K.O. wasn't. Her only successful strategy for maintaining her weight was to weigh herself daily and then make adjustments in her diet.

Even before she'd finished putting on her workout gear, the phone rang again. K.O. could always hope that it was a potential employer, but caller ID informed her it was her sister.

"Merry Christmas, Zelda," K.O. said. This was one small way to remind her that keeping Santa away from Zoe and Zara was fundamentally wrong.

"Did you get it?" Zelda asked excitedly. "Did you get Dr. Jeffries's autograph for me?"

"Ah…"

"You didn't, did you?" Zelda's disappointment was obvious.

"Not exactly."

"Did you even *talk* to him?" her sister pressed.

"Oh, yes, we did plenty of that." She recalled their conversation, thinking he might have manipulated that, too, in order to win her over to his side. The dark side, she thought grimly. Like Narnia without Aslan, and no Christmas.

A stunned silence followed. "Together. You and Dr. Jeffries were together?"

"We went to dinner…."

"You went to dinner with Dr. Wynn Jeffries?" Awe became complete disbelief.

"Yes, at Chez Jerome." K.O. felt like a name-dropper but she couldn't help it. No one ate at Chez Jerome and remained silent.

Zelda gasped. "You're making this up and I don't find it amusing."

"I'm not," K.O. insisted. "LaVonne arranged it. Dinner was incredible. In fact, I gained two pounds."

A short silence ensued. "Okay, I'm sitting down and

I'm listening really hard. You'd better start at the beginning."

"Okay," she said. "I saw Wynn, Dr. Jeffries, in the French Café."

"I already know that part."

"I saw him again." K.O. stopped abruptly, thinking better of telling her sister about the confrontation and calling him names. Not that referring to him as Jim Carrey and Charles Dickens was especially insulting, but still… "Anyway, it's not important now."

"Why isn't it?"

"Well, Wynn and I agreed to put that unfortunate incident behind us and start over."

"Oh, my goodness, what did you do?" Zelda demanded. "What did you say to him? You didn't embarrass him, did you?"

K.O. bit her lip. "Do you want to hear about the dinner or not?"

"Yes! I want to hear *everything*."

K.O. then told her about cocktails at LaVonne's and her neighbor's connection with the famous chef. She described their dinner in lavish detail and mentioned the carriage ride. The one thing she didn't divulge was the kiss, which shot into her memory like a flaming dart, reminding her how weak she really was.

As if reading her mind, Zelda asked, "Did he kiss you?"

"Zelda! That's private."

"He did," her sister said with unshakable certainty. "I can't believe it. Dr. Wynn Jeffries kissed my sister! You don't even like him."

"According to LaVonne I will soon bear his children."

"What!"

"Sorry," K.O. said dismissively. "I'm getting ahead of myself."

"Okay, okay, I can see this is all a big joke to you."

"Not really."

"I don't even know if I should believe you."

"Zelda, I'm your sister. Would I lie to you?"

"Yes!"

Unfortunately Zelda was right. "I'm not this time, I swear it."

Zelda hesitated. "Did you or did you not get his autograph?"

Reluctant though she was to admit it, K.O. didn't have any choice. "Not."

"That's what I thought." Zelda bade her a hasty farewell and disconnected the call.

Much as she hated the prospect, K.O. put on her sweats and headed for the treadmill, which she kept stored under her bed for emergencies such as this. If she didn't do something fast to get rid of those two pounds, they'd stick to her hips like putty and harden. Then losing them would be like chiseling them off with a hammer. This, at least, was her theory of weight gain and loss. Immediate action was required. With headphones blocking outside distractions, she dutifully walked four miles and quit only when she was confident she'd sweated off what she'd gained. Still, a day of reduced caloric intake would be necessary.

She showered, changed her clothes and had a cup of coffee with skim milk. She worked on the Mulcahys' Christmas letter, munching a piece of dry toast as she did. After that, she transcribed a few reports. At one o'clock LaVonne stopped by with a request.

"I need help," she said, stepping into K.O.'s condo. She carried a plate of cookies.

"Okay." K.O. made herself look away from the delectable-smelling cookies. Her stomach growled. All she'd had for lunch was a small container of yogurt and a glass of V8 juice.

"I hate to ask," LaVonne said, "but I wasn't sure where else to turn."

"LaVonne, I'd do anything for you. You know that."

Her friend nodded. "Would you write my Christmas letter for me?"

"Of course." That would be a piece of cake. Oh, why did everything come down to food?

"I have no idea how to do this. I've never written one before." She sighed. "My life is pitiful."

K.O. arched her brows. "What do you mean, pitiful? You have a good life."

"I do? I've never married and I don't have children. I'm getting these Christmas letters from my old college friends and they're all about how perfect their lives are. In comparison mine is so dull. All I have are my three cats." She looked beseechingly at K.O. "Jazz up my life, would you? Make it sound just as wonderful as my girlfriends' instead of just plain boring."

"Your life is *not* boring." Despite her best efforts, K.O. couldn't keep her eyes off the cookies. "Would you excuse me?"

"Ah...sure."

"I'll be back in a minute. I need to brush my teeth."

Her neighbor eyed her speculatively as K.O. left the room.

"It's a trick I have when I get hungry," she explained, coming out of the bathroom holding her toothbrush, which was loaded with toothpaste. "Whenever I get hungry, I brush my teeth."

"You do what?"

"Brush my teeth."

Her friend regarded her steadily. "How many times have you brushed your teeth today?"

"Four...no, five times. Promise me you'll take those cookies home."

LaVonne nodded. "I brought them in case I needed a bribe."

"Not only will I write your letter, I'll do it today so you can mail off your cards this week."

Her friend's eyes revealed her gratitude. "You're the best."

Ideas were already forming in K.O.'s mind. Writing LaVonne's Christmas letter would be a snap compared to finishing Bill Mulcahy's. Speaking of him... K.O. glanced at her watch. She was scheduled to meet him this very afternoon.

"I've got an appointment at three," she told her friend. "I'll put something together for you right away, drop it off, see Bill and then stop at your place on my way back."

"Great." LaVonne was still focused on the toothbrush. "You're meeting Wynn later?"

She nodded. "At six." She should be contacting him and canceling, but she didn't know how to reach him. It was a weak excuse—since she could easily ask LaVonne for his number. Actually, she felt it was time to own up to the truth. She wanted to see Wynn again, just so she'd have some answers. *Was* she truly attracted to him? *Did* he have some nefarious agenda, with the intent of proving himself right and her wrong? Unless she spent another evening with him, she wouldn't find out.

"Are you…" LaVonne waved her hand in K.O.'s direction.

"Am I what?"

LaVonne sighed. "Are you going to take that toothbrush with you?"

"Of course."

"I see." Her neighbor frowned. "My psychic vision didn't tell me anything about that."

"No, I don't imagine it would." K.O. proceeded to return to the bathroom, where she gave her teeth a thorough brushing. Perhaps if Wynn saw her foaming at the mouth, he'd know her true feelings about him.

Six

K.O. had fun writing LaVonne's Christmas letter. Compared to Bill Mulcahy's, it was a breeze. Her friend was worried about how other people, people from her long-ago past, would react to the fact that she'd never married and lacked male companionship. K.O. took care of that.

Merry Christmas to my Friends, K.O. began for LaVonne. *This has been an exciting year as I juggle my time between Tom, Phillip and Martin, the three guys in my life. No one told me how demanding these relationships can be. Tom won my heart first and then I met Phillip and how could I refuse him? Yes, there's a bit of jealousy, but they manage to be civil to each other. I will admit that things heated up after I started seeing Martin. I fell for him the minute we met.*

I'm retired now, so I have plenty of time to devote to the demands of these relationships. Some women discover love in their twenties. But it took me until I was retired to fall into this kind of happiness. I lavish attention and love on all three guys. Those of you who are concerned that I'm taking on too much, let me assure you—I'm woman enough to handle them.

I love my new luxury condo on Blossom Street here in Seattle. And I've been continuing my education lately, enhancing my skills and exploring new vistas.

K.O. giggled, then glanced at her watch. The afternoon had escaped her. She hurriedly finished with a few more details of LaVonne's year, including a wine-tasting trip to the Yakima Valley, and printed out a draft of the letter.

The meeting with Bill Mulcahy went well, and he paid her the balance of what he owed and thanked her profusely. "This is just perfect," he said, reading the Christmas letter. "I wouldn't have believed it, if I wasn't seeing it for myself. You took the mess this year has been and turned it all around."

K.O. was pleased her effort had met with his satisfaction.

LaVonne was waiting for her when she returned, the Christmas letter in hand. "Oh, Katherine, I don't know how you do it. I laughed until I had tears in my eyes. How can I ever thank you?"

"I had fun," she assured her neighbor.

"I absolutely insist on paying you."

"Are you kidding? No way." After everything LaVonne had done for her, no thanks was necessary.

"I love it so much, I've already taken it down to the printer's and had copies made on fancy Christmas paper. My cards are going out this afternoon, thanks to you."

K.O. shrugged off her praise. After all, her friend had paid for her dinner with Wynn at Chez Jerome and been a good friend to her all these months. Writing a simple letter was the least she could do.

K.O. had been home only a short while when her doorbell chimed. Thinking it must be LaVonne, who frequently stopped by, she casually opened it, ready to greet her neighbor.

Instead Wynn Jeffries stood there.

K.O. wasn't ready for their outing—or to see him again. She needed to steel herself against the attraction she felt toward him.

"Hi." She sounded breathless.

"Katherine."

"Hi," she said again unnecessarily.

"I realize I'm early," he said. "I have a radio interview at 5:30. My assistant arranged it earlier in the week and I forgot to enter it into my PDA."

"Oh." Here it was—the perfect excuse to avoid seeing him again. And yet she couldn't help feeling disappointed.

He must've known, as she did, that any kind of relationship was a lost cause.

"That's fine, I understand," she told him, recovering quickly. "We can get together another time." She offered this in a nonchalant manner, shrugging her shoulders, deciding this really was for the best.

His gaze held hers. "Perhaps you could come with me," he said.

"Come with you?" she repeated and instantly recognized this as a bad idea. In fact, as bad ideas went, it came close to the top. She hadn't been able to keep her mouth shut in the bookstore and had been banned for life. If she had to listen to him spout off his views in person, K.O. didn't know if she could restrain herself from grabbing the mike and pleading with people everywhere to throw out his book or use it for kindling. Nope, attending the interview with him was definitely *not* a good plan.

When she didn't immediately respond, he said, "After the interview, we could go on to the Figgy Pudding thing you mentioned."

She knew she should refuse. And yet, before she could reconsider it, she found herself nodding.

"I understand the radio station is only a few blocks from West Lake Plaza."

"Yes…" Her mouth felt dry and all at once she was nervous.

"We'll need to leave right away," he said, looking at his watch.

"I'll get my coat." She was wearing blue jeans and a long black sweater—no need to change.

Wynn entered her condo and as she turned away, he stopped her, placing one hand on her arm.

K.O. turned back and was surprised to find him staring at her again. He seemed to be saying he wasn't sure what was happening between them, either. Wasn't sure what he felt or why… Then, as if he needed to test those feelings, he lowered his mouth to hers. Slowly, ever so slowly… K.O. could've moved away at any point. She didn't. The biggest earthquake of the century could've hit and she wouldn't have noticed. Not even if the building had come tumbling down around her feet. Her eyes drifted shut and she leaned into Wynn, ready—no, more than ready—*eager* to accept his kiss.

To her astonishment, it was even better than the night before. This *couldn't* be happening and yet it was. Fortunately, Wynn's hands were on her shoulders, since her balance had grown unsteady.

When he pulled away, it took her a long time to open her eyes. She glanced up at him and discovered he seemed as perplexed as she was.

"I was afraid of that," he said.

She blinked, understanding perfectly what he meant. "Me, too."

"It was as good as last night."

"Better," she whispered.

He cleared his throat. "If we don't leave now, I'll be late for the interview."

"Right."

Still, neither of them moved. Apparently all they were capable of doing was staring at each other. Wynn didn't seem any happier about this than she was, and in some small way, that was a comfort.

K.O. forced herself to break the contact between them. She collected her coat and purse and was half-way to the door when she dashed into the bathroom. "I forgot my toothbrush," she informed him.

He gave her a puzzled look. "You brush after every meal?" he asked.

"No, before." She smiled sheepishly. "I mean, I didn't yesterday, which is why I have to do it today."

He didn't question her garbled explanation as she dropped her toothbrush carrier and toothpaste inside her purse.

Once outside the building, Wynn walked at a fast pace as if he already had second thoughts. For her part, K.O. tried not to think at all. To protect everyone's peace of mind, she'd decided to wait outside the building. It was safer that way.

By the time they arrived at the radio station, K.O. realized it was far too frigid to linger out in the cold. She'd wait in the lobby.

Wynn pressed his hand to the small of her back and guided her through the impressive marble-floored lobby toward the elevators.

"I'll wait here," she suggested. But there wasn't any seating or coffee shop. If she stayed there, it would mean standing around for the next thirty minutes or so.

"I'm sure they'll have a waiting area up at the station," Wynn suggested.

He was probably right.

They took the elevator together, standing as far away from each other as possible, as though they both recognized the risk for potential disaster.

The interviewer, Big Mouth Bass, was a well-known Seattle disk jockey. K.O. had listened to him for years but this was the first time she'd seen him in person. He didn't look anything like his voice. For one thing, he was considerably shorter than she'd pictured and considerably...rounder. If she had the opportunity, she'd share her toothbrush trick with him. It might help.

"Want to sit in for the interview?" Big Mouth asked.

"Thank you, no," she rushed to say. "Dr. Jeffries and I don't necessarily agree and—"

"No way." Wynn's voice drowned hers out.

Big Mouth was no fool. K.O. might've imagined it, but she thought a gleam appeared in his eyes. He hosted a live interview show, after all, and a little controversy would keep things lively.

"I insist," Big Mouth said. He motioned toward the hallway that led to the control booth.

K.O. shook her head. "Thanks, anyway, but I'll wait out here."

"We're ready for Dr. Jeffries," a young woman informed the radio personality.

"I'll wait here," K.O. said again, and before anyone could argue, she practically threw herself into a chair and grabbed a magazine. She opened it and pretended to read, sighing with relief as Big Mouth led Wynn out of the waiting area. The radio in the room was tuned to the station, and a couple of minutes later, Big Mouth's booming voice was introducing Wynn.

"I have with me Dr. Wynn Jeffries," he began. "As many of you will recall, Dr. Jeffries's book, *The Free Child,* advocates letting a child set his or her own boundaries. Explain yourself, Dr. Jeffries."

"First, let me thank you for having me on your show," Wynn said, and K.O. was surprised by how melodic he sounded, how confident and sincere. "I believe," Wynn continued, "that structure is stifling to a child."

"*Any* structure?" Big Mouth challenged.

"Yes, in my opinion, such rigidity is detrimental to a child's sense of creativity and his or her natural ability to develop moral principles." Wynn spoke eloquently, citing example after example showing how structure had a negative impact on a child's development.

"No boundaries," Big Mouth repeated, sounding incredulous.

"As I said, a child will set his or her own."

Just listening to Wynn from her chair in the waiting room, K.O. had to sit on her hands.

"You also claim a parent should ignore inappropriate talk."

"Absolutely. Children respond to feedback and when

we don't give them any, the undesirable action will cease."

Big Mouth asked a question now and then. Just before the break, he said, "You brought a friend with you this afternoon."

"Yes..." All the confidence seemed to leave Wynn's voice.

"She's in the waiting area, isn't she?" Big Mouth continued, commenting more than questioning. "I gathered, during the few minutes in which I spoke to your friend, that she doesn't agree with your child-rearing philosophy."

"Yes, that's true, but Katherine isn't part of the interview."

Big Mouth chuckled. "I thought we'd bring her in after the break and get her views on your book."

"Uh..."

"Don't go away, folks—this should be interesting. We'll be right back after the traffic and weather report."

On hearing this, K.O. tossed aside the magazine and started to make a run for the elevator. Unfortunately Big Mouth was faster than his size had led her to believe.

"I... I don't think this is a good idea," she said as he led her by the elbow to the control booth. "I'm sure Wynn would rather not..."

"Quite the contrary," Big Mouth said smoothly, ushering her into the recording room, which was shockingly small. He sat her next to Wynn and handed her a headset. "You'll share a mike with Dr. Jeffries. Be sure to speak into it and don't worry about anything."

After the traffic report, Big Mouth was back on the air.

"Hello, Katherine," he said warmly. "How are you this afternoon?"

"I was perfectly fine until a few minutes ago," she snapped.

Big Mouth laughed. "Have you read Dr. Jeffries's book?"

"No. Well, not really." She leaned close to the microphone.

"You disagree with his philosophies, don't you?"

"Yes." She dared not look at Wynn, but she was determined not to embarrass him the way she had in the French Café. Even if they were at odds about the validity of his Free Child movement, he didn't deserve to be publicly humiliated.

"Katherine seems to believe I'm taking Christmas away from children," Wynn blurted out. "She's wrong, of course. I have a short chapter in the book that merely suggests parents bury the concept of Santa."

"You want to *bury Santa?*" Even Big Mouth took offense at that, K.O. noticed with a sense of righteousness.

"My publisher chose the chapter title and against my better judgment, I let it stand. Basically, all I'm saying is that it's wrong to lie to a child, no matter how good one's intentions."

"He wants to get rid of the Tooth Fairy and the Easter Bunny, too," K.O. inserted.

"That doesn't make me a Jim Carrey," Wynn said argumentatively. "I'm asking parents to be responsible adults. That's all."

"What does it hurt?" K.O. asked. "Childhood is a time of make-believe and fairy tales and fun. Why does everything have to be so serious?"

"Dr. Jeffries," Big Mouth cut in. "Could you explain that comment about Jim Carrey?"

"I called him that," K.O. answered on his behalf. "I

meant to say the Grinch. You know, like in *How the Grinch Stole Christmas*. Jim Carrey was in the movie," she explained helplessly.

Wynn seemed eager to change the subject. He started to say something about the macabre character of fairy tales and how they weren't "fun," but Big Mouth cut him off.

"Ah, I see," he said, grinning from ear to ear. "You two have a love/hate relationship. That's what's *really* going on here."

K.O. looked quickly at Wynn, and he glared back. The "hate" part might be right, but there didn't seem to be any "love" in the way he felt about her.

"Regrettably, this is all the time we have for today," Big Mouth told his audience. "I'd like to thank Dr. Jeffries for stopping by this afternoon and his friend Katherine, too. Thank you both for a most entertaining interview. Now for the news at the top of the hour."

Big Mouth flipped a switch and the room went silent. So silent, in fact, that K.O. could hear her heart beat.

"We can leave now," Wynn said stiffly after removing his headphones.

Hers were already off. K.O. released a huge pent-up sigh. "Thank goodness," she breathed.

Wynn didn't say anything until they'd entered the elevator.

"That was a disaster," he muttered.

K.O. blamed herself. She should never have accompanied him to the interview. She'd known it at the time and still couldn't resist. "I'm sorry. I shouldn't have gone on the air with you."

"You weren't given much choice," he said in her defense.

"I apologize if I embarrassed you. That wasn't my intention. I tried not to say anything derogatory—surely you could see that."

He didn't respond and frankly, she didn't blame him.

"The thing is, Katherine, you don't respect my beliefs."

"I don't," she reluctantly agreed.

"You couldn't have made it any plainer." The elevator doors opened and they stepped into the foyer.

"Perhaps it would be best if we didn't see each other again." K.O. figured she was only saying what they were both thinking.

Wynn nodded. She could sense his regret, a regret she felt herself.

They were outside the building now. The street was festive with lights, and Christmas music could be heard from one of the department stores. At the moment, however, she felt anything but merry.

The Figgy Pudding contest, which was sponsored by the Pike Market Senior Center and Downtown Food Bank as an annual fund-raiser, would've started by now and, although she didn't feel the least bit like cheering, she'd promised Vickie she'd show up and support her efforts for charity.

K.O. thrust out her hand and did her utmost to smile. "Thank you, Wynn. Last night was one of the most incredible evenings of my life," she said. "Correction. It was *the* most incredible night ever."

Wynn clasped her hand. His gaze held hers as he said, "It was for me, too."

People were stepping around them.

She should simply walk away. Vickie would be looking for her. And yet…she couldn't make herself do it.

"Goodbye," he whispered.

Her heart was in her throat. "Goodbye."

He dropped his hand, turned and walked away. His steps were slow, measured. He'd gone about five feet when he glanced over his shoulder. K.O. hadn't moved. In fact, she stood exactly as he'd left her, biting her lower lip—a habit she had when distressed. Wynn stopped abruptly, his back still to her.

"Wynn, listen," she called and trotted toward him. "I have an idea." Although it'd only been a few feet, she felt as if she was setting off on a marathon.

"What?" He sounded eager.

"I have twin nieces."

He nodded. "You mentioned them earlier. Their mother read my book."

"Yes, and loved it."

There was a flicker of a smile. "At least *someone* in your family believes in me."

"Yes, Zelda sure does. She thinks you're fabulous." K.O. realized she did, too—aside from his theories. "My sister and her husband are attending his company Christmas dinner next Friday, the fifteenth," she rushed to explain. "Zelda asked me to spend the night. Come with me. Show me how your theories *should* work. Maybe Zelda's doing it wrong. Maybe you can convince me that the Free Child movement makes sense."

"You want me to come with you."

"Yes. We'll do everything just as you suggest in your book, and I promise not to say a word. I'll read it this week, I'll listen to you and I'll observe."

Wynn hesitated.

"Until then, we won't mention your book or anything else to do with your theories."

"Promise?"

"Promise," she concurred.

"No more radio interviews?"

She laughed. "That's an easy one."

A smile came to him then, appearing in his eyes first. "You've got yourself a deal."

Yes, she did, and K.O. could hardly wait to introduce Zoe and Zara to Dr. Wynn Jeffries. Oh, she was sincere about keeping an open mind, but Wynn might learn something, too. The incorrigible twins would be the true crucible for his ideas.

K.O. held out her hand. "Are you ready for some Figgy Pudding?" she asked.

He grinned, taking her mittened hand as they hurried toward the Figgy Pudding People's Choice competition.

Seven

The Figgy Pudding People's Choice event was standing room only when Wynn and K.O. arrived. Vickie and her friends hadn't performed yet and were just being introduced by a popular morning-radio host for an easy-listening station. K.O. and Vickie had been friends all through high school and college. Vickie had married three years ago, and K.O. had been in her wedding party. In fact, she'd been in any number of wedding parties. Her mother had pointedly asked whether K.O. was ever going to be a bride, instead of a bridesmaid.

"That's my friend over there," K.O. explained, nodding in Vickie's direction. "The one in the Santa hat."

Wynn squinted at the group of ladies huddled together in front of the assembly. "Aren't they all wearing Santa hats?"

"True. The young cute one," she qualified.

"They're all young and cute, Katherine." He smiled. "Young enough, anyway."

She looked at Wynn with new appreciation. "That is such a sweet thing to say." Vickie worked for a local dentist as a hygienist and was the youngest member of the staff. The other women were all in their forties and fifties. "I could just kiss you," K.O. said, snuggling close to him. She looped her arm through his.

Wynn cleared his throat as though unaccustomed to such open displays of affection. "Any particular reason you suddenly find me so kissable?"

"Well, yes, the women with Vickie are…a variety of ages."

"I see. I should probably tell you I'm not wearing my glasses."

K.O. laughed, elbowing him in the ribs. "And here I thought you were being so gallant."

He grinned boyishly and slid his arm around her shoulders.

Never having attended a Figgy Pudding event before, K.O. didn't know what to expect. To her delight, it was enchanting, as various groups competed, singing Christmas carols, to raise funds for the Senior Center and Food Bank. Vickie and her office mates took second place, and K.O. cheered loudly. Wynn shocked her by placing two fingers in his mouth and letting loose with a whistle that threatened to shatter glass. It seemed so unlike him.

Somehow Vickie found her when the singing was over. "I wondered if you were going to show," she said, shouting to be heard above the noise of the merry-go-round and the crowd. Musicians gathered on street corners, horns honked and the sights and sounds of Christmas were everywhere. Although the comment was directed at K.O., Vickie's attention was unmistakably on Wynn.

"Vickie, this is Wynn Jeffries."

Her friend's gaze shot back to K.O. "Wynn Jeffries? Not *the* Wynn Jeffries?"

"One and the same," K.O. said, speaking out of the corner of her mouth.

"You've got to be joking." Vickie's mouth fell open as she stared at Wynn.

For the last two months, K.O. had been talking her friend's ear off about the man and his book and how he was ruining her sister's life. She'd even told Vickie about the incident at the bookstore, although she certainly hadn't confided in anyone else; she wasn't exactly proud of being kicked out for unruly behavior. Thinking it might be best to change the subject, K.O. asked, "Is John here?"

"John?"

"Your husband," K.O. reminded her. She hadn't seen Wynn wearing glasses before, but she hoped his comment about forgetting them was sincere, otherwise he might notice the close scrutiny Vickie was giving him.

"Oh, *John,*" her friend said, recovering quickly. "No, he's meeting me later for dinner." Then, as if inspiration had struck, she asked, "Would you two like to join us? John got a reservation at a new Chinese restaurant that's supposed to have great food."

K.O. looked at Wynn, who nodded. "Sure," she answered, speaking for both of them. "What time?"

"Nine. I was going to do some shopping and meet him there."

They made arrangements to meet later and Vickie went into the mall to finish her Christmas shopping.

"I'm starving now," K.O. said when her stomach growled. Although she had her toothbrush, there really wasn't a convenient place to foam up. "After last night,

I didn't think I'd ever want to eat again." She considered mentioning the two pounds she'd gained, but thought better of it. Wynn might not want to see her again if he found out how easily she packed on weight. Well, she didn't *really* believe that of him, but she wasn't taking any chances. Which proved that, despite everything, she was interested. In fact, she'd made the decision to continue with this relationship, see where their attraction might lead, almost without being aware of it.

"How about some roasted chestnuts?" he asked. A vendor was selling them on the street corner next to a musician who strummed a guitar and played a harmonica at the same time. His case was open on the sidewalk for anyone who cared to donate. She tossed in a dollar and hoped he used whatever money he collected to pay for music lessons.

"I've never had a roasted chestnut," K.O. told him.

"Me, neither," Wynn confessed. "This seems to be the season for it, though."

While Wynn waited in line for the chestnuts, K.O. became fascinated with the merry-go-round. "Will you go on it with me?" she asked him.

Wynn hesitated. "I've never been on a merry-go-round."

K.O. was surprised. "Then you have to," she insisted. "You've missed a formative experience." Taking his hand, she pulled him out of the line. She purchased the tickets herself and refused to listen to his excuses. He rattled off a dozen—he was too old, too big, too clumsy and so on. K.O. rejected every one.

"It's going to be fun," she said.

"I thought you were starving."

"I was, but I'm not now. Come on, be a good sport. Women find men who ride horses extremely attractive."

Wynn stopped arguing long enough to raise an eyebrow. "My guess is that the horse is generally not made of painted wood."

"Generally," she agreed, "but you never know."

The merry-go-round came to a halt and emptied out on the opposite side. They passed their tickets to the attendant and, leading Wynn by the hand, K.O. ushered him over to a pair of white horses that stood side by side. She set her foot in the stirrup and climbed into the molded saddle. Wynn stood next to his horse looking uncertain.

"Mount up, partner," she said.

"I feel more than a little ridiculous, Katherine."

"Oh, don't be silly. Men ride these all the time. See? There's another guy."

Granted, he was sitting on a gaudy elephant, holding a toddler, but she didn't dwell on that.

Sighing, Wynn climbed reluctantly onto the horse, his legs so long they nearly touched the floor. "Put your feet in the stirrups," she coaxed.

He did, and his knees were up to his ears.

K.O. couldn't help it; she burst out laughing.

Wynn began to climb off, but she stopped him by leaning over and kissing him. She nearly slid off the saddle in the process and would have if Wynn hadn't caught her about the waist.

Soon the carousel music started, and the horses moved up and down. K.O. thrust out her legs and laughed, thoroughly enjoying herself. "Are you having fun yet?" she asked Wynn.

"I'm ecstatic," he said dryly.

"Oh, come on, Wynn, relax. Have some fun."

Suddenly he leaned forward, as if he were riding for the Pony Express. He let out a cry that sounded like sheer joy.

"That *was* fun," Wynn told her, climbing down when the carousel stopped. He put his hands on her waist and she felt the heat of his touch in every part of her body.

"You liked it?"

"Do you want to go again?" he asked.

The line was much longer now. "I don't think so."

"I've always wanted to do that. I felt like a child all over again," he said enthusiastically.

"A Free Child?" she asked in a mischievous voice.

"Yes, free. That's exactly what my book's about, allowing children freedom to become themselves," he said seriously.

"Okay." She was biting her tongue but managed not to say anything more. Surely there were great rewards awaiting her in heaven for such restraint.

"Would you like to stop at the bookstore?" he asked. "I like to sign copies when I'm in the neighborhood."

"You mean an autographing?" She hoped it wouldn't be at the same bookstore that had caused all the trouble.

"Not exactly an autographing," Wynn explained. "The bookseller told me that a signed book is a sold book. When it's convenient, authors often visit bookstores to sign stock."

"Sort of a drive-by signing?" she asked, making a joke out of it.

"Yeah." They started walking and just as she feared, they were headed in the direction of *the* bookstore.

As they rounded the corner and the store came into sight, her stomach tightened. "I'll wait for you outside," she said, implying that nothing would please her more than to linger out in the cold.

"Nonsense. There's a small café area where you can wait in comfort."

"Okay," she finally agreed. Once she'd made it past the shoplifting detector K.O. felt more positive. She was afraid her mug shot had been handed out to the employees and she'd be expelled on sight.

Thankfully she didn't see the bookseller who'd asked her to leave. That boded well. She saw Wynn chatting with a woman behind the counter. He followed her to the back of the store. Some of the tension eased from K.O.'s shoulder blades. Okay, she seemed to be safe. And she didn't have to hide behind a coffee cup. Besides, she loved to read and since she was in a bookstore, what harm would it do to buy a book? She was in the mood for something entertaining. A romantic comedy, she decided, studying a row of titles. Without much trouble, she found one that looked perfect and started toward the cashier.

Then it happened.

Wynn was waiting up front, speaking to the very bookseller who'd banished K.O. from the store.

Trying to be as inconspicuous as possible, K.O. set the book aside and tiptoed toward the exit, shoulders hunched forward, head lowered.

"Katherine," Wynn called.

With a smile frozen in place, she turned to greet Wynn and the bookseller.

"It's you!" The woman, who wore a name tag that identified her as Shirley, glared at K.O.

She timidly raised her hand. "Hello again."

"You two know each other?" Shirley asked Wynn in what appeared to be complete disbelief.

"Yes. This is my friend Katherine."

The bookseller seemed to have lost her voice. She looked from Wynn to Katherine and then back.

"Good to see you again," K.O. said. She sincerely hoped Shirley would play along and conveniently forget that unfortunate incident.

"It *is* you," Shirley hissed from between clenched teeth.

"What's this about?" Wynn asked, a puzzled expression on his face. "You've met before?"

"Nothing," K.O. all but shouted.

"As a matter of fact, we have met." Shirley's dark eyes narrowed. "Perhaps your *friend* has forgotten. I, however, have not."

So it was going to be like that, was it? "We had a difference of opinion," K.O. told Wynn in a low voice.

"As I recall, you were permanently banned from the store."

"Katherine was *banned* from the store?" Wynn asked incredulously. "I can't believe she'd do anything deserving of that."

"Maybe we should leave now," K.O. suggested, and tugged at his sleeve.

"If you want to know," Shirley began, but K.O. interrupted before she could launch into her complaint.

"Wynn, please, we should go," she said urgently.

"I'm sure this can all be sorted out," he murmured, releasing his coat sleeve from her grasp.

Shirley, hands on her hips, smiled snidely. She seemed to take real pleasure in informing Wynn of K.O.'s indiscretion.

"This *friend* of yours is responsible for causing a scene in this very bookstore, Dr. Jeffries."

"I'm sure no harm was meant."

K.O. grabbed his arm. "It doesn't matter," she said, desperate to escape.

"Katherine does tend to be opinionated, I agree," he said, apparently determined to defend her. "But she's actually quite reasonable."

"Apparently you don't know her as well as you think."

"I happen to enjoy Katherine's company immensely."

Shirley raised her eyebrows. "Really?"

"Yes, really."

"Then you might be interested to know that your so-called friend nearly caused a riot when she got into an argument with another customer over *your* book."

Wynn swiveled his gaze to K.O.

She offered him a weak smile. "Ready to leave now?" she asked in a weak whisper.

Eight

K.O.'s doorbell chimed, breaking into a satisfying dream. Whatever it was about seemed absolutely wonderful and she hated to lose it. When the doorbell rang again, the sound longer and more persistent, the dream disappeared. She stumbled out of bed and threw on her flannel housecoat.

Reaching the door, she checked the peephole and saw that it was LaVonne. No surprise there. Unfastening the lock, K.O. let her in, covering a yawn.

"What time did you get home last night?" her neighbor cried as she hurried in without a cat—which was quite unusual. "I waited up as long as I could for you." LaVonne's voice was frantic. "I didn't sleep a wink all night," she said and plopped herself down on the sofa.

K.O. was still at the front door, holding it open. "Good morning to you, too."

"Should I make coffee?" LaVonne asked, leaping to her feet and flipping on the light as she swept into the kitchen. Not waiting for a response, she pulled out the canister where K.O. kept her coffee grounds.

K.O. yawned again and closed the front door. "What

time is it?" Early, she knew, because her eyes burned and there was barely a hint of daylight through her living room windows.

"Seven-twenty. I didn't get you up, did I?"

"No, I had to answer the door anyway." Her friend was busy preparing coffee and didn't catch the joke. "How are the guys?" K.O. asked next. LaVonne usually provided her with daily updates on their health, well-being and any cute activities they'd engaged in.

"They're hiding," she said curtly. "All three of them." She ran water into the glass pot and then poured it in the coffeemaker.

Katherine wondered why the cats were in a snit but didn't have the energy to ask.

"You haven't answered my question," LaVonne said as the coffee started to drip. She placed two mugs on the counter.

"Which one?" K.O. fell into a kitchen chair, rested her arms on the table and leaned her head on them.

"Last night," LaVonne said. "Where were you?"

"Wynn and I were out—"

"*All* night?"

"You're beginning to sound like my mother," K.O. protested.

LaVonne straightened her shoulders. "Katherine, you hardly know the man."

"I didn't sleep with him, if that's what you think." She raised her head long enough to speak and then laid it down on her arms again. "We went out to dinner with some friends of mine after the Figgy Pudding contest."

"It must've been a very late dinner." LaVonne sounded as if she didn't quite believe her.

"We walked around for a while afterward and went

out for a drink. The time got away from us. I didn't get home until one."

"I was up at one and you weren't home," LaVonne said in a challenging tone. She poured the first cup of coffee and took it herself.

"Maybe it was after two, then," K.O. said. She'd completely lost track of time, which was easy to do. Wynn was so charming and he seemed so interested in her and her friends.

Vickie's husband, John, was a plumbing contractor. Despite Wynn's college degrees and celebrity status, he'd fit in well with her friends. He'd asked intelligent questions, listened and shared anecdotes about himself that had them all laughing. John even invited Wynn to play poker with him and his friends after the holidays. Wynn had accepted the invitation.

Halfway through the meal Vickie had announced that she had to use the ladies' room. The look she shot K.O. said she should join her, which K.O. did.

"That's really Wynn Jeffries?" she asked, holding K.O.'s elbow as they made their way around tables and through the restaurant.

"Yes, it's really him."

"Does he know about the bookstore?"

K.O. nodded reluctantly. "He does now."

"You didn't tell him, did you?"

"Unfortunately, he found out all on his own."

Vickie pushed open the door to the ladies' as K.O. described the scene from the bookstore. "No way," her friend moaned, then promptly sank down on a plush chair in the outer room.

K.O.'s face grew red all over again. "It was embarrassing, to say the least."

"Was Wynn upset?"

What could he say? "He didn't let on if he was." In fact, once they'd left the store, Wynn seemed to find the incident highly amusing. Had their roles been reversed, she didn't know how she would've felt.

"He didn't blow up at you or anything?" Vickie had given her a confused look. "This is the guy you think should be banned from practicing as a psychologist?"

"Well, that might've been a bit strong," she'd said, reconsidering her earlier comment.

Vickie just shook her head.

"He rode the merry-go-round with me," K.O. said aloud, deciding that had gone a long way toward redeeming him in her eyes. When she glanced up, she realized she was talking to LaVonne.

"He did what?" LaVonne asked, bringing her back to the present.

"Wynn did," she elaborated. "He rode the carousel with me."

"Until two in the morning?"

"No, before dinner. Afterward, we walked along the waterfront, then had a glass of wine. We started walking again and finally stopped for coffee at an all-night diner and talked some more." He seemed to want to know all about her, but in retrospect she noticed that he'd said very little about himself.

"Good grief," LaVonne muttered, shaking her head, "what could you possibly talk about for so long?"

"That's just it," K.O. said. "We couldn't *stop* talking." And it was even more difficult to stop kissing and to say good-night once they'd reached her condo. Because there was so much more to say, they'd agreed to meet for coffee at the French Café at nine.

LaVonne had apparently remembered that Katherine didn't have any coffee yet and filled her mug. "Just black," K.O. told her, needing a shot of unadulterated caffeine. "Thanks.

"Why were you waiting up for me?" she asked after her first bracing sip of coffee. Then and only then did her brain clear, and she understood that LaVonne must have something important on her mind.

"You wrote that fantastic Christmas letter for me," her neighbor reminded her.

"I did a good job, didn't I?" she said.

"Oh, yes, a good job all right." LaVonne frowned. "I liked it so much, I mailed it right away."

"So, what's the problem?"

"Well..." LaVonne sat down in the chair across from K.O. "It was such a relief to have something clever and...and exciting to tell everyone," LaVonne said, "especially my college friends."

So far, K.O. didn't see any problem at all. She nodded, encouraging her friend to get to the point.

LaVonne's shoulders sagged. "If only I'd waited," she moaned. "If only I'd picked up my own mail first."

"There was something in the mail?"

LaVonne nodded. "I got a card and a Christmas letter from Peggy Solomon. She was the president of my college sorority and about as uppity as they come. She married her college boyfriend, a banker's son. She had two perfect children and lives a life of luxury. She said she's looking forward to seeing me at our next reunion." There was a moment of stricken silence. "Peggy's organizing it, and she included the invitation with her card."

"That's bad?"

"Yes," LaVonne wailed. "It's bad. How am I supposed to show up at my forty-year college reunion, which happens to be in June, without a man? Especially *now.* Because of my Christmas letter, everyone in my entire class will think I've got more men than I know what to do with."

"LaVonne, you might meet someone before then."

"If I haven't met a man in the last forty years, what makes you think I will in the next six months?"

"Couldn't you say it's such a tricky balancing act you don't dare bring any of them?"

LaVonne glared at her. "Everyone'll figure out that it's all a lie." She closed her eyes. "And if they don't, Peggy's going to make sure she tells them."

Another idea struck K.O. "What about your psychic powers? Why don't you go check out the litter box again?" On second thought, maybe that wasn't such a great idea.

"Don't you think I would if I could?" she cried, becoming ever more agitated. "But I don't see anything about myself. Trust me, I've tried. So far, all my insights have been about you and Wynn. A lot of good my newfound talent has done *me.* You're being romanced night and day, and I've just made a complete fool of myself."

"LaVonne…"

"Even my cats are upset with me."

"Tom, Phillip and Martin?" K.O. had never understood why her neighbor couldn't name her feline companions regular cat names like Fluffy or Tiger.

"They think *I'm* upset with *them.* They're all hiding from me, and that's never happened before."

K.O. felt guilty, but she couldn't have known about the college reunion, any more than LaVonne did. "I'm sure everything will work out for the best," she murmured. She wished she had more than a platitude to offer, but she didn't.

"At this point that's all I can hope for." LaVonne expelled her breath and took another sip of coffee. That seemed to relax her, and she gave K.O. a half smile. "Tell me about you and Wynn."

"There's not much to say." And yet there was. She honestly liked him. Vickie and John had, too. Never would K.O. have guessed that the originator of the Free Child movement she so reviled would be this warm, compassionate and genuinely nice person. She would've been happy to settle for *one* of those qualities. Despite everything K.O. had done to embarrass him, he was attracted to her. And it went without saying that she found Wynn Jeffries compelling and smart and…wonderful. But she was afraid to examine her feelings too closely—and even more afraid to speculate about his.

"You've spent practically every minute of the last two days together," LaVonne said. "There's got to be something."

Shrugging, K.O. pushed her hair away from her face.

"You were with him until two this morning."

"And I'm meeting him at the café in about an hour and a half," she said as she glanced at the time on her microwave.

"So what gives?" LaVonne pressed.

"I like him," she said simply. K.O. hadn't been prepared to have any feelings for him, other than negative ones. But they got along well—as long as they didn't discuss his book.

Overjoyed by her confession, LaVonne clapped her hands. "I knew it!"

K.O. felt it would be wrong to let her friend think

she really believed in this psychic nonsense. She'd cooperated with LaVonne's fantasy at first but now it was time to be honest. "Wynn said he asked you about me before you introduced us."

LaVonne looked away. "He did, but it was just in passing."

"He knew I lived in the building and had seen me around."

Her neighbor shifted in her seat. She cleared her throat before answering. "All right, all right, I was aware that he might be interested." She paused. "He asked me if you were single."

Really? Wynn hadn't told her that. "When was this?"

"Last week."

"Was it before or after you discovered your psychic talents?"

"Before."

Aha.

"Why didn't he just introduce himself?"

"I asked him that, too," LaVonne said. "Apparently he's shy."

"Wynn?"

LaVonne raised one shoulder. She frowned over at the phone on the counter. "You've got a message."

It'd been so late when she finally got to bed that K.O. hadn't bothered to check. Reaching over, she pressed the play button.

"K.O.," Zelda's voice greeted her. "Good grief, where are you? You don't have a date, do you?" She made it sound as if that was the last thing she expected. "Is there any chance it's with Dr. Jeffries? Call me the minute you get home." The message was followed by a lengthy beep and then there was a second message.

"Katherine," Zelda said more forcefully this time. "I don't mean to be a pest, but I'd appreciate it if you'd get back to me as soon as possible. You're out with Dr. Jeffries, aren't you?" Zelda managed to make that sound both accusatory and improbable.

Another beep.

"In case you're counting, this is the third time I've phoned you tonight. Where can you possibly be this late?"

No one ever seemed to care before, K.O. thought, and now her sister and LaVonne were suddenly keeping track of her love life.

Zelda gave a huge sigh of impatience. "I won't call again. But I need to confirm the details for Friday night. You're still babysitting, aren't you?"

"I'll be there," K.O. muttered, just as if her sister could hear. *And so will Wynn.*

Zelda added, "And I'd really like it if you'd get me that autograph."

"I will, I will," K.O. promised. She figured she'd get him to sign Zelda's copy of his book on Friday evening.

LaVonne drained the last of her coffee and set the mug in the sink. "I'd better get back. I'm going to try to coax the boys out from under the bed," she said with a resigned look as she walked to the door.

"Everything'll work out," K.O. assured her again—with a confidence she didn't actually feel.

LaVonne responded with a quick wave and left, slamming the door behind her.

Now K.O. was free to have a leisurely shower, carefully choose her outfit…and daydream about Wynn.

Nine

Wynn had already secured a window table when K.O. arrived at the French Café. As usual, the shop was crowded, with a long line of customers waiting to place their orders.

In honor of the season, she'd worn a dark-blue sweater sprinkled with silvery stars and matching star earrings. She hung her red coat on the back of her chair.

Wynn had thoughtfully ordered for her, and there was a latte waiting on the table, along with a bran muffin, her favorite. K.O. didn't remember mentioning how much she enjoyed the café's muffins, baked by Alix Townsend, who sometimes worked at the counter. The muffins were a treat she only allowed herself once a week.

"Good morning," she said, sounding a little more breathless than she would've liked. In the space of a day, she'd gone from distrust to complete infatuation. Just twenty-four hours ago, she'd been inventing ways to get out of seeing Wynn again, and now…now she could barely stand to be separated from him.

She broke off a piece of muffin, after a sip of her latte

in its oversize cup. "How did you know I love their bran muffins?" she asked. The bakery made them chock-full of raisins and nuts, so they were deliciously unlike blander varieties. Not only that, K.O. always felt she'd eaten something healthy when she had a bran muffin.

"I asked the girl behind the counter if she happened to know what you usually ordered, and she recommended that."

Once again proving how thoughtful he was.

"You had one the day you were here talking to some guy," he said flippantly.

"That was Bill Mulcahy," she explained. "I met with him because I wrote his Christmas letter."

Wynn frowned. "He's one of your clients?"

"I told you how I write people's Christmas letters, remember?" It'd been part of their conversation the night before. "I'll write yours if you want," she said, and then thinking better of it, began to sputter a retraction.

She needn't have worried that he'd take her up on the offer because he was already declining. He shook his head. "Thanks, anyway." He grimaced. "I don't want to offend you, but I find that those Christmas letters are typically a pack of lies!"

"Okay," she said mildly. She decided not to argue. K.O. sipped her coffee again and ate another piece of muffin, deciding not to worry about calories, either. "Don't you just love Christmas?" she couldn't help saying. The sights and sounds of the season were all around them. The café itself looked elegant; garlands draped the windows and pots of white and red poinsettias were placed on the counter. Christmas carols played, just loudly enough to be heard. A bell-ringer collecting for charity had set up shop outside the café and a woman sat at a nearby table knitting a Christmas stocking. K.O. had noticed a similar one displayed in A Good Yarn, the shop across the street, the day she'd followed Wynn. Christmas on Blossom Street, with its gaily decorated streetlights and cheerful banners, was as Christmassy as Christmas could be.

"Yes, but I had more enthusiasm for the holidays before today," Wynn said.

"What's wrong?"

He stared down at his dark coffee. "My father left a message on my answering machine last night." He hesitated as he glanced up at her. "Apparently he's decided—at the last minute—to join me for Christmas."

"I see," she said, although she really didn't. Wynn had only talked about his parents that first evening, at Chez Jerome. She remembered that his parents had been hippies, and that his mother had died and his father owned a company that manufactured surfboard wax. But while she'd rattled on endlessly about her own family, he'd said comparatively little about his.

"He didn't bother to ask if I had other plans, you'll notice," Wynn commented dryly.

"Do you?"

"No, but that's beside the point."

"It must be rather disconcerting," she said. Parents sometimes did things like that, though. Her own mother often made assumptions about holidays, but it had never troubled K.O. She was going to miss her parents this year and would've been delighted if they'd suddenly decided to show up.

"Now I have to go to the airport on Sunday and pick him up." Wynn gazed out the window at the lightly falling snow. "As you might've guessed, my father and I have a rather…difficult relationship."

"I'm sorry." She wasn't sure what to say.

"The thing is," Wynn continued. "My father's like a big kid. He'll want to be entertained every minute he's here. He has no respect for my work or the fact that I have to go into the office every day." Wynn had told her he met with patients most afternoons; he kept an office in a medical building not far from Blossom Street.

"I'm sorry," she said again.

Wynn accepted her condolences with a casual shrug. "The truth is, I'd rather spend my free time with you."

He seemed as surprised by this as K.O. herself. She sensed that Wynn hadn't been any more prepared to feel this way about her than she did about him. It was all rather unexpected and at the same time just plain wonderful.

"Maybe I can help," K.O. suggested. "The nice thing about working at home is that I can choose my own hours." That left her open for job interviews, Christmas letters and occasional babysitting. "My transcription work is really a godsend while I'm on my job quest. So I can help entertain him if you'd like."

Wynn considered for a moment. "I appreciate your offer, but I don't know if that's the best solution." He released a deep sigh. "I guess you could say my father's not my biggest fan."

"He doesn't believe in your child-rearing ideas, either?" she teased.

He grinned. "I wish it was that simple. You'll know what I mean once you meet him," Wynn said. "I think I mentioned that at one time he was a world-class surfer."

"Yes, and he manufactures some kind of special wax."

Wynn nodded. "It's made him rich." He sighed again. "I know it's a cliché, but my parents met in San Francisco in the early 70s and I think I told you they joined a commune. They were free spirits, the pair of them. Dad hated what he called 'the establishment.' He dropped out of college, burned his draft card, that sort of thing. He didn't want any responsibility, didn't even have a bank account—until about fifteen years ago, when someone offered to mass-produce his surfboard wax. And then he grabbed hold with both hands."

K.O. wondered if he realized he was advocating his parents' philosophy with his Free Child movement. However, she didn't point it out.

"In the early days we moved around because any money Dad brought in was from his surfing, so the three of us followed the waves, so to speak. Then we'd periodically return to the commune. I had a wretched childhood," he said bleakly. "They'd called me Radiant Sun, Ray for short, but at least they let me choose my own name when I was older. They hated it, which was fine by me. The only real family I had was my maternal grandparents. I moved in with the Wynns when I was ten."

"Your parents didn't like your name?"

"No, and this came from someone who chose the name Moon Puppy for himself. Mom liked to be called Daffodil. Her given name was Mary, which she'd rejected, along with her parents' values."

"But you—"

"My grandparents were the ones who saw to it that I stayed in school. They're the ones who paid for my education. Both of them died when I was a college senior, but they were the only stable influence I had."

"What you need while your father is here," K.O. said, "is someone to run interference. Someone who can act as a buffer between you and your father, and that someone is me."

Wynn didn't look convinced.

"I want to help," she insisted. "Really."

He still didn't look convinced.

"Oh, and before I forget, my sister left three messages on my phone. She wants your autograph in the worst way. I thought you could sign her copy of *The Free Child* next Friday when—" It suddenly occurred to her that if Wynn's father was visiting, he wouldn't be able to watch the twins with her. "Oh, no," she whispered, unable to hide her disappointment.

"What's wrong?"

"I— You'll have company, so Friday night is out." She put on a brave smile. She didn't actually need his help, but this was an opportunity to spend time with him—and to prove that his theories didn't translate into practice. She might be wrong, in which case she'd acknowledge the validity of his Free Child approach, but she doubted it.

Wynn met her eyes. "I'm not going to break my commitment. I'll explain to my father that I've got a previous engagement. He doesn't have any choice but to accept it, especially since he didn't give me any notice."

"When does he arrive?" K.O. asked. She savored another piece of her muffin, trying to guess which spices Alix had used.

"At four-thirty," Wynn said glumly.

"It's going to work out fine." That was almost identical to what she'd told LaVonne earlier that morning.

Then it hit her.

LaVonne needed a man in her life.

Wynn was looking for some way to occupy his father.

"Oh, my goodness." K.O. stood and stared down at Wynn with both hands on the edge of the table.

"What?"

"Wynn, I have the perfect solution!"

He eyed her skeptically.

"LaVonne," she said, sitting down again. She was so sure her plan would work, she felt a little shiver of delight. "You're going to introduce your father to LaVonne!"

He frowned at her and shook his head. "If you're thinking what I suspect you're thinking, I can tell you right now it won't work."

"Yes, it will! LaVonne needs to find a man before her college reunion in June. She'd—"

"Katherine, I appreciate the thought, but can you honestly see LaVonne getting involved with an ex-hippie who isn't all that ex—and is also the producer of Max's Waxes?"

"Of course I can," she said, refusing to allow him to thwart her plan. "Besides, it isn't up to us. All we have to do is introduce the two of them, step back and let nature take its course."

Wynn clearly still had doubts.

"It won't hurt to try."

"I guess not..."

"This is what I'll do," she said, feeling inspired. She couldn't understand Wynn's hesitation. "I'll invite your father and LaVonne to my place for Christmas cocktails."

Wynn crossed his arms. "This is beginning to sound familiar."

"It should." She stifled a giggle. Turnabout was fair play, after all.

"Maybe we should look at the olives in the martinis and tell them we got a psychic reading," Wynn joked.

"Oh, that's good," K.O. said with a giggle. "A drink or two should relax them both," she added.

"And then you and I can conveniently leave for dinner or a movie."

"No…no," K.O. said, excitedly. "Oh, Wynn this is ideal! We'll arrange a dinner for *them.*"

"Where?"

"I don't know." He was worrying about details too much. "We'll think of someplace special."

"I wonder if I can reach Chef Jerome and get a reservation there," Wynn murmured.

K.O. gulped. "I can't afford that."

"Not to worry. My father can."

"That's even better." K.O. felt inordinately pleased with herself. All the pieces were falling into place. Wynn would have someone to keep his father occupied until Christmas, and LaVonne might find a potential date for her class reunion.

"What are your plans for today?" Wynn asked, changing the subject.

"I'm meeting Vickie and a couple of other friends for shopping and lunch. What about you?"

"I'm headed to the gym and then the office. I don't usually work on weekends, but I'm writing a follow-up book." He spoke hesitantly as if he wasn't sure he should mention it.

"Okay." She smiled as enthusiastically as she could. "Would you like me to go to the airport with you when you pick up your father?"

"You'd do that?"

"Of course! In fact, I'd enjoy it."

"Thank you, then. I'd appreciate it."

They set up a time on Sunday afternoon and went their separate ways.

K.O. started walking down to Pacific Place, the mall where she'd agreed to meet Vickie and Diane, when her cell phone rang. It was Wynn.

"What day?" he asked. "I want to get this cocktail party idea of yours on my schedule."

"When would you suggest?"

"I don't think we should wait too long."

"I agree."

"Would Monday evening work for you?"

"Definitely. I'll put together a few appetizers and make some spiked eggnog. I'll pick up some wine—and gin for martinis, if you want." She smiled, recalling his comment about receiving a "psychic" message from the olives.

"Let me bring the wine. Anything else?"

"Could you buy a cat treat or two? That's in case LaVonne brings Tom or one of her other cats. I want her to concentrate on Moon Puppy, not kitty."

Wynn laughed. "You got it. I'll put in a call to Chef Jerome, although I don't hold out much hope. Still, maybe he'll say yes because it's LaVonne."

"All we can do is try. And there are certainly other nice places."

Wynn seemed reluctant to end the conversation. "Katherine."

"Yes."

"Thank you. Hearing my father's message after such a lovely evening put a damper on my Christmas."

"You're welcome."

"Have fun today."

"You, too." She closed her cell and set it back in her purse. Her step seemed to have an extra bounce as she hurried to meet her friends.

Ten

Saturday afternoon, just back from shopping, K.O. stopped at LaVonne's condo. She rang the doorbell and waited. It took her neighbor an unusually long time to answer; when she did, LaVonne looked dreadful. Her hair was disheveled, and she'd obviously been napping—with at least one cat curled up next to her, since her dark-red sweatshirt was covered in cat hair.

"Why the gloomy face?" K.O. asked. "It's almost Christmas."

"I know," her friend lamented.

"Well, cheer up. I have great news."

"You'd better come inside," LaVonne said without any real enthusiasm. She gestured toward the sofa, although it seemed to require all the energy she possessed just to lift her arm. "Sit down if you want."

"Wouldn't you like to hear my good news?"

LaVonne shrugged her shoulders. "I guess."

"It has to do with you."

"Me?"

"Yup. I met Vickie and Diane at Pacific Place, and we had lunch at this wonderful Italian restaurant."

LaVonne sat across from her, and Martin automatically jumped into her lap. Tom got up on the chair, too, and leisurely stretched out across the arm. She petted both cats with equal fondness.

"I ordered the minestrone soup," K.O. went on to tell her, maintaining her exuberance. "That was when it happened." She'd worked out this plan on her way home, inspired by Wynn's joke about the olives.

"What?"

"I had a psychic impression. Isn't that what you call it? Right there with my two friends in the middle of an Italian restaurant." She paused. "It had to do with romance."

"Really?" LaVonne perked up, but only a little.

"It was in the soup."

"The veggies?"

"No, the crackers," K.O. said and hoped she wasn't carrying this too far. "I crumbled them in the soup and—"

"What did you see?" Then, before K.O. could answer, LaVonne held out one hand. "No, don't tell me, let me guess. It's about you and Wynn," her neighbor said. "It must be."

"No…no. Remember how you told me you don't have the sight when it comes to yourself? Well, apparently I don't, either."

LaVonne looked up from petting her two cats. Her gaze narrowed. "What did you see, then?"

"Like I said, it was about *you,*" K.O. said, doing her best to sound excited. "You're going to meet the man of your dreams."

"I am?" She took a moment to consider this before her shoulders drooped once more.

"Yes, you! I saw it plain as anything."

"Human or feline?" LaVonne asked in a skeptical voice.

"Human," K.O. announced triumphantly.

"When?"

"The crackers didn't say exactly, but I felt it must be soon." K.O. didn't want to tell LaVonne too much, otherwise she'd ruin the whole thing. If she went overboard on the details, her friend would suspect K.O. was setting her up. She needed to be vague, but still implant the idea.

"I haven't left my condo all day," LaVonne mumbled, "and I don't plan to go out anytime in the near future. In fact, the way I feel right now, I'm going to be holed up in here all winter."

"You're overreacting."

Her neighbor studied her closely. "Katherine, you *really* saw something in the soup?"

"I did." Nothing psychic, but she wasn't admitting that. She'd seen elbow macaroni and kidney beans and, of course, the cracker crumbs.

"But you didn't take the class. How were you able to discover your psychic powers if you weren't there to hear the lecture from Madam Ozma?" she wanted to know.

K.O. crossed her fingers behind her back. "It must've rubbed off from spending all that time with you."

"You think so?" LaVonne asked hopefully.

"Sure." K.O. was beginning to feel bad about misleading her friend. She'd hoped to mention the invitation for Monday night, but it would be too obvious if she did so now.

"There might be something to it," LaVonne said, smiling for the first time. "You never know."

"True...one never knows."

"Look what happened with you and Wynn," LaVonne said with a glimmer of excitement. "The minute I saw those two raisins gravitate toward each other, I knew it held meaning."

"I could see that in the crackers, too."

This was beginning to sound like a church revival meeting. Any minute, she thought, LaVonne might stand up and shout *Yes, I believe!*

"Then Wynn met you," she burbled on, "and the instant he did, I saw the look in his eyes."

What her neighbor had seen was horror. LaVonne couldn't have known about their confrontation earlier that day. He'd clearly been shocked and, yes, horrified to run into K.O. again. Especially with the memory of her ranting in the café so fresh in his mind.

"You're right," LaVonne said and sat up straighter. "I shouldn't let a silly letter upset me."

"Right. And really, you don't even know how much of what your college friend wrote is strictly true." K.O. remembered the letter she'd written for Bill Mulcahy. Not exactly lies, but not the whole truth, either.

"That could be," LaVonne murmured, but she didn't seem convinced. "Anyway, I know better than to look to a man for happiness." LaVonne was sounding more like her old self. "Happiness comes from within, isn't that right, Martin?" she asked, holding her cat up. Martin dangled from her grasp, mewing plaintively. "I don't need a man to be complete, do I?"

K.O. stood up, gathering her packages as she did.

Toys and books for the twins, wrapping paper, a jar of specialty olives.

"Thanks for stopping by," LaVonne said when K.O. started toward the door. "I feel a hundred percent better already."

"Keep your eyes open now," she told LaVonne. "The man in the soup could be right around the corner." Or on the top floor of their condo building, she added silently.

"I will," her neighbor promised and, still clutching Martin, she shut the door.

Sunday afternoon Wynn came to K.O.'s door at three, his expression morose.

"Cheer up," she urged. "Just how bad can it be?"

"Wait until you meet Moon Puppy. Then you'll know."

"Come on, is your father really *that* bad?"

Wynn sighed deeply. "I suppose not. He's lonely without my mother. At loose ends."

"That's good." She paused, hearing what she'd said. "It's not good that he's lonely, but… Well, you know what I mean." LaVonne might seem all the more attractive to him if he craved female companionship. LaVonne deserved someone who needed her, who would appreciate her and her cats and her…psychic talents.

"You ready?" he asked.

"Let me grab my coat."

"You don't have to do this, you know."

"Wynn, I'm happy to," she assured him, and she meant it.

The airport traffic was snarled, and it took two turns through the short-term parking garage to find an available space. Thankfully they'd allotted plenty of time.

Wynn had agreed to meet his father at baggage

claim. No more than five minutes after they'd staked out a place near the luggage carousel, a man wearing a Hawaiian shirt, with long dark hair tied in a ponytail, walked toward them. He didn't have a jacket or coat.

K.O. felt Wynn stiffen.

"Wynn!" The man hurried forward.

Wynn met his father halfway, with K.O. trailing behind, and briefly hugged him. "Hello, Dad." He put his hand on K.O.'s shoulder. "This is my friend Katherine O'Connor. Katherine, this is my father, Moon Puppy Jeffries."

Moon Puppy winced. "Delighted to meet you, Katherine," he said politely. "But please, call me Max. I don't go by Moon Puppy anymore."

"Welcome to Seattle," K.O. said, shaking hands. "I'm sorry you didn't arrive to sunshine and warmer weather."

"Thank you. Don't worry, I've got a jacket in my bag."

In a few minutes Max had collected his suitcase and Wynn led the way to his car. "It's been unseasonably chilly," K.O. said, making small talk as they took the escalator to the parking garage. Max had retrieved his jacket by then.

At the car, Wynn took the suitcase from his father and stored it in the trunk. This gave K.O. an opportunity to study father and son. She glanced at Wynn and then back at his father. After the description Wynn had given her, she'd expected something quite different. Yes, Max Jeffries looked like an old hippie, as Wynn had said, but his hair was neatly trimmed and combed. He wore clean, pressed clothes and had impeccable manners. He was an older version of Wynn and just as respectable looking, she thought. Well, except for the hair.

"It was a surprise to hear you were coming for Christmas," Wynn commented when he got into the car.

"I figured it would be," his father said. "I didn't mention it earlier because I was afraid you'd find a convenient excuse for me not to come."

So Max Jeffries was direct and honest, too. A lot like his son. K.O. liked him even more.

They chatted on the ride into Seattle, and K.O. casually invited him for cocktails the following afternoon.

"I'd enjoy that," Wynn's father told her.

"Katherine wants to introduce you to her neighbor, LaVonne."

"I see," Max said with less enthusiasm and quickly changed the subject. "I understand your book is selling nicely."

"Yes, I'm fortunate to have a lot of publisher support."

"He's writing a second book," K.O. said, joining the conversation. It pleased her that Max seemed proud of his son.

"So, how long have you two been seeing each other?" Max asked, looking at K.O.

"Not long," Wynn answered for them. His gaze caught K.O.'s in the rearview mirror. "We met through a psychic," he said.

"We most certainly did not." K.O. was about to argue when she realized Wynn was smiling. "We actually met through a mutual friend who believes she has psychic powers," she explained, not telling Max that her neighbor and this "psychic" were one and the same.

As they exited off the freeway and headed into downtown Seattle and toward Blossom Street, Max said, "I had no idea Seattle was this beautiful."

"Oh, just wait until nighttime," K.O. told him. It was fast becoming dark, and city lights had begun to sparkle. "There's lots to do at night. Wynn and I took a horse-drawn carriage ride last week and then on Friday night we went on a merry-go-round."

"My first such experience," Wynn said, a smile quivering at the edges of his mouth.

"Your mother and I never took you?" Max sounded incredulous.

"Never."

"I know I had some failings as a father," Max said despondently.

"Not getting to ride on a merry-go-round isn't exactly a big deal, Dad. Don't worry about it," Wynn muttered.

That seemed to ease his father's mind. "So what's on the agenda for tomorrow?" he asked brightly.

Wynn cast K.O. a look as if to say he'd told her so.

"I can take you on a tour of Pike Place Market," K.O. offered.

"That would be great." Max thanked her with a warm smile. "I was hoping to get a chance to go up the Space Needle while I'm here, too."

"We can do that on Tuesday."

Max nodded. "Do you have any free time, Wynn?" he asked.

"Some," Wynn admitted with obvious reluctance. "But not much. In addition to my appointments and writing schedule, I'm still doing promotion for my current book."

"Of course," Max murmured.

K.O. detected a note of sadness in his voice and wanted to reassure him. Unfortunately she didn't know how.

Eleven

Wynn phoned K.O. early Monday morning. "I don't think this is going to work," he whispered.

"Pardon?" K.O. strained to hear.

"Meet me at the French Café," he said, his voice only slightly louder.

"When?" She had her sweats on and was ready to tackle her treadmill. After shedding the two pounds, she'd gained them again. It wasn't much, but enough to send her racing for a morning workout. She knew how quickly these things could get out of control.

"Now," he said impatiently. "Want me to pick you up?"

"No. I'll meet you there in ten minutes."

By the time she entered the café, Wynn had already purchased two cups of coffee and procured a table. "What's wrong?" she asked as she pulled out the chair.

"He's driving me insane!"

"Wynn, I like your father. You made him sound worse than a deadbeat dad, but he's obviously proud of you and—"

"Do you mind if we don't list his admirable qualities just now?" He brought one hand to his temple, as if warding off a headache.

"All right," she said, doing her best to understand.

"The reason I called is that I don't think it's a good idea to set him up with LaVonne."

"Why not?" K.O. thought her plan was brilliant. She had everything worked out in her mind; she'd bought the liquor and intended to dust and vacuum this afternoon. As far as she was concerned, the meeting of Max and LaVonne was destiny. Christmas romances were always the best.

"Dad isn't ready for another relationship," Wynn declared. "He's still mourning my mother."

"Shouldn't he be the one to decide that?" Wynn might be a renowned child psychologist but she believed everyone was entitled to make his or her own decisions, especially in matters of the heart. She considered it all right to lend a helping hand, however. That was fair.

"I can tell my father's not ready," Wynn insisted.

"But I invited him for drinks this evening and he accepted." It looked as if her entire day was going to be spent with Max Jeffries, aka Moon Puppy. Earlier she'd agreed to take him to Pike Place Market, which was a must-see for anyone visiting Seattle. It was always an entertaining place for tourists, but never more so than during the holiday season. The whole market had an air of festivity, the holiday mood infectious.

"What about LaVonne?" he asked.

"I'll give her a call later." K.O. hadn't wanted to be obvious about this meeting. Still, when LaVonne met Max, she'd know, the same way Wynn and K.O. had known, that they were being set up.

"Don't," he said, cupping the coffee mug with both hands.

"Why not?"

He frowned. "I have a bad feeling about this."

K.O. smothered a giggle. "Are you telling me you've found your own psychic powers?"

"Hardly," he snorted.

"Wynn," she said, covering his hand with hers in a gesture of reassurance. "It's going to work out fine, trust me." Hmm. She seemed to be saying that a lot these days.

He exhaled slowly, as if it went against his better judgment to agree. "All right, do whatever you think is best."

"I've decided to simplify things. I'm serving eggnog and cookies." And olives, if anyone wanted them. When she'd find time to bake she didn't know, but K.O. was determined to do this properly.

"Come around five-thirty," she suggested.

"That early?"

"Yes. You're taking care of arranging their dinner, right?"

"Ah… I don't think they'll get that far."

"But they might," she said hopefully. "You make the reservation, and if they don't want to go, then we will. Okay?"

He nodded. "I'll see what I can do." Wynn took one last swallow of coffee and stood. "I've got to get to the office." Slipping into his overcoat, he confided, "I have a patient this morning. Emergency call."

K.O. wondered what kind of emergency that would be—an ego that needed splinting? A bruised id? But she knew better than to ask. "Have a good day," was all she said. In his current mood, that was an iffy proposition. K.O. couldn't help wondering what Max had done to upset him.

"You, too," he murmured, then added, "And thank you for looking after Moon Puppy."

"His name is Max," K.O. reminded him.

"Maybe to you, but to me he'll always be the hippie surfer bum I grew up with." Wynn hurried out of the café.

By five that afternoon, K.O. felt as if she'd never left the treadmill. After walking for forty minutes on her machine, she showered, baked and decorated three dozen cookies and then met Wynn's father for a whirlwind tour of the Seattle waterfront, starting with Pike Place. She phoned LaVonne from the Seattle Aquarium. LaVonne had instantly agreed to drinks, and K.O. had a hard time getting off the phone. LaVonne chatted excitedly about the man in the soup, the man K.O. had claimed to see with her "psychic" eyes. Oh, dear, maybe this had gone a little too far....

Max was interested in absolutely everything, so they didn't get back to Blossom Street until after four, which gave K.O. very little time to prepare for *the meeting*.

She vacuumed and dusted and plumped up the sofa pillows and set out a dish of peppermint candies, a favorite of LaVonne's. The decorated sugar cookies were arranged on a special Santa plate. K.O. didn't particularly like sugar cookies, which, therefore, weren't as tempting as shortbread or chocolate chip would've been. She decided against the olives.

K.O. was stirring the rum into the eggnog when she saw the blinking light on her phone. A quick check told her it was Zelda. She didn't have even a minute to chat and told herself she'd return the call later.

Precisely at 5:30 p.m., just after she'd put on all her Christmas CDs, Wynn arrived without his father.

"Where's your dad?" K.O. demanded as she accepted the bottle of wine he handed her.

"He's never on time if there's an excuse to be late," Wynn muttered. "He'll get here when he gets here. You noticed he doesn't wear a watch?"

K.O. had noticed and thought it a novelty. LaVonne wasn't known for her punctuality, either, so they had at least that much in common. Already this relationship revealed promise—in her opinion, anyway.

"How did your afternoon go?" Wynn asked. He sat down on the sofa and reached for a cookie, nodding his head to the tempo of "Jingle Bell Rock."

"Great. I enjoyed getting to know your father."

Wynn glanced up, giving her a skeptical look.

"What is it with you two?" she asked gently, sitting beside him.

Wynn sighed. "I didn't have a happy childhood, except for the time I spent with my grandparents. I resented being dragged hither and yon, based on where the best surf could be found. I hated living with a bunch of self-absorbed hippies whenever we returned to the commune, which was their so-called home base. For a good part of my life, I had the feeling I was a hindrance my father tolerated."

"Oh, Wynn." The unhappiness he still felt was at odds with the amusing stories he'd told about his childhood at Chez Jerome and during dinner with Vickie and John. She'd originally assumed that he was reflecting his own upbringing in his "Free Child" theories, but she now saw that wasn't the case. Moon Puppy Max might have been a hippie, but he'd imposed his own regimen on his son. Not much "freedom" there.

"Well, that's my life," he said stiffly. "I don't want my father here and I dislike the way he's using you and—"

"He's not using me."

He opened his mouth to argue, but apparently changed his mind. "I'm not going to let my father come between us."

"Good, because I'd feel terrible if that happened." This would be a near-perfect relationship—if it wasn't for the fact that he was Wynn Jeffries, author of *The Free Child.* And the fact that he hadn't forgiven his father, who'd been a selfish and irresponsible parent.

His eyes softened. "I won't let it." He kissed her then, and K.O. slipped easily into his embrace. He wrapped his arms around her and they exchanged a series of deep and probing kisses that left K.O.'s head reeling.

"Katherine." Wynn breathed harshly as he abruptly released her.

She didn't want him to stop.

"You'd better answer your door," he advised.

K.O. had been so consumed by their kisses that she hadn't heard the doorbell. "Oh," she breathed, shaking her head to clear away the fog of longing. This man did things to her heart—not to mention the rest of her—that even a romance novelist couldn't describe.

Wynn's father stood on the other side of the door, wearing another Hawaiian flowered shirt, khaki pants and flip-flops. From the way he'd dressed, he could be on a tropical isle rather than in Seattle with temperatures hovering just above freezing. K.O. could tell that

Max's choice of clothes irritated Wynn, but to his credit, Wynn didn't comment.

Too bad the current Christmas song was "Rudolph," instead of "Mele Kaliki Maka."

K.O. welcomed him and had just poured his eggnog when the doorbell chimed again. Ah, the moment she'd been waiting for. Her friend had arrived. K.O. glided toward the door and swept it open as if anticipating Santa himself.

"LaVonne," she said, leaning forward to kiss her friend's cheek. "How good of you to come." Her neighbor had brought Tom with her. The oversize feline was draped over her arm like a large furry purse.

"This is so kind of you," LaVonne said. She looked startled at seeing Max.

"Come in, please," K.O. said, gesturing her inside. She realized how formal she sounded—like a character in an old drawing room comedy. "Allow me to introduce Wynn's father, Max Jeffries. Max, this is LaVonne Young."

Max stood and backed away from LaVonne. "You have a cat on your arm."

"This is Tom," LaVonne said. She glanced down lovingly at the cat as she stepped into the living room. "Would you like to say hello?" She held Tom out, but Max shook his head adamantly.

By now he'd backed up against the wall. "I don't like cats."

"What?" She sounded shocked. "Cats are magical creatures."

"Maybe to you they are," the other man protested. "I don't happen to be a cat person."

Wynn shared an I-told-you-so look with K.O.

"May I get you some eggnog?" K.O. asked, hoping to rescue the evening from a less-than-perfect beginning.

"Please," LaVonne answered just as "Have Yourself a Merry Little Christmas" began.

Eager for something to do, K.O. hurried into the kitchen and grabbed the pitcher of eggnog.

She heard Tom hiss loudly and gulped down some of her own eggnog to relax.

"Your cat doesn't like me," Max said as he carefully approached the sofa.

"Oh, don't be silly. Tom's the friendly one."

"You mean you have *more* than one?"

"Dad," Wynn said, "why don't you sit down and make yourself comfortable. You're quite safe. Tom is very well-behaved."

"I don't like cats," Max reiterated.

"Tom is gentle and loving," LaVonne said.

Max slowly approached the sofa. "Then why is he hissing at me?"

"He senses your dislike," LaVonne explained. She gave Max a dazzling smile. "Pet him, and he'll be your friend for life."

"See, Dad?" Wynn walked over to LaVonne, who sat with Tom on her lap. He ran his hand down Tom's back and the tabby purred with pleasure.

"He likes you," Max said.

"He'll like you, too, as soon as you pet him." LaVonne was still smiling happily, stroking the cat's head.

Max came a bit closer. "You live in the building?" he asked, making his way, step by careful step, toward LaVonne.

"Just across the hall," she answered.

"Your husband, too?"

"I'm single. Do you enjoy cards? Because you're welcome to stop by anytime."

K.O. delivered the eggnog. This was going even better than she'd hoped. Max was already interested and LaVonne was issuing invitations. She recognized the gleam in the other man's eyes. A sense of triumph filled her and she cast a glance in Wynn's direction. Wynn was just reaching into his pocket, withdrawing a real-looking catnip mouse.

Relaxed now, Max leaned forward to pet Tom.

At that very moment, chaos broke out. Although LaVonne claimed she'd never known Tom to take a dislike to anyone, the cat clearly detested Max. Before anyone could react, he sprang from her lap and grabbed Max's bare arm. The cat's claws dug in, drawing blood. He wasn't about to let go, either.

"Get him off," Max screamed, thrashing his arm to and fro in an effort to free himself from the cat-turned-killer. Wynn was desperately—and futilely—trying to distract Tom by waving the toy mouse. It didn't help.

"Tom, Tom!" LaVonne screeched at the top of her lungs.

Blood spurted onto the carpet.

In a panic, Max pulled at Tom's fur. The cat then sank his teeth into Max's hand and Max yelped in pain.

"Don't hurt my cat," LaVonne shrieked.

Frozen to the spot, K.O. watched in horror as the scene unfolded. Wynn dropped the mouse, and if not for his quick action, K.O. didn't know what would have happened. Before she could fully comprehend how he'd done it, Wynn had disentangled Tom from his father's arm. LaVonne instantly took her beloved cat into her embrace and cradled him against her side.

At the sight of his own blood, Max looked like he was about to pass out. K.O. hurriedly got him a clean towel, shocked at the amount of blood. The scratches seemed deep. "Call 911," Max shouted.

Wynn pulled out his cell phone. "That might not be a bad idea," he said to K.O. "Cat scratches can get infected."

"Contact the authorities, too," Max added, glaring at LaVonne. He stretched out his good arm and pointed at her. "I want that woman arrested and her animal destroyed."

LaVonne cried out with alarm and hovered protectively over Tom. "My poor kitty," she whispered.

"You're worried about the *cat?*" Max said. "I'm bleeding to death and you're worried about your cat?"

Wynn replaced his phone. "The medics are on their way."

"Oh...good." K.O. could already hear sirens in the background. She turned off her CD player. Thinking she should open the lobby door, she left the apartment, and when the aid car arrived, she directed the paramedics. Things had gotten worse in the short time she was gone. Max and LaVonne were shouting at each other as the small living room filled with people. Curious onlookers crowded the hallway outside her door.

"My cat scratched him and I'm sorry, but he provoked Tom," LaVonne said stubbornly.

"I want that woman behind bars." Max stabbed his finger in LaVonne's direction.

"Sir, sir, we need you to settle down," instructed the paramedic who was attempting to take his blood pressure.

"While she's in jail, declaw her cat," Max threw in.

Wynn stepped up behind K.O. "Yup," he whispered. "This is a match made in heaven, all right."

Then, just when K.O. was convinced nothing more could go wrong, her phone started to ring.

Twelve

"Don't you think you should answer that?" the paramedic treating Max's injuries asked.

K.O. was too upset to move. The romantic interlude she'd so carefully plotted couldn't have gone worse. At least Wynn seemed to understand her distress.

"I'll get it," Wynn said, and strode into the kitchen. "O'Connor residence," he said. At the way his eyes instantly shot to her, K.O. regretted not answering the phone herself.

"It's your sister," he said, holding the phone away from his ear.

Even above the racket K.O. could hear Zelda's high-pitched excitement. Her idol, Dr. Wynn Jeffries, had just spoken to her. The last person K.O. wanted to deal with just then was her younger sister. However, she couldn't subject Wynn to Zelda's adoration.

She took the phone, but even before she had a chance to speak, Zelda was shrieking, "Is it *really* you, Dr. Jeffries? Really and truly?"

"Actually, no," K.O. informed her sister. "It's me."

"But Dr. Jeffries is with you?"

"Yes."

"Keep him there!"

"I beg your pardon?"

"Don't let him leave," Zelda said, sounding even more excited. "I'm calling on my cell. I'm only a few minutes away." She took a deep breath. "I need to talk to him. It's urgent. Zach and I just had the biggest argument *ever,* and I need to talk to Dr. Jeffries."

"Zelda," K.O. cut in. "Now is not the best time for you to visit."

"Didn't you hear me?" her sister cried. "This is an emergency."

With that, the phone went dead. Groaning, K.O. replaced the receiver.

"Is something wrong?" Wynn asked as he stepped around the paramedic who was still looking after Max.

"It's Zelda. She wants—no, *needs*—to talk to you. According to her it's an emergency." K.O. felt the need to warn him. "She's already on her way."

"Now? You mean she's coming now?"

K.O. nodded. "Apparently so." Zelda hadn't mentioned what this argument with Zach was about. Three guesses said it had to do with Christmas and Wynn's theories. Oh, great. Her sister was arriving at the scene of a disaster.

"Are you taking him to the h-hospital?" LaVonne sobbed, covering her mouth with both hands.

"It's just a precaution," the medic answered. "A doctor needs to look at those scratches."

"Not that dreadful man!" LaVonne cried, pointing at Max. "I'm talking about my cat."

"Oh." The paramedic glanced at his companion.

"Unfortunately, in instances such as this, we're obliged to notify Animal Control."

"You're hauling my Tom to…jail?"

"Quarantine," he told her gently.

For a moment LaVonne seemed about to faint. Wynn put his arm around the older woman's shoulders and led her to the sofa so she could sit down. "This can't be happening," LaVonne wailed. "I can't believe this is happening to my Tom."

"Your cat should be—"

Wynn cast his father a look meaningful enough to silence the rest of whatever Max had planned to say.

"I'm going to be scarred for life," Max shouted. "I just hope you've got good insurance, because you're going to pay for this. And you're going to pay big."

"Don't you dare threaten me!" LaVonne had recovered enough to shout back.

With his arm stretched out in front of him, Max Jeffries followed the paramedic out of the condo and past the crowd of tenants who'd gathered in the hallway outside K.O.'s door.

"That…that terrible man just threatened me," LaVonne continued. "Tom's never attacked anyone like this before."

"Please, please, let me through."

K.O. heard her sister's voice.

Meanwhile LaVonne was weeping loudly. "My poor Tom. My poor, poor Tom. What will become of him?"

"What on earth is going on here?" Zelda demanded as she made her way into the apartment. The second paramedic was gathering up his equipment and getting ready to leave. The blood-soaked towels K.O. had wrapped around Max's arm were on the floor. The scene was completely chaotic and Zelda's arrival only added to the mayhem.

"Your f-father wants to s-sue me," LaVonne stuttered, pleading with Wynn. "*Do* something. Promise me you'll talk to him."

Wynn sat next to LaVonne and tried to comfort her. "I'll do what I can," he said. "I'm sure that once my father's settled down he'll listen to reason."

LaVonne's eyes widened, as though she had trouble believing Wynn. "I don't mean to insult you, but your father doesn't seem like a reasonable man to me."

"Whose blood is that?" Zelda asked, hands on her hips as she surveyed the room.

K.O. tried to waylay her sister. "As you can see," she said, gesturing about her, "this *really* isn't a good time to visit."

"I don't care," Zelda insisted. "I need to talk to Dr. Jeffries." She thrust his book at him and a pen. "Could you sign this for me?"

Just then a man wearing a jacket that identified him as an Animal Control officer came in, holding an animal carrier. The name Walt was embroidered on his shirt.

Wynn quickly signed his name, all the while watching the man from Animal Control.

LaVonne took one look at Walt and burst into tears. She buried her face in her hands and started to rock back and forth.

"Where's the cat?" Walt asked.

"We've got him in the bathroom," the paramedic said.

"Please don't hurt him," LaVonne wept. "Please, please..."

Walt raised a reassuring hand. "I handle situations like this every day. Don't worry, Miss, I'll be gentle with your pet."

"Dr. Jeffries, Dr. Jeffries." Zelda slipped past K.O. and climbed over LaVonne's knees in order to reach Wynn. She plunked herself down on the coffee table, facing him. "I really do need to talk to you."

"Zelda!" K.O. was shocked by her sister's audacity.

"Zach and I never argue," Zelda said over her shoulder, glaring at K.O. as if that fact alone should explain her actions. "This will only take a few minutes, I promise. Once I talk to Dr. Jeffries, I'll be able to tell Zach what he said and then he'll understand."

LaVonne wailed as Walt entered the bathroom.

K.O. heard a hiss and wondered if her shower curtain was now in shreds. She'd never seen a cat react to anyone the way Tom had to Wynn's father. Even now she couldn't figure out what had set him off.

"This'll only take a minute," Zelda went on. "You see, my husband and I read your book, and it changed everything. Well, to be perfectly honest, I don't know if Zach read the whole book." A frown crossed her face.

"LaVonne, perhaps I should take you home now," K.O. suggested, thinking it might be best for her neighbor not to see Tom leave the building caged.

"I can't leave," LaVonne said. "Not until I know what's happening to Tom."

The bathroom door opened and Walt reappeared with Tom safely inside the cat carrier.

"Tom, oh, Tom," LaVonne wailed, throwing her arms wide.

"Dr. Jeffries, Dr. Jeffries," Zelda pleaded, vying for his attention.

"Zelda, couldn't this wait a few minutes?" K.O. asked.

"Where are you taking Tom?" LaVonne demanded.

"We're just going to put him in quarantine," Walt said in a soothing voice.

"Tom's had all his shots. My veterinarian will verify everything you need to know."

"Good. Still, we're legally required to do this. I guarantee he'll be well looked after."

"Thank you," K.O. said, relieved.

"Can I speak to Dr. Jeffries now?" Zelda asked impatiently. "You see, I don't think my husband really did read your book," she continued, picking up where she'd left off. "If he had, we wouldn't be having this disagreement."

"I'll see LaVonne home," K.O. said. She closed one arm around her friend's waist and steered her out of the condo.

Wynn looked at Zelda and sent K.O. a beseeching glance.

"I'll be back as soon as I can," she promised.

He nodded and mouthed the word *hurry.*

K.O. rolled her eyes. As she escorted LaVonne, the sound of her sister's voice followed her into the hallway, which was fortunately deserted. It didn't take long to get LaVonne settled in her own place. Once she had Phillip and Martin with her, she was comforted, since both seemed to recognize her distress and lavished their mistress with affection.

When she returned to her condo, K.O. found that her sister hadn't moved. She still sat on the coffee table, so close to Wynn that their knees touched. Judging by the speed with which Zelda spoke, K.O. doubted he'd had a chance to get a word in edgewise.

"Then the girls started to cry," Zelda was saying. "They want a Christmas tree and Zach thinks we should get one."

"I don't believe—" Wynn was cut off before he could finish his thought.

"I know you don't actually condemn Christmas trees, but I didn't want to encourage the girls about this Santa thing, and I feel decorating a tree would do that. If we're going to bury Santa under the sleigh—and I'm in complete agreement with you, Dr. Jeffries—then it makes sense to downplay everything else having to do with Christmas, too. Certainly all the commercial aspects. But how do I handle the girls' reaction when they hear their friends talking about Santa?"

Wynn raised a finger, indicating that he'd like to comment. His request, however, was ignored.

"I feel as you do," Zelda rushed on breathlessly, bringing one hand to her chest in a gesture of sincerity. "It's wrong to mislead one's children with figures of fantasy. It's wrong, wrong, wrong. Zach agreed with me—but only in principle, as it turns out. Then we got into this big fight over the Christmas tree and you have to understand that my husband and I hardly ever argue, so this is all very serious."

"Where's Zach now?" K.O. asked, joining Wynn on the sofa.

As if to let her know how much he appreciated having her back, Wynn reached for her hand. At Zelda's obvious interest, he released it, but the contact, brief as it was, reassured her.

Zelda lowered her head. "Zach's at home with the

girls. If you must know, I sort of left my husband with the twins."

"Zoe and Zara," K.O. said under her breath for Wynn's benefit.

"Despite my strong feelings on the matter, I suspect my husband is planning to take our daughters out to purchase a Christmas tree." She paused. "A *giant* one."

"Do you think he might even decorate it with Santa figurines and reindeer?" K.O. asked, pretending to be scandalized.

"Oh, I hope not," Zelda cried. "That would ruin everything I've tried so hard to institute in our family."

"As I recall," Wynn finally said. He waited a moment as if to gauge whether now was a good time to insert his opinions. When no one interrupted him, he continued. "I didn't say anything in my book against Christmas trees, giant or otherwise."

"Yes, I know that, but it seems to me—"

"It seems to *me* that you've carried this a bit further than advisable," Wynn said gently. "Despite what you and K.O. think, I don't want to take Christmas away from your children or from you and your husband. It's a holiday to be celebrated. Family and traditions are important."

K.O. agreed with him. She felt gratified that there was common ground between them, an opinion on which they could concur. Nearly everything she'd heard about Wynn to this point had come from her sister. K.O. was beginning to wonder if Zelda was taking his advice to extremes.

"Besides," he said, "there's a fundamental contradiction in your approach. You're correct to minimize the element of fantasy—but your children are telling you what they want, aren't they? And you're ignoring that."

K.O. wanted to cheer. She took Wynn's hand again, and this time he didn't let go.

"By the way," Zelda said, looking from Wynn to K.O. and staring pointedly at their folded hands. "Just when did you two start dating?"

"I told you—"

"What you said," her sister broke in, "was that Dr. Jeffries lived in the same building as you."

"I told you we went to dinner a couple of times."

"You most certainly did not." Zelda stood up, an irritated expression on her face. "Well, okay, you did mention the one dinner at Chez Jerome."

"Did you know that I'm planning to join Katherine this Friday when she's watching the twins?" Wynn asked.

"She's bringing you along?" Zelda's eyes grew round with shock. "You might've said something to me," she burst out, clearly upset with K.O.

"I thought I had told you."

"You haven't talked to me in days," Zelda wailed. "It's like I'm not even your sister anymore. The last I heard, you were going to get Dr. Jeffries's autograph for me, and you didn't, although I specifically asked if you would."

"Would you prefer I not watch the twins?" Wynn inquired.

"Oh, no! It would be an honor," Zelda assured him, smiling, her voice warm and friendly. She turned to face K.O. again, her eyes narrowed. "But my own sister," she hissed, "should've told me she intended on having a famous person spend the night in my home."

"You're not to tell anyone," K.O. insisted.

Zelda glared at her. "Fine. I won't."

"Promise me," K.O. said. Wynn was entitled to his privacy; the last thing he needed was a fleet of parents in SUVs besieging him about his book.

"I promise." Without a further word, Zelda grabbed her purse and made a hasty exit.

"Zelda!" K.O. called after her. "I think we need to talk about this for a minute."

"I don't have a minute. I need to get home to my husband and children. We'll talk later," Zelda said in an ominous tone, and then she was gone.

Thirteen

"I'd better leave now, as well," Wynn announced, getting his coat. "Dad'll need me to drive him back from the emergency room." K.O. was glad he didn't seem eager to go.

For her part, she wanted him to stay. Her nerves were frayed. Nothing had worked out as she'd planned and now everyone was upset with her. LaVonne, her dear friend, was inconsolable. Zelda was annoyed that K.O. hadn't kept her updated on the relationship with Wynn. Max Jeffries was just plain angry, and while the brunt of his anger had been directed at LaVonne, K.O. realized he wasn't pleased with her, either. Now Wynn had to go. Reluctantly K.O. walked him to the door. "Let me know how your father's doing, okay?" she asked, looking up at him.

"Of course." Wynn placed his hands on her shoulders. "You know I'd much rather be here with you."

She saw the regret in his eyes and didn't want to make matters worse. "Thank you for being so wonderful," she said and meant it. Wynn had been the voice of calm and reason throughout this entire ordeal.

"I'll call you about my father as soon as I hear."

"Thank you."

After a brief hug, he hurried out the door.

After a dinner of eggnog and peanut butter on crackers, K.O. waited up until after midnight, but no word came. Finally, when she couldn't keep her eyes open any longer, she climbed between the sheets and fell instantly asleep. This surprised her; she hadn't anticipated sleeping easily or well. When she woke the following morning, the first thoughts that rushed into her mind were of Wynn. Something must have happened, something unexpected and probably dreadful, or he would've called.

Perhaps the hospital had decided to keep Max overnight for observation. While there'd been a lot of blood involved, K.O. didn't think any of the cuts were deep enough to require stitches. But if Max had filed a police report, that would cause problems for LaVonne and might explain Wynn's silence. Every scenario that roared through her head pointed to trouble.

Even before she made her first cup of coffee, K.O.'s stomach was in knots. As she headed into the kitchen, she discovered a sealed envelope that had been slipped under her door.

It read:

Katherine,

I didn't get back from the hospital until late and I was afraid you'd already gone to bed. Dad's home and, other than being cantankerous, he's doing fine, so don't worry on his account. The hospital cleaned and bandaged his arm and said he'd be good as new in a week or so. Please re-

assure LaVonne. The cuts looked worse than they actually were.

Could you stop by my office this afternoon? I'm at the corner of Fourth and Willow, Suite 1110. Does one o'clock work for you? If you can't fit it into your schedule, please contact my assistant and let her know. Otherwise, I'll look forward to seeing you, then.

Wynn

Oh, she could fit it in. She could *definitely* fit it in. K.O. was ready to climb Mount Rainier for a chance to see Wynn. With purpose now, she showered and dressed and then, on the off chance Max might need something, she phoned Wynn's condo.

His father answered right away, which made her wonder if he'd been sitting next to the phone waiting for a call.

"Good morning," she said, striving to sound cheerful and upbeat—all the while hoping Max wasn't one to hold grudges.

"Who is this?"

"It's K.O.," she told him, her voice faltering despite her effort to maintain a cheery tone.

He hesitated as if he needed time to place who she might be. "Oh," he finally said. "The woman from downstairs. The woman whose *friend* caused me irreparable distress." After another pause, he said, "I'm afraid I might be suffering from trauma-induced amnesia."

"Excuse me?" K.O. was sure she'd misunderstood.

"I was attacked yesterday by a possibly rabid beast and am fortunate to be alive. I don't remember much after that vicious animal sank its claws into my arm," he added shakily.

K.O. closed her eyes for a moment. "I'm so sorry to hear that," she said, going along with it. "But the hospital released you, I see."

"Yes." This was said with disdain; apparently, he felt the medical profession had made a serious error in judgment. "I'm on heavy pain medication."

"Oh, dear."

"I don't know where my son's gone," he muttered fretfully.

If Wynn hadn't told his father he was at the office, then K.O. wasn't about to, either. She suspected Wynn had good reason to escape.

"Since you live in the building…" Max began.

"Uh…" She could see it coming. Max wanted her to sit and hold his uninjured hand for the rest of the day.

"I do, but unfortunately I'm on my way out."

"Oh."

It took K.O. a few more minutes to wade through the guilt he was shoveling in her direction. "I'll drop by and check on you later," she promised.

"Thank you," he said, ending their conversation with a groan, a last shovelful of guilt.

K.O. hung up the phone, groaning, too. This was even worse than she'd imagined and she had a fine imagination. Max was obviously playing this incident for all it was worth. Irreparable distress. Rabid beast. Trauma-induced amnesia! Oh, brother.

Wanting to leave before Max decided to drop by, she hurried out the door and stopped at the French Café for a mocha and bran muffin. If ever she'd deserved one, it was now. At the rate her life was going, there wouldn't be enough peppermint mochas in the world to see her through another day like yesterday.

Rather than linger as she normally did, K.O. took her drink and muffin to go and enjoyed a leisurely stroll down Blossom Street. A walk would give her exercise and clear her mind, and just then clarity was what she needed. She admired the evergreen boughs and garlands decorating the storefronts, and the inventive variations on Christmas themes in every window. The weather remained unseasonably cold with a chance of snow flurries. In December Seattle was usually in the grip of gloomy winter rains, but that hadn't happened yet this year. The sky was already a clear blue with puffy clouds scattered about.

By the time she'd finished her peppermint mocha, K.O. had walked a good mile and felt refreshed in both body and mind. When she entered her building, LaVonne—wearing a housecoat—was stepping out of her condo to grab the morning paper. Her eyes were red and puffy and it looked as if she hadn't slept all night. She bent over to retrieve her paper.

"LaVonne," K.O. called out.

Her friend slowly straightened. "I thought I should see if there's a report in the police blotter about Tom scratching that…that man," she spat out.

"I doubt it."

"Is he…back from the hospital?"

"Max Jeffries is alive and well. He sustained a few scratches, but it isn't nearly as bad as we all feared." Wynn's father seemed to be under the delusion that he'd narrowly escaped with his life, but she didn't feel the need to mention that. Nor did K.O. care to enlighten LaVonne regarding Max's supposed amnesia.

"I'm so glad." LaVonne sounded tired and sad.

"Is there anything I can get you?" K.O. asked, feeling partially to blame.

"Thanks for asking, but I'm fine." She gave a shuddering sob. "Except for poor Tom being in jail…"

"Call if you need me," K.O. said before she returned to her own apartment.

The rest of the morning passed quickly. She worked for a solid two hours and accomplished more in that brief time than she normally did in four. She finished a medical report, sent off some résumés by email and drafted a Christmas letter for a woman in Zach's office who'd made a last-minute request. Then, deciding she should check on Max Jeffries, she went up for a quick visit. At twelve-thirty, she grabbed her coat and headed out the door again. With her hands buried deep in her red wool coat and a candy-cane striped scarf doubled around her neck, she walked to Wynn's office.

This was her first visit there, and she wasn't sure what to expect. When she stepped inside, she found a comfortable waiting room and thought it looked like any doctor's office.

A middle-aged receptionist glanced up and smiled warmly. "You must be Katherine," she said, extending her hand. "I'm Lois Church, Dr. Jeffries's assistant."

"Hello," K.O. said, returning her smile.

"Come on back. Doctor is waiting for you." Lois led her to a large room, lined with bookshelves and framed degrees. A big desk dominated one end, and there was a sitting area on the other side, complete with a miniature table and chairs and a number of toys.

Wynn stood in front of the bookcase, and when K.O.

entered the room, he closed the volume he'd been reading and put it back in place.

Lois slipped quietly out of the room and shut the door.

"Hi," K.O. said tentatively, wondering at his mood.

He smiled. "I see you received my note."

"Yes," she said with a nod. She remained standing just inside his office.

"I asked you to come here to talk about my father. I'm afraid he's going a little overboard with all of this."

"I got that impression myself."

Wynn arched his brows. "You've spoken to him?"

She nodded again. "I stopped by to see how he's doing. He didn't seem to remember me right away. He says he's suffering from memory loss."

Wynn groaned.

"I hate to say this, but I assumed that hypochondria's what he's really suffering from." She paused. "Either that or he's faking it," she said boldly.

Wynn gave a dismissive shrug. "I believe your second diagnosis is correct. It's a recurring condition of his," he said with a wry smile.

K.O. didn't know quite what to say.

"He's exaggerating, looking for attention." Wynn motioned for her to sit down, which she did, sinking into the luxurious leather sofa. Wynn took the chair next to it. "I don't mean to sound unsympathetic, but for all his easygoing hippie ways, Moon Puppy—Max—can be quite the manipulator."

"Well, it's not like LaVonne did it on purpose or anything."

There was a moment's silence. "In light of what happened yesterday, do you still want me to accompany you to your sister's?" he asked.

K.O. would be terribly disappointed if he'd experienced a change of heart. "I hoped you would, but if you need to bow out because of your father, I understand."

"No," he said decisively. "I want to do this. It's important for us both, for our relationship."

K.O. felt the same way.

"I've already told my father that I have a business appointment this weekend, so he knows I'll be away."

That made K.O. smile. This *was* business. Sort of.

"I'd prefer that Max not know the two of us will be together. He'll want to join us and, frankly, dealing with him will be more work than taking care of the kids."

"All right." Despite a bit of residual guilt, K.O. was certainly willing to abide by his wishes. She was convinced that once Wynn spent time with Zoe and Zara, he'd know for himself that his theories didn't work. The twins and their outrageous behavior would speak more eloquently than she ever could.

"I'm afraid we might not have an opportunity to get together for the rest of the week."

She was unhappy about it but understood. With his injuries and need for attention, Max would dominate Wynn's time.

"Are you sure your father will be well enough by Friday for you to leave?" she asked.

"He'd better be," Wynn said firmly, "because I'm going. He'll survive. In case you hadn't already figured this out, he's a little…immature."

"Really?" she asked, feigning surprise. Then she laughed out loud.

Wynn smiled, too. "I'm going to miss you, Katherine," he said with a sigh. "I wish I could see you every day this week, but between work and Max…"

"I'll miss you, too."

Wynn checked his watch and K.O. realized that was her signal to go. Wynn had appointments.

They both stood.

"Before I forget," he said casually. "A friend of mine told me his company's looking for a publicist. It's a small publisher, Apple Blossom Books, right in the downtown area, not far from here."

"They are?" K.O.'s heart raced with excitement. A small publishing company would be ideal. "Really?"

"I mentioned your name, and Larry asked if you'd be willing to send in a résumé." Wynn picked up a business card from his desk and handed it to her. "You can email it directly to him."

"Oh, Wynn, thank you." In her excitement, she hugged him.

That seemed to be all the encouragement he needed to keep her in his arms and kiss her. She responded with equal fervor, and it made her wonder how she could possibly go another three days until she saw him again.

They smiled at each other. Wynn threaded his fingers through her hair and brought his mouth to hers for another, deeper kiss.

A polite knock at the door was followed by the sound of it opening.

Abruptly Wynn released her, taking a step back. "Yes, Lois," he said, still looking at K.O.

"Your one-thirty appointment has arrived."

"I'll be ready in just a minute," he said. As soon as the door was shut, he leaned close, touching his forehead to hers. "I'd better get back to work."

"Me, too." But it was with real reluctance that they drew apart.

As K.O. left, glancing at the surly teen being ushered into his office, she felt that Friday couldn't come soon enough.

Fourteen

On Thursday afternoon, LaVonne invited K.O. for afternoon tea, complete with a plate of sliced fruitcake. "I'm feeling much better," her neighbor said as she poured tea into mugs decorated with cats in Santa costumes. "I've been allowed to visit Tom, and he's doing so well. In a couple of days, he'll be back home where he belongs." She frowned as if remembering Wynn's father. "No thanks to that dreadful man who had Tom taken away from me."

K.O. sat on the sofa and held her mug in one hand and a slice of fruitcake in the other. "I'm so pleased to hear Tom will be home soon." Her conscience had been bothering her, and for the sake of their friendship, K.O. felt the need to confess what she'd done.

"The best part is I haven't seen that maniac all week," LaVonne was saying.

K.O. gave her neighbor a tentative smile and lowered her gaze. She hadn't seen Max, either. Or Wynn, except for that brief visit to his office, although they'd emailed each other a couple of times. He'd kept her updated on his father and the so-called memory loss, from which Max had apparently made a sudden recovery. In fact, he now remembered a little too much, according to Wynn. But the wounds on his arm appeared to be healing nicely and Max seemed to enjoy the extra attention Wynn paid him. Wynn, meanwhile, was looking forward to the reprieve offered by their visit to Zelda's.

"I owe you an apology," K.O. said to LaVonne.

"Nonsense. You had no way of knowing how Tom would react to Mr. Jeffries."

"True, but..." She swallowed hard. "You should know..." She started again. "I didn't really have a psychic experience."

LaVonne set down her mug and stared at K.O. "You didn't actually see a man for me in the soup? You mean to say there *wasn't* any message in the cracker crumbs?"

"No," K.O. admitted.

"Oh."

"It might seem like I was making fun of you and your psychic abilities, but I wasn't, LaVonne, I truly wasn't. I thought that if you believed a man was coming into your life, you'd be looking for one, and if you were expecting to meet a man, then you just might, and I hoped that man would be Wynn's father, but clearly it wasn't...isn't." This was said without pausing for breath.

A short silence ensued, followed by a disappointed, "Oh."

"Forgive me if I offended you."

LaVonne took a moment to think this through. "You didn't," she said after a while. "I've more or less reached the same conclusion about my psychic abilities. But—" she smiled brightly "—guess what? I've signed up for another class in January." She reached for a second slice of fruitcake and smiled as Martin brought K.O. the catnip mouse Wynn had given Tom that ill-fated evening.

"Another one at the community college?" K.O. asked.

LaVonne shook her head. "No, I walked across the street into A Good Yarn and decided I'd learn how to knit."

"That sounds good."

"Want to come, too?" LaVonne asked.

Every time her friend enrolled in a new course, she urged K.O. to take it with her. Because of finances and her job search, K.O. had always declined. This time, however, she felt she might be able to swing it. Not to mention the fact that she owed LaVonne… "I'll see."

"Really?" Even this little bit of enthusiasm seemed to delight LaVonne. "That's wonderful."

"I had a job interview on Wednesday," K.O. told her, squelching the desire to pin all her hopes on this one interview. Apple Blossom Books, the publisher Wynn had recommended, had called her in almost immediately. She'd met with the president and the marketing manager, and they'd promised to get back to her before Christmas. For the first time in a long while, K.O. felt optimistic. A publishing company, even a small one, would be ideal.

"And?" LaVonne prompted.

"And…" K.O. said, smiling. "I'm keeping my fingers crossed."

"That's just great! I know you've been looking for ages."

"The Christmas letters are going well, too," she added. "I wrote another one this week for a woman in Zach's office. She kept thinking she had time and then realized she didn't, so it was a rush job."

"You might really be on to something, you know. A little sideline business every Christmas."

"You aren't upset with me about what I did, are you?" K.O. asked, returning to her apology. "You've been such a good friend, and I wouldn't do anything in the world to hurt you."

"Nah," LaVonne assured her, petting Phillip, who'd jumped into her lap. "If anyone's to blame it's that horrible man. As far as I'm concerned, he's unreliable." That said, she took another bite of the slice she'd been enjoying.

Wynn had devised a rather complicated plan of escape. On Friday afternoon he would leave his office at three-thirty and pick K.O. up on the corner of Blossom Street and Port Avenue. Because he didn't want to risk going inside and being seen by his father, she'd agreed to wait on the curb with her overnight bag.

K.O. was packed and ready long before the time they'd arranged. At three, her phone rang. Without checking caller ID, she knew it had to be her sister.

"I can't believe Dr. Wynn Jeffries is actually coming to the house," she said and gave a shrill cry of excitement. "You can't *imagine* how jealous my friends are."

"No one's supposed to know about this," K.O. reminded her.

"No one knows exactly when he'll be here, but I did mention it to a few close friends."

"Zelda! You promised."

"I know, I know. I'm sorry, but I couldn't keep this to myself. You just don't understand what an honor it is to have Dr. Jeffries in my home."

"But…"

"Don't worry, no one knows it's this weekend," Zelda told her.

"You're *sure?*"

"I swear, all right?"

It would be a nightmare if a few dozen of Zelda's closest friends just happened to drop by the house unannounced. Unfortunately, K.O. didn't have any choice but to believe her.

"How are the girls?" K.O. asked, hoping the twins were up to their usual antics. She didn't want Zoe and Zara to be on their best behavior. That would ruin all her plans.

"They're fine. Well, mostly fine. Healthwise, they're both getting over ear infections."

Oh, dear. "You might've told me this before!" K.O. cried. Her mind shifted into overdrive. If the girls were sick, it would throw everything off. Wynn would insist their behavior was affected by how they were feeling.

"They've been on antibiotics for the last two weeks," Zelda said, breaking into her thoughts. "The doctor explained how important it is to finish the medicine, and they only have a couple of doses left. I wrote it all down for you and Dr. Jeffries, so there's no need to worry."

"Fine," K.O. said, relieved. "Anything else you're not telling me?"

Her sister went silent for a moment. "I can't think of anything. I've got a list of instructions for you and the phone numbers where we can be reached. I do appreciate this, you know."

K.O. in turn appreciated the opportunity to spend this time with the twins—and to share the experience with Wynn. At least they'd be able to stop tiptoeing around the subject of the Free Child movement.

"We have a Christmas tree," Zelda murmured as if she were admitting to a weakness of character. "Zach felt we needed one, and when I spoke to Dr. Jeffries last Monday he didn't discourage it. So I gave in, although I'm still not sure it's such a good idea."

"You made the right choice," K.O. told her.

"I hope so."

K.O. noticed the clock on her microwave and was shocked to see that it was time to meet Wynn. "Oh, my goodness, I've got to go. I'll see you in about thirty minutes."

K.O. hung up the phone and hurried to put on her long wool coat, hat and scarf. Grabbing her purse and overnight bag, she rushed outside. Traffic was heavy, and it was already getting dark. She'd planned to be waiting at the curb so when Wynn pulled up, she could quickly hop inside his car. Then they'd be on their way, with no one the wiser.

No sooner had she stepped out of the building than she saw Max Jeffries walking toward her. His cheeks were ruddy, as if he'd been out for a long stroll.

"Well, hello there, Katherine," he said cheerfully. "How are you this fine cold day?"

"Ah..." She glanced furtively around. "I'm going to my sister's tonight," she said when he looked pointedly at her small suitcase.

"Wynn's away himself."

"Pure coincidence," she told him and realized how guilty she sounded.

Max chuckled. "Business trip, he said."

She nodded, moving slowly toward the nearby corner of Blossom and Port. She kept her gaze focused on the street, fearing she was about to give everything away.

"I'm healing well," Max told her conversationally. "I had a couple of rough days, but the pain is much better now."

"I'm glad to hear it."

"Yes, me, too. I never want to see that crazy cat woman again as long as I live."

It demanded restraint not to immediately defend her friend, but K.O. managed. "I see your memory's back," she said instead, all the while keeping a lookout for Wynn.

"Oh, yes, it returned within a day or two. In some ways," he sighed, "I wished it hadn't. Because now all I can think about is how that vicious feline latched on to my arm."

Not wanting to give Max an excuse to continue the conversation, K.O. threw him a vague smile.

"Have you ever seen so much blood in your life?" he said with remarkable enthusiasm.

"Uh, no," she murmured. Since it was her towels that had cleaned it up, she had to confess there'd been lots.

"My son seems to be quite taken with you," Max said next.

As badly as she wanted to urge Max to go about his business, K.O. couldn't ignore that particular comment. Not when Max dropped this little morsel at her feet—much as Martin had presented her with the catnip mouse. "He does? Really?"

Max nodded.

"He talks about me?"

"Hmm. It's more a question of what he doesn't say than what he does. He was always an intense child. As a youngster... Well, I'm sure you don't have time to go into that right now."

K.O. thought she could see Wynn's car. "I don't... I'm sorry."

"Take my word for it, Wynn's interested in you."

K.O. felt like dancing in the street. "I'm interested in him, too," she admitted.

"Good, good," Max said expansively. "Well, I'd better get back inside. Have a nice weekend."

"I will. Thank you." It did look like Wynn's car. His timing was perfect—or almost. She hoped that when he reached the curb, his father would be inside the building.

Just then the front doors opened and out stepped LaVonne. She froze in midstep when she saw Wynn's father. He froze, too.

K.O. watched as LaVonne's eyes narrowed. She couldn't see Max's face, but from LaVonne's reaction, she assumed he shared her resentment. They seemed unwilling to walk past each other, and both stood there, looking wildly in all directions except ahead. If it hadn't been so sad, it would've been laughable.

K.O. could see that it was definitely Wynn's car. He smiled when he saw her and started to ease toward the curb. At the same moment, he noticed his father and LaVonne and instantly pulled back, merging into traffic again. He drove straight past K.O.

Now LaVonne and Max were staring at each other. They still hadn't moved, and people had to walk around them as they stood in the middle of the sidewalk.

K.O. had to find a way to escape without being detected. As best as she could figure, Wynn had to drive around the block. With one-way streets and heavy traffic, it might take him ten minutes to get back to Blossom. If she hurried, she might catch him on Port Avenue or another side street and avoid letting Max see them together.

"I think my ride's here," she said, backing away and dragging her suitcase with her.

They ignored her.

"Bye," she said, waving her hand.

This, too, went without comment. "I'll see you both later," she said, rushing past them and down the sidewalk.

Again there was no response.

K.O. didn't dare look back. Blossom Street had never seemed so long. She rounded the corner and walked some distance down Port, waiting until she saw Wynn's car again. Raising her arm as if hailing a taxi, she managed to catch his attention.

Wynn pulled up to the curb, reached over and opened the passenger door. "That was a close call," he murmured as she climbed inside.

"You have no idea," she said, shaking her head.

"Is everything all right?" he asked.

"I don't know and, frankly, I don't want to stick around and find out."

Wynn chuckled. "I don't, either," he said, rejoining the stream of traffic.

They were off on what she hoped would be a grand adventure in the land of Z.

Fifteen

"This is Zoe," K.O. said as her niece wrapped one arm around her leg. After a half-hour of instructions, Zelda was finally out the door, on her way to meet Zach at the hotel. The twins stood like miniature statues, dressed in jean coveralls and red polka-dot shirts, with their hair in pigtails. They each stared up at Wynn.

"No, I'm Zara."

K.O. narrowed her eyes, unsure whether to believe the child. The twins were identical and seemed to derive great satisfaction from fooling people, especially their parents.

"Zoe," K.O. challenged. "Tell the truth."

"I'm hungry."

"It'll be dinnertime soon," K.O. promised.

Zoe—and she felt sure it *was* Zoe—glared up at her. "I'm hungry *now.* I want to eat *now.*" She punctuated her demand by stamping her foot. Her twin joined in, shouting that she, too, was hungry.

"I want dinner *now,*" Zara insisted.

Wynn smiled knowingly. "Children shouldn't be

forced to eat on a schedule. If they're hungry, we should feed them no matter what the clock says."

Until then, the girls had barely acknowledged Wynn. All of a sudden, he was their best friend. Both beamed brilliant smiles in his direction, then marched over and stood next to him, as though aligning themselves with his theories.

"What would you like for dinner?" he asked, squatting down so he was at eye level with them.

"Hot dogs," Zoe said, and Zara agreed. The two Yorkies, Zero and Zorro, seemed to approve, because they barked loudly and then scampered into the kitchen.

"I'll check the refrigerator," K.O. told him. Not long ago, Zelda hadn't allowed her daughters anywhere near hot dogs. She considered them unhealthy, low-quality fare that was full of nitrates and other preservatives. But nothing was off limits since Zelda had read *The Free Child* and become a convert.

"I'll help you look," Zara volunteered and tearing into the kitchen, threw open the refrigerator door and peered inside.

Not wanting to be left out, Zoe dragged over a kitchen chair and climbed on top. She yanked open the freezer and started tossing frozen food onto the floor. Zero and Zorro scrambled to get out of the way of flying frozen peas and fish.

"There aren't any hot dogs," K.O. said after a few minutes. "Let's choose something else." After all, it was only four o'clock and she was afraid that if the girls ate too early, they'd be hungry again later in the evening.

"I *want* a hot dog," Zara shouted.

"Me, too," Zoe chimed in, as though eating wieners was a matter of eternal significance.

Wynn stood in the kitchen doorway. "I can run to the store."

K.O. couldn't believe her ears. She hated to see him cater to the whims of Zoe and Zara, but far be it from her to object. If he was willing to go to those lengths to get the twins the meal they wanted, she'd let him do it.

"Isn't that nice of Dr. Jeffries?" K.O. asked her nieces.

Both girls ignored her and Wynn.

K.O. followed him into the other room, where Wynn retrieved his jacket from the hall closet. "I'll be back soon," he said.

"I'll put together a salad and—"

"Let the girls decide if they want a salad," Wynn interrupted. "Given the option, children will choose a well-balanced diet on their own. We as adults shouldn't be making these decisions for them."

K.O. had broken down and bought a copy of *The Free Child* at a small bookstore that had recently opened on Blossom Street. She'd skimmed it last night, so she knew this advice was in the book, stated in exactly those words. She might not approve, but for tonight she was determined to follow his lead. So she kept her mouth shut. Not that it was easy.

While the girls were occupied, he planted a gentle kiss on her lips, smiled and then was out the door.

It was now three days since they'd been able to spend time together. With that one short kiss, a lovely warmth spread through her. She closed the door after him and was leaning against it when she noticed that the twins had turned to stare at her. "While we're waiting for Wynn to get back, would you like me to read you a story?" she asked. The salad discussion could wait.

The girls readily agreed, and the three of them settled on the sofa. She was only a few pages into the book when both Zoe and Zara slumped over, asleep. Before Zelda left, she'd said the twins had been awake since five that morning, excited about Katherine's visit. Apparently they no longer took naps. This was something else Wynn had advised. Children would sleep when they needed to, according to him. Regimented naptimes stifled children's ability to understand their internal clocks. Well, Zoe's and Zara's clocks had obviously wound down—and K.O. was grateful.

The quiet was so blissful that she leaned her head back and rested her own eyes. The tranquility didn't last long, however. In less than fifteen minutes, Wynn was back from the store, carrying a plastic bag with wieners and fresh buns. The dogs barked frantically as he entered the house, waking both children.

"Here they are," he announced as if he brandished an Olympic gold medal.

Zara yawned. "I'm not hungry anymore."

"Me, neither," Zoe added.

It probably wasn't the most tactful thing to do, but K.O. smiled triumphantly.

"That's okay. We can wait until later," Wynn said, completely unfazed.

He really was good with the girls and seemed to enjoy spending time with them. While K.O. set the kitchen table and cleared away the clutter that had accumulated everywhere, Wynn sat down and talked to the twins. The girls showed him the Christmas tree and the stockings that hung over the fireplace and the nativity scene set up on the formal dining room table.

K.O. heard Zoe mention her imaginary horse named

Blackie. Not to be outdone, Zara declared that *her* imaginary horse was named Brownie. Wynn listened to them seriously and even scooted over to make room for the horses on the sofa. K.O. was grateful that Wynn was sharing responsibility for the girls, whose constant demands quickly drained her.

"I'm hungry now," Zoe informed them half an hour later.

"I'll start the hot dogs," K.O. said, ready for dinner herself.

"I want pancakes."

"With syrup," Zara said. Zoe nodded.

K.O. looked at Wynn, who shrugged as if it was no big deal.

"Then pancakes it is," K.O. agreed. She'd let him cope with the sugar high. For the next ten minutes she was busy mixing batter and frying the pancakes. The twins wanted chocolate syrup and strawberry jam on top, with bananas and granola. Actually, it didn't taste nearly as bad as K.O. had feared.

According to her sister's instructions, the girls were to be given their medication with meals. After dinner, Zoe and Zara climbed down from their chairs. When K.O. asked them to take their plates to the sink, they complied without an argument or even a complaint.

"Time for your medicine," K.O. told them next. She removed two small bottles filled with pink antibiotic from the refrigerator.

The two girls raced about the kitchen, shrieking, with the dogs yapping at their heels. They seemed incapable of standing still.

"Girls," K.O. ordered sternly. "Take your medicine

and then you can run around." The way they were dashing back and forth, it was difficult to see who was who.

Zara skidded to a stop and dutifully opened her mouth. Carefully measuring out the liquid, K.O. filled the spoon and popped it into the child's mouth. Immediately afterward, the twins took off in a frenzied race around the kitchen table.

"Zoe," K.O. said, holding the second bottle and a clean spoon and waiting for the mayhem to die down so she could dispense the correct dose to her other niece. "Your turn."

The twin appeared in front of her, mouth open. K.O. poured medicine onto the spoon. About to give it to Zoe, she hesitated. "You're not Zoe. You're Zara."

"I'm Zoe," she insisted. Although the girls were identical, K.O. could usually tell one from the other, partly by their personalities. Zara had the stronger, more dominant nature. "Are you sure?" she asked.

The little girl nodded vigorously. Uncertain, K.O. reluctantly gave her the medication. The twins continued to chase each other about the kitchen, weaving their way around and between Wynn and K.O. The dogs dashed after them, yapping madly.

Wynn asked, "Is everything all right?"

K.O. still held the empty spoon. "I have a horrible feeling I just gave two doses to the same girl."

"You can trust the twins to tell you the truth," Wynn pronounced. "Children instinctively know when it's important to tell the truth."

"Really?" K.O. couldn't help worrying.

"Of course. It's in the book," Wynn said as if quoting Scripture.

"You didn't feed Blackie and Brownie," Zara cried when K.O. tossed the leftover pancakes in the garbage.

"Then we must." Wynn proceeded to remove the cold pancakes and tear them into small pieces. Zero and Zorro leaped off the ground in an effort to snatch up the leftovers. Zoe and Zara sat on the floor and fed the dogs and supposedly their imaginary pets, as well.

The yapping dogs were giving K.O. a headache. "How about if I turn on the television," she suggested, shouting to be heard above the racket made by the girls and the dogs.

The twins hollered their approval, but the show that flashed onto the screen was a Christmas cartoon featuring none other than Santa himself. Jolly old soul that he was, Santa laughed and loaded his sleigh while the girls watched with rapt attention. Knowing how her sister felt, K.O. figured this was probably the first time they'd seen Santa all season. K.O. glanced at Wynn, who was frowning back.

"Let's see what else is on," K.O. said quickly.

"I want to watch Santa," Zoe shouted.

"Me, too," Zara muttered.

Wynn sat on the sofa between them and wrapped his arms around their small shoulders. "This show is about a character called Santa Claus," he said in a solicitous voice.

Both girls were far too involved in the program to be easily distracted by adult conversation.

"Sometimes mommies and daddies like to make believe, and while they don't mean to lie, they can mislead their children," he went on.

Zoe briefly tore her gaze away from the television screen. "Like Santa, you mean?"

Wynn smiled. "Like Santa," he agreed.

"We know he's not real," Zoe informed them with all the wisdom of a five-year-old.

"Santa is really Mommy and Daddy," Zara explained. "*Everyone* knows that."

"They do?"

Both girls nodded.

Zoe's eyes turned serious. "We heard Mommy and Daddy fighting about Santa and we almost told them it doesn't matter 'cause we already know."

"We like getting gifts from him, though," Zara told them.

"Yeah, I like Santa," Zoe added.

"But he's not real," Wynn said, sounding perfectly logical.

"Mommy's real," Zara argued. "And Daddy, too."

"Yes, but..." Wynn seemed determined to argue further, but stopped when he happened to glance at K.O. He held her gaze a moment before looking away.

K.O. did her best to keep quiet, but apparently Wynn realized how difficult that was, because he clammed up fast enough.

The next time she looked at the twins, Zara had slumped over to one side, eyes drooping. K.O. gently shook the little girl's shoulders but Zara didn't respond. Still fearing she might have given one twin a double dose of the antibiotic, she knelt down in front of the other child.

"Zoe," she asked, struggling to keep the panic out of her voice. "Did you get your medicine or did Zara swallow both doses?"

Zoe grinned and pantomimed zipping her mouth closed.

"Zoe," K.O. said again. "This is important. We can't play games when medicine is involved." So much for Wynn's theory that children instinctively knew when it was necessary to tell the truth.

"Zara likes the taste better'n me."

"Did you take your medicine or did Zara take it for you?" Wynn asked.

Zoe smiled and shook her head, indicating that she wasn't telling.

Zara snored, punctuating the conversation.

"Did you or did you not take your medicine?" Wynn demanded, nearly yelling.

Tears welled in Zoe's eyes. She buried her face in K.O.'s lap and refused to answer Wynn.

"This isn't a joke," he muttered, clearly losing his patience with the twins.

"Zoe," K.O. cautioned. "You heard Dr. Jeffries. It's important for us to know if you took your medication."

The little girl raised her head, then slowly nodded. "It tastes bad, but I swallowed it all down."

"Good." Relief flooded K.O. "Thank you for telling the truth."

"I don't like your friend," she said, sticking her tongue out at Wynn. "He yells."

"I only yelled because…you made me," Wynn countered. He marched to the far side of the room, and K.O. reflected that he didn't sound so calm and reasonable anymore.

"Why don't we all play a game?" she suggested.

Zara raised her head sleepily from the sofa edge. "Can we play Old Maid?" she asked, yawning.

"I want to play Candyland," Zoe mumbled.

"Why don't we play both?" K.O. said, and they did.

In fact, they played for two hours straight, watched television and then drank hot chocolate.

"Shall we take a bath now?" K.O. asked, hoping that would tire the girls out enough to want to go to bed. She didn't know where they got their stamina, but her own was fading rapidly.

The twins were eager to do something altogether different and instantly raced out of the room.

Wynn looked like he could use a break—and he hadn't even seen them at their most challenging. All in all, the girls were exhibiting good behavior, or what passed for good in the regime of the Free Child.

"I'll run the bath water," K.O. told Wynn as he gathered up the cards and game pieces. Had she been on her own, K.O. would have insisted the twins pick up after themselves.

While the girls were occupied in their bedroom, she put on a Christmas CD she particularly liked and started the bath. When she glanced into the living room, she saw Wynn collapsed on the sofa, legs stretched out.

"It hasn't been so bad," he said, as though that was proof his theories were working well. "As soon as the twins are down, we can talk," he murmured, "about us…"

K.O. wasn't ready for that, feeling he should spend more time with the girls. She felt honor-bound to remind Wynn of what he'd written in his book. "Didn't you say that children know when they need sleep and we as adults should trust them to set their own schedules?"

He seemed about to argue with her, but then abruptly sat up and pointed across the room. "What's that?"

A naked dog strolled into the living room. Rather, a hairless dog.

"Zero? Zorro?" K.O. asked. "Oh, my goodness!" She dashed into the bathroom to discover Zara sitting on the floor with Wynn's electric shaver. A pile of brown-and-black dog hair littered the area.

"What happened?" Wynn cried, hard on her heels. His mouth fell open when he saw the girls intent on their task. They'd gone through his toiletries, which were spread across the countertop next to the sink. K.O. realized that the hum of the shaver had been concealed by the melodious strains of "Silent Night." "What are you doing?"

"We're giving haircuts," Zara announced. "Do you want one?"

Sixteen

Two hours later, at ten-thirty, both Zoe and Zara were in their beds and asleep. This was no small accomplishment. After half a dozen stories, the girls were finally down for the night. K.O. tiptoed out of the room and as quietly as possible closed the door. Wynn was just ahead of her and looked as exhausted as she felt.

Zero regarded K.O. forlornly from the hallway. The poor dog had been almost completely shaved. He stared up at her, hairless and shivering. Zorro still had half his hair. The Yorkshire terrier's left side had been sheared before K.O. managed to snatch the razor out of her niece's hand. Last winter Zelda had knit tiny dog sweaters, which K.O. found, and with Wynn's help slipped over the two terriers. At least they'd be warm, although neither dog seemed especially grateful.

K.O. sank down on the sofa beside Wynn, with the dogs nestled at their feet. Breathing out a long, deep sigh, she gazed up at the ceiling. Wynn was curiously quiet.

"I feel like going to bed myself," she murmured when she'd recovered enough energy to speak.

"What time are your sister and brother-in-law supposed to return?" Wynn asked with what seemed to require an extraordinary amount of effort.

"Zelda said they should be home by three."

"That late?"

K.O. couldn't keep the grin off her face. It was just as she'd hoped. She wouldn't have to argue about the problem with his Free Child theories, since he'd been able to witness for himself the havoc they caused.

Straightening, K.O. suggested they listen to some more music.

"That won't disturb them, will it?" he asked when she got up to put on another CD. Evidently he had no interest in anything that might wake the girls.

"I should hope not." She found the Christmas CD she'd given to Zelda two years earlier, and inserted it in the player. It featured a number of pop artists. Smiling over at Wynn, she lowered the volume. John Denver's voice reached softly into the room, singing "Joy to the World."

Wynn turned off the floor lamp, so the only illumination came from the Christmas-tree lights. The mood was cheerful and yet relaxed.

For the first time in days they were alone. The incident with Wynn's father and the demands of the twins were the last things on K.O.'s mind.

Wynn placed his arm across the back of the sofa and she sat close to him, resting her head against his shoulder. All they needed now was a glass of wine and a kiss or two. Romance swirled through the room with the music and Christmas lights. Wynn must've felt it, too, because he turned her in his arms. K.O. started to close her eyes, anticipating his kiss, when she caught a movement from the corner of her eye.

She gasped.

A mouse…a rodent ran across the floor.

Instantly alarmed, K.O. jerked away from Wynn.

He bolted upright. “What is it?”

“A mouse.” She hated mice. “There,” she cried, covering her mouth to stifle a scream. She pointed as the rodent scampered under the Christmas tree.

Wynn leaped to his feet. “I see it.”

Apparently so did Zero, because he let out a yelp and headed right for the tree. Zorro followed.

K.O. brought both feet onto the sofa and hugged her knees. It was completely unreasonable—and so clichéd—to be terrified of a little mouse. But she was. While logic told her a mouse was harmless, that knowledge didn’t help.

“You have to get it out of here,” she whimpered as panic set in.

“I’ll catch it,” he shouted and dived under the Christmas tree, toppling it. The tree slammed against the floor, shattering several bulbs. Ornaments rolled in all directions. The dogs ran for cover. Fortunately the tree was still plugged in because it offered what little light was available.

Unable to watch, K.O. hid her eyes. She wondered what Wynn would do if he did manage to corner the rodent. The thought of him killing it right there in her sister’s living room was intolerable.

“Don’t kill it,” she insisted and removed her hands from her eyes to find Wynn on his hands and knees, staring at her.

The mouse darted across the floor and raced under the sofa, where K.O. just happened to be sitting.

Zero and Zorro ran after it, yelping frantically.

K.O. screeched and scrambled to a standing position on the sofa. Not knowing what else to do, she bounced from one cushion to the other.

Zero had buried his nose as far as it would go under the sofa. Zorro dashed back and forth on the carpet. As hard as she tried, K.O. couldn't keep still and began hopping up and down, crying out in abject terror. She didn't care if she woke the girls or not, there was a mouse directly beneath her feet…somewhere. For all she knew, it could have crawled into the sofa itself.

That thought made her jump from the middle of the sofa, over the armrest and onto the floor, narrowly missing Zero. The lamp fell when she landed, but she was able to catch it seconds before it crashed to the floor. As she righted the lamp, she flipped it on, provided a welcome circle of light.

Meanwhile, Barry Manilow crooned out "The Twelve Days of Christmas."

Still on all fours, Wynn crept across the carpet to the sofa, which he overturned. As it pitched onto its back, the mouse shot out.

Directly at K.O.

She screamed.

Zero yelped.

Zorro tore fearlessly after it.

K.O. screamed again and grabbed a basket in which Zelda kept her knitting. She emptied the basket and, more by instinct than anything else, flung it over the mouse, trapping him.

Wynn sat up with a shocked look. "You got him!"

Both dogs stood guard by the basket, sniffing at the edges. Zero scratched the carpet.

Zelda's yarn and needles were a tangled mess on the floor but seemed intact. Breathless, K.O. stared at the basket, not knowing what to do next. "It had a brown tail," she commented.

Wynn nodded. "I noticed that, too."

"I've never seen a mouse with a brown tail before."

"It's an African brown-tailed mouse," he said, sounding knowledgeable. "I saw a documentary on them."

"African mice are here in the States?" She wondered if Animal Control knew about this.

He nodded again. "So I gather."

"What do we do now?" Because Wynn seemed to know more about this sort of thing, she looked to him for the answer.

"Kill it," he said without a qualm.

Zero and Zorro obviously agreed, because they both growled and clawed at the carpet, asking for the opportunity to do it themselves.

"No way!" K.O. objected. She couldn't allow him to kill it. The terriers, either. Although mice terrified her, K.O. couldn't bear to hurt any of God's creatures. "All I want you to do is get that brown-tailed mouse out of here." As soon as Zelda returned, K.O. planned to suggest she call a pest control company to inspect the entire house. Although, if there were other mice around, she didn't want to know it....

"All right," Wynn muttered. "I'll take it outside and release it."

He got a newspaper and knelt down next to the dogs. Carefully, inch by inch, he slid the paper beneath the upended basket. When he'd finished that, he stood and carried the whole thing to the front door. Zero and Zorro followed, leaping up on their hind legs and barking wildly.

K.O. hurried to open first the door and then the screen. The cold air felt good against her heated face.

Wynn stepped onto the porch while K.O. held back the dogs by closing the screen door. They both objected strenuously and braced their front paws against the door, watching Wynn's every movement.

K.O. turned her back as Wynn released the African brown-tailed mouse into the great unknown. She wished the critter a pleasant life outside.

"Is it gone?" she asked when Wynn came back into the house, careful to keep Zero and Zorro from escaping and racing after the varmint.

"It's gone, and I didn't even need to touch it," he assured her. He closed the door.

K.O. smiled up at him. "My hero," she whispered.

Wynn playfully flexed his muscles. "Anything else I can do for you, my fair damsel?"

Looping her arms around his neck, K.O. backed him up against the front door and rewarded him with a warm, moist kiss. Wynn wrapped his arms about her waist and half lifted her from the carpet.

"You *are* my hero," she whispered between kisses. "You saved me from that killer mouse."

"The African brown-tailed killer rat."

"It was a *rat?*"

"A small one," he murmured, and kissed her again before she could ask more questions.

"A baby rat?" That meant there must be parents around and possibly siblings, perhaps any number of other little rats. "What makes you think it was a rat?" she demanded, fast losing interest in kissing.

"He was fat. But perhaps he was just a fat mouse."

"Ah…"

"You're still grateful?"

"Very grateful, but—"

He kissed her again, then abruptly broke off the kiss. His eyes seemed to focus on something across the room.

K.O. tensed, afraid he'd seen another mouse. Or rat. Or rodent of some description.

It took genuine courage to glance over her shoulder, but she did it anyway. Fortunately she didn't see anything—other than an overturned Christmas tree, scattered furniture and general chaos brought about by the Great Brown-Tailed Mouse Hunt.

"The fishbowl has blue water," he said.

"Blue water?" K.O. dropped her arms and stared at the counter between the kitchen and the living room, where the fishbowl sat. Sure enough, the water was a deep blue.

Wynn walked across the room.

Before K.O. could ask what he was doing, Wynn pushed up his sweater sleeve and thrust his hand into the water. "Just as I thought," he muttered, retrieving a gold pen.

After she'd found the twins with Wynn's electric shaver, she realized, they'd opened his overnight case.

"This is a gold fountain pen," he told her, holding up the dripping pen. "As it happens, this is a *valuable* gold fountain pen."

"With blue ink," K.O. added. She didn't think it could be too valuable, since it was leaking.

She picked up the bowl with both hands and carried it

into the kitchen, setting it in the sink. Scooping out the two goldfish, she put them in a temporary home—a coffee cup full of fresh, clean water—and refilled the bowl.

Wynn was pacing the kitchen floor behind her.

"Does your book say anything about situations like this?" she couldn't resist asking.

He glared at her and apparently that was all the answer he intended to give.

"Aunt Katherine?" one of the twins shouted. "Come quick." K.O. heard unmistakable panic in the little girl's voice.

Soon the two girls were both crying out.

Hurrying into the bedroom with Wynn right behind her, K.O. found Zoe and Zara weeping loudly.

"What's wrong?" she asked.

"Freddy's gone," Zoe wailed.

"Freddy?" she repeated. "Who's Freddy?"

"Our hamster," Zoe explained, pointing at what K.O. now recognized as a cage against the far wall. "He must've figured out how to open his cage."

A chill went through her. "Does Freddy have a brown tail and happen to be a little chubby?" she asked the girls.

Hope filled their eyes as they nodded eagerly.

K.O. scowled at Wynn. African brown-tailed mouse, indeed.

Seventeen

Thankfully, Wynn rescued poor Freddy, who was discovered shivering in a corner of the porch. The girls were relieved to have their hamster back, and neither mentioned the close call Freddy had encountered with certain death. After calming the twins, it took K.O. and Wynn an hour to clean up the living room. By then, they were both cranky and tired.

Saturday morning, Zoe and Zara decided on wieners for breakfast. Knowing Wynn would approve, K.O. cooked the hot dogs he'd purchased the night before. However, the unaccustomed meat didn't settle well in Zoe's tummy and she threw up on her breakfast plate. Zara insisted that all she wanted was orange juice poured over dry cereal. So that was what she got.

For the rest of the morning, Wynn remained pensive and remote. He helped her with the children but didn't want to talk. In fact, he seemed more than eager to get back to Blossom Street. When Zelda and Zach showed up that afternoon, he couldn't quite hide his relief. The twins hugged K.O. goodbye and Wynn, too.

While Wynn loaded the car, K.O. talked to Zelda

about holiday plans. Zelda asked her to join the family for Christmas Eve dinner and church, but not Christmas Day, which they'd be spending with Zach's parents. K.O. didn't mind. She'd invite LaVonne to dinner at her place. Maybe she'd include Wynn and his father, too, despite the disastrous conclusion of the last social event she'd hosted for this same group. Still, when she had the chance, she'd discuss it with Wynn.

On the drive home, Wynn seemed especially quiet.

"The girls are a handful, aren't they?" she asked, hoping to start a conversation.

He nodded.

She smiled to herself, remembering Wynn's expression when Zoe announced that their hamster had escaped. Despite his reproachful silence, she laughed. "I promise not to mention that rare African brown-tailed mouse again, but I have to tell LaVonne."

"I never said it was rare."

"Oh, sorry, I thought you had." One look told her Wynn wasn't amused. "Come on, Wynn," she said, as they merged with the freeway traffic. "You have to admit it was a little ridiculous."

He didn't appear to be in the mood to admit anything. "Are you happy?" he asked.

"What do you mean?"

"You proved your point, didn't you?"

So that was the problem. "If you're referring to how the girls behaved then, yes, I suppose I did."

"You claimed that after your sister read my book, they changed into undisciplined hellions."

"Well…" Wasn't it obvious? "They're twins," she said, trying to sound conciliatory, "and as such they've always needed a lot of attention. Some of what happened on Friday evening might have happened without the influence of your child-rearing theories. Freddy would've escaped whether Zelda read your book or not."

"Very funny."

"I wasn't trying to be funny. Frankly, rushing to the store to buy hot dogs because that's what the girls wanted for dinner is over the top, in my opinion. I feel it teaches them to expect that their every whim must be met."

"I beg to differ. My getting the dinner they wanted showed them that I cared about their likes and dislikes."

"Two hours of sitting on the floor playing Old Maid said the same thing," she inserted.

"I let you put them to bed even though they clearly weren't ready for sleep."

"I beg to differ," she said, a bit more forcefully than she'd intended. "Zoe and Zara were both yawning when they came out of the bath. I asked them if they wanted to go to bed."

"What you asked," he said stiffly, "was if they were *ready* for bed."

"And the difference is?"

"Two hours of storytime while they wore us both out."

"What would you have done?" she asked.

His gaze didn't waver from the road. "I would've allowed them to play quietly in their room until they'd tired themselves out."

Quietly? He had to be joking. Wynn seemed to have conveniently forgotten that during the short time they were on their own, Zoe and Zara had gotten into his overnight bag. Thanks to their creative use of his personal things, the goldfish now had a bluish tint. The two

Yorkies were nearly hairless. She could argue that because the girls considered themselves *free,* they didn't see anything wrong with opening his bag. The lack of boundaries created confusion and misunderstanding.

"Twins are not the norm," he challenged. "They encourage ill behavior in each other."

"However, before Zelda read your book, they were reasonably well-behaved children."

"Is that a fact?" He sounded as though he didn't believe her.

"Yes," she said swiftly. "Zoe and Zara were happy and respectful and kind. Some would even go so far as to say they were well-adjusted. Now they constantly demand their own way. They're unreasonable, selfish and difficult." She was only getting started and dragged in another breath. "Furthermore, it used to be a joy to spend time with them and now it's a chore. And if you must know, I blame you and that blasted book of yours." There, she'd said it.

A stark silence followed.

"You don't mince words, do you?"

"No..."

"I respect that. I wholeheartedly disagree, but I respect your right to state your opinion."

The tension in the car had just increased by about a thousand degrees.

"After this weekend, you still disagree?" She was astonished he'd actually said that, but then she supposed his ego was on the line.

"I'm not interested in arguing with you, Katherine."

She didn't want to argue with him, either. Still, she'd hoped the twins would convince him that while his theories might look good on paper, in reality they didn't work.

After Wynn exited the freeway, it was only a few short blocks to Blossom Street and the parking garage beneath their building. Wynn pulled into his assigned slot and turned off the engine.

Neither moved.

K.O. feared that the minute she opened the car door, it would be over, and she didn't want their relationship to end, not like this. Not now, with Christmas only nine days away.

She tried again. "I know we don't see eye to eye on everything—"

"No, we don't," he interrupted. "In many cases, it doesn't matter, but when it comes to my work, my livelihood, it does. Not only do you not accept my theories, you think they're ludicrous."

She opened her mouth to defend herself, then realized he was right. That was exactly what she thought.

"You've seen evidence that appears to contradict them and, therefore, you discount the years of research I've done in my field. The fact is, you don't respect my work."

Feeling wretched, she hung her head.

"I expected there to be areas in which we disagree, Katherine, but this is more than I can deal with. I'm sorry, but I think it would be best if we didn't see each other again."

If that was truly how he felt, then there was nothing left to say.

"I appreciate that you've been honest with me," he continued. "I'm sorry, Katherine—I know we both would've liked this to work, but we have too many differences."

She made an effort to smile. If she thought arguing with him would do any good, she would have. But the hard set of his jaw told her no amount of reasoning would reach him now. "Thank you for everything. Really, I mean that. You've made this Christmas the best."

He gave her a sad smile.

"Would it be all right—would you mind if I gave you a hug?" she asked. "To say goodbye?"

He stared at her for the longest moment, then slowly shook his head. "That wouldn't be a good idea," he whispered, opening the car door.

By the time K.O. was out of the vehicle, he'd already retrieved her overnight bag from the trunk.

She waited, but it soon became apparent that he had no intention of taking the elevator with her. It seemed he'd had about as much of her company as he could stand.

She stepped into the elevator with her bag and turned around. Before the doors closed, she saw Wynn leaning against the side of his car with his head down, looking dejected. K.O. understood the feeling.

It had been such a promising relationship. She'd never felt this drawn to a man, this attracted. If only she'd been able to keep her mouth shut—but, oh, no, not her. She'd wanted to prove her point, show him the error of his ways. She still believed he was wrong—well, mostly wrong—but now she felt petty and mean.

When the elevator stopped at the first floor, the doors slid open and K.O. got out. The first thing she did was collect her mail and her newspapers. She eyed the elevator, wondering if she'd ever see Wynn again, other than merely in passing, which would be painfully unavoidable.

After unpacking her overnight case and sorting

through the mail, none of which interested her, she walked across the hall, hoping to talk to LaVonne.

Even after several long rings, LaVonne didn't answer her door. Perhaps she was doing errands.

Just as K.O. was about to walk away, her neighbor opened the door just a crack and peered out.

"LaVonne, it's me."

"Oh, hi," she said.

"Can I come in?" K.O. asked, wondering why La-Vonne didn't immediately invite her inside. She'd never hesitated to ask her in before.

"Ah…now isn't really a good time."

"Oh." That was puzzling.

"How about tomorrow?" LaVonne suggested.

"Sure." K.O. nodded. "Is Tom back?" she asked.

"Tom?"

"Your cat."

"Oh, oh…that Tom. Yes, he came home this morning."

K.O. was pleased to hear that. She dredged up a smile. "I'll talk to you tomorrow, then."

"Yes," she agreed. "Tomorrow."

K.O. started across the hall, then abruptly turned back. "You might care to know that the Raisin Bran got it all wrong."

"I beg your pardon?" LaVonne asked, narrowing her gaze.

"I think you might've read the kitty litter wrong, too. But then again, that particular box accurately describes my love life."

LaVonne opened the door a fraction of an inch wider. "Do you mean to tell me you're no longer seeing Wynn?"

K.O. nodded. "Apparently we were both wrong in thinking Wynn was the man for me."

"He is," LaVonne said confidently.

K.O. sighed. "I wish he was. I genuinely like Wynn. When I first discovered he was the author of that loony book my sister read…" Realizing what she'd just said, K.O. began again. "When I discovered he wrote the book she'd read, I had my doubts."

"It *is* a loony book," LaVonne said.

"I should never have told him how I felt."

"You were honest."

"Yes, but I was rude and hurtful, too." She shook her head mournfully. "We disagree on just about every aspect of child-rearing. He doesn't want to see me again and I don't blame him."

LaVonne stared at her for an intense moment. "You're falling in love with him."

"No, I'm not," she said, hoping to make light of her feelings, but her neighbor was right. K.O. had known it the minute Wynn dived under the Christmas tree to save her from the not-so-rare African brown-tailed mouse. The minute he'd waved down the horse-drawn carriage and covered her knees with a lap robe and slipped his arm around her shoulders.

"Don't try to deny it," LaVonne said. "I don't really know what I saw in that Raisin Bran. Probably just raisins. But all along I've felt that Wynn's the man for you."

"I wish that was true," she said as she turned to go home. "But it's not."

As she opened her own door, she heard LaVonne talking. When she glanced back, she could hear her in a heated conversation with someone inside the condo.

Unfortunately LaVonne was blocking the doorway, so K.O. couldn't see who it was.

"LaVonne?"

The door opened wider and out stepped Max Jeffries. "Hello, Katherine," he greeted her, grinning from ear to ear.

K.O. looked at her neighbor and then at Wynn's father. The last she'd heard, Max was planning to sue LaVonne for everything she had. Somehow, in the past twenty-four hours, he'd changed his mind.

"Max?" she said in an incredulous voice.

He grinned boyishly and placed his arm around LaVonne's shoulders.

"You see," LaVonne said, blushing a fetching shade of red. "My psychic talents might be limited, but you're more talented than you knew."

Eighteen

K.O. was depressed. Even the fact that she'd been hired by Apple Blossom Books as their new publicist hadn't been enough to raise her spirits. She was scheduled to start work the day after New Year's and should've been thrilled. She was, only…nothing felt right without Wynn.

It was Christmas Eve and it should have been one of the happiest days of the year, but she felt like staying in bed. Her sister and family were expecting her later that afternoon, so K.O. knew she couldn't mope around the condo all day. She had things to do, food to buy, gifts to wrap, and she'd better get moving.

Putting on her coat and gloves, she walked out of her condo wearing a smile. She refused to let anyone know she was suffering from a broken heart.

"Katherine," LaVonne called the instant she saw her. She stood at the lobby mailbox as if she'd been there for hours, just waiting for K.O. "Merry Christmas!"

"Merry Christmas," K.O. returned a little too brightly. She managed a smile and with her shoulders squared, made her way to the door.

"Do you have any plans for Christmas?" her neighbor called after her.

K.O.'s mouth hurt from holding that smile for so long. She nodded. "I'm joining Zelda, Zach and the girls this evening, and then I thought I'd spend a quiet Christmas by myself." Needless to say, she hadn't issued any invitations, and she'd hardly seen LaVonne in days. Tomorrow she'd cook for herself. While doing errands this morning, she planned to purchase a small—very small—turkey. She refused to mope and feel lonely, not on Christmas Day.

"Have dinner with me," LaVonne said. "It'll just be me and the boys."

When K.O. hesitated, she added, "Tom, Phillip and Martin would love to see you. I'm cooking a turkey and all the fixings, and I'd be grateful for the company."

"Are you sure?"

"Of course I'm sure!"

K.O. didn't take long to consider her friend's invitation. "I'd love to, then. What would you like me to bring?"

"Dessert," LaVonne said promptly. "Something yummy and special for Christmas."

"All right." They agreed on a time and K.O. left, feeling better than she had in days. Just as she was about to step outside, she turned back.

"How's Max?" she asked, knowing her neighbor was on good terms with Wynn's father. Exactly how good those terms were remained to be seen. She wondered fleetingly what the Jeffrieses were doing for Christmas, then decided it was none of her business. Still, the afternoon K.O. had found Max in LaVonne's condo, she'd been shocked to say the least. Their brief conversation the following day hadn't been too enlightening but maybe over Christmas dinner LaVonne would tell her what had happened—and what was happening now.

Flustered, LaVonne lowered her eyes as she sorted through a stack of mail that seemed to be mostly Christmas cards. "He's completely recovered. And," she whispered, "he's apologized to Tom."

A sense of pleasure shot through K.O. at this…and at the way LaVonne blushed. Apparently this was one romance that held promise. Her own had fizzled out fast enough. She'd come to truly like Wynn. More than like… At the thought of him, an aching sensation pressed down on her. In retrospect, she wished she'd handled the situation differently. Because she couldn't resist, she had to ask, "Have you seen Wynn?"

Her friend nodded but the look in LaVonne's eyes told K.O. everything she dreaded.

"He's still angry, isn't he?"

LaVonne gave her a sad smile. "I'm sure everything will work out. I know what I saw in that Raisin Bran." She attempted a laugh.

"When you see him again, tell him…" She paused. "Tell him," she started again, then gave up. Wynn had made his feelings clear. He'd told her it would be best if they didn't see each other again, and he'd meant it. Nine days with no word told her he wasn't changing his mind. Well, she had her pride, too.

"What would you like me to tell him?" LaVonne asked.

"Nothing. It's not important."

"You could write him a letter," LaVonne suggested.

"Perhaps I will," K.O. said on her way out the door, but she knew she wouldn't. It was over.

Blossom Street seemed more alive than at any other time she could remember. A group of carolers performed at the corner, songbooks in their hands. An elderly gentleman rang a bell for charity outside the French Café, which was crowded with customers. Seeing how busy the place was, K.O. decided to purchase her Christmas dessert now, before they completely sold out.

After adding a donation to the pot as she entered the café, she stood in a long line. When her turn finally came to order, she saw that one of the bakers was helping at the counter. K.O. knew Alix Townsend or, at least, she'd talked to her often enough to know her by name.

"Merry Christmas, K.O.," Alix said.

"Merry Christmas to you, too." K.O. surveyed the sweet delicacies behind the glass counter. "I need something that says Christmas," she murmured. The decorated cookies were festive but didn't seem quite right. A pumpkin pie would work, but it wasn't really special.

"How about a small Bûche de Noël," Alix said. "It's a traditional French dessert—a fancy cake decorated with mocha cream frosting and shaped to look like a Yule log. I baked it myself from a special recipe of the owner's."

"Bûche de Noël," K.O. repeated. It sounded perfect.

"They're going fast," Alix pointed out.

"Sold," K.O. said as the young woman went to collect one from the refrigerated case. It was then that K.O. noticed Alix's engagement ring.

"Will there be anything else?" Alix asked, setting the pink box on the counter and tying it with string.

"That diamond's new, isn't it?"

Grinning, Alix examined her ring finger. "I got it last week. Jordan couldn't wait to give it to me."

"Congratulations," K.O. told her. "When's the wedding?"

Alix looked down at the diamond as if she could hardly take her eyes off it. "June."

"That's fabulous."

"I'm already talking to Susannah Nelson—she owns the flower shop across the street. Jacqueline, my friend, insists we hold the reception at the Country Club. If it was up to me, Jordan and I would just elope, but his family would never stand for that." She shrugged in a resigned way. "I love Jordan, and I don't care what I have to do, as long as I get to be his wife."

The words echoed in K.O.'s heart as she walked out of the French Café with a final "Merry Christmas." She didn't know Alix Townsend all that well, but she liked her. Alix was entirely without pretense. No one need doubt how she felt about any particular subject; she spoke her mind in a straightforward manner that left nothing to speculation.

K.O. passed Susannah's Garden, the flower shop, on her way to the bank. The owner and her husband stood out front, wishing everyone a Merry Christmas. As K.O. walked past, Susannah handed her a sprig of holly with bright red berries.

"Thank you—this is so nice," K.O. said, tucking the holly in her coat pocket. She loved the flower shop and the beauty it brought to the street.

"I want to let the neighborhood know how much I appreciate the support. I've only been in business since September and everyone's been so helpful."

"Here, have a cup of hot cider." Susannah's husband

was handing out plastic cups from a small table set up beside him. "I'm Joe," he said.

"Hello, Joe. I'm Katherine O'Connor."

Susannah slid one arm around her husband's waist and gazed up at him with such adoration it was painful for K.O. to watch. Everywhere she turned, people were happy and in love. A knot formed in her throat. Putting on a happy, carefree face was getting harder by the minute.

Just then the door to A Good Yarn opened and out came Lydia Goetz and a man K.O. assumed must be her husband. They were accompanied by a young boy, obviously their son. Lydia paused when she saw K.O.

Lydia was well-known on the street.

"Were you planning to stop in here?" she asked, and cast a quick glance at her husband. "Brad convinced me to close early today. I already sent my sister home, but if you need yarn, I'd be happy to get it for you. In fact, you could even pay me later." She looked at her husband again, as if to make sure he didn't object to the delay. "It wouldn't take more than a few minutes. I know what it's like to run out of yarn when you only need one ball to finish a project."

"No, no, that's fine," K.O. said. She'd always wanted to learn to knit and now that LaVonne was taking a class, maybe she'd join, too.

"Merry Christmas!" Lydia tucked her arm in her husband's.

"Merry Christmas," K.O. returned. Soon they hurried down the street, with the boy trotting ahead.

Transfixed, K.O. stood there unmoving. The lump that had formed in her throat grew huge. The whole world was in love, and she'd let the opportunity of her life slip away. She'd let Wynn go with barely a token protest, and that was wrong. If she believed in their love, she needed to fight for it, instead of pretending everything was fine without him. Because it wasn't. In fact, she was downright miserable, and it was time she admitted it.

She knew what she had to do. Afraid that if she didn't act quickly, she'd lose her nerve, K.O. ran back across the street and into her own building. Marching to the elevator, she punched the button and waited.

She wasn't even sure what she'd tell Wynn; she'd figure that out when she saw him. But seeing him was a necessity. She couldn't spend another minute like this. She'd made a terrible mistake, and so had he. If there was any chance of salvaging this relationship, she had to try.

Her heart seemed to be pounding at twice its normal rate as she rode the elevator up to Wynn's penthouse condominium. She'd only been inside once, and then briefly.

By the time she reached his front door, she was so dizzy she'd become light-headed. That didn't deter her from ringing the buzzer and waiting for what felt like an eternity.

Only it wasn't Wynn who opened the door. It was Max.

"Katherine," he said, obviously surprised to find her at his son's door. "Come in."

"Is Wynn available?" she asked, as winded as if she'd climbed the stairs instead of taking the elevator. Talking to Wynn—*now*—had assumed a sense of urgency.

Wynn stepped into the foyer and frowned when he

saw her. "Katherine?" She could see the question in his eyes.

"Merry Christmas," Max said. He didn't seem inclined to leave.

"Could we talk?" she asked. "Privately?" She was terrified he'd tell her that everything had already been said, so she rushed to add, "Really, this will only take a moment and then I'll leave."

Wynn glanced at his father, who took the hint and reluctantly left the entryway.

K.O. remained standing there, clutching her purse with one hand and the pink box with the other. "I was out at the French Café and I talked to Alix."

"Alix?"

"She's one of the bakers and a friend of Lydia's—and Lydia's the lady who owns A Good Yarn. But that's not important. What *is* important is that Alix received an engagement ring for Christmas. She's so happy and in love, and Lydia is, too, and Susannah from the flower shop and just about everyone on the street. It's so full of Christmas out there, and all at once it came to me that…that I couldn't let this Christmas pass with things between us the way they are." She stopped to take a deep breath.

"Katherine, I—"

"Please let me finish, otherwise I don't know if I'll have the courage to continue."

He motioned for her to speak.

"I'm so sorry, Wynn, for everything. For wanting to be right and then subjecting you to Zoe and Zara. Their behavior *did* change after Zelda read your book and while I can't say I agree with everything you—"

"This is an apology?" he asked, raising his eyebrows.

"I'm trying. I'm sincerely trying. Please hear me out."

He crossed his arms and looked away. In fact, he seemed to find something behind her utterly fascinating.

This wasn't the time to lose her courage. She went on, speaking quickly, so quickly that the words practically ran together. "Basically, I wanted to tell you it was rude of me to assume I knew more than you on the subject of children. It was presumptuous and self-righteous. I was trying to prove how wrong you were…are, and that I was right. To be honest, I don't know what's right or wrong. All I know is how much I miss you and how much it hurts that you're out of my life."

"I'm the one who's been presumptuous and self-righteous," Wynn said. "You *are* right, Katherine, about almost everything. It hasn't been easy for me to accept that, let alone face it."

"Oh, for heaven's sake, aren't you two going to kiss and make up?" Max demanded, coming back into the foyer. Apparently he'd been standing in the living room, out of sight, and had listened in on every word. "Wynn, if you let this woman walk away, then you're a fool. An even bigger fool than you know."

"I—I…" Wynn stuttered.

"You've been in love with her for weeks." Max shook his head as if this was more than obvious.

Wynn pinned his father with a fierce glare.

"You love me?" K.O. asked, her voice rising to a squeak. "Because I'm in love with you, too."

A light flickered in his eyes at her confession. "Katherine, I appreciate your coming. However, this is serious and it's something we both need to think over. It's too important—we can't allow ourselves to get caught up in emotions that are part of the holidays. We'll talk after Christmas, all right?"

"I can't do that," she cried.

"Good for you," Max shouted, encouraging her. "I'm going to phone LaVonne. This calls for champagne."

"What does?" Wynn asked.

"Us," she explained. "You and me. I love you, Wynn, and I can't bear the thought that I won't see you again. It's tearing me up. I don't *need* time to think about us. I already know how I feel, and if what your father says is true, you know how you feel about me."

"Well, I do need to think," he insisted. "I haven't figured out what I'm going to do yet, because I can't continue promoting a book whose theories I can no longer wholly support. Let me deal with that first."

"No," she said. "Love should come first." She stared into his eyes. "Love changes everything, Wynn." Then, because it was impossible to hold back for another second, she put down her purse and the Yule log and threw her arms around him.

Wynn was stiff and unbending, and then his arms circled her, too. "Are you always this stubborn?" he asked.

"Yes. Sometimes even more than this. Ask Zelda."

Wynn kissed her. His arms tightened around her, as if he found it hard to believe she was actually there in his embrace.

"That's the way to handle it," Max said from somewhere behind them.

Wynn and K.O. ignored him.

"He's been a real pain these last few days," Max went on. "But this should improve matters."

Wynn broke off the kiss and held her gaze. "We'll probably never agree on everything."

"Probably."

"I can be just as stubborn as you."

"That's questionable," she said with a laugh.

His lips found hers again, as if he couldn't bear not to kiss her. Each kiss required a bit more time and became a bit more involved.

"I don't believe in long courtships," he murmured, his eyes still closed.

"I don't, either," she said. "And I'm going to want children."

He hesitated.

"We don't need all the answers right this minute, do we, Dr. Jeffries?"

"About Santa—"

She interrupted him, cutting off any argument by kissing him. What resistance there was didn't last.

"I was about to suggest we could bring Santa out from beneath that sleigh," he whispered, his eyes briefly fluttering open.

"Really?" This was more than she'd dared hope.

"Really."

She'd been more than willing to forgo Santa as long as she had Wynn. But Santa *and* Wynn was better yet.

"No hamsters, though," he said firmly.

"Named Freddy," she added.

Wynn chuckled. "Or anything else."

The doorbell chimed and Max hurried to answer it, ushering LaVonne inside. The instant she saw Wynn and K.O. in each other's arms, she clapped with delight. "Didn't I tell you everything would work out?" she asked Max.

"You did, indeed."

LaVonne nodded sagely. "I think I may have psychic powers, after all. I saw it all plain as day in the leaves of my poinsettia," she proclaimed. "Just before Max called, two of them fell to the ground—together."

Despite herself, K.O. laughed. Until a few minutes ago, her love life had virtually disappeared. Now there was hope, real hope for her and Wynn to learn from each other and as LaVonne's prophecy—real or imagined—implied, grow together instead of apart.

"Champagne, anyone?" Max asked, bringing out a bottle.

Wynn still held K.O. and she wasn't objecting. "I need to hire you," he whispered close to her ear.

"Hire me?"

"I'm kind of late with my Christmas letter this year and I wondered if I could convince you to write one for me."

"Of course. It's on the house." With his arms around her waist, she leaned back and looked up at him. "Is there anything in particular you'd like me to say?"

"Oh, yes. You can write about the success of my first published book—and explain that there'll be a retraction in the next edition." He winked. "Or, if you prefer, you could call it a compromise."

K.O. smiled.

"And then I want you to tell my family and friends that I'm working on a new book that'll be called *The Happy Child,* and it'll be about creating appropriate boundaries within the Free Child system of parenting."

K.O. rewarded him with a lengthy kiss that left her knees weak. Fortunately, he had a firm hold on her, and she on him.

"You can also mention the fact that there's going to be a wedding in the family."

"Two weddings," Max inserted as he handed LaVonne a champagne glass.

"Two?" LaVonne echoed shyly.

Max nodded, filling three more glasses. "Wynn and K.O.'s isn't the only romance that started out rocky. The way I figure it, if I can win Tom over, his mistress shouldn't be far behind."

"Oh, Max!"

"Is there anything else you'd like me to say in your Christmas letter?" K.O. asked Wynn.

"Oh, yes, there's plenty more, but I think we'll leave it for the next Christmas letter and then the one after that." He brought K.O. close once more and hugged her tight.

She loved being in his arms—and in his life. Next year's Christmas letter would be from both of them. It would be all about how happy they were…and every word would be true.

* * * * *